The Burning Season

ALSO BY ALISON WISDOM

We Can Only Save Ourselves

The Burning Season

a novel

Alison Wisdom

HARPER ◉ PERENNIAL

NEW YORK • LONDON • TORONTO • SYDNEY • NEW DELHI • AUCKLAND

HARPER ● PERENNIAL

THE BURNING SEASON. Copyright © 2022 by Alison Wisdom. All rights reserved. Printed in the United States of America. No part of this book may be used or reproduced in any manner whatsoever without written permission except in the case of brief quotations embodied in critical articles and reviews. For information, address HarperCollins Publishers, 195 Broadway, New York, NY 10007.

HarperCollins books may be purchased for educational, business, or sales promotional use. For information, please email the Special Markets Department at SPsales@harpercollins.com.

FIRST EDITION

Designed by Jamie Lynn Kerner

Library of Congress Cataloging-in-Publication Data has been applied for.

ISBN 978-0-06-309758-2

22 23 24 25 26 LSC 10 9 8 7 6 5 4 3 2 1

To Claire

The Burning Season

Prologue

What I've seen the last two years in Dawes, all the wonders, all the unbelievable things:

A man whose legs did not work, whose friends pushed him into the chapel in a wheelchair, healed. Papa Jake pressing his hands down onto the man's thighs for an hour. When he removed them, the man stood up from the chair. A wobbly step, and we all gasped. A miracle.

A little boy, so sick he couldn't eat or talk, couldn't get out of bed, was shriveling up like a dying plant, healed, restored to growth. A miracle.

Trembling hands, stilled. Stiff, pained hands, loosened and soothed. Empty hands, filled. A miracle, a miracle, a miracle.

People abandoning the things they allowed to overpower them in the outside world, to rule them, overthrown: drugs, sex, money, booze. Miracles, all of it.

Traces of heaven—the glory of God falling like light, feathers of the angels. Evidence of the presence of God, a miracle.

Once, a car accident on the freeway, near the exit to

Dawes, a young man not wearing a seat belt, ejected from the car. He's dead, the first responders said. He isn't, said Papa Jake, who worked on the man himself, with his hands, with his voice, refusing to leave his side until the breath of life filled the body back up. See, said Papa. He is not dead. A miracle.

You yourself, says Paul. Look how you've changed. The world had its hooks in you (actual hooks, I imagine, curved and sharp, piercing my skin), and you lost your way, but now look at you. Look at us. A miracle. How can you not look at yourself and see?

One

In the dregs of a hot day, the golden hour, the church family gathers together for a group photo at Papa Jake's house. There are nearly one hundred of us now, and so we spill over the porch steps and into the yard. One of the elders, Kyle, sets up a tripod and directs us into place. He motions for us to move closer together. "Men, stand in the back," he calls out. "Have your wives stand in front of you and hold the babies."

"This way, Rosemary," says Paul, gently guiding me to the step below him. "You look pretty." He is careful not to look at my body but my face as he says this.

"Thanks," I say. He puts his hands on my shoulders.

"Everyone looks good," Kyle shouts. "Ready?"

"Ready," says Papa Jake, who sits with his wife on a wicker bench in front of the whole group, and Kyle sets the timer and runs to his spot. Papa Jake's house is big, Victorian, in a cul-de-sac lined with other big Victorian houses, and these houses are filled with men like Papa Jake and women like his own wife.

It's only after we are lined up that I think about how

stupid I was to wear my hair in a ponytail. It will make my head look tiny in the picture. It will make me look bald.

"Smile," says Kyle now. "One more time." And the flash goes off.

THERE IS A fire that night. This one is close by, close enough that when I wake up in the night, I smell smoke. I wander around the house, turning on lights one by one, thinking that in one of the rooms, I will see a cloud gray and billowing, and we will run out, and everything we have will be gone. Paul finds me in the living room. "It's not here," he says, eyes still squinting with sleep. He walks over to the window and pulls the blinds up, taps the glass. "Outside," he says, and I see that the Wilders' house down the street is on fire. There are five figures standing in front, their backs to us, watching the blaze.

Since the fires began, Papa Jake has instructed us not to call 911. Get out quickly, and then let your house burn. If it looks like the flames are going to move on, going to light up and then eat the houses on either side, we can call 911, but only then. Our yards are big here, though, like gaps in between teeth, and this has never happened. Sometimes the fire burns for days. "There is a season for everything in life," Papa Jake has said. "And this is the season to burn."

"How did you know it was happening?" I ask Paul now.

"I dreamed it," he says.

Paul is always dreaming, and they are, somehow, dreams that make sense, dreams that truly mean something. It can be tedious to listen to him recite their content, but I will myself to listen.

We leave the house and go into the darkness—there are

no streetlights here, in the country—and we join the Wilder family outside their burning house. The parents turn to us, the mother holding two children in front of her body, a hand on each of them, a girl in a nightgown with little rubber flip-flops on her feet and a boy with long, scrawny limbs, a sapling. The third is the oldest, nearly as tall as his father. His arms are crossed, and his body is tense, tight as a bowstring. He doesn't understand, and so he is angry. He stands away from the rest of the group, leaving room enough for a whole other body between them, like a missing person who has been left behind, burned inside the house. "Is everyone all right?" asks Paul in a quiet voice.

"Yes," says the father, Matthew; he is older than us but wears his hair the way the frat boys in school wore theirs, shaggy, curling over their ears, constantly tossed.

"Praise God," says his wife, Amanda. I watch her fingers curl and tighten over the shoulders of her children. "Why us?" she asks, turning to look at me, because she cannot ask Paul herself.

"It's the will of God," I tell her.

"Yes," she says tightly. "Praise His name."

There is a sound like thunder, and we all turn toward the house. "The roof," Matthew says. It has collapsed, sucked down into the cavern of the house. "We should stand back." We all move so that we stand nearly across the street. Around us, lights in other houses go on. The street has woken up. The fire is slow and monstrous. Parts of the house crackle, but mostly it's quiet, and I think of before we came here, when Paul and I used to visit the modern art museum back home, feeling so urbane, and we'd find ourselves tucked into dark little rooms separated by a curtain, standing silently with other silent viewers, watching short films playing on a loop, lights projected on a wall. Art we didn't understand. In a way, this is the same. Something beautiful, created with purpose, but incomprehensible to anyone besides its creator.

"I'm thankful y'all made it out okay," Paul says.

"By the grace of God," Matthew says.

"We got ourselves out," says the oldest son, arms still crossed over his chest. We all look at him, and he looks back, the jut and tilt of the chin. I can tell Paul wants to say something, but this is not his child, and I put my hand on his back. He is quiet.

"Who gave you your legs?" Matthew asks him. "Who put the breath in your lungs?" The boy doesn't answer.

Amanda's daughter starts to cry, and Amanda kneels down next to her and takes her hand off the little boy. He wobbles for a minute, now that he is untethered. "My toys," the girl says. "Ginger the bunny. My Play-Doh."

"Those things don't matter, Abigail," Amanda says.

"But I love them," Abigail says.

"We can only love God," her mother tells her, and I wonder if the message would be different if Paul and I weren't standing here and the other neighbors gathering, if there were no people to hear her comforting her little girl. In our old world, she would have said something different, would have reassured her they would get her new things, new toys, a new stuffed bunny. I know because I would have too, and I'm glad I have no children to comfort. I look at Paul. I can see as he watches Amanda and Matthew with their children, that he feels the opposite way, disappointed he has none to comfort.

"Let's pray," Paul suggests.

We stand together and pray until we are tired and then until we are delirious, and tears turn into laughter, and the night into morning, and until we see the fire not as a destructive, terrible force but as a gift, a source of warmth in a cold world, a bright light to illuminate the truth.

IN THE MORNING, earlier than I would have thought they could organize themselves, a group of townspeople stand in front of our church building with the same signs as last week, the same messages: go home, leave us alone, let Dawes be Dawes. They don't know their home has already changed, that even if we were to go, our fingerprints would remain. *Leave*, they chant. They have heard about the fire, how another house has fallen. They are worried the flames will come for them next. *Leave*, they say. *Leave*. Until the word sounds like nothing but a sound, some other tongue.

There are about thirty of them, a mass of denim and white cotton T-shirts and long-sleeved work shirts, boots on the men, the women in outdated sneakers or cheap flip-flops. Randall, the pastor of the First Baptist Church of Dawes, stands in front of them, facing the church too but not leading the protest, like he is only monitoring his people, not condoning their actions. Paul told me that Papa Jake once thought Randall would make a good member of our church family, but it turned out he was wrong. Randall still embraced the heresies that the rest of us had spurned, and nothing, apparently, would convince him otherwise, not even the prospect of eternal damnation. Papa Jake also told Paul that Randall had smiled—*wistfully* was the word he used—and said, "I'll risk it, brother." Randall is in his forties, older than our own elders by over a decade, and looks like the tutor my old gymnastics gym hired to teach us science after we stopped going to regular school: slight and mild with rimless glasses and fine hair the color of shredded wheat. Whenever I see him, I want to run up and recite the parts of a flower to him; it's the only thing I remember from those lessons.

Randall seems nice. He never chants or shouts. I've never seen him with a sign. I bet he tells his people they shouldn't write nasty things on the signs, though obviously I have no way of knowing for sure; he probably tells them they shouldn't hold any signs at all. But what can he do? He can't stop them. They can do what they want.

I stop near them, still half on and half off my bike. I've just gone to the grocery store, getting things to feed ourselves and the Wilder family, who we've taken into our home and who now have nothing, nothing, to their name but faith. The basket on the bike is heavy, filled with milk, eggs, sliced turkey for lunchtime sandwiches, and I have to keep a hand on the basket to steady it. There are a few other church members watching too, about ten of us.

"Don't they have better things to do?" I ask Sandy, a woman who works at the diner the church owns. "I mean, jobs or kids or farming or something?"

"Dawes is a dying town," she says. "And they think they're trying to save it." She sighs. "What's sad is that they're worried about saving their home when they should really worry about saving themselves."

"Amen," says a man on the other side of me.

Papa Jake and the two elders, Kyle and Lou, come out of the building, and the shouting dies down a little. Papa

Jake leans up against one of the columns of the church's portico, and his arms are crossed, but his face is loose, relaxed. He reminds me of a cowboy resting against a fence, watching the horses run wild, watching them enjoy the muscles in their legs, the wind in their manes, knowing he'll break them soon and they'll be his to command, smiling because they just don't know it yet. He leans over to Kyle and whispers something. Kyle shakes his head and then calls out to the crowd, "Followers of evil!"

"Repent," says Lou, cupping his hands around his mouth like a megaphone. The chanting swells.

"Good to see y'all. Run along, now," says Papa Jake over their voices. "Unless you want to join us for a service." The townspeople hiss. A pit of vipers. "Suit yourselves. Our doors are always open," he says, and he turns and goes back inside.

"He's a class act," says Sandy with admiration. She heads off in the direction of the diner, and the few other church members leave too, but I stay. I prop my bike up against a tree and fiddle with the bike chain. The First Baptist Church of Dawes chants on, and I wait there under the tree until they get tired and lower their signs and walk back to their cars. Their shoulders slump. Randall cleans his glasses with the hem of his shirt. It's time for them to return to their homes or their jobs or the fields in their dying town.

When I get back to our squat brick house, the carton of milk is wet with its sweat, and as I'm transferring everything inside, I drop the eggs. When I open their carton to inspect the damage, I see that all but three are broken. I drop the yolks down the sink and throw the shells in the trash, but when I turn the disposal on, that's broken too. I put the last three eggs into the refrigerator carefully, perfect and whole and safe.

AS HAS BECOME customary the day after a fire, we all gather in the chapel to repent, to praise God, to sit in His presence. We spend all afternoon and evening here, breaking for water, sometimes for a meal, but often we continue on, sustained by the adrenaline of encountering holiness. It is exhausting, yes, but few good things come naturally in this life, so here in Dawes we will ourselves to do what is hard, to push our bodies, our minds, our spirits. "Your body is a blessing and a curse," Papa Jake likes to remind us. "It's both strong and weak." But the weakness is what makes it trainable, like a big, dumb dog, and the strength that allows us to persist in the training, the molding. It's our minds and spirits that are harder to will into submission. But that's the reason we're here—to work, to submit, to create lives that mean something.

Paul and I walk into the chapel together before we go to our respective sides. Amanda and I sit together, Abigail beside her. Our husbands and sons and brothers are across the aisle, one pew behind us so that they can see us all the time. This is because a woman is a thing of beauty, and isn't it right, Papa Jake has told us, that we admire beauty? Isn't it right that we keep our most precious things in our sight?

Amanda wears one of my dresses, and it is big on her, too long and too wide, and the hem drags on the ground when she walks. Abigail is still in her nightgown. She didn't want to take a bath, threw a big fit in which she writhed and wept. Matthew wanted to pray over her, but Amanda told him to let her be. And so now she is here, smelling of smoke.

At the back of the chapel, there are raised voices, and we all turn. Brother Lou, wooden and strange, is holding his arms straight out like he's stopping someone, ready to push them away. A trim, gray-haired man, old enough to be the father of anyone here, stands before him in short sleeves, khakis. "You are not welcome," Lou says in a loud, firm voice. "Please go."

But the man remains, looking past Lou, searching, and because he is not my father, I watch him. Other women do not. This man could be their father, finding them when they do not want to be found, trying to see them when they do not want to be seen. You belong only to God, Papa Jake has taught us. Only to God and to us. "Your pastor said anyone can come," the father says. "Your website says it's an open-door service."

"Not this one," Brother Lou says, and he places his hands on the man's shoulders and pushes him away. A few other men, Paul among them—Paul, who is always ready to serve—come alongside Lou for backup. "Jennifer!" the father yells. "Jenn! Jennifer Bell!" Three rows in front of me, Jennifer is still, rigid. She does not turn. The father cries out one more time, and then the door is shut, and he is gone. The other men return a few minutes later, and the service can begin.

Our chapel is a small building with white pillars coated in fine dirt the color of sawdust and meticulously laid tan brick, in lines as straight as an army regiment. There isn't even a real sign outside, just one of those black ones where you slide in the white plastic letters. The inside of the chapel is plain too, with neat rows of pews leading up to a short stage adorned with a cross and a pulpit. But what fills it—what we fill it with—is extraordinary.

"There are people," Papa Jake says, "who want you to think they know the truth, but here's the real truth"—he smiles—"they don't." He laughs and shrugs. "And they'll go to great lengths to convince you they're right and you're wrong or we're wrong, that everyone else is wrong or, worse, that everyone is right and there's no truth at all. These people are like serpents with two heads, and they're speaking out of both of them at once, that's how bad they want you to believe them. Two heads, two tongues, one for each of your ears. One head tells you what the world says, that you're fine, that everything is fine, that you're perfect, never change. The other head tells you you're wrong, that you've never been right, but they know how to help you. How to change you.

"Maybe you listened to one of those heads. Maybe you've listened to both of those heads. But look. You didn't change. You weren't fine. You weren't fulfilled. You didn't hear the voice of God, not with them. The voice of God doesn't exist beyond these walls, outside the borders of our town. That is why we left those other places. That is why we left the people we once cared about. We left, and we"—he stamps his foot, grinds the heel of his boot into the ground—"crushed the heads of those snakes, those serpents." The s's hiss when he speaks. We clap for him, we clap for the truth, for the walls of our church, for the borders of our town, for the heels of boots, for the strength to bring our feet down and crush the liars. We weep for them, even as we show them our power. The lost, the lost who want to grab us by those heels we will only use to crush them, grab us by our ankles and pull us down into their pit. We weep for the weak they will take, who aren't strong enough to fight back. We weep for the people we left behind.

"We are the lucky ones," Papa Jake says, and as he lifts his hands, music swells, and Amanda slides down the pew and into the aisle, where she twirls. Eyes closed, dancing. She moves clumsily, my too-long dress tangling around her feet, but she doesn't stop. "Yes!" Papa Jake says. Abigail joins her too, grabbing at her mother's hand, even though Amanda's eyes are still closed, and it could be anyone's small hand reaching for her. She holds it tight, squeezing and swinging Abigail's arm. Abigail's movements look joyful, her body communicating happiness, but her face is still serious, like she is thinking hard about how she moves with her mother. "This is a picture of heaven," Papa Jake says, reaching out from the pulpit toward all of us. "Look what this family has lost today. Their home still smolders, all their things are charred, but they delight in the gifts and wonders of the Lord."

Behind me, a woman named Renee calls, "Look at the angels! Look how the angels surround them!" I look, and I see nothing. No angels, no light, I hear no beating of wings. But others around me have shielded their eyes from the blinding glory of the angels around Abigail and Amanda.

"Join us!" Amanda cries, extending her arms toward the women's side of the church. Even now, filled with glory, she does not address the men. The men dance less freely than we do, as if they are unsure of how to let their bodies move. Some speak languages I do not understand, inhabiting even in worship a world wholly other than the smaller, lesser one where I live and move. The men remain careful in the frenzy of the service not to let the boundaries of these spheres—theirs and ours—loosen and slip away. They maintain their uniqueness, their difference from us. I find Paul in his pew, still sitting, head in hands, his body sharp, and I know he is experiencing a vision. Later, he will tell me about it, and I will listen.

"The angels," Renee says again. Her voice cracks.

I still do not see them. But I stand and go to Amanda and Abigail. I take the girl's other hand, and she looks up at me with big, solemn eyes. Her nightgown has a blue smudge on the chest. Toothpaste from the morning, dripped from her mouth. At our house, she used the same spare toothbrush as her mother, and she came to Amanda, still holding the toothbrush in her mouth and pointing to where the foam had landed on her nightgown. It's fine, her mother told her, wiping it with her finger. We'll wash it. But where? Abigail asked.

"Do you see the angels?" Abigail says to me now.

"Do you?" She doesn't answer, so I don't either. "Close your eyes," I tell her. "I'll close mine too."

We dance together with our eyes closed, the three of us, and I only open mine when I feel something landing in my hair, on my shoulders. Feathers, small and white. They fall from the ceiling. Papa Jake has turned the lights off, and in the dark, the feathers are so white they glow. Abigail picks one out of her hair. She holds it between her fingers, examining it like a jeweler looks at a diamond, inspecting it for flaws. Then she looks at Amanda and me in wonder.

"The angels," she says.

Two

Dawes is a small town. Not dusty, though. Everyone thinks small towns in Texas are dusty, the land brown and tan, ochre, yellow, soil crumbling between your fingertips, wind blowing sand and dust so that grit coats your teeth if you smile, fine dirt that gets under your nails. But that's only part of Texas—the Panhandle, up north, all red dirt and dust storms, and South Texas, brush country beneath clear skies. Then there's East Texas with its swamps, lurid algae skimming the water's surface, alligators beneath, and West Texas with its flat, drab land. But then, even further west, there are mountains and rivers that cut through canyons like snakes.

Dawes is not dry, is not on a swamp, sits squarely in the middle of the state, does not have mountains or rivers or anything worth mentioning. When you take the exit off 87 to get to Dawes, there is a sign that says it's the crossroads of Texas. Lots of towns in Texas claim this title. I don't know who deserves it.

It is a sleepy town, and slow, but not still. Not stagnant. There is a downtown here, storefronts with brick facades, big windows that overlook the street. A cobbler, a bakery, a dim little antiques store, a folksy restaurant with an old wagon wheel out front, fake flowers wrapped around its spokes.

When we first got here and walked through downtown, we passed by a barbershop in which a man sat in a chair looking out the window, arms crossed over his round belly, frowning. The shop was empty of customers. For a while, every time I passed, I saw him sitting in that chair, the kind that swivels, watching through the window, but then eventually, he was gone, the shop was closed, then completely vacant. The man might still be here in Dawes, and I've just never seen him. He might be one of those men with the signs, a chant on his lips. But we cut our own hair here, in our kitchens, on our front porches. We sweep up the hair with brooms, into dustpans or out into the yard, giving the birds something soft to build their nests with.

Beyond the strip of downtown are the houses we occupy, the neat lines of ranch-style houses built in the town's more recent history: squat boxes alternating in tan brick, orange brick, brown brick, up and down the streets. Next are the Victorians in a nest of their own, a pretty little enclave for the church leadership. These homes are older, bigger, have wraparound porches, the kind you know had rotten floors and weathered, chipping paint before the church came in to restore them.

We all have lawns we keep mown. In the spring and into the summer, the grass is green and healthy. By the time September rolls around, the grass is scorched from a long summer that begins in May and ends—when?—sometimes in October, sometimes November, and the grass by then is yellow and brittle. We are on the cusp of summer now, the third one Paul and I have spent here, each day hotter than the last.

Past our little brick houses are the houses with the real land, working ranches with livestock, owned by people who have lived in Dawes their whole lives. I like to walk past them, the horses and cows and sheep, say hello. Once I put a bag of baby carrots in my pocket—they were almost bad, gone a little whitish in our refrigerator—and walked to the closest of these properties, one with a small herd of goats that grazed near the fence closest to the road. Reaching my hand through the fence, I fed them the carrots and watched their jaws moving nimbly as they ate, but later I worried that carrots were bad for them, that I'd hurt them somehow, made them sick. I went back a week later to check on them, and they were fine, but I've never gone back to feed them again.

Here, we, the church, own a gas station just off the freeway and, in the center of town, near the Victorians, a grocery store and a diner. Once, all these places were independently operated but, like everything else in town, dying, and so with the money we took from our old lives and gave to Papa Jake, we saved them. It is impossible to own the town's park and playground, but we might as well, since no one else uses them. The town is shrinking as its residents age. Meanwhile, the church is growing, bringing babies into the world, babies who turn into children who hang from the monkey bars, who pump their legs on swings, going higher and higher and then jumping off while their mothers hold their breath until they land. We own the hardware store. We bought the dying video rental store, got rid of all the tapes and DVDs. Now it sits empty while we wait for the Lord to tell Papa Jake what to do with it. One day, we will own it all. The houses, the buildings, the stores, the roads, the land, even the animals that live on it. "A new promised land," Papa Jake told us. "All we have to do is take it."

AFTER THE SERVICE, our bodies are spent from the hours of movement, our muscles loose as string, our souls somehow both more full and less, cleansed and emptied of earthly wickedness, replaced with light. "What a day," Amanda sighs as we walk up to our house. "I'm wiped out."

"Me too," I say, "so I can't imagine how y'all are feeling."

"Grateful," says Amanda, taking my hand. "We're so thankful to you and Paul for sharing your home with us."

"Of course," I say. I do not tell her what she surely already knows, that this has nothing to do with my own generosity but with the expectations Papa has for all of us. The fires—there have been three in all, including the one that took her family's home—mean that people have had to squeeze in where they can, however they can. Papa Jake and Caroline, his wife, are housing one family already. The other family was able to move into a new house right away, left vacant by a local man who died and whose heirs quickly sold to the church. Kyle and Lou live together, each with his own floor in a rambling Victorian next to Papa Jake, and they've offered to take the Wilders in once they clean out the guest rooms, which they have filled with all kinds of junk. "Men," said Amanda when she heard this, rolling her eyes conspiratorially at me. I smiled knowingly, but

Paul has always been neat, minimalist. When we moved to Dawes, into this house, he walked through room by room with a trash bag, sweeping every surface clean of whatever trinkets had been left behind by the previous owner. Of the two of us, I am the one who lets things collect and build, who allows everything to move toward chaos.

Inside, Paul and Matthew are still talking, laughing occasionally. They've talked the whole walk home. Paul, I know, will miss him when they leave—he has always been the kind of man who treasures a friendship with another man. The fact that I am not a man feels like just another of my shortcomings.

"We're going to turn in, if that's okay," Amanda says as we walk in. Abigail is quiet and wide-eyed in her arms, clutching her mother around the neck. "It feels like it's been a hundred years since this morning."

"Wait," I say. "Let us get out of y'all's way—there's bread in the pantry, peanut butter. Jelly in the refrigerator. Why don't you eat something and just stretch out a little without us hovering over your shoulder?"

Before I even finish talking, the boys are moving toward the kitchen, and Amanda lets them. "You sure?" she asks me, but she looks relieved.

"Make yourselves at home," I say, and Paul looks over, smiles approvingly: good little hostess. I always was, I think. Paul and I retreat to our bedroom, leaving the Wilders to forage in our kitchen. When we shut the bedroom door behind us, Paul surprises me, taking me in his arms and kissing my neck, touching my cheek, pushing a lock of my hair behind my ear. Like a reflex, I lift my arms for him to take my dress off. He does. In the kitchen, the Wilders are quiet, uncomfortable in a strange home or too tired to acknowledge each other. I lift a finger to my lips.

I unhook my bra, and I watch Paul look at me, his hand moving toward my breasts, another reflex, muscle memory, heart memory. I think of the other afternoon on the steps outside of Papa Jake's house, Paul's careful hand on my arm, the way he made sure not to look at my body. I take a step back, away from his hands, just out of reach, so that he has to look but cannot touch. I feel both disdain and desire—this small bit of power I have to wield; this weakness of his. He is supposed to be the strong one. He comes to me, unbuckling his belt, and it feels suddenly important he undress himself. I won't help. Make your choices, Paul. Look, watch.

I move so I am standing over the bed, and I want him to push me down on it, and he does, and we're kissing and moving together as quietly as possible, and my brain is empty, my body weightless, spineless, borderless, and I want more. *You always do*, I imagine Paul saying, and Paul is right; I hate him for it and love him for it, for knowing me so well, knowing what I want, and never giving it to me. *I'm never enough for you*, that Paul says. "Harder," I tell him, keeping my voice low. I want him to bite me, to bruise me, and I must say these things out loud because he stops, and I cry out before he covers my mouth with his hand. "No," he says, and now he is the one filled with desire and disdain, pulling out, leaving me empty and alone. He takes his hand off my mouth. "Don't ask me to do that again." He storms off to the bathroom, closes the door. I hear the shower turn on, the weak spray of water against the tile. The rest of the house is quiet.

This is what I get for asking, for showing my weakness. The wrong kind of weakness. Here we love weakness, and we hate it. We value strength in our convictions; we sharpen our wills like iron, but our spirits—those should remain without strength, as white and delicate as eggshell. I pull the flat sheet off our bed and wrap myself in it so that my shoulders are bare and the rest of me is covered, clothed in cascading white. I go into the bathroom and sit on the lid of the toilet, my knees up and my arms around them. I think of Paul, angry and washing the failure of my body off his own. I think of one long ago summer when my parents sent my sister and me to a Christian camp our neighbors' daughters were going to, how all the girls there had to wear one-piece swimsuits with T-shirts layered over them when we swam in the sun-warmed lake, how at night we listened to grown-ups in dusty sneakers tell us about our mistakes. Our sins, our Sin. The problem our bodies created. We prayed all the time, multiple times a day, and nothing happened. We sang, and nothing happened. We asked God to speak to us, and nothing happened. My family went to church every Sunday, unless we were traveling for my gymnastics meets, and still nothing happened. Until Paul and I came to Dawes.

Churches are everywhere in Texas, every kind of church. In Houston, just in the neighborhood where Paul and I once lived, there were hundreds, millions. We had an old Baptist church made of orange brick with three cracking concrete steps leading to the front doors, an orange cat the same color as the bricks often lying on those steps when we walked by, the services there attended by older people, the ones who lived in the neighborhood decades before Paul and I moved in. I imagined that inside the church there would be pews and hymnals in holders built into the backs of the pews. They would sing traditional songs. There would be an organ.

Also in our neighborhood: a Church of Christian Scientists in a building so plain and gray it looked like a bunker. I don't know much about Christian Scientists, so I can't picture what the inside of the church looks like. If I had to guess, I would say like a library—quiet and somber, with books or informational pamphlets inside a little kiosk near the entryway. I think they're like Scientologists, Paul said once. I guess science is very important to them, I said.

But later I googled it, and it turns out I was wrong; it was the opposite—they don't believe in medicine, so I suppose science isn't important to them, after all. We understand that here. It feels threatening—why do you need proof when you have faith? Back then, when I told Paul what the Wikipedia entry said about the Christian Scientists, he rolled his eyes. Who doesn't believe in medicine, he said.

Around the corner and down the street from us was a very hip church, with paintings and candles and fair-trade coffee made by real baristas, and inside the sanctuary, the lights were always low, and almost everyone held a cup of coffee wrapped in a sleeve made of recycled paper and printed with the church's name in black ink. The few times we woke up early enough to make it to church, Paul and I, this was where we went. Inside, the floor was polished concrete, and the walls were white, like an art gallery. They prided themselves on being different from other churches. The pastor loved to talk about wine, all the places he'd visited and drunk in—Mendoza, Napa Valley, Tuscany. Anytime

you want to come over to my house, he said, you're welcome as long as you bring us something good to drink while
we talk.

Then there were several megachurches in the city
too, which meant they met in sprawling campuses or sta-
diums they bought from sports teams, which meant every
service was packed. The pastors at these places are slick.
The churches they operate are like machines, with gears and
grinding teeth. The pastors smile with white teeth, they
blink a lot, they tell their congregants that good things are
coming to them if only they'll just believe. Speak it into
existence, the life that you want, the things you desire. God
wants to give you what you want. He wants to give you
everything. It's like every Sunday they get fed cotton candy,
marshmallows, croissants, Papa Jake says, but what they
need is meat, potatoes, vegetables. What I give you is the
meat, he says. It's a steak dinner. What I give you is the truth.

When Paul gets out of the shower, he glances at me and
sighs and then focuses on his reflection in the mirror. The
light bulbs are awful, bulbous things over the mirror, like
the sad vanity of an aging starlet, and in their light, among
the peach tile and paint, Paul's skin looks hot and pink.
Everything in the bathroom is a shade of peach, the color
of sand, a sunset, like whoever designed this bathroom had
been dreaming of the beach. When we walked through this
house for the first time, we flipped on the switch in here and
both cringed. It could be worse, Paul had said.

Could it? I'd asked, and he'd shrugged.

Lime green? he'd said.

"I'm sorry," I say now.

"It's shameful," he says, watching me in the mirror. "It's not what God wants for us."

"I know."

"Things have to be different," Paul says. "Your body is a temple, Rosie. God's never going to give us what we want if you ask me to disrespect it. It's offensive to God and to me, and honestly it should be to you too."

"Pray with me?" I ask.

He sighs. "Okay," he says, and there in the bathroom, he kneels beside the toilet where I perch, wrapped in white like his pretty bride. He holds my hand and asks God to forgive us, to forgive me. While he prays, I think of woods and witches, sacrifices and stone tables, magic and miracles. And then it is over. We open our eyes and take each other in. Forgiveness makes us new creations, new eyes to see, new selves to be seen.

"Want a sandwich?" Paul asks.

"Yeah," I say, and I follow him back into the bedroom, where I drop the bedsheet and pick up the clothes he just took off me, and I dare him to look at me as I dress, but he doesn't. The strong one after all. We go into the kitchen, vacated now by the Wilders, and eat peanut butter sandwiches made from the heels of the bread, all that remains.

Three

In the morning, the men go off to the church office to assist Papa Jake in whatever church business he needs to conduct, and Amanda begins the school day for the children, moving from the kitchen table to the back porch to the living room, trying to find the perfect spot. She is an ineffectual teacher, easily distracted and unclear in her expectations, and the younger two children are wild, the older one sullen. He even disappears at one point, sneaks out the front door while we prepare lunch for everyone.

"It's okay," Amanda says when we discover Gabriel is gone. "He's old enough that he doesn't really need any more schooling. It's fine if he isn't great at math." She shrugs. "I'm not either."

So far Abigail and Troy, the middle child, have read from the Bible, prayed, and drawn pictures of the God-thoughts they've had, and now they are looking at a big atlas, lying on the floor studying it the way my friends and I used to read magazines at junior high sleepovers: "Twenty Tricks to Drive Him Wild," "Find the Right Swimsuit for Your Shape," "Which Lipstick Is the Color of Your Energy?" We studied those pages like diviners reading bird bones, listened to them like they were oracles. This atlas had been in their car, their only major possession spared in the fire. Signs of God's providence, Amanda said.

"Every day we pick a country," Amanda explains to me, "and pray for that country. One day God will call Troy to leave us and go to a far-off place to preach His word. Now we're trying to figure out where he'll go." Troy is ten, with tan hairless arms and legs, and spent twenty minutes this morning trying to climb the fence in our backyard before he got splinters in both hands and cried while Amanda rubbed his shoulders and I bent over his palms with tweezers. While Amanda talks, he tears off the corner of a page in the atlas. With two fingers, he rolls it into a tiny ball and then flicks it away, and it disappears from sight immediately.

"Abigail will, of course, stay here with me," Amanda says, running a hand through her daughter's ponytail, the girl's face solemn. "My baby forever."

"That's sweet," I say.

"That's part of why we came here," she says. "Everyone grows up too fast out in the world. There are so many scary things out there, trying to rob our children of their chance to just be kids. You know?"

"I do."

"I don't know if I'll keep up the schooling with her once the boys are old enough to go to the training school," she says. "It's hard work."

"I used to be a teacher," I say. "Before."

"Oh?" says Amanda, sitting up so that she is cross-legged on the floor. "Take a break," she tells Abigail and

Troy. "Go outside and play." She points in the direction of the backyard, and the kids stand up, leaving the atlas open on the carpet. "Don't climb the fence," she calls, and then we hear the back door fall closed.

"Language arts. Seventh graders," I say.

"You could be Gabriel's teacher," she says.

"In another life," I say.

"Did you like it?"

I did. I was good at it, pushing myself to be the best, the most well-liked, the most well-prepared, the teacher whose students had the highest test scores. Paul was working long hours, trading at an oil and gas company, so I did too, staying up at the school late, grading and planning, and then coaching the cross-country team in the fall, the tennis team in the spring. At night, we'd come home, exhausted, to our apartment, a little set of rooms in a duplex near the bayou, and we'd slump toward and against each other in a weary, desperate way. Summers were better for us, even with the heat. At night, we would spread out a picnic blanket in the front yard, under the sprawling oak tree, and read and drink wine and eat cheese and fruit we bought from the farmer's market two blocks over. Even when the oak tree died and had to be cut down, we sat out there anyway; we used the stump as a table for our feast until the landlord took that away too, ground it down to nothing.

"Yes," I tell her. "But this is better."

Amanda spreads her legs out, stretching, and she is barefoot, toes peeking out from the hem of my dress. She cocks her head to the side. "I was remembering your Reclamation," she says.

"You brushed my hair," I tell her.

She nods. "And you cried. So much. It was so hard for you to leave that old life behind."

"I was ready to leave it," I say.

She watches me closely, as if she is looking for the tears I cried two years ago. "They didn't seem like happy tears."

The women, strangers, had surrounded me in an office at the back of the chapel. I wore a strange dress that didn't belong to me, long and white like a wedding gown and too tight in the chest, and every time I breathed I worried a button would pop off. Amanda's hands had been in my hair, pulling it off my neck, braiding it, twisting it, pinning it so that my head felt heavy. My feet were soft from being soaked in a small tub of water. I don't know what my face looked like, though I know there were hands fluttering around it, applying eyeshadow and blush, coating my lashes in mascara; I didn't look in the mirror. I wasn't encouraged to. My face, my body—these were not mine. They were being reclaimed by my husband and my Father. The wedding Paul and I had before wasn't enough for Dawes, not enough for God, but this, my Reclamation, would be.

The women told me I looked beautiful. They told me if I didn't stop crying, they would never be able to finish my makeup. They told me they loved me already. I was a sister now, a friend. Never mind I had been both those things before, to other people, but those times, they told me, did not count. They told me they had prayed and had seen that I was supremely gifted by God, that He would use my life if I let Him. We can tell you've spent your whole life putting God in a box, they said. We're telling you now to open the box. Open the box and be free.

"I had done bad things," I say to Amanda now.

"Haven't we all," she says. "But it was a beautiful Reclamation. The glory of God was full that day."

People had been dancing and murmuring and shouting and laughing then too, a dreamy madness covered us like a cloak, and Paul was so happy, finally, happy with me, happy that we were here. It looked like freedom. I wanted what Paul had, and I asked God to give it to me. The lights went out, a gasp of darkness, and then light again. This time it was blinding. Then a cloud descended on us, blanketed us, twinkling and light. "Is this glitter?" I asked Paul as it fell, and people wept.

"It's the glory of God!" Paul said, and he tilted his head back as if he were going to drink those tiny particles of floating light, but he kept his eyes closed, his mouth closed, and it clung to him. It stuck in his beard like stardust.

"You're shining," I told him.

"So are you!" he said. And I could barely believe it, but I was. I looked at my arms, clad in the unfamiliar white dress, long sleeves, and they sparkled.

"It was very special," I say now. The front door opens, and we turn to see Gabriel come in, clothes sooty, like he has been up a chimney, a black mark streaking across his face like a meteor in a pale sky. In his arms, he holds a few black objects. "I found stuff," he says. "Some of our stuff."

"Oh, honey," Amanda says. "Did you go home?" The boy nods, looking not at his mother but at the things in his hands, his fingers twitching slightly around them. Amanda sighs. "It's not safe in there. You could have gotten hurt! And whatever's left—those things are tainted now."

His face contorts, as if someone has tightened it with a wrench. "Tainted," he echoes.

"God said no to them," his mother tells him.

"You'll get new things," I offer. In a year, when he is thirteen, I won't be able to speak to him, but now he is still a child and it's fine. All the women are mothers, even those of us without children, our unborn babies promises we made to the church when we joined.

He looks at me with surprise, like I am a vase of flowers or an egg in a carton that has just spoken. "I don't want new things," he says, arms full.

"You didn't even have much," Amanda says, glancing over at me, perhaps fearing I am making silent judgments, believing that she and Matthew have spoiled the children, given them everything they wanted, when everyone here knows that belongings, stuff, are trappings of a world we have rejected. I try to keep my face blank—a vase of flowers, a single white egg.

"But I liked it," he says. His voice cracks, and he looks at the ceiling. The boys I taught were still young enough that they sometimes cried over a bad grade or a friend's slight, reluctantly and with burning pink cheeks, and it was painful for everyone present, and I excuse myself to the bedroom. A gift, I think, for this boy I could have known in a different life.

"Maybe that's why our house burned down," I hear Amanda say as I head out of the room. "Maybe it was because you cared more about your comfort than the presence of God." I close the door before I hear Gabriel's response.

If I stand in just the right spot and press my cheek against the glass, I can see the ruins of the Wilders' house from our bedroom window. We have left the remains of the burned-down houses in place, either as a warning or a tribute or a trophy or some combination of those things. I asked Paul if it would decrease the property value on those streets, to have a blackened home sitting there like a dead tooth. He laughed and said no, the town belongs to us now, us the church, us this family of people, and things like property value don't matter to us. We'll never leave Dawes, not until we leave the world altogether.

I picture Gabriel, shaggy hair and whole body like a scowl, picking his way through the charred bones of their house even though nothing good remained for him there. He was only going back to a corpse, looking for a heart that had already stopped beating, searching for life in a thing that was lifeless and had nothing left to offer but ghosts.

Four

The children are asleep on the queen bed in the guest room, and the adults go outside so that we can talk and laugh without disturbing them. Years ago, back in Houston, I would have opened a bottle of wine, and we would have stayed outside until we were drunk, mosquito-bitten, and windblown. But tonight I pour lemonade Paul made himself, with real sugar, real lemons, and our glasses sweat and leave rings on our patio table. The men mostly talk only to each other, like Amanda and I aren't here, leaving us to our own quiet conversation, heads close together, our voices like water flowing under a bridge only the men cross. When we arrived in Dawes, Papa Jake's wife, Caroline, took me around without Paul, walked me down the streets, through the small downtown. Things work a certain way here, she said, we have to be careful not to step on any toes, not to insert ourselves into situations we haven't been invited to join. Here, men like to speak to men. "Have you been out of the country before?" she asked.

"Paul and I went to Italy a few years ago," I said. "Before we came here."

"Good," she said. "Do you speak Italian?"

"A little. But not really. I could ask where the bathroom was but not much else."

"Remember how people would be speaking Italian all around you, and you could hear them but you didn't really listen because none of it would make any sense anyway?" she asked. "When your husband is talking to another man, pretend you're back in Florence, that they're speaking Italian."

"But what if they do talk to me?" I asked. "Do I just ignore them?"

"Then answer," she said. "You don't want to be rude."

"I actually received two prophecies today," Paul says now.

"Would you like to share them with us?" Matthew asks, running a finger down the glass in front of him, tracing the path of a bead of water slipping down.

"I'd love to hear, honey," I say.

"That's good," Paul says, "because they're both about you."

"Me?" I ask.

"'You talkin' to me?'" Matthew says. "'There's no one else here.'" He looks at us. "*Taxi Driver*," he says. "De Niro. Remember?"

"Matthew," says Amanda. He picks up his lemonade like he's going to drink it, but then he puts it down again. He is quiet.

I had thought things were fine after my misstep last night, but this makes me unsure. "In the first one," Paul says now, "we were in the desert. And then it started to rain, and I thought that would be a good thing, all the rain. But then it turns out we weren't just in a desert, we were in a canyon, and the canyon starts filling up." He pauses here, frowns at the glass of lemonade in front of him, as if he can look into the glass and see the miles of sand, filling, miraculously, with water.

"Is that it?" I ask him. "Is there more?"

"No," he says. "I mean, no that's not it. There's more, but not much. We got rescued. I don't even know how. It was just all of a sudden we were standing up above the canyon looking down as it filled up with water."

Amanda reaches over to squeeze my hand, like this has really happened, and Paul and I were the ones who narrowly escaped catastrophe, not them. "So it's a good prophecy," I say. We were out of harm's way. Dawes was the cliff we stood on to watch the waters rise below us. I think of my high school English teachers and all those papers I had to write about the symbolism of this story or that poem, and I feel like they would be proud.

"No," says Paul. "Because it started raining again, and we looked up, and that's when I saw we weren't fully out of the canyon after all. We had just made it up to a ledge, and the water was getting higher and higher. And this time we didn't go anywhere. We were just stuck."

"Oh," I say.

"Yeah," says Paul. "I feel a little embarrassed telling you this in front of company." Here, Matthew says *no, no, don't*, to Paul, and Amanda echoes her husband, but says it only to me, into the night air around us. Paul looks at Matthew, brown eyes big, full of sorrow. "We have a good marriage," he says. "You know? But maybe this means something is coming for us."

"It isn't," I say. "God won't let it. We won't let it."

"There's no us apart from God," Paul says and frowns. I look down at the table, ashamed, my body saying so with its shape, the curve of my back, my neck bent.

"What's the other one?" Matthew asks. "You said you received two today. Maybe they make sense together. Like part one and part two of the same message."

"Oh, right," says Paul. "It's not as big." He shifts so that he is facing me head-on, and I look back up at him. "Rosemary, I think we need to cut your hair."

"Oh," I say. "Okay." My hair is long and dark and thick. Even though I am only thirty-two, it has thin threads of gray running through it, and when I wear it in a braid, the strands snake down and wind through it. I used to think of my hair, my face, my body much more than I do now. Once I cared about my body in a different way, and I spent so many years of my life developing each individual part, forcing it to be its best, and now I've changed; for him to say he will cut my hair feels both as major as cutting off a finger and as trivial as trimming a fingernail. A loss and not a loss. I want to know, though, how my hair has offended anyone, why God wants me to get rid of it. "Vanity," Paul says, as if he's reading my mind. "That's what God told me."

"God knows the heart," Amanda says to me, nodding.

Vanity, I think. I didn't even know any was left in me. Only my most dowdy clothes survived our move from Houston to Dawes, ankle-skimming dresses, anything shapeless, high-necked, sack-like—which is to say, not much. Before we left Houston, one day Paul brought home two shopping bags of loose dresses, button-down shirts paired with long skirts, brand-new, all the tags still on, and we haven't had to shop since. Tonight I am wearing an opaque white nightgown with a Victorian collar that my college roommate Tess got me as a gag gift at my lingerie shower. "You better wear that," Tess said. "It's from Anthropologie, so you know I spent a lot of money on this joke."

"All right," I tell Paul. "There are scissors in the drawer in the kitchen next to the dishwasher."

"Now?" he asks. He is surprised by my readiness but also, I think, pleased, proud of his amenable wife.

"Yes," I say.

"I can cut it," Amanda says to me. "I can make it look nice."

"Nice doesn't matter," Paul says. "That's not the point. That's not what God wanted."

"Someone can direct me," Amanda suggests, careful to address only me. "Someone can tell me where to cut, and I'll do it however they want."

Paul nods and goes inside to get the scissors. Amanda scoots herself away from the table and comes to stand behind me, running her hands through my hair. "It will be fine," she whispers into my ear. "You have good bone structure." Paul comes out, holds up the scissors.

"They're dull," I tell him.

"Do it in sections, then," he says to Amanda, and I feel her hands at my shoulders.

"No," says Paul. Her hands move again. "Shorter," says Paul, and now I feel her hands again, fingers like scissors holding a piece of my hair between them, grazing my earlobe. "Yes," he says.

She cuts. It is dark out here, evening, and the only light

we have is a fixture above the back door that glows wanly and attracts June bugs whose bodies ping and zip against the plastic. "These scissors are dull," Amanda confirms. "But we're making progress." It is only when there is something to be blown away that I notice it's a breezy night, and the inches of my hair begin to separate and scatter, though not very far. They look like little flattened animals. I imagine birds using the strands for their nests. But I know that Paul hates a mess, and so when this part is over, I will get our broom from the kitchen pantry and the dustpan, and I will sweep it all up, throw it all away, and I will go about my life. I will be a person with short hair. Paul always liked my hair long.

He stands across the table from where I sit, one foot up on the chair he had been sitting in, his elbow on his bent knee, serious face in hand, watching me. He looks like a pirate or like an athlete, listening to the coach dissect the play. "I don't know if those two messages were related," he says. "I don't see how they would be."

"Maybe it's Rosemary's vanity that's coming for you," Matthew says. "Vanity's a deadly sin." He is looking at me too but blankly, the way you look at the muted TVs in the waiting rooms of doctors' offices.

"I think they're two separate things," Paul says. "It's something else. This—the hair—it's not a big deal."

"No," I say. "It's fine. It's good."

"The other thing could be, though," says Paul. "We just don't know what's coming."

I picture it, this vague amorphous bad thing growing, taking shape. I remember how one night, before Dawes, we went to dinner after work, and we were about to pay our bill when Paul said, "Man, everyone at work is getting sick, and I know I'm going to get sick too. I can feel it." His tone was light, though, and the whole evening had been a lovely one, so I took his complaint in stride; besides, it was an opportunity for me to take a particularly nurturing, wifely interest in him, take care of him, worry needlessly over his health, in a way he liked. It was like a little game, a role I was playing. It was sweet.

"We have that medicine you can take," I said. "That kind that's supposed to cut your odds of getting sick in half if you take it right away."

"Yeah," he said, scribbling his signature on the check. "I guess I can take that." He looked up at me and smiled, not looking too sick. "Let's get out of here," he said. He tossed the pen on the table, and out we went.

At home I dug through the medicine cabinet, found the box of pills, and tossed it to Paul. He caught it and tossed it back to me. "It's too late," he said, shaking his head. "I'm already sick." He walked into the kitchen, so I followed him there.

"Seriously?" I said. "There's no way." I glanced at the clock on the microwave. "Thirty minutes ago you said you were worried you might get sick. Not even thirty minutes!"

Paul shrugged. "I probably already knew I was sick and didn't want to tell you."

"Maybe you're just tired," I suggested. "And why wouldn't you want to tell me?"

"You're probably right." He didn't look at me when he spoke. Instead he walked past me, opened the refrigerator and poured himself a glass of orange juice and took a long sip. "Vitamin C," he said.

"I'm tired too," I said.

"Maybe you're also sick," he said matter-of-factly.

"I'm not. I'm just tired."

"Okay," Paul said. He held his hands up, palms facing me, surrendering. "I'm just tired, not sick. Is that better?" He finished the glass of orange juice and put it in the sink. Then he stalked out of the kitchen and back toward our bedroom.

"Well, now you're lying," I said, following him into the master bathroom, where he was putting toothpaste on his toothbrush. His hair was sticking up on the side, a sign he had just been running his hand through it, evidence of his exasperation with me.

"Rosie, I just want to go to bed," he said. "I don't feel good, and you said you're tired too, so let's just go to bed." He stuck the brush in his mouth, and with his free hand, he rubbed at a smudge on the mirror.

"I don't feel like it," I said. "And you're being kind of rude."

He rinsed his mouth and spat and rinsed again. "I'm not," he said. "But I'm done with this conversation."

"I had a bad day," I told him. "I feel upset. I needed to talk to you, and now you can't help me because you're sick."

He looked at me as he dried his hands on the towel hanging by the sink. "A bad day," he said. "Really? Funny how you didn't mention your bad day at dinner. Are you sure you aren't rewriting the past just because you're upset now?"

"Just say you're sorry I had a bad day. How hard is that?"

"I'm sorry," he said robotically, moving past me into the bedroom. "Tomorrow will be better."

"I wish you would let me take care of you," I said, sitting next to him on the bed. "Can you just take the medicine?"

"No," he said. "Because it won't help. But if it makes you feel better, you do a good job taking care of me, I promise." He put his hand on my leg, but it felt heavy and perfunctory there. I leaned in toward him anyway.

"That's not true," I said.

"It is," Paul said. He looked tired around the eyes—even sick, possibly—but he reached over and touched my cheek. "And like I said, tomorrow everything will be okay."

He was right. The next day was better. It always was until it wasn't, and we couldn't get back to the better days on our own.

"All done," Amanda says now. Scissors still in hand, she goes to stand beside Matthew, cocks her head to study me. She begins to cry. Now we all watch her.

"Is it that bad?" I ask her. I ask Paul. Paul says nothing, but Amanda shakes her head. "It's just uneven," she says. She holds a hand up so that it partially obscures her face. "I think everything is catching up to me," she says. "The fire."

"It's a lot to take in," Paul says.

Amanda's face crumples, and she nods. Matthew pulls her to him. "And I'm pregnant," she says. She smiles and cries at the same time, a little sputtering sound.

Paul claps his hands together and swoops over to Matthew, who sticks his hand out, and the men shake, and Amanda smiles at me, wiping her nose. "Four months along," she tells me.

"God has blessed you," I say, and I stand up too, hair falling off my shoulders, more for me to sweep up before the birds can carry it away, and I go to her. I hug her. When she steps back, she holds her dress against her body so that I can see the gentle curve of her expanding body. She is small-boned, small-framed. It seems impossible this is a body that has borne three children, that is growing a fourth. My body seems hardier, sturdier—I never lost my gymnast's build, strong and hard—and it has borne none, grown none. I pull away and smile at her. "Thank you for cutting my hair," I tell her. "I love it."

LATER, AFTER I have showered and gotten in bed, Paul comes in, and he looks at me as he undoes his belt and slips off his pants, pulls his shirt off over his head. Paul is tall and lean. He ran cross-country for our college, and even though he stopped any serious training years ago, he retains that look, strong enough, patient enough to run and run and run without stopping. "Hey," he says.

"I look like a little Victorian child who was forced to work in a factory," I say.

"Right," says Paul. "They had to cut your hair off so it wouldn't get stuck in one of the machines and scalp you."

"Exactly."

He disappears into the bathroom and reemerges with a toothbrush in his mouth, stands in the doorway of the bathroom brushing for a minute and disappears again.

"You aren't wrong," he says when he comes back out and climbs into bed. "You do look a little like that."

"Rude," I say, but we both laugh. We lie on our backs and look up at the ceiling. There is a watermark that stretches a foot each way, and it's shaped like Europe. One night we looked at it and tried to pick out all the places we'd been together: Barcelona would be there, on the coast. Paris up north. Florence, I think, over there. *Is that the Duomo?* Paul asked. *What else would it be?* I'd said. Afterward, when Paul went to sleep, I cried.

"Did God really tell you that?" I ask him now. "About my hair? Or are you punishing me for last night? Or for something I don't know about?" There was no story before he delivered that proclamation, no imagery for him to paint, no desert, no flood, and I am curious whose voice he heard say I should cut my hair.

"Rosie," Paul says, but his voice is gentle. "That isn't how this works. I heard it from the Lord." He rolls over to face me. "I don't want to punish you."

"Are you sure?" I ask.

"Positive," he says. "We're past that now. Thanks be to God."

"Thanks be to God," I say.

"Besides," he says, "it will grow back."

A few hours later, I wake up in the night and hear someone crying. It isn't me, and it isn't Paul, and so I roll over and go back to sleep.

IN THE MORNING, I go to the kitchen to make pancakes for everyone, using the three surviving eggs from my last trip to the grocery store. When I throw the eggshells away, I see my lopped-off hair sitting in a pile on top of the other trash. I reach down and touch it; it seems softer here than it ever did on my head, though I don't know why. I pinch some of the hair and close my hand around it, go into the backyard, away from the house, and throw it into the grass. Let the birds use it after all.

Five

The first time I cheated on Paul, we weren't married, and for a long time I told myself that it didn't count. We were in college and had just started dating (one reason it didn't count—we were in college, young, shouldn't have been tied down—and the second, that we barely knew each other. It was easy to forget about him when I didn't really know him in the first place). A group of girls drove to Austin one Friday night, and we went to this frat party in a shabby two-story house made of ancient wood, and the house seemed to list side to side, and every step we took—up the front porch, up the stairs—creaked.

I got drunk, draining endless Solo cups full of cheap beer and bad mixed drinks. There was a boy there with curly dark hair, and the two of us walked up those creaking stairs into a room with a Texas flag hanging over the bed. I let him take my clothes off and put his hands and mouth all over me until my body felt hot and weak. Did I think of Paul? I can't remember. I didn't know this other boy's name, but the next day I was ashamed of this and told the girls his name was Cory, and that we only kissed before he ran to the bathroom to throw up, a scene I'd watched in a movie. "Don't tell Paul," I begged them.

"It was only kissing," said Tess. "It doesn't count." I took the lie, swallowed it, and believed it. Even now I can't remember his face. He looks like a thousand boys I've known. No one special. He doesn't count.

The second time, I was home for Christmas break. A few months later, in the spring of our senior year, Paul would propose, and I knew he would. But one night, I was alone, my parents at my father's office Christmas party downtown, and my little sister, Bree, out of town on a ski trip, and I ran into my high school boyfriend in the frozen food aisle of the grocery store, lonely and glowing under the fluorescent lights. By this time, the parties and reunions during holidays had stopped; the lives we'd all created away from home had become our real lives, and the ones we'd visit here felt too small. Even though I loved my parents, it was lonely to be back. With no real friends around, I felt like the borders that made up my body, my person, began to dissolve until I was only floating from place to place, disembodied, vaporous. I had stopped gymnastics years before, but I longed to be in a gym again, concentrating only on my body and what I could make it do. I told my mom how I was feeling—unsteady and so out of sorts—but she brushed me off. "You're okay," she said. "Go for a run. Or maybe try cutting out sugar? Or dairy? You'll be fine." I'm falling apart, I told her, crying. "Everyone feels that way," she said. If that was true, how did anyone ever exist in the world? It was so hard. But then that night when I saw a familiar face, a familiar body at the grocery store, I thought *aha*! This was the thing I was missing. This could make it better.

We made small talk and quickly established that neither of us had anything else to do, so we went home together under the pretense of watching a movie and had sex on the bed I'd slept in since I was a little girl. This too barely counted, though it happened two more times while we were home, because we'd never had sex when we were together in high school, and it just felt like we were settling some score. Did I think about Paul? Yes. No. I pushed him out of my head and let my body be occupied only by itself and then by this other person, a boy I used to know. We never spoke again. I ignored the Facebook messages he sent me, I didn't answer his calls. Eventually I blocked his number. I said yes when Paul proposed because I loved him, he was so good and gentle, and I was lucky to be loved by him too.

At my bachelorette party, I fucked a stranger. I waited until my bridesmaids were asleep and went down to one of the bars. There were bars everywhere. We had found cheap plane tickets to Mexico and went to an all-inclusive resort my father paid for, and everything was on the beach: our rooms, the restaurants, the bar, the other bar. We were drunk the whole time. I met a man, and the night air was cool and salty, and we walked in the sand and each held a drink. When we finished them, we left the empty glasses in the sand.

Paul and I got married in August. I was twenty-two when I started teaching. I was very young but didn't feel that way. I never told Paul about the others, and what I told myself was this: things would be different. I would be different. I would be content and happy, secure in my marriage to a man I loved. I felt guilty that I did not feel more guilty, and I knew that was another reason I had to be different, better. I had never loved any of the others. Only Paul. And as far as Paul knew, he was the only person I'd ever slept with. This wasn't true: in high school, I had sex with my friend's older brother once when he was home from his freshman year of college and then for several months with a boy from another school; neither was my boyfriend, and I kept them both secret from my friends, so it felt like the truth when I told Paul he was my first. To be fair, I wasn't his, either—he had slept with a girl he had briefly dated freshman year, a choice he described as calculated and pragmatic. He had begun to resent his virginity; it seemed embarrassing to still be holding on to it, and this girl was nice and pretty and obliging. Tess pointed her out to me once when we were all out at this horrible, dark bar we liked to go to. She had a heart-shaped face and curly hair that reached to her waist. "She's a slut," I said to Tess, and she agreed.

Paul and I had been married for seven years when I met Nick. He taught Texas history in the classroom next to mine, and one night when Paul was out of town, all the seventh-grade teachers came to my house for pizza and beer, and when everyone left, Nick stayed. I was curious about what it would be like to sleep with someone else again, if it would feel bad or good or a combination of both, and I was lonely too, though I only realized it when Nick was there and Paul wasn't. In college, Paul had been a boy. Now he was a man with a job and a wife, who was gone so much, away at the office and on business trips, and without him there, I felt myself disappearing again. How could I be here without someone else to show me that I was?

Everyone said when you got married, life would be better because you had a partner, someone who saw you and knew you and understood you, and I had that, I thought, with Paul—but I was still alone. I spent every available minute with Paul, but when I looked at him, and sometimes when he spoke, when I spoke, I realized we were separated by a chasm that could never be bridged. How could he truly know me? How could I know him? Our heads were filled with thoughts, beautiful ones and ugly ones, that the other would never know. "What's going on in that head of yours?" Paul used to ask me, grinning, certain that whatever was going on in there was something that would only make him love me more, and I would shake my head. "Just thinking," I'd say.

The other thing was this: we had begun trying to get pregnant, and the possibility of a baby had unmoored me, the idea of sharing my body with something else. I wasn't an idiot; I understood that I had always been generous with my body, offering it to my coaches for training, to competition judges for their scrutiny, to men for pleasure, but the coaches always stayed on the outside, their hands on my body often but fleetingly, the judges touched me only with their eyes, and the men, yes, had been inside me, but they always left.

By then, my friends had babies. This was Texas, after all; we married young, became young wives and then young mothers and then just plain old mothers. My old teammate Sonja had relocated to the East Coast after her gymnastics career ended with an injury her sophomore year of college, and she was constantly reassuring me I had plenty of time. "Women here don't even start trying till they're, like, thirty-five!" she said. "Your eggs are nice and young." Tess, meanwhile, already had two children and was always bitching about them, how she never wanted to have sex anymore; how her old life was dead, she was forever tethered to her house, her husband, her children; how nursing had made her tits long, droopy, and flat—"Like paddles," she said once. "I could row a boat with them."

"You make it all sound so dreamy," I'd said.

"It is, though," she said, sighing. I didn't believe her. The strange, expanding body, leaking all the time; the breasts that would balloon to monstrous proportions only to inevitably deflate into boat-paddle tits. The blood, the shit, the crying. And that's just pregnancy. Then there's more blood, shit, and crying, only some of it your own. But Paul and I diligently tried anyway, and I preemptively began to mourn the loss of my life as I knew it even before it had begun to change.

Still, though, I harbored a thought I never told Paul: when I was a gymnast, we understood that we could push our bodies so hard they would break—after all, we aimed to exist in an eternal state of girlhood, just outside womanhood, and so we didn't care if we didn't have periods, couldn't have babies—and a part of me still hoped that maybe I actually had broken my body, rendered it useless in this regard.

When Nick went into the kitchen that night Paul was gone and came back with two more beers, grinning as he handed me one and noting that it wasn't late yet, not really, and maybe there was something good on Netflix, I saw my chance, an opportunity to reclaim my life, to revel in my body. I craved it, the adrenaline, that old feeling of being together and the even older feeling of being together with someone new. But I was alone when Nick took off my clothes, alone when I pulled him into the bed I shared with Paul, alone when he left, and even more alone after Paul got home.

I didn't want to tell Paul, of course. I hadn't ever wanted to tell him before, but this time finally counted: I hadn't been drunk, we weren't newly dating, it hadn't been unfinished business from long ago, and I had meant my vows when I made them at our wedding. But look what I had done. For a couple of weeks after Paul returned, I felt so bad and so far away from him that I thought if I told him, it would be one less obstacle keeping us apart, that if he knew, I could make it up to him. So I sat him down one night and cried, and he put his hand on my leg and waited for me to finish. "Get it all out," he said, his brown eyes full of care. I could barely stand to look at him, so instead I focused on his hand on my leg, the long fingers and the neat nails. "Did something happen at school? What could possibly be so bad?"

"This," I said, and told him.

"Okay," he said. That was it. The discussions came later—angry ones—but that was it at first: resignation, acceptance, a sense that he had seen this coming all along. Maybe he had. I thought maybe he had known all along, about the nameless frat boy, about my high school sweetheart, but I think had he known, he wouldn't have held that back from me. He was angry, of course, a righteous anger, and he would have used that information against me like a dagger,

letting the words pierce me until they drew blood. I understand now he never knew, and I have never told him about
the others. (I had only let them kiss me, touch me—even
Paul's old roommate one summer night when Paul was out
of town—and compared to what other things I had done,
these were nothing; but they meant the same thing, that I
could never be content, that my body was too wild, could
not be contained.)

For a month after that, I pursued his forgiveness furiously. Guilt replaced loneliness. I cooked him elaborate
dinners, I bought lingerie and wore it for him, I got the
name of a counselor for us to see, I cried until I made myself sick, I was docile and submissive like the wife I thought
he might want. I never tried to convince him to sleep in on
Sundays instead of go to the church service I knew he liked;
I made sure I was always the first one up, the first one ready.
Another month passed and another. I told him I thought
we should try harder to get pregnant, maybe see a fertility
doctor. I told him about all those years without a period as
a girl, said maybe it was finally catching up to me. He said
that right now we couldn't provide a stable home environ-
ment for a child, and I promised I would make it so.

Finally, I asked him if he would leave me. It was that
night, when I asked if he was going to leave, that he told
me about the Church of Dawes and his prophesy. He had
grown up going to a private Christian school, from pre-K
to senior year, and together we had maintained a nominal
interest in religion, attended Sunday services when we felt
like it, but this was something else. I'd never heard him talk
about prophecies before, and I had to pay close attention,
because it was like he was speaking a different language

and if I stopped listening for a second, I would lose the thread of what he was saying.

"I had this dream," he said. "There was this basket, and we were inside it together, and we were happy." He wasn't looking at me. He was jiggling his right leg and watching it, like it wasn't his own leg, like it wasn't his brain that was telling his leg to shake.

"We can be happy," I told him. I put my hand on his leg, but he shook me off.

"Someone was holding that basket so we wouldn't fall or anything," Paul said, raising his eyes to look at me. He paused.

"Who was it?" I asked, because I thought I was supposed to. "Who was holding the basket?"

"It was God," he said.

It was like Paul had gone through a third transformation, from college boy to man to something else. Somewhere in the midst of my groveling, he had shed his old life and put on a new one like he was putting on a coat. He said his old friend Lou, a relic of Paul's childhood, was instrumental in the church's founding, and he wanted us to go.

"Lou?" I'd asked. "The weird one?"

Lou and Paul grew up together on the same street, the best street ever, according to Paul, full of boys and bikes and skateboards and basketball hoops. It meant a lot to Paul, who's an only child, to have that. His parents have always been odd. Thanksgiving was their designated holiday, the one we spent with them every year, and it was always strained, always uncomfortable. They were pretty removed from Paul's life as he grew up, too entangled in their own to pay much attention to where he was going or what he was doing or who he was with. He used to say he could never imagine growing up another way, that he was always fine with being on his own. After all, he may have been lonely within his quiet, lovely house, but outside he was a part of a pack of boys, roving and wild. Eventually, though, Lou moved away, and Paul grew up, and the two lost touch.

Paul mentioned Lou off and on over the years, but just as another boy in the stories he'd tell about the mischief he got into as a child. There was never anything remarkable or memorable about Lou in any of these stories; the boys all blended together, forming for me a faceless blur of boyhood. They weren't Lou and Michael and Russell and Will but one single organism, all one breath of names. But during our senior year, Paul came home from hanging out with Michael, in town for a visit, flopped down on the couch, and said, "Remember that guy Lou from my old street? Listen to what Michael just told me about him." Apparently, Lou went off the deep end a little bit in college, only not in the typical kind of way: he didn't get anyone pregnant, didn't flunk out of school, didn't get into drugs. Instead, he became religious. "So?" I asked. We went to church sometimes too, Paul more often than me.

"No, I mean in a big way," Paul said. Paul's friend said that for a while, Lou would preach on campus, standing on a crate and yelling through a bullhorn at passersby about repentance and their eternal salvation. "And he has a giant cross he drags around with him," said Paul. "Michael says the cross has wheels, so really he wheels it around with him, like to class and stuff."

"Cuckoo," I'd said, and Paul had agreed then, but here we were years later, and things had apparently changed.

I was stunned. I had a million questions. Later, after we had verbally committed to Dawes, I logged in to Paul's Facebook while he was out getting his hair cut and found messages between him and Lou. They were infrequent and unexciting at first, just two guys reminiscing about childhood and catching up about adulthood. But then a few months later came the first mention of Dawes—previously Lou had only mentioned that he worked at a church—and as I read on, I could see what was happening: Paul was being recruited, the same way I had been back at the gym, college scouts visiting practice and sitting off to the side, observing, examining, seeing which of us would be able to cut it. Here was Lou evaluating Paul's potential; here was Lou selling his. Honestly, he barely had to try; Paul was so broken, ready to share intimate details not only about his life but mine. All my failures, all my shortcomings. *You can both start over here*, one of Lou's messages said.

Yeah, said Paul. That was his only response. *Here's my number, call me*, Lou wrote back, and then there was nothing from Paul after that, though I suppose a phone call came later. But the words that Lou used, the promise of a new start, were the same ones Paul said to me too. They had worked on both of us.

"They're changing lives," Paul said to me that night, and it was then that I could see he was as desperate as I was, that what he meant was they could change our lives. "They're saving people," Paul said.

"I'll do anything," I told him.

Six

The Wilders have officially been shunted along to Kyle and Lou, and I've been cleaning up after them when Paul comes home, calling for me. "In here," I say from the laundry room, where I'm washing sheets and towels they used.

He pokes his head in. "Got a text from Lou. It's baby time," he says. "People are already heading over there."

"Which baby?" I ask, stuffing another round of sheets into the mouth of the washing machine.

"Friedrichs'," he says, already out of the room. Through the tiny window in the laundry room, the afternoon sun is already high, its light relentlessly yellow and cheerful, a bright, burning daffodil in a blue field. It will be hot when we gather outside their house, but I think of Julie Friedrich, pale as milk, her hair barely a shade darker than her skin, laboring now in her bedroom, and I think it's better to be outdoors, sticky in the spring heat, than inside that house, sweating and pushing a child out into the world.

By the time we get to the Friedrichs' house, people are already assembled. Some are scurrying around, making preparations for the party this will become; others are already dancing, twirling, singing, physically manifesting the joy God has put inside them. I think suddenly of Amanda, how we spent hours on the lawn outside her burning house, crying and praying, our bodies both worn out and so, so alive. The fire bright and wild in the darkness, like jagged red, orange, yellow mountains crumbling and reassembling themselves over and over. "Paul," I say. He looks at me. "What would happen if there was a fire right now?"

"Like, here and now?" he asks, gesturing at the Friedrichs' small house. I nod, but he shakes his head. "It wouldn't happen. It only happens at night."

"But what if," I ask.

"Well," he says. "I guess we'd let it burn, like always."

"What about Julie, though?"

"What about her?" he asks, holding open the gate to the backyard. "Kyle! Smells great, man." Kyle is already at the grill, tongs in hand, laughing with the men who mill around him, occasionally turning hot dogs over, flipping patties. The air smells like meat and flowers—the azaleas are blooming, bright and pink—and my stomach turns. At one birthing celebration, Kyle had smoked ribs, and the new mother, spent after labor, requested a plate of them. Papa Jake took a picture of her on his phone, smiling and sweaty and red-mouthed, sticky-fingered, and put it on the church's Instagram. I do not have a phone or an Instagram account, not anymore, but Paul has both, and he showed me. It got three hundred likes.

"Rosemary," a woman named Missy says as we walk up. "Look at your hair! Hey, can I get your help for a sec? Can you fill up this pool?" She points at an inflatable baby pool to my left, a picture of a pink-tailed mermaid winking up at me from the pool's floor, and hands me a hose, already running, the water streaming from its mouth onto the grass.

"Of course!" I chirp, and Paul squeezes my shoulder, excusing himself. Missy leaves me too, to drag out a sprinkler in another part of the yard. As soon as she turns it on, the children run to it, leaping through the spray, drenching themselves and laughing and slipping on the wet grass. By the end of the day, the yard will be torn up with muddy craters and divots made by wild little bodies, grass trampled by two hundred feet. Before I can even finish filling up the little pool, a naked toddler I recognize as belonging to Missy plops herself down in it to splash. I hand her the hose, and she is delighted by the water spewing out of it. She sprays herself first in the face, then the tummy, and then points the hose toward a group of men talking with their backs to her. "Do with it what you will," I tell her, and make my way to the shade of an oak tree, far out of the water's reach, and sit on the ground.

People have arranged themselves around the yard into positions of prayer, solitary, some of us still and some of us moving, driven by the Spirit. Amanda, one of these who is never still, is wearing a different long dress now, Caroline's maybe. This one fits her better, and when she spins in the sunlight, I can see the outline of her legs.

Across the lawn, Paul has joined Lou and Kyle near the grill, and two small boys, shirts off and in baggy swim trunks, slip through the trio like little fish toward another baby pool. The bodies of the men bend to avoid being touched, and Lou calls after the boys to be careful, but of course they don't turn around. Paul and Kyle laugh, Paul's eyes crinkling, but Lou smiles woodenly. At first glance, Lou seems normal—he's okay-looking, handsome enough in a private-school-boy way. Maybe at some point he was even normal, and it was his rebirth as a follower of Papa Jake that made him so withdrawn and short, emptied him out.

Suddenly, though, the men are no longer laughing but frowning, Kyle with one arm drawing them both nearer, three heads together looking at the screen. "Oh no," I watch Paul's lips say, and then I see him look up, searching for me, and I stand. I step out of the shadows, but I don't go to him. In front of me, Amanda has stopped spinning. She turns around. "Something is wrong," she says.

Paul strides over to me and takes my hand. "The baby is here but isn't breathing," he says. "Papa just texted from inside. We need to pray now. I'm going to gather everyone in a circle, for strength. Will you help?"

"Of course," I say, and Amanda nods too, and the three of us scatter, grabbing everyone we see, the children too, though they do not understand the urgency, and they complain and pull away before their mothers drag them back. We create one circle in the backyard, fast, and there is another in the front yard. We grow quiet as we assemble.

I stand next to Amanda, who holds my hand and Abigail's hand—Abigail, who materialized out of the throngs of children still wearing her nightgown, wet and sticking to her little body. On my other side is Lou, and we do not hold hands. It's funny, because a circle by definition is unbroken—otherwise, what is it?—but even in this moment, we have a side for women and a side for men. This means there are two little gaps in the circle where the women's half ends and the men's half begins.

We flank this house to offer the best kind of protection we can, turning our backs to anyone who doesn't belong to us, but I always think: Those two gaps, couldn't they let anything in? The thought frightens me, as does the thought of the baby inside, breathless and unmoving, and I squeeze Amanda's hand next to me, and she squeezes back, a quick pulse like a heartbeat.

The quiet breaks as Renee begins to pray in a loud voice, warbling with emotion. Renee is always the first to speak, her words the ones to break the dam, and sure enough, others begin to shout and pray, offering prophecies, words over this child. The baby is a boy, the baby is a girl, the baby will be a great leader, the baby will be a good follower, with gifted hands, gifted language—but the fact that they're contradictory, Papa Jake has told us, doesn't make any of them untrue. The world is a complex place; we must try to hold two opposing ideas in our heads at the same time, reconcile them to each other. And so we ask to think like God, to know what He knows, see what He sees. I close my eyes and somehow I try to think only of the baby and not think of the baby at the same time.

The circle is vibrating, trembling with the messages of the Lord, when we hear the back door shut, slamming, and we all look up, and there is Papa Jake, red-faced and sweaty as though he himself has labored. He seems loose, spastic, like his limbs control only themselves and there is no greater body governing their movement, and he runs toward us, to Lou beside me. The two men grab at each other's arms. "A miracle," says Papa Jake in a low voice, and Lou closes his eyes. Papa Jake turns to all of us now, reaching out to the entire circle, like he can gather us all, hold us all. "A miracle!" he cries. We erupt, embrace. Amanda scoops up Abigail and kisses her neck, then turns to me and kisses me too, on my bare neck, no longer hidden by my hair, like I too am her child. She laughs when she pulls away. Across the circle my eyes find Paul. He is crying. The people in the front yard begin to stream in, beckoned by the sound of rejoicing, and we fold them into our celebration.

"We called the baby back to us," Papa Jake says, eyes shining. "The Lord gave me a name for her, and I called it, and she came back."

"The baby's a girl?" asks Lou.

"Lily of the Valley," Papa Jake says. "But we'll just call her Lily." He holds his hand up. "Shh," he says. "If we're quiet, we can hear her crying." We hush, and we do.

"How is Julie?" Matthew Wilder calls.

Papa Jake nods. "She's good," he says. "Worn out after such a long labor, as you can imagine. And weak. This was difficult for all of us."

Around the circle, the children squirm, anxious to go back to the sprinklers, which are still going, making arcs of water across the grass. Papa Jake laughs. "Be free," he says to them. "Go crazy. Knock yourselves out."

"But not really," says Caroline, his wife. "Please. We've had enough frightening things for one day." Her own children run past, her daughter's long braid thick as a rope whipping behind her. Caroline comes and stands next to Papa Jake, slips her arm around his waist. "Should we have the women go in and see her? Deliver their words to her?" she asks, looking up at him. She is tiny and light, a shining dragonfly with gossamer wings.

"Yes," says Papa Jake. "I'm sure you're all starving."

Caroline nods. "I'll gather the troops." All she does is look at us, and she brings the few dozen of us together like magic; we line up and follow her through the gate to the front yard, a streak of women and a little flock of girls, all in long sleeves, long dresses, cutting across the Friedrichs' small front lawn. A car driving past slows down in front of the house, and we all turn to watch it, tense, alert. We wait to endure whatever wickedness comes flying out the car's open window, but it's only an old woman scowling at us from the passenger seat, and we stare back to remind her we are the ones who belong here. Then she is gone.

Caroline stands on the top step leading up to the house, facing us, and I think of how I used to take my students on field trips, looking at them with both worry and pride as they lined up outside the museum or other place where we had to be well-behaved, a place with even more rules than our normal place. Caroline holds her hands up to silence us, though we are mostly quiet already. I am close enough to her, at the front of the line with Amanda, that when she lifts her hands, I can see circles of dampness under her arms. "You know the drill," she says. "No lingering, no conversation besides sharing your words with Julie. No touching the baby. In and out." We all nod, and Caroline opens the door. The air-conditioning rushes out at us, and we step inside.

I love to see the homes of other people, though the houses we all live in were mostly already furnished when we arrived. But if you look closely, there are still clues about the kind of people who live there, what's left out, what is put away. Here, in the living room, the blinds are open.

THE BURNING SEASON | 63

There is a couch covered in striped fabric, a matching arm-chair, a side table in tan wood topped by a lamp, the bulb burned out, a fat globe-shaped vase brimming with freshly cut pink flowers sitting on the coffee table. I recognize the flowers from the bushes in the front yard. I like to imagine Julie, nine months pregnant, clipping them herself, assembling them in the vase, giving herself something beautiful.

"This way," says Caroline, and she marches us down a dark hall to a bedroom door behind which Lily of the Valley is still crying. Caroline opens it a crack and peeks in. "Hey, girl," she coos loudly over the baby's wails. "Are you ready for us?" Julie must nod because Caroline says, "Good," turns, and tells us that we will go in two at a time, and she will stand at the door monitoring us. "You're up," she says to Amanda and me, and now she swings the door open for us to step inside.

The air in the room is thick and sweet. The ceiling fan whirs overhead. There is no quilt on the bed, but the sheets are pristine, white, bright against the dull blue paint on the walls. They must have changed the bedding after the birth, and somewhere in the house the washing machine rocks and shakes, taking those soiled things and making them clean. The dryer rumbles too, filled with tiny baby clothes, warming them for the girl to wear. Julie sits on the bed, her legs under the sheets, the top half of her shrouded by some loose white garment. Near her hairline, around her forehead, the hair curls, the way mine used to after I finished running. The rest of her blond hair tumbles down over her shoulders, and she looks regal, like a woman in a painting. In her arms, the baby is swaddled in a white blanket, wrapped up tightly, continuing to cry. Julie has trails running down her face, from her eyes, from her nose. She has been crying too.

"Congratulations!" says Amanda. She approaches the side of the bed so she is closer to the baby. "I think she's hungry."

"I nursed her," Julie says. "But I don't think it worked."

"It will eventually," Amanda says. She leans over. "Your milk isn't in yet. Want to try while I'm here? Sometimes you just need someone else to make sure their latch is deep enough."

"Not now," says Caroline.

"Okay," Amanda says, stepping back, collecting herself. "The Lord told me that Lily will be a good wife someday and a good mother, like you." Amanda has received visits like these each time she's given birth and has heard all the blessings we could offer, and I wonder how many of us told her that her boys would grow into men of great faith, that they would lead their households well, that Abigail would be a good wife and mother. It's funny that God gives us all visions and knowledge of these same gifts for all these babies, odd the things that get left out. Strength in tiny girls, gentleness in little boys. Paul, though, has always been gentle. I always imagined him as a sweet little boy, the kind who crawls into his mother's bed on stormy nights and curls up close to her. The kind of man, now, who cries when a baby has made safe passage into the world. When I met Paul's mother, I assumed she would be gentle like Paul—where else would he have learned such tenderness?— but she was reserved and serious, a mother whose affection was limited to a cool pat on the shoulder. She was not a mother who would pull the covers of her bed back for her scared little boy, who would weep over the birth of a baby. This realization made me love Paul more; his softness was simply innate, nurtured by no one, but present nonetheless.

"Thank you," Julie says to Amanda, and the baby squalls, pushing at the confines of her swaddle.

"She'll fall asleep soon," Amanda says. "I promise." She looks at me, my cue.

"She'll be a good listener," I say. "She already is. Papa Jake told us she answered to her name and came back to you."

For a moment, Julie doesn't respond. On the bedside table, there is a small chrome clock, the old-fashioned kind with the bells on top, like two ears on the round face of a teddy bear. I watch the second hand tick wildly around, unstoppable. Lily cries more softly now, and I think that maybe Julie is waiting for her to stop so that she doesn't have to speak over her. But then she says, "Yes." That is all. I look over at Caroline, who is watching us intently. "She came to Papa," Julie says.

"And to you," I say.

"If it was a girl, I was going to name her Evelyn," Julie says. "I had a doll named Evelyn when I was little." Her voice is tight, like there are still tears somewhere but she cannot find them to let them spill.

"You did have a girl, honey," Caroline says.

"Thank you, Rosemary," Julie says.

"Let's bring in the next girls," Caroline says, and holds out her arm so that Amanda and I will follow. The next women come in as we exit. The baby is still crying.

"Poor little thing," says one of the women in the line. "She must be hungry."

"Or cold," says another. "Or hot."

"I hope it's not anything worse," says the first, and then Amanda and I leave the line behind and find our way to the back door, through the laundry room, where little piles of tiny clothes sit on top of the dryer.

"Oh," says Amanda when she sees them. She reaches out a hand, touches a onesie with the tips of her fingers. "The clothes get me every time."

"So sweet," I say, and I open the door to the backyard where the celebration has begun in earnest. Amanda leaves, off to find her children or her husband or simply another woman to talk to—and Paul comes up to me and hands me a bending paper plate with a hot dog on it.

"They didn't have any relish," he says. "Sorry."

"Thanks," I tell him, taking the plate and lifting the hot dog to my mouth. Paul stands beside me, with his hands in the pockets of his shorts, watching Lou and Kyle set up a little speaker on one of the folding tables that holds bags of chips, sweaty rows of lettuce, cheese slices, tomatoes.

Paul sighs. "Rosie," he says, and it sounds like he is going to cry again, and I look up, my mouth full. "I want a baby."

I swallow. "I know," I say. "We're working on it."

"It's taking so long," he says.

"Paul, I'm old. I mean, not old old, but did you know girls are at their most fertile when they're, like, sixteen? I'm twice that age."

Paul nods but doesn't look at me, looks past me, over my head. When he is worried, he gets this little crease right between his eyebrows, and the space between his eyes and brows shrinks. He looks like a little baby hawk. "Yeah," he says. "Okay."

"Hey," I say, and reach out to touch his elbow. His shirt is thin, and it sticks to his hot, damp skin. "It will happen."

"It doesn't look good for us," he says, "not to have a baby."

I know this. I feel it. People will begin to wonder, if they haven't already. Surely they have. "God will bless us," I say. "I know it."

"I had an idea," Paul says. "While we were praying for Lily of the Valley."

"I'm open to suggestions," I tell him.

"I need to clear it with Papa first," he says. "Before I tell you. Just to see if it's even a possibility." He stands up on his tiptoes, even though he is already so tall, and scans the crowd. "Actually, I see him, I think I'm just going to go now."

"Oh," I say, "okay. I'll be here." He nods again, trots away. I stand alone and eat my hot dog and watch Paul approach Papa Jake, who is talking to another man, and stand quietly, dutifully, until they finish and the other man walks away. Papa Jake claps his hand on Paul's shoulder.

The conversation is brief—they are close, the situation is certainly already known to Papa Jake—and even before Paul walks toward me, grinning, I can tell that whatever his idea is, Papa Jake has agreed to it. *Yes*, I see him tell Paul. *Thank you*, Paul says, relieved and giddy. Now it is his turn to shake Papa Jake's hand, and this time, Papa Jake pulls Paul into a hug, and they pat each other's backs.

"That was easy," I say as Paul returns.

"When you have a word from the Lord, it is," he says. "Okay, you ready?"

"Yes," I say.

"You're going to help Julie with Lily of the Valley!" he says. "You're going to come over here and pray with Julie and help her with whatever she needs, and each time she's going to pray over your womb." He reaches over to me and puts both hands on my stomach. "Like this," he says. "Hands right here. This is how I saw it in my vision. And you're going to touch her stomach. She's going to transfer some of her fertility to you." He pulls his hands away and takes a step back.

"Sounds easy enough," I say. "I'll do it."

"I'm glad," Paul says. "Papa said just give Julie a couple of weeks, and then you can start. And just think! This could be a new practice for our entire church! We could be helping future couples get pregnant more easily. Someone has to be the first to do something, right?" He is so eager, looking at me. Gone is the baby hawk, and he looks like a golden retriever instead, all happy, ready energy. "I'll take your plate," he says. "You should go sit in the shade. It's hot." It is as if I'm pregnant already.

Paul walks toward the trash cans, which are already overflowing and surrounded by flies darting around the old food, the crumpled plates and napkins. On his way, he is stopped by men who want to talk with him, laugh with him. My husband has always been the kind of man other men love—athletic, a good sport, quick to joke and offer a hand—and because women see men loving him, his value increases. In college, girls would tell me how lucky I was to be with Paul. What about *him*? I always wanted to say. Isn't he lucky to be with me too? "It's the other way around," Tess said once after I'd complained about this. "He's not good enough for *you*." I didn't believe her, but I appreciated her being on my side. In fact, it felt so good to be told how special and wonderful I was that it wasn't until later, after Paul and I got engaged, that it occurred to me that maybe Tess saw something in Paul that I didn't. When I asked her, she hesitated before saying, "Rosie, my love, if you're happy, I'm happy." And I was.

More women file out of the house, two by two, come out and find their husbands, their friends, their children. In a moment, I will find friends too, the other women. I won't stand here alone even if I'd like to. They will tell me my hair looks nice, that the new cut flatters my face. I will thank them. I will tell them of Paul's vision, his insight, even though it makes me look bad, reveals the vanity Paul saw in me, and the women will judge me, will tell their husbands later, and their husbands will admire Paul, a decisive man of faith, of action. This is a gift I can give Paul. A gift that is easy to give, though it is not the one he wants. That one is much harder.

I walk up to a group of women standing in the shade of the oak tree I sat underneath earlier in the afternoon. "Rosemary," says one. "Your hair! You look so chic. Very French."

I smile and touch a piece by my ear. "Thank you," I tell her.

Seven

At the end of the birthing celebration, Papa Jake gathers us all around, sunburned and weary, the Friedrichs' yard rutted and wet, and tells us that tomorrow will be a healing ceremony. It will be open to the public, he adds. He often tells us we are making a name for ourselves, that people are hungry for the truth. They have begun to talk about us, this little church in this little town, great in power, gifted by the Lord. Just look, Papa Jake has said before, we have nearly three thousand followers on Instagram now.

As we clean up and begin to leave, another car slows down in front of us, and one by one we look up as it idles. Behind that one is another, then another—a whole line of them coming down the street, slow-moving, like a funeral procession. "Oh, come on," says Paul. "This is so stupid."

"A car drove past earlier," I say, trying to recall what it had looked like—blue? Black? I know it was dark, with rust spots shaped like continents on the body. I imagine the middle-aged son of the old woman punching words into his phone, getting on Nextdoor to rally the troops. Here's the address, let's go.

The driver of the first car lays on the horn and speeds off. Then the driver of the second car also honks, a pathetic little bleat, and when it passes us, the next honks too, this one deeper, older, a goose, not a lamb. One by one, they honk and pass and hurry away, but the last one—a jacked-up red truck with mud on its big tires—stops and is silent. We wait, frozen. I imagine the window suddenly rolling down, revealing a man with a gun pointing at us, easy targets. I imagine them tossing a flaming bag of dog shit at our feet. I imagine a muscled arm throwing a writhing, moving burlap sack out the window, snakes spilling from its wide-open mouth when it hits the pavement. We are still, silent. When we arrived, Papa Jake told us not to underestimate them. "Beneath the simplest guise can lie an impenetrable darkness," he warned. "You think they're harmless? Dumb old country folk? Look closer. I guarantee they're looking closely at us."

"For fuck's sake," Paul says now under his breath as the truck idles, engine rumbling. "Completely immature." But I think of Julie upstairs in her room, and Lily of the Valley, both of them adjusting to this strange new world in which they are now a mother and a child, and the sound of anger slicing it open, and I am relieved when finally the truck's tires squeal and it passes, its horn going and going until it is out of sight, like lungs screaming until there is no air left.

In the morning, before we go to the healing service, Paul gets his phone out and shows me the church's Instagram account. "Look," he says, tilting the phone screen toward me. "I took the picture Lou put up for the service today."

The picture is a three-quarters profile shot of Papa Jake

from yesterday, filtered in black and white, and he is laughing in a photogenic way, the dimple in his cheek deep, smile lines radiating from around his eyes. He has a good jawline, a full head of hair, nice teeth. Objectively, he is attractive, though I am sure I'd never fuck him. There is something both artificial and superficial about him that repels me, like the silver film on one of those scratch-off lottery tickets, the shiny little square covering what is inevitably going to be a disappointment.

Beneath the photo is information for the healing service—who is eligible ("the sick, the weary, the wounded"), who to contact to arrange a visit. I think of the old Paul, angry and weeping and open as a wound, opening up Instagram, searching for this page, scrolling through the pictures and feeling, for the first time in a long time, hopeful. "You have a good eye," I say, and take my hands away from the phone.

He holds the screen at a bit of a distance, as if it will help him see the image anew, and studies the picture. "I think so too," he says.

WHEN WE ARRIVE at the chapel, Paul and I go inside together and take our seats. For public services, married couples are allowed to sit together. It would make people uncomfortable to see us divided, to walk in with someone and immediately be separated.

Papa Jake stands at the door with Kyle—strange, stilted Lou shunted away, given another job—and they welcome in the strangers. There are not many. There never are, though Papa Jake always says that however many we have is the right amount. Today, a couple the age of my parents. A group of three young women, probably in their twenties.

A man on his own. Outwardly, none of them look sick, but they must be. Caroline comes over to the three girls, who move as a unit, and she hugs each of them, separating them, and they relax into a little line and follow her to the front. Two are wearing jeans even though it is hot, muggy, but one is wearing a dress, the same azalea pink as the flowers growing on the bushes outside the Friedrichs' home, bright and cheery. Her legs are tan and look so long, there's so much skin to see. I watch her take a sweater out of her purse and drape it over her shoulders. "I miss my legs," I whisper to Paul.

"I think they're still there," he says. "Under all the fabric."

"God's not going to tell you we should cut them off too, is He?" I ask.

"Hilarious," he says, but he grins.

The girls sit in the first row next to Caroline, whose children sit on her other side. Caroline has a daughter and three sons, the girl the oldest. When the daughter, Ruth, got her period last year, Papa Jake announced it during a service, Caroline cried, and Ruth sat statue still, hands in her lap. "So grown up now," Papa Jake had said. "I can hardly believe it." The bow on Ruth's head, as large as a predatory bird, twitched, the only sign of the girl shivering.

I feel sorry for her; I imagine she must be lonely. When Paul and I first came to Dawes, she was inseparable from a girl named Erin, only a few years older, their heads always together, shoulders touching, fingers often intertwined. But there are some ages when a few years' difference between girls means very little, and some when it means a great deal, and Ruth and Erin have reached the latter stage.

Ruth, despite her father's announcement, still looks like a child, but Erin does not, her legs lengthening, her face thinning. I have watched the older girl leaving Ruth behind, staying close to the women instead, signaling to all of us that she's grown now, ready to leave behind childish things and marry one of the young men here.

When that time comes for Ruth, there will be lots of men lining up to marry her. She is a pretty girl. She looks like her mother. I've heard that Papa Jake keeps a list in his office of all the births and birthdays of the girls, their names in a column written in black ink. Beside each name, another name, in pencil so he can erase and replan, a man, a boy. A husband.

Papa Jake emerges from the left side of the stage—he refigured the front of the chapel when he bought it, so that now there is a raised platform with wings and curtains like a theater—and lifts his hands as he walks out. We all stand to receive him, and he grins at us. He extends his hands to the newcomers, and I cannot see their faces, only the backs of their heads as they too behold Papa Jake, this man who will heal them.

"Welcome," he says. "Brothers and sisters, welcome to Dawes." Applause erupts; someone whistles. "I know why you're here. We're going to get to you, I promise, but we are going to do a few other things first."

Papa Jake is meticulous about the order of events during services. Sometimes it's impossible to gauge exactly how things will go—the Spirit moves in mysterious ways—but Paul has told me that Papa Jake comes to every service with a plan. "First things first," he says now. "We're going to see a miracle." Again, we clap. I find the whistler: a middle-aged man who looks like a beaver, with two fingers in his mouth like buckteeth.

"Though we are special here," he says, "though God has set us apart and equipped us, we are not untouched by sickness. Or the passage of time. Or death. It's the way the world works, even for us. Them's the breaks." He shrugs, then holds up a finger. "But not today.

"Could I ask the sick to please stand?" he asks. "Not if you're a guest, though, not unless you want to. You can stay seated. We don't want anyone to feel uncomfortable presenting themselves in any way." He smiles. "My friends, though, my brothers and sisters here—I don't care if you're uncomfortable. Stand up." We all laugh at the joke of his bossiness, his wish to embarrass us.

A few stand up. Two of the people standing are sick every week. One is a very tall man, with long arms and big hands he holds up in the air, as though he is preparing to catch something large. His name is Erik with a K, like a Viking. I've asked Paul before if he knows what he's sick with, and Paul rolled his eyes and said, "I think he's looking for attention."

The other is a woman named Molly, married to someone Paul is close to, a quiet man named Richard, who used to be a science teacher. She too has some unspecified chronic illness, though unlike Erik, she looks unwell. There's no way of knowing what she has, but if it's something serious, it's killing her slowly, and if it's anything else, then it's a lesson from the Lord. She has very rosy cheeks, like a fever is always burning, but beneath that, her skin is pallid; she looks wan and tired.

I've always wondered if Molly makes herself sick, if it's

all in her head, psychosomatic or attention-seeking, like Erik. Regardless, we pray for her during our healing services. We hold her in our hearts. Erik too, even if he is a liar.

A third man standing is a friend of Paul's, Franklin Aaron, whose name I struggled to remember for months. Whenever anyone said it, I heard it with a comma separating the two names, the way they'd be written in an attendance book: Franklin, Aaron. Franklin has a broad chest, broad shoulders, and a beard that makes him look serious, so that when he smiles, it seems like only the top half of his face is happy. He looks like he could cleave a log in half with an axe. Something about him makes me uncomfortable, and so I always hold myself at a distance from him. Like Erik, he looks healthy.

But as Papa Jake scans the sick standing in front of him, it is Franklin Aaron on whom his gaze stops. He comes down from the stage, descending the carpeted steps, and stands in front of the first pew. People in that row lean away, scoot over, create a little window for Papa Jake to call through. "Brother Franklin," Papa Jake says. "You are sick." It's unclear if it's a question or an observation.

"I am, Papa," Franklin says.

"Come on, then, friend," says Papa Jake, and Franklin, bear-broad, squeezes himself out of the narrow pew and makes his way to the stage to stand beside Papa Jake. We all clap. With his hands half in his pockets, the tops of them ruddy and too large to fit inside entirely, Franklin watches us watch him. I wonder what we look like to him. I imagine we look the same, like someone made a stamp of Paul and me and then stamped it up and down the pews, filling up the chapel, the same image over and over: young, healthy, well-groomed pairs of men and women.

"Ready?" Papa Jake asks Franklin, but even before Franklin says yes, Papa Jake's hands are on his head, cupping his ears like earmuffs and then moving down, searching for hidden illness the way a diviner looks for gold beneath the surface of the earth. The hands are on his shoulders now, then his arms, feeling the biceps, circling the wrist but not all the way, fingers not meeting, like a broken bracelet. He puts his hands on Franklin's neck and then moves down to his chest. They stop there and then pull back, as if singed by a heat from within. "Here," Papa Jake says. Franklin nods. "Your lungs." Franklin is silent.

"Today," Papa Jake says, turning to us, "we are going to cure him. God is going to cure him! We are going to call to God, bring Him here, and demand healing for our brother. Join me."

We will, we tell him. We will.

"All right," Papa Jake says. We quiet down. "You know what to do." He puts his hands by his side, and as he lifts them up, slowly, slowly, we begin to hum.

We are quiet at first. God speaks the language of the angels, a tongue known by only a few among us, but Papa Jake received a God-thought that if we sang to Him in a song without words, without our normal voices, if we reached a certain pitch, the right frequency, we could summon Him. And so we do. As Papa Jake raises his hands, we hum more loudly, and when his arms are straight up in the air, we open our mouths and sing the song with no words. The sound becomes an otherworldly thing, disembodied as if it is the air itself that is moaning.

The lights blink off, the way they did during my Reclamation, when Paul and I began to shimmer, but this time they are back on in the snap of two fingers, and the glory of the Lord rains down on us, alighting in our hair, caught on the men's shirt collars, dusting our faces. It stops soon, but it is enough—God has heard us calling. "Here He is!" Renee cries, always eager to show us what she sees. I see nothing, nothing at all.

Onstage, Papa Jake has turned to Franklin, and he has a hand on Franklin's chest and a hand on his back, and though he must be talking, praying, directing, we cannot hear him over our own voices. But what I can see is this, the tension, the building, escalating of something we cannot understand: Papa Jake's hand pressed hard into Franklin's chest, his other hand on Franklin's shoulder, desperate fingers gripping the fabric, Papa Jake's legs weakening, knees bending, as if it is this sick man who is holding him up. As if Papa Jake is caught in a current and Franklin, body rigid, unmoving, is a rock, a tree root, keeping him from drowning.

But then Franklin begins to cough. Again, we do not hear the sound over our voices, but we see the gesture of a person with a cough. He bends in the middle. He puts his curled fist to his mouth. Papa Jake thumps him on his chest, more of a slap, and then does it again as Franklin coughs, and then again and over and over, until Franklin jerks away, completely doubled over. A woman cries out.

Papa Jake walks over to Franklin, who is now on his hands and knees, and puts his hand on the other man's broad back, bends so that his head is close to Franklin's. He thunders his fists now, both of them, on Franklin's back, as though he is a table and Papa Jake is a child, hungry and waiting for his supper, demanding to be fed.

Franklin tenses, forehead pressed to the floor, back no longer like a table, but curved like a bridge. We cannot see his face. Papa Jake raises his hands, arms straight, and our sound grows louder again. He begins to lower them, and we let our voices weaken, until we are only humming. Franklin is on the floor coughing, body shaking, then he starts to heave, before he's on his back, spent, arms out to the side, and Papa Jake staring at his body. He finds Brother Lou in the first row and says, "The jar! Quick!" Lou springs up, a glass mason jar in his hand, and rushes it to Papa Jake, who grabs it and picks up something gray and wet off Franklin's chest. He drops the lump in the jar, tightens the lid, and sinks to his knees, holding the glass container in one hand above his head. Lou kneels beside Franklin and with a rag dabs at his face, his mouth, his forehead. When he pulls the man up to sitting, we can see that the front of Franklin's shirt is wet. With one hand, Franklin rubs at his eyes, like a tired child.

Now Papa Jake kneels beside Franklin too. It is silent in the chapel, besides Papa Jake saying to Franklin, "Do you want to see it?"

"What is it?" Franklin asks. "The . . . sickness?"

"I don't know what else it could be," Papa Jake says.

"I don't want to see it," Franklin says.

"I do," says Lou, and Papa Jake hands him the jar. It's as if the rest of us aren't here anymore, and I wonder for a second if maybe we aren't. That God came here and we went away.

Papa Jake stands up and offers a hand to Franklin, who

takes it and lets himself be pulled up to his feet. The pastor wraps him in a hug and whispers something in his ear before releasing him and turning him to face us. "Praise God," Papa Jake says.

"Praise God," we repeat.

"This man is healed," Papa Jake says.

"God has healed him," we say as Franklin trembles. "We have healed him."

"Rest," Papa Jake says to him. "Go."

Brother Lou puts the jar on the podium Papa Jake often stands behind to preach, and he hooks his arm through Franklin's and leads him back into the wings from which he came. The mass in the jar on the podium just sits there, does not breathe, does not ooze, does not reach with tendrils up the sides of the jar.

When I was ten, my dad killed a snake we found in our front yard, severing its head from its body with a shovel. He used the shovel to scoop the head into a glass jar just like the one holding Franklin's sickness, and even apart from its body, the mouth yawned, showing its fangs, while its abandoned body still moved on the hot pavement of the driveway. Only a reflex, my dad said, but I marveled at the paradox in front of me—movement where there was no life, breath with no lungs. The world grew at once bigger and less clear, expanding to such a size that I couldn't see it well at all; there was just too much of it to take in at once. This place, it turned out, was more complex than I understood it to be; it contained impossible things happening right in front of my eyes. A snake breathing without a body. Illness captured in a jar. Fires starting from nothing. A baby growing in hostile ground. Things that are but shouldn't be.

"I think we need a break," Papa Jake says. "Just a quick one? I think we have sandwiches." He looks to Caroline in the front row.

"On a table outside the church," she says, giving him a thumbs-up. "Unless the protesters took them."

"Great," says Papa Jake. "Take a break to eat, and we'll meet back here in twenty." Caroline hurries down the aisle, her children trailing after her, one of the boys stepping on the heels of his brother in front of him so the boy trips, foot popping out of his shoe.

"Wow," says Paul as we rise to file out to the lobby. "That was incredible. I want to talk to Franklin." He isn't anywhere we can see, though, and I wonder if he is still in the wings, in the dark, listening to us, searching his body for signs of disease.

"It's incredible," Paul repeats. "Seriously unbelievable."

"Yes," I say.

"I mean, you'd think it wouldn't be," he says. "After all we've seen. We've seen so much since we've been here. But I guess miracles are always kind of unbelievable, right?"

I turn around and see the strangers who have come here. They are gathered in a loose bunch at the front of the church, a little group who are strange to each other but even stranger to us. Or we are strange to them. Though, truthfully, it is both. The force of people behind us pushes us into the lobby, and the newcomers are out of sight.

Paul and I take our sandwiches outside. Next to us, a giant truck peels out of the parking lot, its big tires bouncing, the body of the truck tilting on the turn. The windows are down, and I can see a hairy elbow sticking out. Paul frowns. "Where are they going?" he asks. "No one is supposed to leave."

I shrug. "Not our problem."

"It could be," Paul says. But he relents, and we sit on the curb of the parking lot with some other couples eating their sandwiches, and we all talk about the service, about the people we know, the ones we left behind, who were sick, who are sick, the ones who won't ever know true healing. If only they would come here, we say, and join us—knowing, still, that part of the reason we are special is that they have not come here, they have not joined us. How special is something that anyone can be a part of?

Molly and her husband, Richard, are sitting with us, eating in silence. Molly is watching their children playing in the parking lot, jumping off the curbs, spinning around the post of the handicapped spot sign. She picks the crust off her sandwich and lets it drop to the ground. For a moment, it looks as if Richard might say something to her, but then he does not.

Sweating in the spring heat, we finish our sandwiches and go back inside, where we wait for another miracle.

Eight

After the second part of the service, Paul and I stand outside where the sun is starting to set. "I need to stay," he says. "Just for a little bit longer. I need to find Franklin. You could come with me, but I know you don't like him."

"That's fine," I tell him. "I'll take one of the bikes."

"Great," Paul says. "I'll see you at home, then." He squeezes my arm, a pulse like a kiss, and turns back to go inside the chapel.

I take the bike leaning against the building and walk it to the street. When I am out of sight, out on the country roads, I will hop off for a moment and tie my dress off to the side so that I can pedal more easily.

It's the beautiful, liminal time of day, right before night falls. I think of the baseball coach at my high school who also taught driver's ed, tapping the window as I drove and saying, "This time of day is when the most accidents happen." The sky is gray and lavender, the color of a pigeon's breast, the grass of the sprawling pastures a quiet, somber green as evening settles in.

These houses and fields and cows and horses belong to

the townspeople whose work or loyalty has kept them tethered to Dawes. When the church settled here, lots of people
left. But not everyone, of course, could, and some could but
just refused; but even some of those have begun to leave
now. And when they do, we buy their homes, their busi-
nesses; we stake another inch of the town for the church.
"For the Lord," Papa Jake says.

My family had a ranch too, out near La Grange, but it
was—it is—a ranch in name only, the kind of ranch that
lots of families in Houston own: not a way to make a living, but a way to escape the living you've made. When I
was growing up, my whole family would go there to relax
by the pool or shoot skeet or sit in the rocking chairs on
the wide porch my parents added at great expense the year
after they bought it. I remember telling Paul, the first time
I brought him there, how sad I would be to live in a place
where I never saw animals beyond dogs and cats, even if I
drove an hour or two outside the city. I liked the neighbors'
cows, the lazy flick of their tails and the way they plopped
down in the shade, or the nearby house with a large pen of
goats I always said hello to when we passed.

Tonight there are two cows outside the fence of one
of the houses I pass as I take the long way home. Standing there in the road like they almost belong there, they
startle as I approach. I stop and lean my bike against a
fencepost and look around to see that most of the cows
are still within the boundary of the fence, watching the
two escapees—and now me—warily. I walk a few feet up
the fence line to see that the gate is wide open, the lock cut
so that it dangles uselessly against the gate's metal bars.

I think about walking up to the house and knocking on the door to let the owners know the cows are out, but the house is set pretty far back on the land, and people have guns here, fingers ready on the trigger in case a stranger traipses across their land. I picture myself getting shot, then Papa Jake's hands on my body, digging inside for the bullet, dropping it into a jar with a plink, fingers stained red as he holds it up. *Look at how the Lord guided my hands.* I decide to leave the cows to their fate.

But as I bike back toward my home, I pass a different tract of land and notice a few more cows outside their fences, and then a horse. Now that I know to look, I see open gate after open gate. Someone has cut the locks on all of them. I wonder if the same person left food on the ground or something to lure the animals out, but I'm pedaling too quickly to look. It's not my problem anyway. Then I hear a man's voice behind me hollering at the cows and I'm relieved that they're being caught.

Inside one of my shoes, a tiny rock is pressing itself into my skin as I pedal, so I stop and remove it, but as I'm slipping the shoe back on, a truck slows down beside me: the same truck that sped away from the parking lot at lunch. Now I'm able to see the people inside it—two young recruits the church picked up in Austin a few months ago. The driver, Tyler, has just graduated from college; aside from the children, he's one of the youngest members of the church. "The Lord really changed him," Paul said to me when Tyler first got here. "He was just a boy, but Papa and Lou and Kyle, they've made him into a man of God now." To me, though, he still seems like a boy, youth and power and confidence coursing through him. The other is called Young Jake, to differentiate him from Papa Jake. He's compact and short, built like a child's wooden block.

"Hey," Tyler says, leaning across Young Jake. "Did you see all those animals? Making a run for it, I guess. Is that what you're doing?"

"Just going home," I tell him.

"Want a ride?" he asks. "We can throw your bike in the back." He is tan and pretty, but has the type of mustache college guys grow to be funny, sun gold, the hair on his head a shade lighter, the kind of man who used to spend Sunday afternoons getting drunk at the pools of apartment complexes he didn't actually live in.

"Yeah," I say. "I do."

"You do?" he asks.

"It will be dark soon. And you offered."

I worry for a second I've taken it too far, that he was hoping I'd fuck up and he could get me in trouble with whichever man is in charge of me, but then he grins. "Okay," he says. "Come on, then." Young Jake slides out of the truck and hoists the bike into its bed and then opens the door for me to climb into the cab.

"Oh, no," I say. "I'll ride in the back."

"My mom'd kill me," he says, "if I didn't give my seat up to a lady."

This, I know, is absolutely one step too far, but it's that distance which propels me into the passenger seat beside Tyler, who both repulses and attracts me. It's thrilling and uncomfortable, that old rush of adrenaline that comes with desiring and being desired. I want him to want me, and I want to reject him, to crush him. I feel nearly reckless, like I am standing on a cliff's edge, peering over, wind building, lifting my skirt, the ends of my hair. One gust and I'm over. "Take a left up here," I tell him.

"You got it," he says, and takes the turn. "You're Paul's wife, right?"

I'm looking out the window. A stray dog sniffs along the grass at the edge of the road and lifts its head, trots off out of sight. "Did y'all let those cows out?" I ask.

Tyler raises his eyebrows and puts one hand to his chest, the other loose, casual on the steering wheel. "I'd never," he says.

"Okay," I say, laughing even though it isn't that funny, and suddenly I am fifteen again, alone with a boy, both hopeful and terrified he will reach for my hand, feel the calluses there from the years of uneven bars, my tough hands so unlike the soft pink ones of other girls. I look down and find that I have been clenching them into fists.

Tyler laughs too. "The cows will be fine. Farm animals are stupid. They'll just stay wherever they're put."

"The locals will retaliate, you know," I say. "Then what?"

Tyler shrugs without looking over. "I hope they do," he says. "They don't belong here anymore. We do. Besides, where's the fun in letting a good old-fashioned feud die out?"

"Here." I tap the window, and he turns right. Our street is just a minute away, and with an ache in my stomach, I suddenly realize how profoundly stupid I am. Standing on the edge of a cliff—what did I think was waiting for me below? Rocks to break my bones, a river to swallow me up. "Actually," I say. "I'll just get out here. I'm close enough. I can walk."

"Nah," he says, eyes on the road ahead. "I'm going to drive you right up to your house."

I don't answer. "It's this street, yeah?" he asks in the silence. "Or the next?"

"The next," I say. The street where Paul and I live passes by us in a flash, and we come up on the next turn. "Here. Another left." My voice is cold, and I cough as if there's something in my throat, as if that's the problem.

"Hey," he says, glancing over at me. "You said you wanted a ride." His voice is lilting and his tone playful. He's amusing himself. I am the cow, too dumb to see she isn't where she should be. We take the left.

"That one," I say. "With the red mailbox."

"You should get Paul to mow the yard," he says as we pull into the driveway. All the lights are off inside. He puts the truck into park with a lurch, and we all rest, frozen, engine and bodies humming. "Should I walk you in?"

"I'm fine," I say. "Thanks for the ride." I hesitate, my hand on the inside of the door. "Could you do me a favor and not tell anyone about this? I just got scared biking in the dark, and I wasn't thinking. I'd hate for anyone to get the wrong idea."

Tyler frowns, making his mustache twitch. "Are you ashamed to be seen with me?" he asks, faux offended.

"Come on," I say.

He laughs. "As long as you don't happen to mention the great animal escape to anyone, we're good."

I nod and get out of the cab. From the back, Young

Jake waves. Even his hands are blocky. Short, square fingers ending in short, square nails. "We'll take the bike back to the church for you," he says.

"Thanks," I say. I go up to the front door and pretend to look for a hidden key in a derelict flower bed by the front door. I am hopeful that whoever lives here isn't home; it's possible no one lives here at all. Dying Dawes. Satisfied by seeing me kneel in the dirt, I suppose, or impatient, Tyler and Young Jake drive off. When the truck is out of sight, I walk back toward home.

Paul will wonder where the bike is. I'll tell him it got a flat tire. I can tell him about the truck, about Tyler, how he and Young Jake saw me and stopped, offered to take the bike back. Asked if I wanted to ride in the bed of the truck with the bike. That would be okay. I think of Young Jake's mom, somewhere in Texas missing her nice-mannered son. I, of course, declined the offer. I live just around the block. We all waved goodbye to each other, and I continued home on foot, night falling around me, the fire colors of evening turning blue black.

Did you see the cows out? Paul might ask.

What cows? I would say.

I think about the animals, how confusing it would be for them to see that open gate, to know that all it takes is a few steps and then a few more until you're free, if you even want to be free; you probably don't even know. But, then, to wonder, where would you go when you left?

THAT NIGHT, LYING in bed, I find myself remembering the year in college when Paul took up mountain biking. He spent a ton of money on a fancy bike, the special shoes that clip in, the spandex so brightly colored that he looked like a parrot when he wore it. He went to the trails in the park by campus every afternoon for a month, watched YouTube videos of guys biking along narrow ridges of mountains, the sky a tumbling and perilous blue behind them. Then one day he just stopped. "I'm tired of it," he said with a shrug. After that, he only used the bike for riding to and from campus, and when we moved to Houston, on leisurely rides through our neighborhood. I used to think this period of our life, this time in Dawes, was like that, a passing obsession that would eventually be buried. But every day we stay. The luster hasn't worn off yet. The truth Papa Jake gives us here—it makes the whole place shine.

And yet there are still times when I think about leaving Dawes, alone: When I'm tired. When I'm bored. When I hear the rush of cars on the freeway at the edge of town. When it's hot, and I have to run errands anyway and have to walk or ride my bike because Paul won't let me drive the truck. When I have something to say but don't say it. When Paul is mad at me or frustrated with me, even though I'm trying my hardest to not be frustrating. When we're praying and my mind wanders. When we're singing and my mind wanders. When Papa Jake is preaching and my mind wanders. When it's nighttime and I'm in those last few minutes of being awake, like now, when everything is a hazy sort of purple gray behind my eyelids, and the divide between who I once was and who I am now feels thin, and I can't stop myself from thinking of my parents and my sister, my friends, my old job, the old house with the ground-down stump in the front yard.

And so I make myself think about when I got to college

for my freshman year. I hated it. Everything felt wrong. If I wasn't in class, I was thinking about leaving or I was scolding myself for choosing this school when clearly another would have been a better fit, or I was watching enviously as pairs and groups of people walked past me on their way to lunch or the library or to the coffee shop I was too scared to go to alone. They all looked just like me, only they were happy. They looked around and thought about how lucky they were to be here, how perfect it all was.

"You'll be fine," my mom would say when I called home, always at times when my roommate was out of the cramped room we shared. "Just think about how in a few weeks you'll have made all kinds of friends and learned all kinds of things," she said. "Think about in a few *years*. You'll be happy, honey. I'm sure." I didn't believe her, but she promised it would all be worth it, and that all the things worth doing in life are hard. You've never been good at sticking it out through the hard things, she told me. Maybe now's the time that changes.

I don't think I even know the moment it started to feel worth it, what series of events triggered it, but I do remember that one day I woke up and realized I was happy. When I left college, I had a degree, a best friend, a job. I had Paul.

It was only one semester where I thought about leaving all the time, and then I just didn't anymore. It's been two years that we've been in Dawes, longer than that first semester away at school, but that was one semester out of eight. This is two years out of the rest of my life.

It's infinitesimal. In the long run, it's nothing.

Nine

Once Paul has a plan, he executes it. And so exactly two weeks after Lily of the Valley is born, Paul drives me to Julie Friedrich's house.

When we pull up outside, Julie is sitting on the steps, the same ones where Amanda and I waited the day she had her baby. She does not have her baby with her now. She doesn't stand up when she sees the truck, but she waves when she sees me. Julie and I have no special relationship, neither of us particularly drawn to the other. Sometimes before a big meet or after a bad one, my mother would take one look at me and say, "Honey, you're vibrating." Something within me had been unsettled, dislodged, struck by an outside force like a tuning fork, leaving, my mother said, the air around me troubled and humming. The first time I had a conversation with Julie, I understood what my mother had seen in me: a sensitivity that wasn't completely pleasant, a disturbance in the air. But Julie and Caroline are close; from behind, they even look like the same person, all that blond hair. Paul rolls the passenger side win-

THE BURNING SEASON | 93

dow down and leans across the seat I've just left. "Rob isn't
here, is he?" he calls.

"Nope," Julie says.

Paul nods, and I turn to say goodbye to him. "Have a
good time," he says. "Let yourself help and be helped." He
looks meaningfully at my stomach. "Please."

"I will," I tell him, and he says he'll pick me up before dinner. Julie and I watch as he pulls into the driveway,
backs out, and leaves the way we came.

"He could have gone straight," Julie says, "and cut over
on Grovewood." Outside her house, the azaleas wink and
dip in the breeze. If she's pruned any of them since the baby
was born, I can't tell. Soon, any minute now, it will be too
hot for the azaleas—their lives are so bright but so short—
and their heads will shrivel up and fall to the ground.

"Is the baby sleeping?" I ask.

"I doubt it," Julie says. "She's never sleeping." Julie is
all one pale color, and her hair is pulled back into a bun,
the ends poking out from under the grip of the elastic so
they look a little sharp, pointed. The skin around her eyes
is soft and dark.

"Oh no," I say. "What's she doing now?"

"Crying, probably." She holds a finger up, cocks her
head. "I think I can hear her."

"I'll go in. You can stay out here." But she doesn't make
a move to get up anyway. When I stand up, I see she has
stretched her legs out, pulled the dress up over her knees to
expose them to the sunshine. Her legs are pale too.

Inside, I don't hear the baby crying, and I am relieved
for a moment, but then I think back to her birth, the silence

that must have followed her entrance to the world, blue, unbreathing, not crying, and I walk through their small house, panicking, until I find the little bassinet next to Julie's bed, and there is tiny Lily of the Valley, swaddled tightly, a pacifier lying next to her head. Her little brows are knit so she looks angry even as she sleeps, the hair so light they're almost invisible, only suggestions of eyebrows. I leave her and go back to the living room, sure Julie will come in when she's ready.

Around the room are various devices in which you can put babies: a swing, some kind of pillow with an indentation in the middle, a bouncer designed to look like a puppy. What do you do with a baby that won't sleep? I guess put her in the swing, put her in the bouncer, lay her on the pillow, strap her to your chest, rock her in the crib. Go outside, close the door. Wait.

There is nothing for me to do here, but I feel strange and lazy sitting on the couch, so I find the laundry room and move the clothes from the washer to the dryer, and I start a new load, a small bundle of clothes sitting in a basket on the floor: a long dress that could be a nightgown or a regular dress, it's hard to tell, men's shirts, men's underwear. Rob's. Rob, I know, worked for an oil and gas company in Houston, probably not far from Paul's company, and he looks like every single guy I saw downtown whenever I picked Paul up at the office. He's fair but not pale like Julie, with light brown hair. Average height, average weight. It's easy to imagine him in a suit, holding a briefcase, eating a taco on his way back to the office with his tie slung over his shoulder so he doesn't drip salsa on it. Rob is fine and nothing more. I feel nothing for him. I can't imagine touching him, being touched by him. My body rejects the thought, and I am thankful.

Lily of the Valley begins to cry, and I half expect to hear the front door open, for Julie to rush into the house, but beneath the crying, there is only the thump of the dryer and nothing else. I go to her bed and pick her up, but she fights against the swaddle, pushing at the fabric until her tiny fists punch through the folds, and so I lay her down on the bed to unwrap her, leaving the swaddle blanket behind. I carry her into the living room, bouncing her and shushing her, but she seems to be approaching anger, her little body hard and strong as she writhes.

Once, when Tess was over with her first baby, the baby began searching around my breasts urgently while I was holding him. "Lunchtime," Tess had declared. "Though you think he'd be able to tell which boobs belong to him. He spends so much time fucking attached to them." Maybe, I think, Lily is hungry. I try to cradle her in my arms and put her at my breast, not because I have milk to offer, but just to see if she's hungry, but she resists. I adjust her so that her stomach is pressed against my shoulder, and I pat her back and bounce, like I've seen Tess do, all to no avail. There's a phone, a landline on the side table next to the couch, and I move toward it, thinking I could call Paul if I needed to—his cell phone number hasn't changed since I first met him, and I know it as well as my own, the one I used to have—but I stop myself. I'm not a baby person, never have been, but through careful and practiced enthusiasm and tenderness, I've managed to convince Paul I am, that I would be happy to have one, that I'd be happy to have his.

I open the front door and step outside into the heat, and

that does it. Lily's crying slows until it's a pitiful intake and release of breath. "Look!" I say to Julie. "She's happy!" But then I see that Julie isn't there. She's gone.

TWO HOURS LATER, Julie reappears, first as a tiny figure, a little doll, walking around the corner. I stand up with Lily of the Valley and move to the sidewalk so she sees us waiting for her. She must spot us, but she doesn't speed up, just continues at a steady, unhurried pace. When she gets closer, she says, "Hi," but doesn't offer to take Lily. She is sweating, the baby hairs at her temples curling with moisture. "I just needed to get out of here."

"She's not crying now," I say, and I can hear the accusation in my own voice: *You said she was always crying, but look. Listen.* Julie blinks. "She was crying, though," I say. "She stopped when I took her outside."

"Let's go in," Julie says. "I think I bled through this pad already. And look." She points down at her breasts, the two dark, wet circles on her dress, one side larger, a lake, the other only a puddle. She walks past me and opens the front door to show me in, but still does not take the baby.

"Were you walking the whole time?" I ask. I think of the blood she mentioned, the weakness of the body. The strength.

"No," she says, and I realize how sore she must be, how tender, and the baby starts crying again, as if she too is in pain and doesn't want us to forget that. It would be shocking to have a home and lose it, trade it for something new and cold. Shocking too to be a home, house a little being for months, and suddenly the home of your body is empty again, and I remember when I left for college, when I got married, when I left my mother for a final time to come to Dawes. How being a mother is an endless series of good-byes. Who could stand it?

"Come sit," I tell her. "I've got the baby."

Julie eases herself down onto the couch so that she is reclining, white ankles peeking out from her dress, an ancient Greek woman on a chaise. "I'll nurse her," she says over the crying, unbuttoning the dress and removing a breast from a soft pink bra, her nipple large and dark. She reaches for the baby, and I hand her over, but when Julie puts her up to her breast, she doesn't latch. Lily's mouth is open, surrounding Julie's nipple, like the gaping mouth of a shark about to swallow a tiny fish, but she doesn't close her mouth around it. "There's something wrong with this baby," Julie says, looking up at me.

"No," I say, though who knows, maybe there is. "I think lots of women have a hard time breastfeeding."

"It's like she doesn't even want to be here," Julie says. "Maybe she isn't supposed to be." She still has one hand behind Lily's head, and with the other hand, she pinches the skin around her nipple.

"God brought her to us," I say.

"But what if it wasn't God?" Julie asks. She looks up at me now, bluish shadows under her eyes.

"There's no one else here but God," I say. "We invited Him here. Can I take the baby? Or get you something to drink?" Lily of the Valley is still crying. Her eyes are wide open, and her mouth is open too, the lower lip pressing against Julie's breast.

"What if," Julie says over the baby's cries, "when we opened the door of heaven to let Him in, something else got in too?"

"That isn't how it works," I tell her, though I think of standing outside her house, and those two little chinks in the armor of our circle.

"God moves in mysterious ways," Julie says. Just then, the baby stops crying, and we both look at her. She has found her way at last. She eats. "Finally."

"Thank God," I say with genuine relief, and we sit without speaking, listening to the baby eat, and I want her to never stop, to eat and eat until she is full and there's no room left inside her for doubt, for fear, for anything else trying to get in.

Ten

When Paul picks me up in the late afternoon, he asks how it went. "Fine," I tell him.

"Fine?" he asks. "I feel like I'm your dad picking you up from a slumber party. Just fine?" He looks over at me and grins and reverses the truck out of the driveway, and I look back at the house, where the curtains are closed.

"Actually," I say, "it was kind of weird."

"The praying part?" he asks. "With the hands." He takes his hands off the steering wheel just for a second, fingers spread wide, like he's ready to catch a basketball.

"Oh, fuck, Paul," I say. "I totally forgot. It was so weird, Julie seemed off, and I was trying to help her, and I forgot."

"Rosie," he says. He keeps his eyes fixed on the road, hands on the wheel. "You can't say fuck."

"I'm sorry, Paul," I tell him. "I can get her to do it next week. Next week will be better anyway. I'll be fertile then."

Paul sighs. "Okay," he says. "It's fine. I'm just disappointed."

"Me too," I say. "But maybe I could just ask Amanda to pray over my womb. I bet she would."

"That's not the way it works," he says. "It has to be someone who's just given birth."

"How do you know?" I ask. "Is it possible you're wrong?"

"God," he says, and that answers both my questions at once.

Our house is close—I would have walked if Paul hadn't insisted on driving me—and now we are almost there. We pass by the Wilders' house, silent and charred black, like the bones of a massive, ancient offering to the gods. "I wonder how they're doing," I say. They've moved into their new house now, a lavender-painted Victorian in the same cul-de-sac as Papa Jake. Paul went over to visit them last week, and when he came home, he did a lot of heavy sighing, which I ignored, until finally he admitted he wished we had been allowed to move into the empty house on the cul-de-sac. Papa always says I'm his right-hand man, Paul said, hurt in his voice. I do so much for him, even when I don't want to. Why wouldn't he pick me?

You know Papa loves you, I said, and he shrugged.

"So Julie seemed weird?" Paul asks now. "Rob says she's been having these really bad dreams. Crying in her sleep and stuff."

"Dreams about the baby?"

"About the fires," Paul says. "Rob said the other night, she shook him awake and told him she smelled smoke. She made him check every room and even, like, go around the house feeling the walls in case the fire was inside them."

"Poor Julie," I say. "I understand why it would be scary."

"God doesn't want us to worry," Paul says. "If a fire

comes for them, there's no stopping it. A season for everything, right? There's a time to build and a time to burn."

"Right," I say. We pull up into the driveway, our house
whole before us.

AFTER DINNER, WE wipe down the kitchen table and get
out the calendar. It's big, the kind that covers a desk, and
every month when my period starts, Paul retrieves it for
me, hands me a pen, and watches as I record the dates of
my cycle. I put a dot for the day my period begins; I count
fourteen days and draw a little flower on the fourteenth
day, I count fourteen more and put a star: this is the day my
period will start, or this is the day I am pregnant. That day
will be a relief, a releasing of pressure, an exhalation, or it
will be a tragedy. The rest of the calendar is blank, these
three little marks like tiny islands in a stark white sea.

This is something that Paul admires about me. "Like
clockwork," he says whenever he watches me update the calendar, standing over my shoulder. The fact that my body
can do something so regularly, just the way it's supposed
to, the way God made it to work, while the rest of me—my
brain, my heart, my soul, I'm not sure—can't quite be de-
pended upon, that, to him, is astounding. I tried to tell him
once before that I felt the opposite about my body, how it had
let me down, ending my gymnastics career. He'd laughed
when I said career. "You were twelve," he said. "How can a
twelve-year-old have a career?"

"You peak very early in gymnastics," I said, even
though he was wrong: I'd been fifteen. Plenty old, and lucky
to last that long. "You're on the clock once your body starts
changing." Pendulous breasts, widening hips—so much

more weight to hurl through the air. It's such a narrow window of time when your body is just right for gymnastics. My teammates and I worried over the appearance of hair, the emergence of breasts, the arrival of our periods. We thought that if we trained hard enough, if we pushed ourselves far enough, we could trick our bodies into thinking we weren't aging, and we could exist in a state of perpetual girlhood.

But a body works by its own rules. One day after practice, in the privacy of my own bathroom, I stripped off my leotard and found a red streak on the soft white lining of the crotch. I peed and wiped—more red. I wrapped a towel around myself and found my mother in the kitchen. I held out my leotard to her, inside out with the rusty mark visible. "It happens," she said. "It happens to everyone. It means you're a woman now. It means someday you'll get to be a mother. Now, would you like to try a tampon or do you want a pad? I'll warn you, though, you'll be able to see the bulge of it through your leo."

I quit the next year. My body did nothing I asked of it. Bleeding, crying, erupting, growing, shifting its shape. I tried punishing it, but it didn't care. "You've never worked harder," my coach observed with disgust, "and improved so slowly." The day I left the gym, I didn't realize it would be my last time there. I just didn't feel like going back the next day or the next day or the next week, and finally, my mother went in for me and cleaned out my locker, which held only deodorant, a warm-up jacket with no matching bottoms, a too-small leotard, and a box of tampons because my mother was right, the bulge of the pad was very visible in a leotard. My body was mine, finally, but I didn't want it. I didn't want something that would not obey.

Now I sit in front of the calendar, and Paul leans over me. "See?" I say, tapping today's date with the pen. "We're here, and then next week, we'll be here, and I'll go see Julie then." Now I tap the flower, next week's little daisy. When I draw a flower, I always put five petals, never a stem or leaves. Just the petals and the round center, a perfect circle. A decapitated flower. I look up at Paul, who is frowning and nodding at the calendar, like he is memorizing it, even though there is so little to look at. "What?" I ask.

"I'm worried you did it on purpose," he says, coming around the table and taking the seat across from me.

"Did what?"

"Forgot," he says, making air quotations with his fingers, "to have Julie pray over you."

I roll my eyes. "Paul," I say. "I'm sorry. Honestly, it was a weird day. Julie didn't seem entirely okay, and Lily cried almost the whole time. I wasn't even thinking about it. But it will be fine. I'm not even ovulating yet."

"Rolling your eyes is disrespectful," he says.

"You're right," I tell him. "I'm sorry."

Paul covers his face with his hands. "I'm sorry too," he says. "This is hard for you. Harder for you than me. It's your body."

"It is," I say. "But listen. Say we never get pregnant. And there's no baby. It wouldn't be the worst thing, would it? We would still be happy."

He looks at me, his eyes dark and serious, animal eyes.

"We'll do what we need to do. We don't want people to think you're really and truly barren."

"Right," I say, twisting the pen in my hands. "You're right."

"You're not *really* barren," he says. "You can't be. You're just having difficulty."

We don't want people to think I'm barren, to wonder about the landscape of my body, empty, not only lifeless but unable to sustain life. Like a desert, scorching sand under sun. Like miles of ice and snow, so cold, so blindingly white.

But those places are beautiful, aren't they? Dunes like silk, ice like crystals. Photographs of them on the walls of homes, spas, offices. Magic places where no one lives. We treasure them, we don't want anyone to spoil them. And they don't want to be spoiled. God made those too, I want to tell Paul. He loves them for what they possess and not just for what they could become.

"So," I say, tapping the calendar with the pen. "Next week."

"Next week," he echoes. "Okay." He lowers his hands and reaches one across the table. He opens it, closes it, opens it again, until I put the pen down and place my hand in his.

IN BED, I can't sleep. I am thinking of the calendar, and I am thinking of Paul, pinning his hopes and dreams on those dates, the pen marks I've made. The combination of a person's hopes and dreams, a day of the month. It's simple, black and white. As black as the ink, as white as the page it's on. But what I haven't told Paul—the true thing I've forgotten, the purposeful action I've taken—isn't forgetting to tell Julie to place her hands on my body and pray.

When I was little, I played with dolls: first, the baby dolls with the floppy middles and the plastic heads that were heavier than the rest of their soft bodies so that when you tried to sit them down, they tipped forward, bending in the middle like they had just been punched in the gut. Their eyes would blink closed, traumatized by the ignorance you displayed—how could you not know this would happen? How could you not know you couldn't put your baby down safely?

As I got older, I had bigger, stiffer dolls with long hair you could brush and braid, and they came with catalogues full of clothes you could buy for them, and matching ones for yourself. They had limbs you could twist and turn, a head you could spin all the way around if you wanted. Once my sister, Bree, accidentally yanked her doll's arm out of its socket, and my mom took the doll and boxed her up, the doll lying in there like she was in a tiny casket, waves of her dark synthetic hair arranged dramatically underneath her, and she shipped her off somewhere. When she came back to Bree, her arm was reattached, a removable soft cast placed around it, and tucked at her feet was a letter detailing all the adventures she had at the hospital. *I got to eat ice cream*, the note read. *And the doctors were super nice and helped me feel better!* After that, the cast became an element of all the stories we dreamed up for the dolls. Our babies were always injured. They fell off a horse, they fell off a bike, they got into a car accident, they jumped off the roof. They didn't have easy lives, these children of ours. The stories we built around them were always so much more interesting than they themselves were.

In high school, I never had that assignment where a classmate and I had to be parents to an egg and take care of it and change its eggy diapers and listen to its imaginary eggy cries and make a budget so we could feed it and send it to college, and I never wanted to, even though I liked the idea of working so closely with a boy. I imagined, in this assignment that never even happened, that my partner and I would bicker over the needs of this egg and then, naturally, fall in love. Then I thought about smashing the egg and laughing because it wasn't a real baby anyway, even less real than my limp baby doll. Years later, I told this to Paul one morning when I was making breakfast, holding a cool little egg in my hand. "Wow," he said. "That's kind of fucked up."

In college, we all talked about having babies someday, what we would name them, if we wanted boys or girls. I couldn't imagine wanting either, but I said Adelaide for a girl, Ethan for a boy. Then we all got married young so that we would have plenty of time to just enjoy being married before we started having babies. We talked about our desires to be young moms, smooth and beautiful with tight bodies that bounced back right away. This part I knew I could do, if it came down to it; I've always been good at punishing myself. We would have all our children before we turned thirty. It only got harder the older you got.

After Nick, I truly thought a baby could make everything right again. As if Paul were an angry god and I was just a stupid, fucked-up peasant, I thought I could sacrifice something to appease him. Giving up my freedom, my body, seemed like the only thing big enough to matter. But those months and months of trying had been half-hearted on my end. I didn't pay any attention to timing. Tess had told me to buy ovulation tests to get just the right window, to hold my legs in the air after sex, to cut out dairy, grains, any processed food, to try acupuncture. I bought ovulation tests in bulk, narrow paper strips I held under the stream of urine. I always, always got pee on my hand. I ate clean, I let a soft-spoken woman stick needles in my back; I even went to some fancy spa and sat on this toilet-like contraption that billowed steam from its bowels, promising to cleanse and renew my parts. "Vagina facial?" I said to Tess. "Vaginal aromatherapy?"

"Steamed pussy," she said.

I monitored my body for signs of fertility, the swelling and cramping of menstruation, the secretions of ovulation. Despite all the years of gymnastics, I was like clockwork. I still am. I tracked my cycles on an app on my phone, one that showed butterflies and flowers on the screen on my most fertile days. Paul's mother would ask us when we were going to make her a grandmother. "We're working on it," Paul told her.

"Well," she said. "Don't keep your cell phone in your pocket, honey. It can make you sterile."

I didn't get pregnant, though, and when we got to Dawes, I prayed and prayed that I would. Everyone here promised this was a special place, blessed by the Lord, the spot where our issues would be resolved, where we would get what we wanted from our lives. God loved to see new children added to His holy family, and now that we were here, doing what He asked of us, I was sure He would give us a baby, the very thing, I believed, that would fix our problems. We would be a team, partners working together on the biggest, most important project of all: raising a child, nurturing a life. There was a story we could build around the baby—no broken arms or hospital visits, but a happier one, no broken babies anywhere. It would be the opposite: a baby restoring wholeness to a broken thing.

It has not happened, either the baby or the wholeness. I love Paul, and if I had a baby, I bet I would love it, but I don't want one, not as a person, not as a sacrifice to save our marriage. *We* want a baby, but I do not.

This is a problem. There's a verse in the Bible I'd never heard before I got here, but have now memorized, about how children are like arrows in the hands of a man, how happy and blessed a man is who has a quiver full of them. But whenever I hear it, I think of what an arrow does, what it is designed to do. "Be fruitful and multiply," Papa Jake always says. "What did you think He meant?"

I knew nothing of my own fertility until I started paying attention to it, learning my body like a new language. I have banked, all this time, on Paul knowing nothing about my fertility either. He knows what I have told him. There are five days, really, I could get pregnant. He thinks there is one, only one.

But even though we are diligent about sex on the flower days, I know it won't happen unless the clock I've been watching breaks—because I've pushed everything back by a week. During the week of my period, I throw my pads away in the kitchen trash can, shoving them down deep beneath the onion skins, paper towels, cracked and empty eggshells. Then on the week I'm fertile, I remain untouched, like the flower in the garden we're told not to pluck, the apple on the tree we're told not to pick.

Next month Paul and I will get the calendar out and look at it together again. He'll hand me the pen, and I'll count fourteen days from the flower, make a mark. "There," he'll say. "By then we'll know we're pregnant. This is the month, Rosie." And I know he'll truly believe it. It's possible, I think, that someday I will end up pregnant. It's possible my body's clock will change. It's possible to make mistakes, to count incorrectly and get the days all mixed up. This is what I'll say if Paul ever finds out that every month I make a mistake making the calendar, that I put the flower on a day when I'm likely not fertile. *I'm sorry*, I'll say. I'll weep. *I've been so desperate, I wasn't thinking, I got confused.*

But I don't think he'll find out. My body is a mystery to Paul. I know it's wrong, that I'm doing something bad, that I'm a bad wife, that I'm weak, that I'm a liar, just as Paul suspected. This too is a kind of adultery, only the person I'm cheating on is the version of myself Paul believes in. But I guess she doesn't exist anyway. The worst that could happen is that Paul finds out and is angry, or he begins to suspect I've deceived him, and if it's the latter, well, I can shift the dates around again; after all, bodies are funny, fickle things.

Sometimes when I can't sleep, I pray, and so that's what I decide to do now. I ask for forgiveness, for deliverance, and tomorrow I'll make another sacrifice, whatever I need to do.

Eleven

Another house catches fire overnight. This time it belongs to Richard and Molly Moore. Paul and I go out of our way to drive past the ruins the next morning as we head to the church for prayer and worship, but the fire is already out. Papa Jake told Paul that the neighbors across the street, Dawes locals, called the fire department as soon as the blaze started around midnight, and despite the family's pleading they leave it burning as God wished, the firefighters put it out anyway. So now the house stands, half-burned, and we wonder if this is enough to satisfy God, or if He will take another house. "They should have let it burn," Paul says as we drive away.

Inside the chapel, I take a seat by Amanda and her daughter. "Hey," Amanda says, squeezing my knee. "The Moores, this time. Did you see?"

"Paul drove me past it just now," I say. "God's power is mighty."

"Praise His name," Amanda says. "But it didn't burn all the way."

"It burned enough, though."

Her daughter, on the opposite side of her, leans forward, and I give her a wink. She grins and sits back, swinging her feet, legs covered by her long dress.

"It should have burned all the way," Amanda says, smoothing her dress over the roundness of her belly. She sees me looking and smiles. "Almost five months now," she says. "I'm finally showing. Here, feel." She takes my hand and sticks it on her stomach, and I'm not sure if there's some movement, a fluttering, within her I should be feeling, so I let my hand linger for a moment and then take it away.

"A gift," I say. "Thank you."

"Oh, Rosemary," she says. "It will happen for you. I know it will."

"We're prayerful and hopeful," I say, casting my eyes down at my own stomach, invisible, empty and flat beneath my dress.

"I heard you're working with Julie Friedrich," she says.

I nod. "Paul received a God-thought, and Papa Jake confirmed it. He thinks I can absorb her fertility the way the men receive the anointings of the dead." I put my hands out the way I saw Paul do in the truck, like I was gripping an invisible basketball.

Amanda is nodding, her chin wrinkling as she frowns. "Makes sense," she says. "Touch is very important. The laying on of hands."

"Of course," I say.

"Hey," she says abruptly. "Julie's here. She's in the back with the baby." I look over my shoulder and see her standing near the door. Now that I'm listening, I hear Lily of the Valley crying, and I watch Julie bouncing her, the fabric covering her knees quaking as Julie moves up and down.

"She should feed that baby," Amanda says. "She's hungry." She leans in, angling her head toward mine, speaking in a low voice. "I heard Julie's seeming crazy. Is that true?"

"Not crazy," I say, feeling surprisingly protective of Julie. "Exhausted. Overwhelmed."

Amanda nods. "It's hard becoming a mother."

Papa Jake emerges from the wings and raises his hands to greet us, and we all clap for him. Someone whistles. A woman yells, "Papa!" He grins. He raises both his hands again, this time to quiet us.

"The work of the Lord will not be thwarted," he says. We watch him looking for someone in the congregation, and we know when he finds them because he grins again. "Stand up," he says, lifting both hands as if he can make them stand with magic. "The Moores."

They stand up, the four of them—Richard and Molly and their twin boys, younger than Abigail. I imagine the boys waking up, realizing that this time it's them, the holy fire is happening to them. "These faithful brothers and sister stood up against the world for what was right, for the will of God," Papa Jake says. "The world approached them in the guise of helpers, saviors, but they were wise enough to know that only God can help us. Only God can save us." We cheer. Yes! God alone. And you, Papa. You. "This time," he says, "the world pulled ahead. The holy fire didn't burn the way God intended, but next time." He raises a finger, as if he is pointing to God Himself. "Next time, brothers. Next time, sisters."

Next time, we answer. A promise or a threat or both. Molly and Richard are still standing, though she has let the boys sit down, and she keeps a hand on the shoulder of the one closer to her.

"Let us celebrate," Papa Jake says, and we don't even have to ask why or what for. We leap to our feet, we move out of the confines of the aisles as music swells. I spot Paul, who is kneeling between the pew behind him and the pew in front of him, his hands covering his eyes and his mouth moving, but I can't hear him. I wonder what he's seeing.

Suddenly there is the sound of glass shattering at the back of the chapel. For a moment, I wonder if it is some new ritual Papa Jake has envisioned, but then I hear screaming, and I whip around, drawn to the sound of an outside force making its way inside our sanctuary. Julie Friedrich is in the back, frozen and silent. Lily is crying. On the floor to her right, not even a foot away, lies a brick. We look to the other window on the other side of the door, and that is broken too. From where I am in the aisle, I cannot see a second brick, but I know it must be there.

We stand stunned, before Papa Jake bellows, "Devils! Look what they've done!" All they've done is break the glass, but what they could have done is understood, had that brick been a few inches further in, had Julie and Lily of the Valley been standing a few inches further out. "Look what they've brought into our house," Papa Jake says. "They've let the evil in." We have been silent, in shock, but with his voice, we find our own. We shout in anger and we wail, we moan; we tell God He must punish the wicked, we ask that He show no mercy.

Julie hasn't moved, and I realize I should go to her, that someone should. I rise and hurry to where she stands, splinters of glass like ice around her feet. "You're okay," I say, and I'm not sure if I'm asking or telling. There is glass in her hair. She looks up at me and holds the baby toward me, and I take her. A tiny bead of blood blooms on Lily's cheek. I press my finger to it, but when I take my finger away, it blooms again. I turn around and see that Amanda is behind me with Abigail. "She has a little cut," I tell her.

"I'll take her," Amanda says. "You help Julie." I transfer the baby to Amanda, who wipes away the blood and then holds her upright, patting and shushing her, and her crying slows. I turn to Julie and pick the glass from her hair, the tiny pieces like ice in my palm.

"She doesn't want to be with me," Julie says. "She's happier with Amanda."

"She's scared," I say. "I'm sure you are too."

"I think maybe that isn't my baby," Julie says.

Everyone has started drifting toward the back of the church, pressing in closer to us. Paul emerges from the crowd and puts his hand on my back. I hold my hand out to him, still cupping the little bits of glass, and he guides me toward a trash can in the corner of the chapel, by the doors. Julie follows and stands by me as I brush the glass off. "Take her home," Paul says. He presses the truck keys into my hand. I ask him where Rob is, and he shrugs. "No clue," he says. We both look to Julie, and she shrugs too.

"He left almost as soon as the service started," she says. "But he seemed like he was up to something."

"Okay," Paul says politely, glancing over at me. "Why don't I just go find him and meet you back at the house?"

"Good idea," I say, and Paul squeezes my shoulder and jogs off.

"The enemy has been emboldened by their victory against God's fire," Papa Jake calls from the front. "They attacked us here! They tried to kill a mother and her child. But they won't win! They don't have God on their side." People have their hands up already, as soon as Papa Jake began to speak, and some are swaying, listening to the voices of angels, to music only they can hear.

"Come on," I say to Julie. "Let's go." I put my arm around her and open the door, the bright morning light invasive in the dim chapel. I look over my shoulder at Papa Jake, who is watching us. He nods at me. "Thank you, Rosemary," he says. "Care for her. Care for your sister. God bless you both."

God bless you both, the people say, and I shut the door behind us.

Twelve

In the truck, we are quiet. The radio is tuned to a station Paul likes, playing a sports show with the volume turned very low so that the voices feel private, their conversations urgent and furtive. They repeat the names of players that I barely recognized in my old life, but now when I hear them, I find myself missing these people I do not know, who I would never even recognize if I saw them. I think about tuning the radio to find music—Julie is only a few years older than me, I think, we would have grown up listening to the same bands—but I am already feeling fragile, and Julie seems even more breakable, and I think the nostalgia might actually split us open, kill us. So I turn the radio off. I haven't driven in a long time, and so it's easier than I'd think to sit with the silence and focus on what my hands and eyes and feet are doing: tapping the brake as we roll toward a stop sign, pulling the handle for the turn signal, checking the mirrors as we make a left.

I expect Julie to ask about Lily, when she will see her again, who will feed her in the meantime, but she does not. When I glance at her, she's looking out the window, the back of her head to me, and I see her face reflected in the glass, like a ghost in a mirror. "Julie," I say because I want to remind us both that she is here, a person, not a spirit caught between worlds. I think of those times, with the boys who were not Paul, how my body had started to feel too light to exist on earth, and I know this is when bad things happen. I say her name again.

She turns to face me. "What?" she asks.

"Nothing," I say. "Just making sure you're okay."

"I'm fine. Here," she says suddenly, pointing at her house, and I make a sharp turn into the driveway I nearly passed. I stop the truck and turn it off and follow her into the house without asking. She lies down on the couch, puts her feet up, and I notice they are bare, and now I can't remember if she had even been wearing her shoes in the first place.

I fill up a glass with water from the kitchen sink and bring it out to Julie, but she sets it on the coffee table and doesn't take a sip.

"Can I get you something else?" I ask. "I could make you a sandwich?"

"Where is the baby?" she finally asks.

"Amanda took her," I say. "Remember? She'll bring her back soon. You should rest."

I expect her to say nothing else, but she sits up. "Did you know I knew Caroline in college?" she asks. "Before she married Papa."

"No," I say. "But I know y'all are close now."

"We lived on the same hall our freshman year," she says. "At Westbury." This I knew—that Caroline and Papa had met at Westbury University, a wealthy Baptist school in a small town not too far from here. There are others too who came to Dawes from this school.

"Tell me more," I say to Julie because I want to hear it, and because there is a tone of voice a person gets when they want to tell a story, a note that says listen to me, I have something to say. When she starts to speak, I realize there were other times too, when I've heard that same note, said in the same way: *I wanted to name her Evelyn. There's something wrong with her. I think this isn't my baby.*

She tells me that Caroline is who she has always been, a golden child, Julie says. Hearing this, I imagine a golden sewing needle, delicate and sharp; that is what Caroline is. "And Papa?" I ask.

"He's just the same too," Julie says. "He's always been special." Yes, I think. Golden in a different way—flashier, like an expensive watch, not a needle. At their school, so many girls were golden in just the way Caroline was: privileged and pretty, smart but not threatening. But while the other boys were rough or funny or athletic, Jake was something else. Magnetic, enthralling, but untouchable. He never dated anyone until he dated Caroline. The rumor was that he never even proposed to Caroline, that she woke up one day knowing she was officially off the market. A ring came later. It just showed up one day sparkling on her finger, winking in the light like a cold and brilliant eye, but if there was a proposal story, no one ever heard it. Oddly fitting, I think, for Jake and Caroline. Too special for an ordinary engagement.

Julie says there was a joke about the little city that housed Westbury—an oddly sized place, too small to be a proper city but a metropolis compared to Dawes—that you could stand on any street corner, throw a rock, and hit a church, but truthfully there were only two churches that anyone at the school went to.

One of the churches was the cool one: moody and artsy, candles burning in the corners, dripping wax onto the floor that stayed there week after week, the slow accumulation of it a kind of art installation. The people who attended wore sneakers and band tees, thick-rimmed glasses. The girls wore bangles on their arms, hippie clothes they ordered from Nordstrom, Free People.

The other church was earnest. This was where Julie, Jake, and Caroline went on Sundays, and then Sundays and Wednesdays, and then every free moment they had. Hearts on the sleeve, hands in the air during worship. People spoke in tongues, and everyone believed it, took it in good faith that this was a true manifestation of the Spirit. People received prophecies, and these too were believed. Healings, yes, Julie saw those too.

But after church, they all went to eat tacos or burgers or went to the pool on warm days. They worked out at the student center, they studied at the coffee shop. They were normal. It was only that their faith was intense.

Every year during spring break, the church took a group of upperclassmen on mission trips to underserved places. One year, Julie says, she heard the pastor just spun a globe, closed his eyes, and pointed, stopping the spinning globe with his index finger. "We're going to Ukraine!" he said. What if he had landed on Paris? London? I ask. They would've gone to Paris or London, I guess. Surely even people in fancy cities need saving, Julie says sharply.

But the year Julie went, Caroline and Jake were going

too, and the trip was to Nicaragua. They would spend two days in Managua, then head out to a rural village for a few more days, then take the last two days to rest and play at a modest hotel on the beach. The girls all bought one-piece bathing suits.

The country: a few hours away from the city in a hot van, on a bumpy road. The scenery changed from gray to tan and green, and dust clouds floated up to the windows as the van knocked along. They would be staying in a house owned by a church in-country, twenty minutes' drive from the village. The girls would help with the children and women in the community, the boys would build things, break things down, swing tools. On their way out to the village each morning, they passed cows in fenceless pastures and chickens roaming in front of small homes. Children peeked and waved at them from behind thin curtains flapping in open windows.

Some of this Julie does not say. Some of it I fill in on my own: the color of the land, the unflattering swimsuits, high necked and athletically cut, the chickens, the children at the window. Some of the details of the churches, I realize, those too are my own, how I envision them, with the candles burning, the rich girls clinging to bohemia, the fervent crowd at the other church, hands in the air, testifying, starving. Those voices on the radio in the truck—I long for a world besides this one.

There was a village boy, Julie says, who was wild. He ran like an animal through the village, spun like a storm in the heat. Did not sit through the lessons the girls taught. He spat and scratched and hit the women. He did not have a mother, Julie says. No one would claim him as their own.

He belongs, a woman said in Spanish, to the village. A burden. This woman who was not his mother was the one who every day tried to contain him. Sometimes she would pick him up and hold him on her lap under the shade of a tree by the school, her arms a straitjacket around him. His little chest heaving in and out, body working to run even when he was sitting still.

Usually the mission team ate breakfast at their house, lunch at the village prepared by the women there, and then piled in the van to go back to the church for dinner. But on the last night, the village threw a big party, and the team ate dinner with the locals. There was singing and dancing, and one of the guys from the church's mission team borrowed a guitar from a man in the village. He sang praise songs from their church back home, and soon it was a full-blown worship service. They were all so tired from the week, from the work of course, but from the community too, from the overwhelming exposure to poverty, from the relentless engagement with other people, some who didn't even speak the same language, and between the food and the music and the relief of leaving soon, a kind of mania began to build, a frenzy. Hands thrust into the sky, eyes closed, people wept and danced, people sunk to their knees. Julie felt like she had been lifted out of her body, flung out so she could see everything from a higher vantage point, a view more like God's. What did the villagers do? They sang, Julie says. They danced. We all danced together. She says she can still remember watching Caroline, the bright head of blond hair like a light, as she spun and bobbed, Jake moving beside her but not touching her. The wild boy tore through the crowd. There was the sound of fabric ripping. Caroline stood still, the sky bright with color behind her, and held her tissue-thin skirt together, but it slipped, and everyone could see her legs, tan and firm, and the pale whisper of pink underwear. The boy was laughing at having ripped her skirt. Three girls flanked Caroline, shimmied her away, hiding her from view. Women from the village followed, each offering the clothes off their backs.

The woman who was not the mother of the boy picked him up—he was a small thing, slight but hard and fast as a knife—and she took him to the porch where she sat down on a white plastic chair and held him tightly. He pushed against her embrace, getting an arm loose, flailing, knocking her in the nose, which bled.

The sun was setting, so that bright color began to fade in the dusky light, but when there was still enough light to see by, Julie watched Jake and another boy from the church walk over to the wild boy and the woman. Jake held a tissue out to her, but she couldn't remove her arms from the boy in her lap, and so Jake held it up to her nose, applying pressure and then gently wiping away the blood.

The other boy with Jake, Julie knew, was one of the fluent Spanish speakers on the team, and he'd had a busy week as an interpreter. Jake was crouched down beside the pair, looking at the woman and speaking to her. Even when he paused for his friend to translate, he didn't break eye contact with the woman. In her arms, the boy growled and thrashed. Julie watched her shake her head, watched Jake and Andy continue talking, watched her hand move from her mouth to her eyes. By then, Caroline was back, wearing a skirt made of thick, stiff fabric like drapes, and she stopped to speak to Jake. She nodded, squeezed the shoulder of the woman, and walked toward Julie. Julie grabbed her by the arm. "What's happening?" Julie asked.

Caroline's eyes were shining. "Oh, Julie," she said. "Jake received a word from the Lord. He's going to heal that boy."

"But he isn't sick," Julie said. "Is he?"

Caroline nodded. "Spiritually he's sick. That's why he's like that. Jake says it's like a demon you have to cast out. He attacked me. You saw it. Who knows what could have happened next?"

At first, no one else paid attention to the quartet under the cover of the porch. The party was in full swing, and Jake and the woman and the boy were off to the side. The woman slid out of the chair, still holding the boy, until his two feet were planted on the dirt floor, and she put her hands on each of his shoulders. Jake put his hands on the boy's shoulders too, and miraculously, the boy went still. He did not try to run away. Julie breathed in. Everyone had their eyes closed but the boy, who was looking around at the dancers, at the people he saw every day, at the strangers he'd only seen this week and who would in an hour be gone from his life forever. Jake moved a hand to the boy's forehead, and beneath Jake's fingers the boy began to squirm again. Julie and Caroline watched. "See?" whispered Caroline. "It's working."

Then the boy began to thrash, and Caroline whispered again. "Look," she said. He knocked the woman's hands away, and she stutter-stepped backward, and then the boy shook off Jake too. The boy began to shout. People began to listen, to watch, then to gather. Jake leaned over to the translator, spoke something into his ear. The translator nodded. "La cuerda?" the translator called. "Does anyone have a rope?"

And a rope materialized, was handed to him and Jake, who led the boy, still fighting, to a fence near the white chairs. The woman trailed behind them, weeping, and another woman from the village came to her, embraced her, led her away so the Americans could work. Another boy from the mission team joined them, helped hold the wild boy down, as they wound the rope around his wrists. "Loosely," Jake said, overseeing. "Gentle. Be careful." But the rope couldn't be too loose or he would escape, and so the loops around his wrists chafed as he struggled.

"God," Jake said, "heal this boy. Heal Your child. Free him from this devil inside who wants to enslave him and keep him from fulfilling Your will." He said these things over and over, and the boy kicked, his fingers curled and uncurled, forming useless fists. Whatever was inside the boy, Julie says, was being bound beneath his skin, within his soul, and soon would be cast out into oblivion. She wondered if she would see it, when it was finally loose, before its existence ended. The woman who wasn't his mother stood by and cried.

Poor woman, I say, and Julie looks at me quizzically. No, she says. Lucky woman.

Now it was fully dark, but clear, and the stars twinkled, and the air smelled thick and warm, and mosquitoes buzzed around their ankles. Mothers took their children by the hands, led them home, carried their pots and pans home too. Still, the boy was tied to the fence. Still, Jake spoke, pleading to God. Others came and laid their hands on the boy, prayed over him. People moaned and spoke in husky, strange voices. There were hands everywhere. Julie put a hand on the boy's ankle, which was bumpy with mosquito bites, and below her, Caroline had a hand on the boy's foot. Every time Jake placed his hands on the boy's body, he went still. When he moved away, the boy struggled again, he howled. Do you see? Julie asks now. That power?

Finally, the boy's head hung, his muscles slackened. When his body went loose in the ropes and the mission team held him there, bolstering him, Jake nearly collapsed too. He sunk to his knees, his chin dropped to his chest. Julie worried that perhaps the boy had passed what was inside him to Jake, and it was nesting there within, but then she heard the voice of God—rest, He said, and Julie knew that was all Jake was doing. The woman ran over to the boy, wrapped her arms around him, and he looked at her blankly. She called to some men from the village, who untied him and carried him away.

The mission team helped Jake up, and they walked back to the van, two boys supporting him as he weakly stumbled through the darkness. The ride home was quiet. The next morning, they left the countryside and went to the beach.

"And then?" I ask.

"We flew home," Julie says.

Listen to me, her voice had told me. Listen to me. "What do you think happened?" I ask.

"I just told you," Julie says.

"To the boy, I mean."

Julie shakes her head. "I just told you," she says again. She takes a thin elastic from her wrist and uses both her hands to scoop her hair up and back, and I think of the glass that glittered in her hair an hour ago, like ice, like diamonds, sharp things hidden in the softness. She wraps the black band around her hair. "He healed him," she says.

"Praise be to God," I say.

"A miracle," Julie says.

"Praise be to God," I answer.

"You already said that," she says.

The front door opens. "Knock, knock," a voice says before the body it belongs to steps inside. It's Amanda, empty-handed, and Caroline behind her, holding Lily of the Valley. The baby's little head lolls in the newborn way, her mouth making a tiny pink O as she adjusts to the shadows inside the dim house, the cool whir of the air-conditioning. She has a tiny Band-Aid on her cheek. Julie puts her hands out for the baby, and I am relieved to see her do it. "She's happy," she says.

"She just ate," Amanda says.

"Missy Wilson nursed her," Caroline says. "That woman is a milk-making machine. Lily latched on right away like she was starving."

"Maybe she is," Julie says. "Is she?"

"No," I say.

"Maybe," Caroline says, studying the baby. "She's a scrawny little thing."

"Some babies are like that," Amanda says. "No big deal."

"We'll just be praying about it," Caroline says.

"Did anyone find Rob?" Julie asks, but she doesn't look up from the baby. With a fingertip, she traces the outline of Lily's face, avoiding the Band-Aid.

"He's on his way right now," Amanda says, looking at me.

"Julie, do you need anything else?" I ask.

She shakes her head. "I'm much better now, thank you. I was just shaken up."

"We all were!" says Caroline. "That was frightening. But Papa is going to talk to Randall."

"Good," says Julie.

"Imagine being evil enough to shoot a gun into a church," Caroline says.

"A gun?" I ask.

"What do you think shattered the window?" Caroline asks. I look at Amanda, who says nothing.

"A brick," I say. "I saw a brick on the floor."

"No," says Caroline. "Someone shot at us. Someone from the town. Probably from Randall's church."

"Did you see a brick?" I ask Amanda.

She glances over at Caroline. "I don't know," she says. "Papa Jake says it was a gunshot."

"Oh," I say. We are all silent. The air-conditioning turns on, a rattle and then a hum. Lily of the Valley's eyes snap open.

"Oh no," says Julie, her body tensing reflexively. I think she might hand off the baby to us, but she just stares at her, dull-eyed, and the baby stares back, alert.

"Oh, Jules," Caroline suddenly says. "You know what you need? A nice, long shower." Amanda glides over and lifts the baby from Julie's arms, swaying, her lips close to Lily's little flower petal ear, and Caroline gently pulls Julie from the couch. They disappear down the hallway to the master bathroom, and I hear the water running.

"I really have to pee," Amanda says. "So bad. Can you take Lily? See if she'll let you put her in the swing, and then we can all leave when Caroline's done." She's already handing me the baby, who feels like a loaf of bread in my arms—a warm, still little bundle.

The swing is in Julie's room, right beside the bed, and I strap her into it, then press an assortment of buttons until the swing begins to move and the mobile of stars above the seat spins. The door to the bathroom is cracked open, and inside there is singing, barely audible above the running water, just the suggestion of words. Though I know this is an intrusion, I peek in.

Julie sits in the bathtub as it fills, and Caroline perches on the white rim, her fingers combing gingerly, tenderly through Julie's light hair, like she is looking for something precious. Caroline is singing in a soft voice, not a hymn but a song I can remember from another life, and in the water, Julie smiles. When Caroline turns the water off, I recognize the lyrics immediately. Julie laughs, and then Caroline laughs, and I almost do too. I sneak out, back to the living room, where Amanda sits.

"Everything okay in there?" she asks.

"Yep," I say.

"Good." She nods, then cocks her head to the side. "Is that—Britney Spears?"

"Yep," I say again, and she nods again, and together we wait and listen. I am sad when Caroline's singing fades out.

"EVERYONE'S ASLEEP," CAROLINE says when she emerges. "Let's go."

Outside, the sun is hot and bright, and we fan ourselves with our hands. Papa Jake's truck, hulking and blinding in the sunlight, sits in the driveway next to Paul's truck, which looks decrepit beside it. "Thanks for helping," Caroline says.

"Thanks be to God," I say, "that no one was seriously hurt."

"Praise His name," Caroline says, nodding.

"I didn't know you and Julie knew each other," I say. "Before."

Caroline cocks her shiny head like a golden retriever. "We were sorority sisters," she says. I imagine them getting ready for parties together, Britney playing tinnily from someone's laptop speakers.

"Was she the same then?" I ask.

"She's always been sensitive," Caroline says, "if that's what you mean. Very attuned to the Lord."

"What a gift."

"Yes," Caroline says. "And, Rosemary, I'm going to help Julie for a while, until she's in a better place. I'll give you a call when she's ready for you again. Sound good?" I nod, relieved. "Perfect," she says. "We'll see you tonight." She and Amanda pull out first, and I follow them. As they pass by the remains of Amanda's house, I wonder if they talk about it, if Amanda turns her head, or if Caroline makes her look at it. Are you watching? Another act of heaven, cutting both ways. A gift or a punishment depending not on the story told but on the listening to it, depending on not what is said but what is heard.

"HAS PAPA EVER done an exorcism?" I ask Paul on our way to the chapel for an evening service. We are in the truck. I have been in the truck so much of the day, driving between places, and I am tired.

Paul frowns but doesn't look at me, keeps one thumb hooked around the steering wheel. We pass by a man washing his car in the dying light, a black and white dog jumping to snap at the arc of water from the hose. He looks over at us as we pass but does not wave. "Yeah," Paul says, "but not too many. Maybe only a couple?"

"When?" I ask.

"Once in college, I think," Paul says. "Or maybe not long after? In South America somewhere? Uruguay?" He looks at me now and smiles. "Clearly I was paying very close attention." I smile too, put my hand on his leg and squeeze, friendly pressure but nothing more. "Why do you ask?"

"No reason, I was just thinking about it," I say.

"Actually," Paul says, "I'm hazy on the details, but there was a little boy in the village in Uruguay or wherever, and he was wild. Violent, I think. They had to keep him tied up with a rope all the time. Anyway, when Papa met him, he knew the boy was possessed, and he cast out the demon, but immediately these chickens just started freaking out, pecking at each other like crazy, and they realized he had cast the demon into the chickens."

"Then what?" I ask.

"Papa and his team—Lou may have been there—held the chickens down and cut their heads off one by one."

"Wow," I say. "That is super gross."

"Very messy," Paul agrees. "But then again, the work of the Lord is rarely tidy."

"You're telling me," I say.

"I know you know," Paul says, smiling again, and we park at the back of the lot where there are no other cars. I wonder why, but then before we get out of the truck, Paul says hey, and I turn toward him and he kisses me.

IN THE CHAPEL, the panes in both of the back windows have been removed, and the gaping rectangles they leave are covered up with pieces of plywood, darkening the space. I think suddenly of the gym where I trained, which was cavernous, windowless, so that you never knew what the weather was until you walked out after practice. Inside the gym, it was only you, your body, your coach and his hands. The chalk, the mat, the bars, the vault. The weather didn't matter because there was no outside world. This, I think, is true here too. Nothing outside this space matters.

During the service, I watch Papa Jake carefully as he preaches. Some people you can tell are uncomfortable in the world just by the way they move, how they hold them-selves, where they put their hands, where they look when they talk to you. But everything about Papa Jake feels easy. He wears cowboy boots when he preaches, keeps one hand in his pocket when he talks to us. When he says something funny, he smiles but doesn't grin; he isn't too proud of him-self when he's clever, but he doesn't hide his awareness of his own charm. This is appealing. He keeps a small Bible in his back pocket, where it's made a rectangular outline in his jeans, and takes it out from time to time while he speaks, but he never looks at it.

Everyone sitting in the chapel nods as he speaks. Yes, God, yes, Papa. Paul sits across the aisle and one row be-hind me, and I nod too so he sees me. "God reveals things to us all the time," Papa Jake is saying. "That's why we have to always listen. God's truth is ongoing. He didn't stop revealing His truth to us just because time kept marching on. God doesn't get tired of the truth."

We clap for him. We say yes! We nod our heads. Every word a rope on our wrists, rubbing us until our skin is red but not letting us go.

IN THE MORNING, Paul tells me about a dream he had. We have been lazy and haven't gotten up yet, the comforter pushed down at the foot of our bed because of the heat. "The chapel was burning down, and all the windows were broken out," he says. "Like someone had thrown a brick through every window."

"I thought someone shot into the windows," I say.

"They did," says Paul, looking up at the ceiling. "This was just a dream."

"Did God give you this dream?"

"Yes," says Paul, still staring up and frowning. "I think."

It sounds like a normal dream, the kind inspired by the events of the day or the past. It makes sense he would dream of smashed windows and fire. "Was Julie in your dream?" I ask.

He shakes his head. "No. She wasn't anywhere. Instead it was you by the window." He closes his eyes, tight the way you do when you're afraid of what you'll see when you open them again. "You weren't moving, and I was screaming at you to come, but you wouldn't turn around. You were just looking through the open window, and then I thought maybe you could just climb through it."

The window with its remaining glass, like broken teeth in the mouth of a boxer. Flames licking the frame of it. I close my eyes too, and can see it. I open them.

THE BURNING SEASON | 133

"I shouted at you to climb out the window," he says. He turns and lies on his side to face me. "And then you turn, and I see you're pregnant. Like, nine months pregnant. And I realize you can't fit through the window, but I don't know why you aren't moving, and then I notice something else: you're tied up with a rope. You're stuck."

I roll over so that we are face-to-face. I touch the dark stubble on his cheek. "It's just a dream. It sounds like an anxiety dream, like the one I always have about having a final in a class I didn't know I was taking."

"You looked at me," Paul says. "And you didn't even try to escape, and then you said something."

"What?"

He looks at me, dark eyes sorrowful. "'Let me burn.'"

Thirteen

True to her word, Caroline calls me a week or so later to tell me Julie is doing much better and is ready for me to come back over. "I don't want to go," I say to Paul.

"Too bad," he responds merrily. He takes me in the truck to Julie's, and on the way, he tells me that yesterday Papa Jake had a sit-down with Randall, and I picture the two men, squaring off like army generals, a peace treaty on a makeshift desk between them. "He says he didn't know anything about the attack," Paul says.

"Maybe he didn't," I say.

Paul shakes his head. "This could get bad," he says. "God doesn't like His people to be messed with."

"That wouldn't make it bad, then, right? If God lets it happen, then it isn't bad."

"You're right, Rosie," he says thoughtfully. "Thank you. That doesn't make it bad. It makes it just. Fair." He pulls into Julie's driveway and taps the side of his head. "No one knows the mind of God."

I look at the front door of the Friedrichs' house. "I don't want to go today," I say. "Can't you just say I'm sick?"

"Rosie!" Paul says, but he's laughing. "That's not a good attitude."

"If you take me home, we could do something else instead," I say. "Something more fun." I don't mean it suggestively, but it comes out that way. My fertile window ended last week, so we should be fine. Or maybe I need to just give in, let my body do what it will, let Paul do with it what he wants. For so long, I've welcomed people into my body with no thought other than "I want this." If I gave my body a job, like building a home for a baby, maybe it wouldn't want anything else anymore. I could have a baby. Stay here. Stay with Paul.

When I look at him, he smiles but looks a little sad. "Rosemary," he says.

"I just love you," I say. "I can't help it."

"You'll be ovulating soon," he says. "In just a few days."

"All right," I say. "Okay. Fine. I'll go. Look at me, having a good attitude." I smile big, showing all my teeth, and Paul laughs again. As I open the door and slide out, he calls my name.

"I love you," he says through the open window. And I am glad, but in my head I hear this: No one knows the mind of God. How that explains so much and so little, complete and unsatisfying. That's what I am thinking when Paul tells me he loves me, but then Julie opens the front door, and Lily of the Valley is crying, and I go inside.

THE HOUSE IS tidy and there are lines in the carpet where Julie has pushed the vacuum back and forth. The lines are neat and straight, like she picked up the vacuum at the end of each row and carried it so there wouldn't be extra lines.

"The vacuum drowns out the crying," she explains. "I just put her in the crib and turn it on, and I forget she's even there."

"Oh," I say. "That's good." We are sitting cross-legged on the smooth, clean carpet. Lily is lying on her back under the arc of a mobile attached to a quilted mat. Her eyes are open, and her little limbs flail and kick. I jingle the toys above her, and she looks toward the sound. "You look good," I tell Julie, and she does. Her cheeks are pink today, and her hair is clean and shining. She's wearing a white dress that makes her look like a Nordic maiden at a midsummer festival; all she's missing is a crown of flowers on her head.

"I feel good," Julie says. She reaches over to the coffee table and feels around with one hand until she finds what she's looking for and brings it to her lap: a shiny length of rope, golden with a tassel at each end, like a two-headed snake. "I got so rattled by the window thing, but it's like after that, something cleared inside my head. Caroline and Papa came over and prayed with me. They said I seemed under attack, and I think I have been. You know Caroline used to pray with me in college too?"

"I didn't know that," I say.

She sees me looking at the rope in her hand. "Oh," she says, holding it up between two fingers. "It's a graduation cord I just found in a closet. It took me a few minutes to figure out what it was. Isn't it funny? I've been teaching myself to tie knots."

"Why?"

"Just keeping my hands busy," she says. "It calms me

down." She holds up the rope, and I watch her hands twist and pull, like she is a magician, performing.

"That's so great," I say. "What does Rob think?"

"Who knows," she says. "He keeps disappearing. Sometimes I wake up in the night, and he isn't there. Then in the morning, I ask him where he was, and he says he was in bed next to me the whole night."

"Maybe he was," I say. "And you were dreaming."

She shakes her head. "He's having an affair," she says. "I just don't know with who. It's not you, is it?" She laughs, but the sound is cold.

"Oh, goodness, no," I say.

"Well, I can't blame him," she continues. "For doing it. It's wrong, I'm not saying it isn't. It definitely is, but it's understandable. I haven't been myself in so long. First being pregnant, and then with the actual baby."

"Having a baby is a big deal," I say.

"It never felt right," Julie says. "I should have known something was wrong."

"How could you have known?" I ask her, though maybe the signs were there all along that Rob was an asshole. They probably were. I'm sure there were signs with me too, if Paul had known what to look for. I would know, I think. I would know how to spot a bad one.

"All the other women talked about feeling bonded right off the bat, and I didn't," she answers. "That should have been a sign."

"You didn't feel bonded with Rob?"

She stares at me. "No," she says. "I meant the baby. I didn't feel bonded with the baby." She looks down at Lily, who has grown tired, her little rib cage rising and falling. She watches her mother, though I can't tell if she's trying to make meaning from the sounds Julie makes, or observing the golden cord moving in her hands like a serpent.

"Oh," I say, trying to think back to what she'd said before, but it's hard for me to follow the thread of the conversation now that the context has changed. "I think that's normal too."

Julie shrugs. "Anyway, I feel like it's going to get better." She leans in, and the tips of her long hair skim Lily's forehead. The baby reaches up with a tiny hand. "I hear the voice of God again," she says. "It's so clear. It sounds like a bell, ringing, but there are words if you listen carefully. He's telling me what to do."

"Praise God," I say. Lily's fingers clench around Julie's hair. Julie unwraps the tiny fist and sits back up. The baby begins to cry. Julie offers her the cord instead, tied in a knot like a bow. Still crying, Lily takes it.

"And now I think I can help you," she says over the sound. "I haven't forgotten. I was so overwhelmed before, but now I think He has anointed me with His power to share with you."

Still seated, I pick up the baby, and Julie hands me a pacifier, which I put in Lily's mouth. For a minute, she cries around the pacifier, but then she accepts it, and her eyes close, though she still holds the cord, fingers around the tassel. "I think she's tired," I say. "I'll put her down for her nap, and then we can pray."

Julie stands up and comes around the mat to take Lily from my arms, then puts her back on the mat, keeping the pacifier pressed into her mouth with one finger. "Leave her," Julie says, and motions for me to stand. "I want her to hear that we serve God in this house and no one else." There's something in her voice that sounds authoritarian, powerful.

"Okay," I say, watching Lily, whose eyes are open again. She is listening.

"Let all who have ears hear," Julie says. "Okay." She shakes out her shoulders, loosening her body, and takes my hands and puts them on her stomach, which is soft and rounded, still, under her dress. "I think it should be like this," she says, then puts her hands on my stomach. "Yes. This feels right. Ready?"

"Ready," I tell her, and she prays, and I listen, and I feel nothing but hands on my body. At one point she presses into my stomach, hard, and I almost fall back. I am imagining myself with a baby inside my body and then a baby outside of my body, in my arms, on my breast. I want to see who the baby looks like—me? How vain, to crave seeing your own likeness replicated in miniature, but I do. No matter how I try, though, I can't see anything but the shape of the baby, no other details. This baby could be anyone's. I open my eyes and realize I'm crying. "Shhhh," Julie says softly, her eyes still closed, her hands still on my belly but gentler now. "You're all right."

On the floor, Lily is watching her mother quietly, unblinking, as if she really is listening to her after all.

THAT NIGHT, I make pasta with a sausage sauce simmering with peppers, onions, and diced tomatoes, and our small house smells full and warm. I pick out the tomatoes before I eat my dinner, creating a little red fortress on my plate. "I only put them in there for you," I tell Paul.

"I know," he says. "It's nice. Thank you."

"You're welcome," I say.

My stomach is unsettled, and I'm not hungry. For a moment, I think of telling him about the picture I held in my head while Julie prayed, that featureless, blank child, but I don't. Then I think about telling him about Julie. What would I even say, though? She's weird, I'm uncomfortable, I think her life is sad and hard and lonely. What could Paul do with any of that?

"I want to have sex tonight," Paul says, and I look up. The plate below him is empty, and he's absentmindedly fiddling with his fork. "Isn't tomorrow the day?"

"Yes," I say, "but it's not tomorrow yet."

"But didn't Julie pray over you today?"

"Will it make you feel bad after if we do?" I ask.

"No," says Paul, shaking his head. "Besides, couldn't you have done the math wrong on the calendar? Couldn't you be off by twenty-four hours?"

"No," I say quickly, instinctively. But I picture the baby I cradled, and I say, "Maybe."

Paul raises both hands and smiles. "There you go!" he says. "See? It works." He stands up from the table, leaving the plates there.

"Right now?" I ask.

"Why not?" he says.

In our bedroom, we turn the lights off and undress. We kiss, and Paul runs his hands over me. He pauses for a moment on my stomach, and I wonder if he is feeling anything there, a promise, energy passed from Julie to me, but then I think I imagined it. When he moves inside me, I'm close, my body responding that yes, it wants this too, but it wants more, as it always does, and this time I tell it no; I say, this is what you have.

THAT NIGHT I dream of Paul staring out the bedroom window; everything outside is dark. His back is to me, so I go to him and put my hand on his shoulder to find that his body is burning hot, like a flame is building below the surface of his skin. When he turns to face me, his mouth opens, and black ash spills out. I run away from him and his wide black mouth, but when I leave the house, instead of the front yard, I find myself in Julie's bedroom. She is in the bathtub, holding Lily of the Valley. *I'm scared*, Julie says. I tell her not to be, the house won't burn down—look, she's surrounded by water. *No*, says Julie. *I'm scared because I want it to.*

Fourteen

When Paul has a bad night of dreams, he wakes up exhausted, no matter how many hours he's slept. This is how I feel after I dream of Paul consumed by an unseen fire, of Julie and Lily of the Valley hiding in the bathtub. I do not tell him, though. I am both eager to leave the house and reluctant to go to Julie's, but she calls to say she doesn't need me, that Caroline is coming over today. So I stay home and clean and do laundry, finish a crossword puzzle, and fall asleep in the shade of the backyard, Paul coming and going as he always does.

But even in the background of my day, he has been strange, like a tiger at the zoo pacing the length of his cage, keeping a black eye trained on the faces and hands and legs and heads past his bars. He snaps at me and then is tender, apologetic, pushing a lock of hair behind my ear, grazing my cheek with his finger. After dinner, he sits down on the couch and pats the cushion next to him. I sit. The lamp on the table next to us, like everything that came with the house, is ugly, but its light yellow glow is almost romantic. In the old days, we would have made out here, a movie playing in front of us on the TV. In this house, we don't have a TV. "Is this because we had sex last night?" I ask.

"What?" he says. "No." He clears his throat and points at the coffee table, where the calendar sits. Paul angles himself to face me. "Well," he says. "I've been praying all day that tonight's the night. Or that last night was. Have you?"

"Yes," I say.

"Okay," he says, nodding. "Great." He slaps his hands on his knees, like we've just settled something, meeting adjourned, good talk.

"Great," I echo.

He looks across the room at the clock hanging where the TV should be. "Listen, Rosemary," he says. "Something's going to happen tonight, and you might not like it, but it'll be good, I promise."

Someone knocks at our door. "Paul," I say, but he stands up before the knocking is even finished, and opens the door, and a group of men come into our house.

"Thanks for coming, guys," Paul says. There are three of them: Brother Lou, who stands like a nutcracker in the doorway; Richard Moore, husband of the sick Molly; and Franklin Aaron, sick himself and now healed, the mass of his illness living in a mason jar in Papa Jake's office. Lou and Richard are roughly the same height as Paul, and they are all wearing button-downs and jeans, and it looks like Paul has just multiplied himself, populated our house with more versions of him. Franklin is so much larger than the other men, I almost feel sorry for them. "Hi, Rosemary," says Franklin, lifting a massive hand. I do not answer him.

"Paul?" I say instead, standing up. "Should I get coffee going?"

"No," says Lou. "We can get started. We know tonight is an important night."

"Oh," I say.

"We were just talking about it," Paul says, crossing the room and putting a hand on my waist.

"I'm sorry, I'm a little confused," I tell him, but I don't want to seem rude or unhappy, so I smile after I say it, at Paul and then at the other men, even Franklin. My husband smiles back, but the others don't.

"They're here to help, Rosie," he says, then looks at Lou. "Should she be on the couch? Or the bed? What's best?"

Lou gives a little shrug. "It's your preference," he says. "Whatever you're the most comfortable with."

"The couch," I say.

"That's fine," says Lou, "but I was really talking to Paul."

"The couch is fine," Paul tells them. With his hand on the small of my back, he walks me to the couch and helps me sit down, as though I'm very breakable. "I think you lay down," he says to me.

I lie back and close my eyes. I feel someone adjusting a pillow so that it's underneath my head. A hand touches my arm, and my body flinches before the hand is gone again. When I open my eyes, it's still Paul in front of me. It was only Paul, then, touching me.

"We're just going to pray," Paul says. "Nothing to worry about. Just try to relax." He puts his hand on my stomach and presses down, a command: be still.

The other men come closer, and I watch them position themselves around me, and I feel like I am a broken car on a racetrack, a faulty but treasured instrument surrounded by busy men, a pit crew whose job it is to fix it so the driver still has a shot to win the race. "We're ready," says Paul, giving a nod to Lou.

But Brother Lou frowns, the stiff corners of his mouth bending just a little. "Not quite," he says. "Is there a blanket?" Paul says nothing. "Is there a blanket?" Lou repeats, and I realize he is asking me.

"Linens are in that closet," I say, pointing to a door near the kitchen. Franklin Aaron nods, and I feel embarrassed, like he's going to open the door, and all my underwear or maxi pads are going to tumble out. When he puts his hand on the doorknob to the closet, he looks at me and I nod. He takes out a queen-sized flat sheet and hands it to Lou, who shakes it out, and he holds it up, turns his head away. I do not see him anymore. I do not see them at all.

"Lift your dress up," Lou says. "To right under your, ah, breasts, so that your stomach is exposed. Paul, you may help."

On my back, I inch up my dress and look down at my stomach, my legs, warm white in the glow of the ugly lamp. I am cold. Then Paul lowers the sheet, covers my bottom half, tucks the sheet underneath my feet. Now I see them all again. I am only a midsection; I am only a short-haired head.

"We want there to be as few barriers as possible," Brother Lou says. I think that if they could get below my skin, they would. Make a slit with a paring knife, plunge their hands inside. Paul looks uncomfortable. "All right," says Lou, and it isn't a question.

There are now eight hands on me, all of them on my stomach, below my rib cage, above my hipbones. I worry that hands will find their way up my dress, tug down the sheet and then my underwear, that there will be a sudden and sharp pain, and I'll gasp and cry and struggle while the other hands hold me down, or that all these things will happen but I won't fight, I'll be silent and yielding. But their hands are still and warm, their touch is light. I remember the gym, the coach's hands on my body bending me, stretching me, the only barrier between his hands and my skin a thin leotard. This, I tell myself, is fine.

"God in heaven," says Lou, and I don't listen past that. These prayers are not for me. I know they are praying for healing, for a ready womb, for new life, praying for me, interceding on my behalf, asking God to forgive me, to let me carry a child as He intended. They are praying for Paul, for virility, for strength. They thank God for Paul, they pray I can make him a father. I pray too, silently, privately. My prayers are small, half-formed things, newborn birds whose wings can't keep them up, whose feathers are still sharp and new and slimy from the egg. Please, I pray over and over. Please. Please. I keep my eyes closed, so everything is dark.

Afterward, the men step back, and Paul holds out his hand to help me up. "See?" he says. "Not so bad."

"Not at all," I say.

"Well," says Lou, "y'all go on in, and we'll be right out here."

"Where?" I ask, though I'm not sure what I'm asking.

"Into the bedroom," Paul says softly. "They'll be out here praying."

"The door will be shut," Lou says. "Of course."

"Of course!" says Paul, and he laughs, the sound short and harsh, like a cough.

"Remember, as few barriers as possible," Lou says. "We want to be close without being intrusive, so we'll sit by the bedroom door, with our hands on it, and pray."

"All fine," Paul assures him, and the two men shake hands, like they're concluding a business deal, and I'm only the secretary, simultaneously necessary and unimportant. "Come on," Paul says to me in a soft voice, taking me by the hand and leading me into the bedroom. "You were a trooper. You did exactly what needed to be done."

"I just lay there," I say.

"What else would you need to do?" Paul says. He shuts the door behind us, and I can hear Lou and the other men making room for each other so that everyone can place a hand against the door. Then it is silent.

Paul and I lie down on the bed, though we are still dressed. I begin to undo my dress—it has stupid buttons down the chest, and my fingers feel weak and clumsy—but Paul stops me. "Just lift it," he says. "Since they're out there, I think we should try to make this as fast as possible."

"All right," I say, and obey. Paul arcs his back and undoes his pants, slides them down, boxers still in them.

"Do you mind?" Paul says, gesturing toward his penis.

"Not at all," I say and touch him, my husband, but I think of Franklin Aaron. Can I help it? I don't know. Maybe I can and just don't. But I do feel a rush thinking of him picturing me behind the door, the body he has just touched.

"Ready!" Paul calls when he is, but he doesn't move. His body is straight and strong above me; he props himself up with both arms and doesn't look at me but at the head-board. Outside the door, I hear someone clear their throat, and then I hear nothing and then I hear the sound of the men calling God here, a humming that grows louder and louder.

"Now," I hear a voice say above the humming—Brother Lou, I think—and then Paul moves inside me, and I am startled. The humming like cicadas in the summer. The Fourth of July when my family went to the river, and it was so dark, and in the tall grass, we heard them whirring. *What is it?* my sister asked. *What's that sound?*

"It's okay," says Paul. "It's almost over." Disembodied, separate from the people in the chapel, from my own throat, in which there is nothing now but a choking tightness, the humming sounds like it's coming from the walls, the carpet, the headboard Paul was staring at.

Then we are finished. I have not moved at all. *What else would you need to do?* Paul shudders and collapses. "Okay," he calls, and the humming stops. "I'm sorry," he says to me in a low voice. "Was it awful?"

"Yes," I say, and his face falls. "It's fine."

"We won't have to do it again," he says. "I promise. But put your legs up for a minute?"

"Okay," I say, and I raise my legs. Everything is wet.

Naked, Paul walks to the door and puts his hand on it. "Hang on just a second," he calls to the men. He steps into his boxers and his jeans and pulls a T-shirt off the top of the dresser.

"Take your time," says Brother Lou. I lower my legs and pick up my panties and go to the bathroom. I turn on the light, which hums too, and I shut it off and pee in the dark.

"Ready?" Paul asks when I come out.

We open the door, and there they are, looking at us expectantly, and Paul nods. They all nod back. "Thank y'all so much," says my husband. "We are grateful to you and to God who has brought us here."

"Yes," says Brother Lou. "Praise God."

"Praise Him," says Franklin.

"Praise Him," says Richard Moore.

"Amen," I say, and we walk them out.

When we are alone again, Paul reaches for me and says my name. "Come here," he says gently. "Please."

"No," I say. His hand drops to his side, I turn my back to him and walk to our bedroom. To his credit, he lets me go alone.

Fifteen

Julie calls our landline in the morning and asks if I can come over after the afternoon service; Rob is fasting all day with Papa Jake, and they decided to have a feast at sundown to celebrate, men only. Of course, I tell her. Paul is waiting, standing nearby as I talk. She mentions that she needs help with something. "Caroline agrees with me that things aren't right," she says. I don't ask her what she means; honestly, I don't care. Everything—my body, my brain—feels tender, like it's all been worked too hard. So I just say, "Sure, Julie, I'll see you later today."

Outside it looks like rain, and Papa Jake dedicates the afternoon service to prayers for rain because the spring has been strangely dry, and the summer is coming, long and unrepentant in its heat. While he speaks, Renee stands up and does a dance in the aisle, her long hair in front of her face as she crouches close to the floor before springing up. Papa Jake says she is moved by the Spirit of the Lord, her motions will bring rain. Later, when he holds a hand up and says stop, listen, and we hear the sound of rain falling outside, Renee collapses to her knees, thanking God.

Papa Jake asks the sick to stand, a private healing service this time, and though the usual people rise from their seats, he gazes out at them and declares that there is no one for the Lord to heal today. I watch Erik, the Viking, take this in. He looks thin and sallow, his wrists frail, his body trembling; it's like looking at someone who is already dead. When he sits, it's a collapse, as if his body just couldn't keep itself upright any longer. The Lord has given us rain, Papa Jake says. Today he has chosen to heal the earth instead.

We make a tunnel down the aisle, clasping hands across the gap, rearranging ourselves so that women only hold hands with women, men only hold hands with men, and Missy dances down the aisle, under the archway of our hands, as we speak words of delight over her. Then Papa Jake sends the sick down the aisle too, and they let themselves be touched and held by us as we break our tunnel apart so that we may heal them. Of course, the hands that really matter belong to Papa Jake, who receives each of them with an embrace at the end. Molly, whose house burned down, who is relentlessly sick, whose husband listened at the door last night as I had sex with my husband, walks by me, and I feel suddenly like I should touch her, and I grab her thin arm. She stops and looks at me with round owl eyes, and I let her go. Her arm felt hot under my hand, like a pot of water simmering on the stove. I think of the dream I had of Paul, standing by the window, ash spilling out of his endless mouth.

"God is here," Papa Jake says as he touches the sick. "We've brought Him here. Can you feel Him? Can you feel the angels? They've carried Him down here on their shoulders. Do you see them?"

I see Julie step forward from the tunnel, unencumbered—where is Lily?—and she spins down the aisle, smiling. "Look at the beauty of God," Papa Jake says. And then Amanda joins her, holding her hands, then Amanda's daughter, who follows her everywhere, goes too, the beauty, Papa Jake says, the beauty of it all, and then we are all going down the aisle, the tunnel falling apart, person by person, all of us letting go.

AFTER THE SERVICE, I try to get Julie's attention from across the room to see if she's ready to leave, and when I think her eyes are on me, I gesture toward the front door before I realize she is looking past me at someone I don't see. "She'll be right behind you," Paul says, shrugging. "Come on." When Paul drops me off at the Friedrichs' house, I sit on the front step to wait, but then it begins to rain again. There's no gradual buildup to it, just sudden heavy drops that fall hard like little nails. I stand flush against the front door, trying to stay underneath the narrow awning hanging over the porch, but I'm still getting wet, so I turn and wiggle the doorknob, just in case. I know Julie won't mind if I wait inside for her. It's unlocked, and the door opens.

My shoes are muddy from the rain-soaked ground outside, so I slip them off by the door. In another room, Lily of the Valley is crying. Julie must have somehow made it home before me after all and now she's in the back with Lily, trying to get her to stop crying, or nurse her or dress her or change her diaper, all the things the girl does not want done. I walk past the empty kitchen and living room and down the dark hallway, and the crying grows louder. "Julie?" I call. She doesn't answer, and I worry: she's sick or unconscious; she's hurt herself; she's gone, left Lily of the Valley behind, this time for good. I look first in the bedroom she shares with Rob and which Rob has maybe shared with someone else, then their bathroom. Both empty. Lily's crying sounds hoarse, as if she has been screaming for hours. I should have gone to her first, and I rush into the room set up as the nursery. Julie had only recently moved Lily from the bassinet in the master bedroom to the nursery, and even with Lily crying and therefore very much alive, the room somehow feels strange, sterile. But I can see through the slats in the crib that Lily's in there on her back, and I am relieved until I get closer.

She is tied up, her body spread out into an X. Limbs extended, wrists attached with—what? shoelaces—to the slats of the crib. Her ankles are tied the same way, but with the golden graduation cord, cut in half. Mismatched crucifixes are propped up in the four corners of the crib. I recognize two from the Friedrichs' house: a small pewter cross that hung on the bathroom wall above the light switch, the other covered in brightly colored stones that used to hang near the kitchen sink. I remember looking at it once as I washed the dishes for Julie.

I loosen the knot of one lace tying down her wrist, and immediately that little hand shoots up, reaching for something, grabbing at the air. My hands are shaking too much to get the second undone. I rush back to the kitchen, where I find scissors in the knife block, then carefully slide a scissor blade between her wrist and the shoelace and cut. Then I try to cut the cords around her ankles, but the glossy braids are thick and slippery, and I wonder how Julie did it. I go to work untying the knots instead, and they slip out easily, then grab the baby and hold her tightly. She feels clammy, sweaty, as if her whole body has been crying. "Shhh," I tell her stupidly. I find her pacifier on the changing table and give it to her. The laces and severed cord lie in the crib like snakes.

I hear the front door open. Lily and I stand in the gray light of the nursery, her breath calming gradually in the jerky way my own once did when I used to cry hard. I've learned how to stop the tears now, tamp them down. But this—I don't know where to go. The window doesn't open. I could run past Julie. Poor Julie. Poor Lily of the Valley. What a stupid name.

Julie walks into the nursery but stops when she sees me. "Rosemary," she says. "You have to put her down."

"You tied her up," I say.

"I had to," she says. "She isn't who you think she is. I know what it looks like, but what you think is happening isn't really happening."

"I don't know what's happening," I tell her.

"That's why she's always crying. And why she hates when I nurse her," Julie says. "Have you ever heard of a baby like that? Something isn't right."

"Let's figure this out together," I say. "We can figure it out. She's okay. She isn't hurt."

"She's not right," Julie says again. "I've been trying to tell you. Something got in. In her. We can let something evil in if we aren't all so careful. When we're calling God, if anyone does it wrong, any one person! It must have been a mistake, that something got in, that we let in. But I think we can get rid of it."

I think of the boy Julie told me about. How could I not?

A pen full of headless chickens, blood on the brown dirt. A rope.

"We can't do this, Julie," I say.

She looks nervously at Lily in my arms, as if whatever she thinks is inside Lily might make its presence known. A cascade of ashes from her mouth, her nose, her eyes. "God told me I needed to do this, and He said you would help," Julie says, raising her eyes to meet mine. "He specifically said you, Rosemary! Haven't you felt that? Didn't He tell you too? This is why you're here!"

"I'm here so I can get pregnant," I say gently. "Remember?"

She rolls her eyes. "You aren't going to get pregnant," she says. "God told me that too. I felt it when I put my hands on you. Your body isn't a good home for a baby. It's all—" She waves her hand vaguely. "Wrong."

"Wrong," I echo, thinking of that anonymous baby I'd imagined myself holding the day she put her hands on my stomach. I want to tell her my body isn't wrong, but I can't because I think it might be true—the emptiness of my body not a landscape of beauty, not a desert of sculpted dunes, but a bleak countryside, flat and gray, a city draped in polluted, choking air. In my arms, Lily of the Valley begins to whimper. I look down at her; her mouth is a sad little worm. At the sound of the baby, Julie flinches. "Let me call Paul," I say. "Or Rob. Or Papa. Let's tell them what God told you."

"Not them," says Julie.

"Who, then?"

Julie says nothing. She is still standing in the doorway, but it's like she has begun to droop, or like something in the floor is reaching up, attaching itself to her wrists, her hips, her neck, and pulling her down very slowly. "Caroline," she says. "Please." Lily begins to cry in earnest now, and Julie covers her ears with her hands.

"Okay," I say. "I can call her." I hold tightly to Lily, grabbing a thin blanket from the top of the changing table, and slip past Julie. Our shoulders touch. She doesn't follow me, and when I look down the hall, she isn't in the door-way, and I wonder if she is sitting in the nursery now, in the rocker she tried to nurse the baby in.

I know Caroline's number is on a list of important ones on a Post-it note on the refrigerator, and awkwardly cra-dling Lily, I dial it. I hope she won't answer and I can call Paul, who will know how to fix the situation, instead, but she picks up almost immediately. "J?" she asks.

"It's Rosemary," I say. "Something's wrong with Julie. She's—"

"Where's Lily of the Valley?" Caroline interrupts.

"I have her. I'm holding her. Julie's in the nursery, I think." Lily begins to cry angrily.

"I'll be right there," Caroline says. "Take the baby out of the house. Y'all need to go."

"I don't want to leave Julie alone," I tell her, but Caro-line isn't having it.

"I said I'm coming," she says, and hangs up the phone.

"Julie?" I call. "Caroline's on her way. I'm going to take Lily outside to see if it calms her down."

"No," Julie says from somewhere in the back of the house, and I know I should go back and check on her be-cause now she's saying wait, shouting that Lily can't be re-moved from the house, can't be let loose, but I keep going.

I go out the front door and run down the steps without stopping to put on my shoes. Outside the rain has stopped, but the sidewalk is wet and the sky is gray, and as I walk down the sidewalk, the trees above me, oak trees with full branches, drip water on my head and on Lily. Calm now, she blinks in my arms, and I start to run.

Sixteen

I stand, with Lily still in my arms, by the stop sign at the end of Julie's street, waiting for someone—Caroline, I suppose—to tell me what to do. But when Caroline does appear, turning onto the street in a car I don't recognize, she does not stop for us. Instead she drives right past us as if she doesn't see us at all and turns into the driveway of Julie's house, hurrying out of the car and through the front door. I'm unsure whether I should follow. It seems callous and cowardly to wait out here, but at the same time, what good could I serve in there, especially with Lily? I walk down the block a few houses, approaching Julie's, but then stop, as though there is a force field surrounding the house repelling me, and instead walk back toward the stop sign. Lily's eyes are open, and she looks at the trees overhead, her mouth in an O like she's about to coo, but no sound comes out. She blinks, tree branches, snatches of white sky reflected in the dark of her eyes. All is quiet, and I think of the day Lily was born. That eerie stillness, the fear. The broken circle, the gap in the link we made in the backyard. We could let anything in.

After a few minutes, when neither Caroline nor Julie has come out, I pace with Lily, rounding the corner and then coming back past the stop sign, toward Julie's house, and then turning again. Back around the corner. My arms are tired. Finally, I sit cross-legged on the wet sidewalk by the stop sign and drape Lily across my lap, her body in the hollow my legs make, her head on my thigh. She lifts her arms, as though she is showing them to me, and I grab one wrist to see if there is any sign of the restraints. And there it is—a series of red marks like little bracelets. But the tiny cut on her cheek from the broken glass has healed. She is very sweet in my arms, and still, I think, I do not want this for myself.

I stroke her faint eyebrows, the jut of bone beneath her skin, until her blinking slows and then stops altogether, eyes closing. Her lips loosen around her pacifier, and then it just rests there, against her bottom lip. I don't know if I should push it back in or pluck it out and eventually decide to do nothing.

Finally, Paul pulls up in his truck, the passenger side window rolled down. "Ready?" he asks.

"Can you help me with this?" I gesture toward the sleeping Lily on my lap.

Paul nods, and the truck gives a lurch as he shifts it into park. He comes around and smiles down at us. "Wow," he says. "You two are beautiful together. Should I just—?" He bends, reaching for Lily, and I cup her head in one hand as we awkwardly make the transition. Beneath my dress, my thigh is sweaty and damp from where she rested. "She's so cute!" he says. He's a natural, sure and gentle, body reflexively swaying as soon as he takes her. "I never loved my husband more than when I saw him hold Bella for the first time," I remember Tess saying. Paul is tender with Lily, but I love him no more and no less.

I situate myself in the passenger seat of the truck, and he passes her back off to me. She startles, arms jerking momentarily up before relaxing again, and I think of how her arm shot up, desperate, when I untied the first knot. "Oh, Paul," I say. "It was awful."

"I'm so sorry, Rosie," he says. "Hey, hold her really still, okay? I'm going to drive as carefully as I can."

"She'll be fine," I say. "Do you know if Julie's okay? I haven't seen her or Caroline come out."

"Papa says she is. All things considered. He should be there any minute now. Rob too."

"Julie thinks he's having an affair," I say.

"Huh," says Paul, eyes on the road ahead as we turn onto our street. "Rob would never do that."

But I feel certain he's lying, and we are both silent. When we pull up into our driveway, our house is dark and the sky is dark, even though the sun won't set for several more hours. We stay in the truck even after Paul has turned it off. "Now what?" I ask.

"What do you mean?" Paul looks at me, the crease in the middle of his eyebrows deepening.

"Lily," I say. "What do we do with her? Is someone coming to pick her up? We don't have diapers or anything. And she's probably so hungry. I think babies are supposed to eat a lot. Right?"

"Well, she's asleep," he says.

"Yes, Paul, I see that," I say, and he frowns at the bite in my voice. "Sorry," I say.

"I'll call someone," he says. "Y'all go in, and maybe you can lie down with her on the bed or something."

"Okay," I say. Paul gets out and hurries around to my side, opens the door, and gently helps me out of the truck, as if I've just been in labor, pushed the baby from my body into this dark world. He guides me into the house and I climb into bed, cradling Lily like she's a football, and Paul puts a blanket around us and kisses my forehead. "I'll figure everything out," he says. "Just rest."

I don't want to close my eyes, afraid that if I do, I will see Lily of the Valley bound in her crib, silent and still and cold this time. Or I'll see Julie or I'll see Paul or I'll see myself, burning or drowning or dying or lost. Afraid I'll see a pen of headless chickens with bloody necks, tumorous lumps breathing and beating in glass jars, a brick through every window, coming for us. But—a miracle—I sleep and do not dream. I am completely empty. Nothing left in me at all.

I WAKE TO singing. The room is dark except for the lamp on Paul's side of the bed, but he's not here. On the foot of the bed sits Missy, singing softly, Lily of the Valley on one of her breasts. The nipple of the other glistens in the glow of the lamplight. "Hi," she says. "Sorry. If I'm not completely topless, my bra gets wet."

I pull myself up so I'm sitting against the headboard. "I don't know what that means," I say.

She swipes a finger against the shining nipple and holds it up. "She can only nurse on one at a time, but they both leak. I don't know why God hasn't given me twins so we can make use of all this milk."

"Oh," I say. God, I think, the indignity of it all. "What time is it?"

"About seven thirty," Missy says. "I'm just finishing up here, and then I think Paul said y'all are going to give me a ride home, and we'll get everything taken care of."

"Thank you," I say, relieved. "I wasn't sure what we were going to do with Lily."

"Okay," Missy says to the baby, gazing down at her. "All done, baby girl." She slides a finger into Lily's mouth, and Lily pops off her breast. "Why don't you go get Paul, and I'll get her all burped and changed and everything?"

"Great," I say. I notice there's a box of diapers on the floor next to our dresser and atop it, a box of wipes. As I leave, Missy begins singing again. I think of Caroline washing Julie's hair and singing Britney Spears, and I want to throw up.

Paul is sitting on the couch in the living room, frowning at his phone, but looks up when he hears me. "Just got an update from Papa and Caroline," he says. "Julie is doing much better."

"That's great," I say. I sit down next to him and put my head on his shoulder. He reaches an arm around me to pull me closer. "Where is she?"

"Not sure," he says into my hair.

"She shouldn't be alone," I say. "Someone should be with her all the time for a while, I think. Maybe Caroline? Maybe we could do shifts or something."

"Well," says Paul. His voice is so careful I scoot away from him so I can see him better. "Caroline and Jake are taking her somewhere."

"Where?"

"Rosie," Paul says, holding up his hands. "I don't know. Somewhere else. She can't be here. Honestly, she's dangerous. To all of us. Unpredictable."

"Where did she go?" I ask again. "What about Rob?"

"What about him?"

"He's her husband," I say. "And what about Lily?"

He sighs.

"All ready!" sings Missy as she walks into the living room, cradling Lily in her arms. "All fed, all clean. Got a good burp. We're good to go!"

Paul slaps his thighs heartily as he stands up. "Wonderful!" he says. "Missy, let us give you a ride home. I can't thank you enough."

"It's no problem," she says. "It's a tragedy she's all alone."

"She isn't," says Paul. "She has us."

WHEN WE PULL up to Missy's house, her brood of children runs out barefoot from the house into the wet grass, calling for her. In the illumination of the truck's headlights, I can see a fine spray of rain falling. Missy climbs out of the truck, and they swarm her, clinging to her legs, pulling on her skirt, standing on her feet, reaching and needing and begging. "Look at the baby!" she says, pushing me and Lily toward them, but they do not care; they've seen babies before and are therefore unimpressed.

"Missy, seriously, you're a lifesaver," Paul says.

Missy smiles and nods demurely at Paul. "You are so welcome," she says to me. "Let me know if you need anything, okay?" Her children are wild in the yard, tumbling and running and still somehow touching their mother, a hand grazing her each time they pass. "I better go," she says.

"Here's Lily of the Valley," I say. Lily blinks as if she is finally noticing the dampness of the air touching her face.

"Oh, of course," Missy says, leaning toward her. "Goodbye, sweet girl." She brushes her lips to the girl's forehead and then she says, "Okay, troops, inside." The children twirl around her, little nymphs, wildlings.

"Ready?" Paul says to me, and opens the passenger side door.

"Wait!" Missy calls. She's hurrying toward us, full breasts bouncing as she cuts across the grass. In her hand she has a car seat. "We have an extra," she says. "I can put it in for you real quick."

"Amazing," says Paul. "Thanks." Missy slides the seat across the bench of the truck's back seat, there are a series of clicks, and then she takes the baby from me and straps her in. My arms feel light and free. Lily whimpers as she is buckled.

"There we go," Missy says. She closes the door for me, and Paul closes his door, and now here we are together. It is night now, fully dark.

"Paul," I say.

"Don't," he says.

"Paul!" On the dashboard, Paul's phone begins to buzz and tremble. He reaches for it. "Do not answer that," I say. "I need to talk to you."

He looks at the screen and slides his thumb across it. "Paul here," he says, and listens. "You're kidding." He listens again. "Be there in a minute." He hangs up without saying goodbye, and he does a U-turn in the middle of the street. When we pass Missy's house again, the porch light stares like a bright, unblinking eye.

"Is it Julie?" I ask. "Where are we going?"

"No," he says. "There's a fire."

"Whose house?" I ask, glancing at the truck's clock. "It's so early."

"No one's," he says. "First Baptist of Dawes."

"Randall's church? Was it a holy fire?"

"No," Paul says. "How could it be a holy fire?"

"What do you mean? Why wouldn't it be?"

"It just isn't, Rosie, trust me," he says. "Fuck. We're going there now."

"Why do we care about the church burning down?" I ask. "What does it have to do with us?"

"Use your brain," Paul snaps. "What do you think it has to do with us?"

"Did we burn it down?" I ask. Paul says nothing. We turn a corner, and the flames are before us, fiery tentacles thrusting through the church's windows. But it's a smaller fire than the one that ate the Wilders' house, amateur in comparison, honestly, and anyway, the fire department is already there taming it, the flames shrinking. Paul swings into the parking lot and jumps out of the truck without turning off the engine. Papa Jake is there, Lou and Kyle too, standing, to my surprise, with Randall. All of them watch the firefighters in their giant suits and hats, holding the hoses like they're gripping the long slithering neck of a serpent. I want to see too. I want to get closer. I get out of the truck, I stand behind the men, a little off to the side. They do not turn.

"Doesn't look too bad," Paul says by way of greeting. "Lucky it's been so wet today."

"Hey, Paul," says Randall.

"I'm sorry about your building, Randall," Paul says. "What a mess."

"I appreciate that," Randall says. "And I appreciate y'all coming out here." He looks to the other men, who stand with their arms crossed. Then he turns just a bit more, enough so that I can see his face, enough that he can see me. He nods at me so quickly I almost miss it; the flickering of the dying flames reflects in the lenses of his glasses for just a second before he turns back to the other men. I step back toward the truck, slink away into the shadows like a rat exposed to light.

"Of course," says Papa Jake, scratching the back of his head with one hand, a little boy in the principal's office, both caught and unyielding. "Though I'm not sure what it has to do with us, exactly."

"Brother, this has to stop," Randall says.

"The fire?" Papa Jake answers. "Looks like the boys are taking care of it."

"No," says Randall. "You know what I mean."

"We haven't done a thing," says Kyle. "And y'all keep coming after us. But we just take it. You probably burned your own church down."

"Kyle," Paul says, placing a hand on his shoulder. "Randall, we're sorry. We are. We wish we could give you some answers, but we just can't. We aren't responsible for this."

"All right, then," says Randall. He extends his hand toward Paul, who shakes it, and then offers his hand toward the others. One by one, the men shake Randall's hand. I climb back into the truck, where Lily is still asleep.

"You know who I bet it was?" I say when Paul gets back in the car. "Tyler. The young one. He seems—destructive."

"Rosemary," Paul says. "That's not appropriate."

"Sorry," I say as he pulls out of the parking lot.

"Look. We're fighting a great battle. Sometimes you have to do things you don't want to do in order to win the war. We had to send a message."

"You didn't have anything to do with this," I say. "You didn't even know about it."

Paul sighs. "We're all one body, Rosie," he says. "But I've done a lot for this church. A lot you don't even know about."

I wonder if Paul wants me to ask. What, Paul? What have you done that I don't know about? Share your secrets with me, show me what you have done. Show me what you can do. But I don't, and the three of us go home in silence, unspoken, unknown things heavy among us, as thick as the smoke pouring forth from the burning church behind us.

Seventeen

When we get home, there's a bassinet on the front porch. As we get closer, I recognize it from Julie's house—a pretty wicker basket with a muslin lining, perched on curved legs that rock from side to side. "Rob said he would bring it by," Paul says, picking it up. He puts it in our bedroom, on the floor next to my side of the bed, and I carefully place Lily in it. As I do so, she wakes up, but I don't know what I'm supposed to do about that. I don't even know when babies go to sleep. It's nine o'clock. Do I just leave her there?

"When is someone coming to get her?" I ask Paul, following him as he walks out of the bedroom, back down the hallway, into the kitchen. "What's this?" I point to a bottle warmer sitting on the counter next to a brown paper grocery bag.

"A bottle warmer," says Paul.

"I know it's a bottle warmer," I say. "I'm not an idiot."

"You asked," he says. He reaches past me and opens the refrigerator, pulls out a small container of breast milk, then dips his hand into the brown paper bag and pulls out a plastic baby bottle. He hands them both to me. "Do you know how to do this?" he asks.

I sigh and take them. "I can figure it out."

"It's just for a little while," Paul says. "Until Rob is ready to have her back. He needs some time."

"Why wouldn't someone else take her?" I ask.

"Because this makes the most sense," he says. "There aren't many people here with the room to spare. Everyone else has their own children already."

I press some buttons on the bottle warmer—it looks like a small rocket ship, sleek and aerodynamic, expensive-looking, and I wonder where it came from—until a little clock appears and starts a countdown. I turn back to Paul and lean against the counter.

"What?" he says. "Why are you looking at me like that? I don't get why you're being so combative with me. We want a baby. Here is a baby."

"'Here is a baby'?" I ask. "Seriously?"

"There's something else too," he says. "Okay? Another reason. I should've led with it, I guess."

"Okay," I say warily.

"Papa had a prophecy, about Lily of the Valley and Julie," he says. "And about you."

A basket held by unseen hands. A canyon filling with water, a flash flood building, unstoppable. Vanity and a pair of scissors. I am a thing, always a thing. The bottle warmer beeps. I open it, letting loose a small cloud of steam. The bottle feels hot. Too hot? How can you tell?

"Lily is a special baby," Paul says. "Julie was right that she isn't just an average baby, but otherwise she had it all wrong. God has imbued her with so many gifts. Ears to hear, eyes to see. That's how Papa was able to call her back to him during her birth."

"Okay," I say. "Tell me the story."

"Papa saw a castle," he says. "Moat, drawbridge, tall towers. Those skinny little flags, you know? And there are all these armies approaching the castle. They come one after the other, with swords and horses, then with fiery arrows, then a battering ram. But the castle stands strong. It looks like it's never going to fall." He pauses.

"But it does," I say.

"Exactly," he says. "The crowd of knights or soldiers or whatever they are part and turn, they're looking at something behind them, and you can't see what's coming, but you know it must be something powerful. Finally, you see it's a little girl. She stands before the moat." Paul lifts his hands, his palms facing me. Hands that have built things, hit things, created things, fingers that have touched all parts of me, palms that have held my face, hands that I have held and kissed. They seem strange to me now. So white, bloodless. "The girl makes the castle fall."

"I'm the castle," I say.

"You're the castle," Paul says. "Lily is the girl."

"That sounds bad," I say. "I don't want to fall." A lie. I do want to fall, I always have. That was how I'd ended up in gymnastics in the first place, because my mother was tired of watching me teeter at the edge of high places. At the gym, falls would happen fast, but there was always a split second in the air that felt euphoric, almost worth the pain of the bad landing, and even that, the pain, had an element of ecstasy too—the bruises, the scrapes, the pulled muscles.

If I'm going to be a cold, dark castle, I want to feel the earth beneath me shake from the horses' pounding hooves, the heat from the arrows, the charge of the battering ram. I want to see the mess that's left when I finally give up. Look, I imagine Paul saying, you're something new now.

"No, no," says Paul, shaking his head. "The castle is really your womb, and Papa says it's like there's a fortress surrounding it. Lily is going to make you fertile. She's going to fix you."

"Thank you, Paul, for sharing," I say. "Now I'm going to feed Lily."

Paul grabs my wrist, and I turn back to him. "Rosie, there's more. This is something we have to do."

From our bedroom, Lily lets out a little cry. "I have to go," I say, pulling away from him. "I need to figure out what to do with this very special baby."

"They're going to make you leave," Paul says, and I stop in the doorway.

"What?" I say, turning back around. "Why?" He's still slouching against the kitchen counter, his strong back curved forlornly and his head hanging.

"Because you can't get pregnant," he says. "Everyone knows we've been trying, and it isn't working. Papa thinks it's because you don't truly believe. And he says I'm unduly suffering being tethered to you. No weak links, he said."

I think of Julie. *Anything can get in.* And the ropes. I imagine the gold cord she'd tied around Lily, only now long enough to be wrapped around Paul and me, binding us together, Paul suffocating while I struggle to keep him in the constraints. My heart races, but everything outside of my body feels like it has slowed down, taken on a sheen of unreality. "Oh," I say. I can't tell if I'm relieved or sad. I've failed at so much in my life already. "Papa would do that to us?"

"Not us," says Paul. "You'll have to go. Not me."

"Ouch," I say. Lily cries, building momentum.

"I'm sorry," he says. "It's the truth. I could always get remarried here."

"But would you?"

Paul thinks for a moment, eyes toward the ceiling. "I would," he says finally. "I deserve it."

"You do," I say. He nods and wipes his eyes. You never cry, he told me once in college. It wasn't true. I cried all the time, but my mother had told me when I started gymnastics that tears should stay in the locker room, in the car on the way home from practice, in my bedroom with the door closed. I'm going to teach you, Paul said, to cry in public. That didn't sound the way I meant it, he said, and we laughed.

"I love you," he says. "So much. I don't want you to go. That's why I'm worried."

"So what do we do?"

"What we've been doing," Paul says. "Pray for a miracle. Wait for God to show us what he can do. Let Lily stay."

"I'm going to feed her," I say, and Paul nods.

"Wait, though. Rosie?" he says. "Is Papa wrong? Do you still believe?"

I have loved Paul for so long. What would I be without him? I'm afraid I wouldn't be anything at all. Once, in college, we drove to Big Bend, just the two of us, south and south and south until we could touch Mexico. We went hiking in the park's rambling deserts but got lost—

somehow, the map didn't match the trail—and Paul saved us, kept a cool head, kept us moving, and eventually got us back to camp safe and sound. Another time, right after we started dating, there was a big spring storm, and a tornado warning siren wailed in the night like a frightened child, and Tess hadn't been home. I was scared, alone in my shitty third-floor apartment, and so I called Paul. Just keep talking to me, he said. You'll be okay. Just stay on the phone. Then: Did you hear that?

Hear what? I asked.

A knock. I was quiet, I listened. Over the cry of the siren and the thrashing of the storm, there'd been a knock. I left the bathroom where I had been hiding and opened the front door of the apartment. Outside the light was gone, sucked out by the storm, leaving only wind and rain in its place, and there was Paul, his cell phone to his ear.

"Of course I believe," I say as he leans against the kitchen counter.

"I'm so happy," he says. "Thank you. I love you. God is going to do big things here, for us. Now go feed Lily."

But in the bedroom, the baby has fallen back asleep. I sit down on the edge of the bed to wait in case she wakes up, and when it doesn't seem she will, I walk back to the kitchen. Paul is gone. Outside maybe, to call Papa and debrief. I put the bottle back in the refrigerator. I don't even know if it was ever the right temperature, and it all feels like a stupid, useless effort.

AT THE SERVICE the next day, Papa Jake tells us two things. The first regards Julie and her sudden removal. The demon, the something else Julie felt, was not inside Lily of the Valley, but Julie herself. Surely we'd all noticed something about her was amiss? We all nod. Yes, Papa, we had. I look at Caroline as she listens to her husband. Her face is still, revealing nothing. A woman, Papa explains, is in a vulnerable position after she gives birth. All of her strength goes toward the expulsion of the baby, and imagine the weakness left when all that force is gone. An empty body that doesn't know what to do without its charge will take anything, allow anything. "This is why mothers must be strong," Papa Jake says. "The strongest of us all." He has all the mothers stand up, and we clap for them until our hands sting. I watch Amanda, stomach growing, housing a baby, Abigail clutching one hand, Troy the other.

"Paul and Rosemary will be taking care of Lily of the Valley while Rob gets his footing," Papa Jake says. "Will y'all stand real quick?" We do. Before the service, Amanda strapped Lily to my body with some kind of long, linen wrap she wound around me until I felt constricted. "Snug," said Amanda. "And hands free!" Paul gives a little wave as everyone claps for us. Lily's eyes are wide open. "Listen, if y'all have any extra baby items lying around, take them by Paul's house, will you?" Papa says. Everyone says they will. And that is the end of Julie's story here in Dawes.

The second story he tells us is about the fire. "Some of them think it was us," Papa Jake says. "And others among them think it was God! 'See?' they say. 'You are not the only ones whom God touches with flame!' But we know God has no covenant with them. They are strangers to Him. He gives them no gifts, and He gives them no struggles. You might say, okay, well, if He doesn't care about them, why doesn't He punish them?" He pauses here, looks around at us. Waits. "Because," he finally says, "God can't be bothered. When you see an earthworm struggling through the dirt, do you step on it? Of course not. There's no need to be cruel. But do you stoop down to help it? Push your finger into the soil, give it level ground to inch along on? Of course you don't do that either!

"So, look," Papa Jake continues. "Their fire could have been caused by faulty wiring. Plain old bad luck. Could have been an angry parishioner." He shrugs. "Who knows? All we know is it wasn't us."

I find Tyler in the congregation. There he is, right beside Young Jake, whose ears stick out from his square head, and it could be my imagination, but I think they burn red with shame.

I zone out for the rest of the service, rubbing Lily on the back the way I've seen mothers of babies do, and I think about the fire. Imagine finding just the right place to start it, imagine the thrill of the little flame taking hold, knowing it was only going to grow bigger and stronger, and if you stood too close to it, it wouldn't stop for you simply because you made it—it would swallow you up too. Light from your fingertips, heat on your face.

I look down at my feet, sticking out from my long dress on the floor. I watch them like they are about to disappear if I look away even for a second, dissolve into the carpet or up into the air of the chapel. My fingers on Lily's back suddenly feel the same way—temporary. I shake them out until the feeling comes back. But by the time it goes away in one place, it's back somewhere else: my ears, my neck, my abdomen. I need to get out of here. I jostle Lily awake, shifting slightly in my seat, just enough to disturb her, and predictably, she wails, and I stand, giving an apologetic look to those around me, who give me a sympathetic look as I hurry outside.

In the warm air, Lily takes a deep breath and begins to settle, straining in the wrap as she adjusts herself. It was a half-hearted cry to begin with. I stand in the sun. It is hot in Texas in the spring, and spring is about to turn to summer, violent and heavy. I stand there with Lily in that spot until my head swims but my flesh feels hot and the top of my head, my hair, burns to the touch.

Eighteen

Over the next week, people bring by baby things: a swing, bottles, a special brush to clean the bottles, tiny fingernail clippers, breast milk in small plastic bags, breast milk in small plastic containers, a little instrument to suck snot from her nose, some kind of reclining chair you carry around from room to room so the baby always has a place to rest. Better to wear her, though, the mothers tell me. Better for attachment. I want to tell them I don't want her to be attached to me, a stranger who is not her mother, not anyone's mother, but instead I smile and say she does love to be worn. I wonder, again, if she misses Julie.

Someone else brings me a stroller, and suddenly Lily of the Valley and I have the world at our fingertips. Every day, twice a day, we say goodbye to Paul if he's here, then I load Her Majesty into her royal carriage, and we walk down the driveway. In the mornings, we take a right. In the evenings, a left. Then we walk until she cries. But until she does, I belong only to me. The sun on my face, the cracked sidewalk beneath my feet, the dress on my legs, the sweat on my back, the stroller's handle clutched in my fingers—I feel it all. I worried the other day when my body felt impermanent, so fleeting and unfixed, but all the walking has helped. With every step I'm gaining muscle, more body, more weight to keep me attached to the earth.

I've always assumed the world got smaller when you had a baby, reduced to the size of a nursery, but now I think maybe it gets a little bigger. It has for me, anyway, the boundaries of my world expanding to as far as I can walk before Lily cries. Paul tells me he feels like I'm cheating on him. "With the stroller," he says quickly when he sees my face. "I just miss having you girls around when you're not here." I wonder if Rob misses Lily.

We settle into a routine. When I describe our nights to Amanda, she tells me Lily is a good sleeper. I can't imagine what a bad sleeper would be like, because she makes noises all night long, grunting like a little piglet, crying when she wakes up hungry, breathing deeply and then quickly and then loudly, each shift causing me to start awake. Every morning I feel hazy, loose, and it is only when we stroll out into the daylight that I start to solidify. During the day, Lily eats all the time. I think of Missy's shining nipple the first night, and I wonder if Julie's milk has dried up or if her breasts still fill and ache, a constant reminder of what she has lost. Then I wonder if she feels it's a loss at all, or if it feels like a relief.

After Lily eats, she plays, which is a dumb thing to call it because all she can do is lie on her back and look up at the world above her. I find her shiny things and hold them in front of her face: spoons, a small mirrored compact that used to hold powder, aluminum foil. The last I crinkle, and the sound makes her glare at me, so I stop. We stroll. I wash the bottles over and over and over again. She naps in various places. The bed while I lie next to her, a blanket on the floor, her special reclining chair, her bassinet, my arms. Once a day I put her on the floor on her tummy because Amanda said if we don't, she'll get a flat spot on her head. "Gabriel has one," she said. "First child learning curve." Paul rubs Lily's head every night, checking to make sure there are no flat spots developing.

After doing that and feeding her the last bottle of the evening, Paul has me lie down on our bed, and he puts Lily on my stomach and prays over us. Sometimes she is still, compliant, like a warm little blanket over my body, like the floppy-bodied toy dolls Bree and I played with, and others she squirms so violently and cries so loudly that Paul has to hold her on top of me and practically shout the prayer. I wonder if Lily remembers the cords, the ties.

Everyone is so nice to me, all the women. I am acceptable to them now, exhausted and softened by Lily, no more sharp, dangerous edges they might cut themselves on. A woman without children is a judgment against a mother, and now I am not quite either of those, but still—I am acceptable. I feel as unlike myself as I ever have. I wonder if Paul misses me or he even sees that I have gone.

One evening, about a week after Randall's church burns down, Paul and I are finishing dinner out on the patio in the backyard, Lily reclining in her portable chair, when we hear a knocking. Paul cocks his head to one side.

"Should I see who it is?" I ask, already scooting my chair back from the table. "Or do you want to?"

"Hello?" a voice calls. "Paul?"

Paul frowns at me, shrugs. "We're in the back," he calls,

cupping a hand around his mouth. "Come on through." To me, in a low voice, he says, "I think it's Tyler. He was coming by to pick something up."

Out of sight, the gate latch lifts with a little screech, and Paul turns awkwardly in his chair to see who's coming. But he stands when he sees who it is.

"Hey, there," says Randall. He has his hands up, palms open and facing us, like he's showing us he comes in peace. I wonder if he thinks we're crazy. I would. He looks at our plates on the table, then at Lily. "I could come back later if that would be better."

Paul stares at Randall with a statue-like blankness as he registers the sight of the man, a near stranger in his backyard—but the moment is brief, and he puts his hand out for Randall to shake. I stand without meeting the pastor's eye, and I stack the dinner plates and silverware but leave our glasses on the table.

"You can leave Lily out here," Paul says, smiling at her. "She's happy."

"How are you?" Randall asks. It is only when I get to the door that I realize he was speaking to me.

I glance at Paul, who nods. "Fine," I say. "Thank you." But by then, Randall has already shifted his attention back to Paul, and I go inside, precariously cradling the plates as I open the back door.

I put the dishes in the sink, which overlooks the side yard, but I can't see the men. As far as I know, Paul and Randall have never had a conversation, just the two of them. I return to the back door, and even before I crack it open an inch—just enough so I can see them—I can hear their voices. No one sounds angry, though I know Paul wouldn't sound it, even if he was; he isn't like Lou, who is always minutes away from red-faced frustration, or Kyle, who loves to jab and poke at people's tender spots, everything jolly and hilarious until suddenly it isn't. But nor is he like Papa Jake, honey sweet and insincere. Paul genuinely listens, and weighs his words before he speaks.

Paul's back is to me, but I can tell that his arms are crossed over his chest. At one point, he swats a mosquito at the back of his head, then scratches. Randall, too, waves a hand in front of his face. It hasn't rained since the day Julie left; I don't know how we have so many mosquitoes when there is no wet place for them to lay their eggs.

I hear Randall saying something about insurance, the church fire.

Paul shakes his head. "I don't know what to tell you, man," he says. "These old buildings have bad wiring. My brother is an electrician, and he used to tell me that all the time. He used to check our wiring every six months." Paul is an only child; hearing him lie so deftly stuns me for a moment, but Randall, oblivious, nods.

"Of course," Randall says. "You're right, but everything was up to code. We'd just had a guy out to fix this blinking light in the sanctuary, and he did a whole walkthrough."

"Maybe your guy didn't check things as well as you thought," said Paul. "I really hate to be rude, Randall, but I just don't understand what this is about. What do you want us to do?" What Paul doesn't say, but I hear: What do you want from *me*?

Randall looks toward the door, and for a second, I worry he'll tell Paul the back door is cracked, the air-conditioning escaping—no man will tolerate that, the money dissolving into space—but he only looks at our buzzing light fixture, the light reflected in the lenses of his glasses like fiery little planets, and doesn't see me. He runs a hand through his hair. I wonder if he has ever been married. I wonder, so briefly it doesn't count, what he looks like naked. He is more slight than Paul, his body narrow like a paintbrush. "I know most of y'all don't have bad intentions," he says. "Sometimes people do things they shouldn't do, without the blessing of the boss, so to speak. I know that from personal experience. But look—the insurance company thinks we burned our own church down."

"Well," says Paul evenly, "maybe some of your people did that without your blessing. So to speak."

"Paul," says Randall, and suddenly he really is my old science tutor at the gym, with that note of frustration and exhaustion in his voice, and Paul must hear it too because he stands up straighter, like he's been caught sleeping in class. "Please. I came to you because—well, I don't know you well, or at all, really. I don't know any of you well, not even Jake, but I've watched y'all plenty. You seem like a good guy. You're thoughtful, and I know you've got Jake's ear."

I want to see Paul's face, to see if he is at all moved by Randall's appeal. Both men are silent. "I don't know who's responsible for the fire, Randall," Paul finally says. "Truly. I'm sorry. I'm not as important here as you might think. I don't know much about what goes on." Another lie.

"Just think about it," urges Randall. "Will you? We need the insurance money to fix the damage. We can come up with some story that works for all of us—the guys who started the fire did it accidentally, we don't want to press charges, just want the insurance money—and we can all put it behind us."

Paul shifts his weight to one foot, uses the other to scratch his calf. Another mosquito. "If anything changes, Randall, we'll let you know," he says, sticking out his hand.

Randall looks at Paul's hand for a moment, then extends his own. "I appreciate it, brother," he says, and looks toward the back door. This time he sees me, and gives a slight nod. I curl my fingers around the door, then release. A little wave. "Tell your wife good night for me, and my apologies for interrupting your dinner."

"Will do," says Paul, clapping his hand on Randall's shoulder and steering him toward the gate. I stand up and hurry to the sink, where I start to wash our plates. I'm about to dry them when Paul comes in through the back door, somehow both cradling Lily and holding our two water glasses.

"Well, that was weird," he says, coming up behind me and putting the glasses in the sink. He takes Lily into the living room, and I hear the whir of her swing and a chime as a tinkly little song begins playing.

"What did he want?" I hand Paul a clean plate as he comes back into the kitchen, and he puts it back in the cabinet. Then he turns to face me again, his hair messy from the humidity of the nighttime air.

"He wanted us to take the blame for the fire," he says. "Obviously we won't."

"Obviously," I say. I open the silverware drawer and

place the two forks and two knives inside, and they wink brightly at me in their holders. "So what are you going to do?"

"Nothing," says Paul. "Tell Papa, I guess, that Randall is snooping around."

"Good idea." I wash the glasses, dry them, hand them to Paul. He puts one away and refills the other from the water pitcher we keep in the refrigerator. "I wonder how he knew where we lived."

"I thought about that," Paul says. "It's a little alarming. I'll mention that to Papa too." He pauses. "You don't think he was trying to get to Lily, do you? I didn't think of that until just now."

"Paul," I say. "Randall seems nice. Harmless."

He takes a drink and places the glass on the counter beside him, swallows, and points to me. "That's exactly what he wants you to think. I'm going to take a shower. It's so humid out there."

"Sounds good," I say.

"By the way," he says as he turns to leave the kitchen, smiling, "you left the door open a crack when you went inside. We don't want the AC getting out and the mosquitoes getting in."

I go into the living room and watch Lily in her swing. I think of the things I could be doing while she's happily occupied, but it feels like there are at once too many options and too few, and before I can decide, she starts to cry. I feel my shoulders slump. Wash a dish. Put it away. Feed the baby. Feed her again. All the endless things. I get her out of the swing and go once again into the kitchen.

Nineteen

I had a teacher in high school who used to say, "Here comes trouble," every time I entered his classroom. Embarrassed, I would tug down my shirt so the sliver of skin at my midriff shrunk to nothing. In the tanning beds, we put little stickers by our hipbones, letting the silhouette bake into our skin—a flower, a butterfly, a heart—and we let our shirts rise, our jeans lower, but this wasn't for him, this tiny secret of pale skin. I was suddenly uncomfortable thinking of its presence. All those years in the gym, training to have eyes on me, eyes that would scrutinize every movement, looking for flaws and missteps, and it was this—a high school hallway, a teacher, a pale heart on my hip—that made me uncomfortable. I was never clever enough to say anything back to him the way some girls would have, and so instead I would smile and sit down, say nothing. The year after I graduated, he got in trouble himself for fucking a student.

"He probably wanted to fuck *you*," Tess said when I told her the story. "That was the trouble he was hoping for."

"Probably," I said, laughing. But I worried he knew

something I didn't. Maybe he felt it in the air. Some coming trouble, amorphous and hazy but definitely there, a trembling under his feet, a change in the wind. Later I could tell too when trouble was coming. It was a feeling that started in my skin, that lightness, a promise that things would come apart, like stitches in thin fabric ripped apart.

A few days after our visit from Randall, I see Franklin Aaron in the grocery store, in the baking aisle. I rode my bike there, took the long way, the hilly road, and I sped down the declines and up the inclines, pumping until my muscles ached pleasurably. I didn't really need to go to the store, but Paul has taken Lily of the Valley over to visit Rob, and I want to feel myself somewhere else, have the eyes of someone else on me. Someone who isn't a baby. I can hand the cashier money, can let my fingers touch theirs. At the end of every day with Lily, I feel simultaneously desirous of and revolted by the idea of another hand on my body. Here, though, is Franklin Aaron crouching down, a red basket in his hands, at his knees, as he studies a row of peanut butter jars. "Hi," I hear myself saying—or not myself as I am now, but the self I used to have, like an old friend I thought had gone away, and I am both terrified of and thrilled by her return. I want to ask her how long she will stay.

Franklin Aaron looks up, craning his neck to glance behind him, in case I'm addressing someone else, and then turns back to me in surprise. I smile. "Rosemary," he says politely. "Hi. How are you feeling?"

This response was more than I expected—I assumed he would frown and ignore me, slide his cell phone out of his pocket and text Paul about my misbehavior as soon as I walked past. If I thought I would be in trouble, thought

I would get caught, why did I do it? Because I am a stupid girl, because I haven't changed at all. I am who I once was. Do you know what that means? a voice inside me asks. You're still here. You are who you once were. "I feel okay," I say. "Tired."

He raises his eyebrows. "Good tired?" he asks. "Did it work? The prayers?"

"No. I just haven't been sleeping well," I say. "Lily of the Valley seems to be very hungry at night." I laugh a little.

"Of course," he says, clapping a hand to his face. "I don't know how I forgot y'all have Lily now. No wonder you're tired."

It's true that Lily has splintered my sleeping, but also true that when I do sleep, I have bad dreams. Last night I dreamed that I went into Julie's house, but this time Lily was strapped down by lines of teeth encircling her ankles and wrists. When Julie came in, she opened her mouth to yell at me, and I saw that her mouth was yawning and black and missing its teeth.

"How are you feeling?" I ask Franklin.

"Me?" he asks. He stands up, a jar of peanut butter in his big hand. Now he towers over me, and it delights me to look up at him, the kind of joy that comes with seeing something so much bigger than yourself, a mountain, the ocean.

"Your lungs?" I say, raising my eyebrows. I feel my hand go instinctively to my chest—showing my lungs—and his eyes follow my hand there, for only a second before he looks at the row of baking supplies on the shelf beside him. A heat begins to prickle beneath my skin.

"Oh," he says. "Yeah. I'm fine. Much better."

"Praise God," I say. He looks down at me again, then past me.

"Paul here?" he asks.

"Oh, no," I say. "Just me."

He smiles. "Just you, huh," he says. "Hey, look—have you ever had this kind of peanut butter? I usually get Jif, but all they have is this."

"Let me see," I say, taking a step toward him, feeling a bright pleasure wink inside me.

He faces the label toward me but doesn't hand over the jar, so I come closer to examine it.

"Well?" he says. "What's your professional opinion?"

"Oh," I say, glancing up at him again. "I've never claimed to be a professional. But in my humble layman's opinion, all peanut butter is good peanut butter." He laughs, and I feel the way I did when I climbed into Tyler's truck on the side of the road, when I walked up the creaking stairs in that frat house, when I shook the hand of the strange man on the beach in Mexico.

"Hi!" someone behind me chirps, and I turn to see Amanda coming down the aisle, Abigail and Troy in lock-step behind her. "Rosie, we'll give you a ride home," she says. "Matthew drove us. He's waiting in the car." She does not acknowledge Franklin until he greets her, and then she responds with a chaste nod. Franklin holds a hand out to Troy, and the two shake, Franklin's hand covering the boy's so completely I think of an animal devouring a smaller one. "Y'all have a good afternoon," Franklin says. We all thank him. Troy watches him until he turns out of the aisle, and then he grabs a package of chocolate chips and puts them in his mother's basket. She takes them out and puts them back on the shelf. "No," she says.

"Thanks," I say to Amanda as we head toward the checkout.

"You're welcome," she says, putting her things on the conveyor belt. "Be careful," she says without looking at me.

"I don't know what you're talking about," I say, but I look down because my cheeks are hot. I pull Abigail's braid, and she grins at me. She's lost a tooth.

"Okay," Amanda says. Now she pulls Abigail's braid too and winks at her son. "All right, everyone," she says. "Let's load up."

In the parking lot, we all wave at Franklin Aaron, who smiles at us, tight-lipped, no teeth, and holds up a hand.

"He's tall," Troy says.

"Very," says Amanda. "Do you think he could be a giant?"

"Rosemary, do you think that he's a giant?" Abigail asks.

"Probably," I say.

"Giants are bad," Abigail says. "Like Goliath."

"Giants are trouble waiting to happen," Amanda says, looking at me, holding the car door open so I can climb in past the children's car seats.

Trouble, I think. Here it comes.

I AM NOT the only one sleeping poorly; Paul is unsettled too, waking me up every night with half words I cannot understand, though somehow he never hears Lily of the Valley when she cries. In the morning, he's tired, and though he doesn't always remember his dreams, he knows that the voice of God, the messages of the angels, came to him in the night. He's been on edge lately; we all have. We came out of the chapel one night to find that Papa Jake's tires had been slashed, the rubber split open like a mortal wound. They have an arsenal of weapons, he announced. Guns, knives. But only we have God. But it is hard not to worry what will be next.

I'm listening more carefully, Paul says. Every night, I'm listening and watching for the visions God sends me.

What are you dreaming about? he asks me. Julie again?

I hesitate because I do dream of Julie, yes. And Lily of the Valley, but not only them. Sometimes I dream of a dusty village in Central America, a boy tied to a fence. Sometimes it is Lily of the Valley tied to the fence, and there is blood in the dirt, but I don't know whose blood it is. Randall coming into our backyard, then into our house. We only see him in the shadows, in the corners, holding his hands up, asking me, *What are the parts of the cell? Can you tell me what an enzyme does? Did your husband start the fire?* I tell him no, no, no.

Lily and her mother's teeth biting down on her flesh.

Something sneaking in through the gaps of our circle enveloping the Friedrichs' yard. We hear it before it comes, like a train whistle, and the ground shakes. We aren't ready, Amanda says to me, her hand in mine. We aren't ready. Where are my children? she asks. But all the children are gone. I can't see them either.

I am letting Franklin Aaron cover my body with his, we are in an unfamiliar bed, but then he begins to cough and cough, shuddering and then choking as something lodges in his throat.

I am on the beam, dismounting, counting on only a second in space before I hit the mat, but instead I don't come down, and I am stuck there, spiraling in the air. Everyone claps for me. Don't cry, my mother says from a chair in the gym. Don't cry until you're alone.

I dream, of course, that I am disappearing. Ever since Julie left, I've felt desperate to remind myself of the world around me, the hardness of it, its sharp corners, cold air. It's making me reckless. What if Amanda hadn't interrupted my conversation with Franklin Aaron?

Do you ever dream I'm not here? I've asked Paul before. But the answer is always no. You're everywhere, he says.

Yes, I finally say to Paul. Julie again. Julie every night.

She's fine, he tells me. Listen to what God said last night. Listen to the picture He created in my head. Look at the gift He gave me.

But then what he tells me are frightening things, not gifts at all. And I'm in every dream, even if I'm not. You couldn't recognize yourself? Paul asks. You were the rope. The basket of fruit, and the flies around it, you're both. In the desert, when I'm dying of thirst, you're the sand in the cactus that spills out when I cut it open.

You're scaring me, I tell him.

No, he tells me again, desperate for me to understand these images the way he does. These are God's promises. Don't you see it?

He keeps going. The fire again in the chapel, me begging him to leave me behind and let the flames eat me up.

Me pregnant and dressed in white and covered in feathers. An angel, he says. Beauty. A treasure chest that rattles and shakes like something is trapped inside. You have the key, Paul tells me. You are powerful! You can let it out. Let what out, I ask. But he doesn't know. A deer in quiet woods, a frozen lake where you can see the fish swimming beneath the glaze of ice, a giant clutching me in his fist, carrying me away. But you're smiling. You're happy, he says. I don't know where you're going, but you're happy.

That's all I want, Paul says. I dream about it every night. For you to be happy with me, with God.

I am, I tell him.

That makes me feel better, he says, but at night, he still thrashes in his sleep, and I let him grab me, put his hands in my hair. I feel scared to sleep in my house, worried that something is in it, visiting Paul and me, tormenting us as we sleep, but eventually all is dark, and then all is light again, and still he is touching me when I wake, fingers tangled in my hair.

Twenty

One morning a few days later, as I'm about to take Lily for a walk, Paul tells me I need to help Sandy at the diner; the girl who was going to woke up sick. "They even said they'll make you your very own name tag," he says, grinning. "Enticing?"

"An offer I can't refuse," I say. "But what about Lily?" I feel the lure of the stroller sitting in the dark of the garage, the hour of freedom it allows me.

"Rob wants to see her again," Paul says. "He's going to introduce her to Jennifer." Rob has proposed to Jennifer Bell, and they're planning to marry soon, though Amanda says Jennifer would prefer a fall wedding, when the weather is cooler. When I heard the news of their engagement, I ached for Julie. Julie, who knew all along.

"I was just going to stroll her," I say. "Can you wait for a little bit? I'd hate for her to get off her routine."

"You know what, I'll stroll her over to Rob's," Paul says, walking over and taking her from my arms. "You can bike to the diner."

The restaurant doesn't have a name. We only call it the

diner, though it looks like it used to be a Waffle House. The outside is yellow and tan brick, with tall, smudgy windows overlooking the parking lot, and inside there are smooth-backed booths, the kind without any upholstery or cushion, and freestanding tables, and the floor is a terracotta orange. It's the kind of place that looks like everything will feel sticky from years of customers dripping syrup as they eat pancakes, but whenever I've been in here, I've been surprised by its cleanliness; appearances are very important to Papa Jake.

At the diner, Sandy hands me a brown apron and, as promised, a name tag whose individual letters spell out ROSMARY. "You forgot a letter," I say.

"No one likes a know-it-all," she says. Sandy is built a little like the beach houses we used to see in Galveston: top heavy, supported by long, skinny stilts. Her roots have been showing the same amount since the day she arrived in Dawes over a year ago. Whenever I see her, I wonder how that's possible, if her hair could actually just grow like that. She hands me a notepad and pencil with no eraser. "Take the orders," she says. "And clean the tables."

I wait on Brother Lou, who orders oatmeal and cleans his glasses on the hem of his shirt, hands and body rigid like his joints don't work. He's joined by Tyler, who let those poor cows out. Tyler is engaged to be married now too, to Erin, Ruth's former best friend. "Nothing for me," he says when he arrives. When I look at him, all I see is an image of him with a can of gasoline, standing in a darkened sanctuary and laughing.

I wait on a group of three old men in button-down shirts and Wranglers; they're locals, and don't look at me when I hand them their food, but they do say thank you into the plates I give them. "Have a great day," I say because it's polite and also because Sandy told me not to say anything beyond information about the menu and the bill, and I like the idea of annoying her. I've already decided that if Randall comes in, I will make polite small talk; I will answer the questions he asks.

After a while, I wait on no one. I sit at a booth in the front of the restaurant and look out the window. When Sandy comes by, she tells me I will need to refill the ketchup bottles before the lunch rush. "Remember," she says. "Everything you do has the potential to bring glory or shame to the name of the Lord." Sandy is from another sad nothing town a few exits down the freeway. She has no husband, no children that we know of; like the rest of us, she gave everything to Papa Jake when she joined. Unlike the rest of us, who were from well-off families, who were well-off ourselves, many who knew Caroline and Jake from their college days, everything she had wasn't much. When she speaks to me, she says don't shame the Lord, take the orders, bus the tables, but what she means is *you are not above me. You are not above this.*

The bell at the front door dings. Two men and a woman walk in, and I stand up. The older man has the buttoned-up, rigid look of my own father, whose voice I hear suddenly in my head. *Look sharp, Rosie.* "Anywhere?" this man asks.

I nod. "I'll grab some menus and be right there."

They sit at a table in the corner, a booth and two chairs, the woman—a mother—slides into the booth, leaving her husband and son to sit by each other in the chairs. She is about my mother's age, and she even resembles her a little. They are the same kind of woman. Their hair is an ashy sort of blond, the color of weak sunlight, though my mother's hair may now be grayer. I have no idea. Lately I've been thinking of her. For a long while, I did not, I pushed her down the stairs of my brain into the darkness of the basement, and I closed the door. If she has pounded or screamed, I have not heard her. Have I been cruel? Maybe it's because of my time with Lily of the Valley, the days I spent with Julie. What is Julie now that she is gone? What is my mother now that I have gone? A mother still or something else? What am I as I care for this baby who isn't mine but who calms when I hold her, stills when I sing to her, who without me would not be cleaned, would not be fed, would not have any kind of mother at all?

"Breakfast is being served for a few more minutes if you'd like that," I tell them, handing the menus out one by one.

"Coffee," the father says. They all nod. The son looks at me and stares. He has curly dark hair. His wedding ring finger is naked, but on his right hand he wears a college ring, gold and chunky.

"Hey," he says. "Do I know you?"

"No," I say.

"Did I know you?" he asks.

"I don't think so," I say, but my brain is scanning all my memories, and he's in every one I find—at the summer camp where I volunteered after my freshman year, in my college psych class in the freezing science building, at the dingy bar we went to on Thursday nights. Boys, men, all the ones I've ever seen and been with and known. He is any one of them. I don't want to look at him closely in case he is someone more. This is when I cannot be trusted.

"Colin Bell," he says. "Did you go to UT? I know I know you."

"Colin," his father says, opening a menu. "Let her go, please."

Now I look at the father, and I recognize him, his voice frantic in the chapel, face red, looking for his daughter, Jennifer Bell. Now they are all here, a mother, a father, a brother. The daughter is here too, of course, but she is unreachable. She is in love or something like it.

"I didn't go to UT," I say.

"But did you visit?" he asks. "Everyone visited Austin, right? I'm sorry, this is going to drive me crazy."

"I'll be back with the coffees," I say.

"We need you to help us," the father says when I come back. Colin Bell is looking at his phone, eyebrows knit together like he is trying to concentrate, but I'm sure he's just scrolling, idly, compulsively.

"I can take your order," I say. I pull out the little notepad, the pencil without an eraser, the green metal circling the top like a sharp crown.

"Our daughter is here," the mother says. "She's getting married."

These desperate people. I want them to go. "Look," Colin says, pressing the screen and scrolling. He holds it out. A picture of Jennifer Bell in an Instagram post. She is in a long dress, standing in a field of bluebonnets, and her hair ripples down her back. She is laughing, and Rob Friedrich's arms are around her. A tiny diamond winks on her left-hand ring finger. The light around them is gold.

"Is this hers?" I ask, and I mean her account, because how did she do it, and Colin says yes, but he must have misunderstood me because I look, and it isn't her name there, but Rob's. The picture was posted yesterday. They must have seen it, somehow, and come straight here.

No one from the church is in, this in-between time that isn't quite lunch yet; only the three men from the town remain, though I cleared their plates an hour ago. I want so badly to hold the phone and scroll through all the pictures, to call my mom, the only other person whose number I have memorized. "Can I see it for a second?" I put my hand out, and Colin gives me the phone, still warm. I look through the pictures Rob has posted. There are none of Julie, none of Lily of the Valley. Only pretty Jennifer, a sunset over a field, Rob grinning with his arm around Papa Jake's shoulder. In one, they are in the backyard of the Friedrich house; there are children running behind them, and the yard is green and wet, stripes of mud at their feet. There are no women because we are lined up in the front, waiting to go inside to see the new mother and her baby. The caption says, "Papa Jake, the man, the myth, the legend."

"Thank you," I say. "But I don't know that I can help you."

"Is there anyone who can?" the mother asks.

"Not here," I say.

"I'm not even sure what we're asking," the father says. "Maybe if you could—" The bell above the front door dings again, and I excuse myself and step around the corner.

It's Paul, with Papa Jake and Richard Moore, the husband of Molly. Paul glides over to me and gently kisses my cheek. "Look at you," he says. "Before you ask, Lily is with Rob; I'm going to get her after lunch. I just couldn't resist

seeing you in your apron." He grins. "Brown is a very flat-
tering color on you," he says.

I elbow him good-naturedly, and he laughs. The men
laugh too.

"Well, it's good to see y'all," I say to Paul and the air
around the other men. "I wonder how Molly is feeling today."

"A little better," Richard says, stepping forward. "Slightly
more energy today. I'll tell her you were asking after her."

"Caroline is well too, Rosemary. Thanks for asking,"
Papa Jake says, grinning. I look at him, his white teeth. We
all have nice teeth here. "I'm just teasing," he says. This is
the closest I've been to him since Paul told me that Papa
would make me leave. But there is something about him
that still seems far away and untouchable, the way an actor
appears on a TV screen: he's there with you in your living
room, but it's only a flat, unreal version of him, a thinly
drawn character appearing to you in pixels of light. I look at
Papa Jake and try to see the tan boy in the fraternity T-shirt,
sweating in the dirt in Nicaragua, but I can't. Perhaps he left
that boy tied to the fence in the village too.

"Praise God for her health," I say. "Sit anywhere you
like."

"Thank you, Rosie," Paul says, touching my waist, and
the men glide past me and sit at a table in the middle of the
restaurant. As they do, I see Papa Jake see the Bell family.
He's been listening to something Richard Moore is saying,
and he laughs at the right time and nods at the right time,
but he is watching Jennifer's family. The three men from
the town scoot out from the table, and the sound makes

Papa Jake look toward them. He nods at the men as they stand.

"Rosemary," Papa Jake says when I bring over the menus, "do you know who those people are in the corner?"

"No," I say. "I didn't ask. But one of them is wearing a UT class ring, so maybe they're just passing through on their way to Austin."

"Maybe," Papa Jake says.

"Could be people looking for healing, Papa," Paul says. "Maybe they got the wrong date and meant to come on a healing day."

"I know one way to stop the speculating," Papa Jake says. He scoots his chair back a little, his hands on the table, full of energy. He stops and looks up at me. "Turkey club," he says. "And a side salad." Then he rises from his seat and heads over to the Bells.

In front of their table, he sticks a hand out to the father, to the mother, to the son. I take Paul's and Richard's orders and tell them I'll be right back, and Paul touches the hem of my apron, but when I glance down at him, he isn't looking at me at all.

I drop the ticket off in the kitchen, where Sandy is taking inventory. "Papa Jake's here," I tell her, and she perks up.

"I'll take care of his table," she says.

I go to the bathroom and look in the mirror. Tonight I will trim my hair around the ears where it has gotten a little shaggy. Maybe I can ask Paul to trim it in the back. He'll want to know why, and I will say I want to look lovely for him, and don't I?

When I step out of the bathroom into the dark hallway,

Colin Bell is there. He doesn't say anything. "Do you need your check?" I ask.

"I really don't want to be a creep," he says, holding his hands up to show his innocence. "But you look so familiar."

"You've said that," I say, and I know it's rude, but it feels thrilling to speak to a man this way, to be dismissive; I feel strong. From where I stand, I can see that Papa Jake has rejoined Paul and Richard at the table, where Sandy is now setting down glasses of water for them. I step back so they are out of sight.

"Do you know Jennifer?" he asks.

"Not really," I say. I see him looking at my hair. "What?" I ask. I try not to touch the hair curling around my ears, at my forehead, but my fingers want to float up, high and away.

"Did you used to have long hair?"

"Yes," I say. "I need to go take care of the other tables." But I don't go. Instead, I move closer to him, into the shadow of the hallway. The light overhead is burned out, which is good because I want to be hidden, even from myself.

"What's your name?" he asks. "Oh, never mind. I see it." He looks up from my name tag to my face. "Rosmary?" He says it like *Rosalyn*.

"They forgot the *E*," I say.

"Rosemary," he says. "Like the herb."

"Exactly like the herb."

He smiles. "Did we go to camp together? Did you date my friend? Did I date you?" he asks. He laughs, and I do too, but then I think oh no, oh yes. The boy with the Texas flag over his bed, my head and body light with cheap alcohol. That boy too was someone I have met a thousand times since then. This could be him, or it might as well be. If it is, then this doesn't count, this conversation. It's happened before.

"Whatever it was," I say, "it was in a past life."

"I'm going to figure it out," he says, pointing at me and squinting his eyes. "Then I'm going to come back and tell you."

"You're staying in town?" I ask.

He nods. "My parents want Jenn to come home," he says. "We won't leave until she does."

"Good luck," I say.

"I'll see you around," he says. "In this life or another one." He grins. His teeth are white and pretty, like Papa Jake's, like Paul's, like mine. I want to stick my finger in his mouth, see if he bites it.

"This is the only life I've got right now," I say, "so if you want to see me, it will have to be here."

"Deal," he says and sticks out his hand.

I put my hand out too, but I wait for him to grab mine. He does not shake it, only holds it gently, and I can feel each of his fingers, and when I do, I feel mine too. Now he squeezes, light pressure, and then I am squeezing back. Here I am, in a body, and it is mine.

"Goodbye," I say, and step back out into the yellow light of the diner, where everything feels too bright and hard: the orange tile floor, the tables and chairs, the windows and the landscape they frame, the hot, sharp summer. Colin Bell has green eyes.

I check on Paul's table. They are eating, passing the

ketchup bottle, stabbing wilted lettuce with a fork. "Did Sandy get everything y'all need?" I ask.

"You disappeared," Paul says.

"Light-headed," I tell him, touching my forehead. "The heat. I went into the bathroom and splashed water on my face."

"Poor girl," he says. "You're probably just tired." He looks at the other men. "Lily isn't what I'd call a champion sleeper." They all commiserate with sympathetic murmurs, and Paul reaches over and takes my hand, the same hand that Colin Bell held, and I almost jerk it away, but I make myself leave it. Now Paul is the last man to have touched me.

Papa Jake is watching me. It feels as if he is touching me as well, or seeing something the rest of us cannot.

"Anything else?" I ask the men.

"Nothing for me," says Paul.

"I'm good," says Richard.

"Thank you, Rosemary," says Papa Jake.

The bell over the door dings again, and we all look up. The Bell family is gone.

THAT NIGHT, PAUL asks me if I knew the family in the diner. "Not at all," I say.

"They're the family of Jennifer Bell," Paul says. "They came right out and told Papa they aren't leaving without her." He shakes his head. "Why would they come after her? She left them behind. Why can't they understand that?"

"They love her," I say.

"What's out there," Paul says, "what they have to give her, none of that is real love. If they loved her, they'd let her be saved. That's what a real mother would do."

"My mother hasn't come after me," I say. "Neither has yours."

"They love us enough to let us live our own lives," Paul says. "And to let us do what we know is right." I think of how his parents could barely be bothered to tend to him when he lived in the same house, how strange it would be if suddenly they felt motivated to track him down here. But my parents did love me—I suddenly think of my mom doing my hair before a meet, before I could do it myself. All the products she used, the sprays, the gels. Sometimes she would create an intricate braid winding like a labyrinth, the bun at the crown of my head always tight and shining. My mother wasn't always a gentle person, but her hands were. She would comb her fingers through my hair, down to the tips, loosening tangles and snares I never even knew I had.

"What if it means they don't love us enough?" I ask.

Paul looks at me, his eyes as serious and dark as a soldier's boot. He has a scar on his cheek where the family dog bit him when he was two, though you can only see it when he shaves. "If you were on a ship," he says, "the *Titanic*, for example, and it was sinking, and there weren't enough lifeboats, your mother would tell you to get on one. She thinks there's a chance the ship might not sink, they might get rescued before the whole thing goes under, but is she willing to risk your life?" He shakes his head. "Of course not. She'd let you go."

"I guess she has," I say. I feel like I'm about to cry, and I look down at Lily of the Valley, having a bottle in my arms, so Paul won't see if I do.

"We were chosen by God to be here," he says. "What

else can our parents do but let us go? They know we're the lucky ones."

IN BED, I lie awake and think of Jennifer Bell's mother, and then I think of my own. She told me once that when I was very little, I couldn't differentiate between her body and my own. I touched her the way I touched my own body— unthinking, mindlessly. "It made sense," my mother told me. "You came out of my body, and honestly, I don't know if it's healthy, but I always thought of your body as an extension of my own." An arm, a leg, a hand, a daughter.

As I grew up, the space between us grew. I went to school, I went to swim class, jumping in the water alone, my mother behind a wall of glass in a row of other mothers. This separation unnerved me. I understood she was her own person and I was mine, but I also understood the world better with her nearby. Without her, I craved the sensation of contact, the feeling of brushing up against something great and unyielding to tell me oh yes, here you are. Without that, my body didn't cooperate. It told me it didn't belong, and I panicked at the looseness of my skin and bones, their untrustworthiness. I learned to test them.

At school, I climbed to the top of the jungle gym, higher than anyone else, and stood there wobbling until I jumped down, over and over until I got a note sent home saying someday I would break my neck, and could my mother please tell me to stop. In swim class, I made myself sink to the bottom by telling myself I was made of stone, and I stayed down there until my head swam too and my vision freckled, and a teacher lifted me up under the arms, and together we broke through the surface, gasping.

"You want to be a daredevil?" my mom asked. "Go for it. But you're going to learn how to fall without killing yourself." When I turned five, she signed me up for gymnastics.

"Let's see what you can do," the coach said at my evaluation. He told me to spread my legs, like open scissors before you cut, before you bring the blades together. Then he pushed me down until my legs were nearly flat against the floor. "Can you go down further?" he asked. I shook my head. "You can," he said, and he manipulated my legs, his hands cold, until they were just the way he wanted them. "Told you," he said, grinning. Next, he bent me over backward, the way I didn't think my body could bend, my back compressing, my stomach stretching, a perfect arc. "Reach for the floor with your hands," he said. "Reach until you find a place to land."

He took me over to the bars and told me to jump up, but to keep my elbows bent and my chin above the bar. In a swift, smooth motion, he pushed up my legs so I was upside down and spun me around on the bar until the world was right side up again. "Now do it forward," he said. "Lean forward like you're going to roll over the bar." I rolled, expecting to feel the hand that had been on my back in every other task he had me do, but it was only me, no one else, and I let go. I tumbled to the floor. I looked up at the coach. "That's fine," he said. "Get up. Do it again." Get up, get up—he would say it again and again until we finally learned to say it to ourselves.

"She's strong," the coach told my mom. "And she doesn't care about falling."

"No," said my mother. "She wants to fall."

"We'll whip her into shape," the coach said, winking at me. "We'll turn the falling into flying." I was so little, and now I think I've made this up, the way I remember that wooden frat house in Austin swaying in the night breeze, a detail, an emotion that wasn't there, but I knew even then that I needed something extreme to be satisfied—the flying, the falling, the world in a blur. For years after that day, I tested my body and learned what it could do. I felt the adrenaline of mastering a new skill, but also the head rush of failure, the bruises, the hot tears, sore muscles, the blooms of blood springing up from chapped palms. These things, too, I loved. I went home and showed my parents after every practice, proudly revealed each mark on my skin, every tight muscle.

"Battle wounds," my father said approvingly. He loved it, how strong I was, how tough, but I can't remember him ever tending to those wounds. My mother, though, held my hands and looked at the rips there clinically, regarding them as she did any injury on her own body: practically, gently if not with great tenderness. She neither praised me for my bravery nor begged me to quit, never asked me to find a sport that would be kinder to my body.

She told me that sometimes at night she would dream that she was performing too, going through my routines, particularly when there was a skill I was struggling with, her subconscious forgetting that there was a difference between us, between her body and mine. The truth is, of course, our bodies were never the same, but hours and hours of training separated my body from my mother's even more. Mine hardened, hers softened, and I started to feel embarrassed that there was ever a time when I felt so connected to the actual physical person of her, not just the idea of her, my mother, the person whose job it was to care for me. But now I find myself longing for that, for her, and I wonder if there is a part of her even now, even though we are separated by so, so much, that still regards me as an extension of her own self. A broken arm, a sore leg, a calloused, bleeding hand, a daughter, gone away.

Twenty-One

It is the middle of the night, and Lily is awake. I know before she cries, my body anticipating it, and my eyes are already open when she makes a sound. We have been together, Lily and I, for two weeks now. Paul, as always, is asleep.

I lift Lily out of her bassinet and creep out of the bedroom and into the living room, where I place her in the swing and turn the mobile on to distract her while I make her a bottle. When I turn on the kitchen light, brightness floods the room; the kitchen is an ocean of light, and I am the island in it. I'm readying her bottle when I see Paul's phone, charging in the outlet by the toaster, instead of on his nightstand in the bedroom.

I want it. I want to scroll through his photos, his text messages, shop online. I have a sudden memory from just before we moved here, and Bree was texting me over and over, confused and mad and hurt. Before I could respond to one message, she would send another, an avalanche of sadness and anger rushing toward me. "Look at this," I said to Paul, angling the phone toward him.

"Just give it to me," Paul said as I watched the green bubbles pop up, one after the other. "You don't need it anymore, and in a few days, no one will be able to reach us at all."

I thought about putting the phone in his open palm and being done with it. We were saying goodbye to my sister anyway. We were leaving everyone. But I wasn't ready. "I'm just going to keep it until we have to go," I said. "I'll turn it off now." That night, after he was asleep, I turned it back on as I lay in bed, and shielding the bright screen with my hand, I read the messages once and then again. Finally, I sent her a message that said I would find a way to tell her when we got to where we were going. I said someone would let me use their computer, I was sure, just to let her know I was okay, happy, that things were better with Paul.

I press the button of Paul's phone, and it lights up. He doesn't have a passcode, and this makes me smile; he trusts I won't break this one rule, at least. But here I am. I look at the screen, everything calling to me. Green box, white phone. Green box, white speech bubble. Blue box, white envelope. Gray box, black camera. I open the photos. Lily's bottle beeps, so I take it and the phone into the dark living room, and we sit on the couch together. It's tricky to hold the phone, the bottle, and the baby, but I manage a tenuous grip on all three.

Paul has only a few pictures saved: a wobbly-kneed baby horse born in Dawes the day we arrived, the chapel with a hot blue sky behind it, our house, a picture of me in our front yard that first spring when the azaleas were blooming. I can remember when he took it. I was wearing a white dress, and Paul said, "You look so pretty in front of the flowers. Stay there." He held up the phone, and I smiled, a reflex: this is what you do when you see a camera. I swipe, and I disappear, replaced by myself again, this time with Paul, and we are young. Newlyweds, when we lived in the house with the big tree in the front yard, just a few streets over from the bayou. It was snowing at the time he took the picture, barely, and the whole city went collectively insane over it, all of us outside in jeans and sweaters watching the flakes fall before they hit the ground and were gone for good. "It's a Christmas miracle!" I remember saying, and Paul laughed. Christmas had passed a few days ago, was over. "Just a miracle," he said. I close the photo album and go back to the home screen. Paul has deleted Facebook, but I feel a rush when I see the sunset-colored square of the Instagram app, the white outline of a camera inside it. I open it.

The feed consists of pictures belonging to men in our church. There must be rules around when to post, what to share, but no one's ever needed to tell me what they are. Paul's own profile has all the same pictures from his photo album, except the one of us in Houston. I'm about to search for Colin Bell when I'm suddenly distracted by something on the feed of photos shared by the accounts Paul follows: a picture of Caroline, posted by a user named sweet_caroline, standing in front of a cluster of azalea bushes, laughing into the camera, a hand pushing a lock of golden hair behind her ear. Caroline has her own account, one that Paul apparently follows. I think of the day I called her from Julie's house, how quickly she answered it, and I wonder if Caroline has her own cell phone. Caroline, breaking the rules. Caroline, above the rules.

Her photos are carefully curated, artful; she has a good eye. Even the grid made by her photos is pleasing, full of dusty pinks and mellow tans, the green of dark earth and spry leaves and bright plants, everything cohesive. They are mostly pictures of her and her children but especially the littlest one, a boy, and the oldest, Ruth, whose period Papa Jake announced during the service earlier this year. There are two middle children, but they aren't as beautiful as the girl, nor as sweet as the baby boy with his stout toddler legs, and are featured less. In one picture, Caroline is holding the baby, his belly looking soft as a puppy's, and biting his leg playfully, her white teeth barely on the flesh. She looks directly at the camera. He is laughing, eyes closed and head back. Underneath she has written, "I'll eat you up, I love you so." Caroline in a long pink dress on the wraparound porch, smiling without teeth, her daughter's head on her shoulder. Caroline in a field I think I recognize, backlit in the waning afternoon, holding the hands of her older children, who in turn are holding the hands of the younger ones. Caroline sweeping the wood floors, one of her boys with his own miniature broom sweeping beside her. Caroline's lovely children arranged in a patch of bluebonnets, all their clothes carefully coordinated. It is strange to think of Caroline, as powerful as a woman can be here, still taking pains to make her life look appealing to those in the outside world, those she has shunned. But if I had my own phone, if I could do what Caroline does, arranging the color scheme of her photos just so, filtering Dawes so that it looks idyllic, nostalgic for a simpler time, maybe I would too. I could justify to my family, my friends, everyone looking in that I had made a good choice, that I was living a special life that I, not them, was chosen for.

Caroline has a picture from inside the church too, in black and white, of all of us in our pews. I can tell it was taken on a healing day because we are sitting together, men and women together, in pairs. Papa Jake is onstage, hands up and head bowed, alone. Caroline must have been standing at the very back of the church, in the middle of the aisle. I look for myself, but I can't figure out which one of these women I am. It is only when I locate Paul, who is just a bit taller than most of the other men, that I find myself in the crowd.

I find the picture we posed for on the front porch of Papa Jake's Victorian home, all of us cascading down the steps and spilling into the yard. Instinctively, I look for myself again, and I'm alarmed when once again I seem to have disappeared. Where have I gone? I examine the picture more carefully, and there I am, with my hair pulled back in a tight ponytail. I remember worrying I would look bald, and I do. But my face is familiar to myself, and that comforts me.

You look familiar. Do I know you?

I put the empty bottle on the end table and hoist Lily onto my shoulder. As soon as she burps, I put her back in the swing—just for a minute, I tell myself. I have one more thing to look for. I find the search box in the app and type in *Colin Bell*. There are many results, but the first one is the right one, a tiny circle filled with a tiny picture of his head, dark hair longer and more unruly. I touch the circle, and I am taken away to a new page, the squares of his photos loading. The first one I see is of him and a golden retriever in a green park, both smiling, squinting in the sun. The most recent one is a picture of him with Jennifer. "Missing this one today," he wrote beneath it. The picture is a little overexposed so their skin is milk pale.

"Rosie?" Paul calls from the bedroom, and I jump. I close out Instagram and shove the phone in between two couch cushions. When I don't hear him coming down the hallway, I pick up Lily and the bottle and the phone and go into the kitchen, drop the bottle in the sink, and plug in the phone again. I carry her back into the bedroom, change her diaper and swaddle her in the dark, and place her in the bassinet. "Bad dream?" Paul whispers.

"Lily was hungry," I say.

"Wow," he says. "I didn't even hear her."

"Oh," I say, and for a minute, I want to throttle him, but then I remember that even if he had heard her cries, I would still be the one getting up with her.

Even after Paul and Lily fall asleep, I am still wide awake, the adrenaline of using a phone, of breaking the rules and getting away with it, still coursing through my veins. I think of Colin and Caroline, and then I think of my sister. The morning after I reassured her that I would check in from Dawes, I woke to find my phone gone, the charger coiled limp and useless on my bedside table. I found Paul in the kitchen, making coffee. His phone was on the kitchen counter, but mine was nowhere in sight. "Good morning," he said, watching my eyes as I scanned the room for my phone. "It's a new day." The rest of the day, I kept walking into rooms and realizing I was looking for my phone, a habit. I never saw it again. What was one more night of silence between the rest of the world and me? Much more than I understood. That was the last time I had any contact with my sister.

IN THE MORNING, when Paul wakes me up, Lily is silent. I peer into the bassinet anxiously, but she's alive, awake and squirming in her swaddle. She's gotten one hand free, and it touches her face, which makes her frown, as if she does not control the hand and where it goes. "Did you have any dreams last night?" Paul asks, excitement in his voice. He is wearing a T-shirt and gym shorts, his hair sticking up like a little boy's after waking. I lift Lily up and unwrap her from the swaddle. Her other arm shoots out, and then she touches her face with both hands. Her diaper has leaked, and she's covered in pee.

"Umm," I say, going to get a clean diaper. I don't remember any dreams. When I think of last night, all I can picture is Colin Bell, his Instagram photos, Paul's phone in my hand. But I feel sure Paul wants me to say yes, I did dream, so I do.

"Was it about a fire?"

"Yes," I say again. I should give Lily a bath, but I just don't feel like it. I peel the soaked pajamas from her and decide to wipe her down with a wet wipe instead.

"I knew it!" said Paul. "I was praying this morning, and I heard God tell me to ask you about your dreams. Then the next thing I knew, my phone rang, and it was Papa. There was a holy fire last night."

"Whose house?" I say.

"The Carsons'," he says. "They're fine. It's only the two of them, so Papa has already secured a new house for them."

"Praise God," I say, walking to the kitchen with Lily, Paul trailing behind us.

"I feel like you're not understanding this, Rosemary. Do you know what this means?"

"No?" I say. I hand him the baby while I start making a bottle. Last night's bottle is gone from the sink, already washed and put away by Paul, who cannot stand to let something be out of place. I look at the empty sink and feel glad I don't have to wash another bottle and irrationally annoyed that Paul didn't give me a chance to do it.

"You had a God dream," he says, swaying with Lily. "God shared with you about the fire, and you were open enough to receive it. Did you tell God to send it to you?"

I shake my head.

"It must have been me, then. Wasn't it, Lily? Wasn't it?" Paul says as he looks down at her. The warmer beeps, and I take the bottle out, wiping the condensation on my nightgown. I sit down at the table, and Paul hands the baby to me. As soon as I take her, she starts rooting around until she finds the bottle, touching it with both hands, her precious thing. "I've been telling God you need a miracle," he continues. "Before I went to bed, I invited Him to come in."

Suddenly he reaches toward me, and I flinch.

"Relax," he says, laughing. "Did you think I was going to hit you?" He plucks something from my hair and shows it to me—a white feather, curved like a smile. "An angel has been here," he says, sitting down beside me at the table. "See?"

"Paul," I say. "It's from the pillow."

"The pillows aren't down."

"It's from something else, then. The couch. I don't know."

Paul leans his head back and groans. "You aren't even trying, Rosemary," he says. "Be excited with me."

"I'm sorry," I say. "It's very exciting. I'll pray for more gifts from God."

"Just wait," he says. "When there's another fire, I bet you'll have another dream. I bet you'll see it. We'll ask God together for Him to show you."

That night, I do not dream of fires or of anything I can remember, but the Moores' house—the second one, the new one—burns down anyway and this time takes Richard with it.

Twenty-Two

It has been three days of praying for the resurrection of Richard Moore, three days of our dark clothes. Tonight we will be allowed to change clothes and shower; until then we sit with our own stench, endure our unwashed bodies. My navy dress smells like sweat and bug spray and all the foods I've cooked in our tiny kitchen. Amanda gave me a headband she was wearing at our day two service and put it on me herself, pushing my dirty hair off my forehead. "Better," she said, winking. Last night I tried to give Lily of the Valley a bath, but Paul stopped me. "Even babies need to follow the rules," he said. When he left the room, I tried to clean her body with wet wipes, but Lily still smells sour, her little outfit yellowing from spit-up.

When we finally reach the last day, the last hour of praying that God would resurrect Richard Moore, Richard has stayed dead. We are weary from showing our grief and our hope, the weeping and dancing, using our bodies and voices to show the depth of our feelings. God has told some of us that we must fast. Others He has told not to speak; others, still, have been given new voices, a new language, to speak in. Paul has been dreaming both asleep and awake. Sometimes his eyes roll back so far in his head that I only see white. "Don't be afraid," he told me before, but it's hard to feel scared by something you once watched sixth-grade boys do in the cafeteria. This morning he picked another feather out of my hair as we walked into the chapel, holding it up and grinning. "You're sprouting," he said. "Maybe you're the angel."

During the service, I let my thoughts drift toward Colin Bell. I replay the conversation between us in the dark hall of the diner, the feel of his hand on mine; I watch the scene in my head the way I might watch a movie, with pleasure and interest. I want to stay there, in my head, but I know that lingering too long in a memory or a fantasy is dangerous. You might never make it out again. So I go back to observing the real people around me. Being here in a real world is dangerous, too, but in a different way.

I watch Molly Moore, especially, and her children. We have been confused by this fire because we didn't expect God to take the life of one of our own, especially one so young, not even forty, Paul said, especially a father. We will never speak it out loud, but we know that there is a hierarchy here; some people are more expendable than others, and fathers and mothers are among the least expendable. Paul has been particularly stunned by Richard's death. Sometimes he is grief-stricken, crying in the shadows of our house, and at other moments he seems angry, lost. "This wasn't supposed to happen," he said.

"How do you know that?" I asked. "This one wasn't, but the other fires were?"

"Yes," he said, and that was it.

But last night I went out to the backyard with a spaghetti sauce jar whose lid I needed him to loosen, and he was standing in the back corner by the fence with the jasmine, his back to me as he talked on his cell phone. I stayed in the doorway and listened, the same way I did when he was out here with Randall. "How could this happen?" he was saying. "Are we responsible? I just don't understand it." I took a step forward and let the door fall shut behind me. He looked up and waved. "The Lord moves in ways we can't understand," he said into the phone, like he was answering his own question.

Molly has always been weak, and is now so debilitated by grief that she is flanked by women on either side of her at all times, propping her up. Her two boys stick their hands past the women, trying to grab at their mother's skin, her dress, anything by which they can tether themselves to her. Sometimes she acts like she doesn't notice them, and other times, she seems as desperate to touch them as they do her. Other women, other mothers, try to take the children, distract them, offer their own bodies to them for comfort, but the boys push them away. Today Molly has her hair in a long braid down her back, and one of the boys keeps tugging at it like she's a bell he's trying to ring. One of the women steadying her is Caroline, who keeps an arm around her waist, while her own children sit on a separate row.

The unusual thing about Molly is she doesn't cry. Her children don't cry either; the death is too new, too abstract for their tears. The pain, the real kind, the kind that lasts, will come later. But Molly understands he has gone somewhere else, a bright, shining place he would never want to leave, and now that the three days have passed, she knows he won't be back, that everything is ending. But still she has not, that I've seen, cried. Maybe her mother told her not to cry in public. Maybe she has spent all her tears crying before this, being sick and still having to be a wife, a mother. When I grabbed her that day as she went down the aisle, through the arches we made with our arms, and she looked at me, she wasn't startled or alarmed, wasn't surprised to feel me touching her. I think of all the people who must have touched her regularly—her husband, her children, her friends, Papa Jake—what was one more hand on her body?

"It is over," Papa Jake says from up front. "Let us grieve. Let us wail."

And we do, because God has not restored life to the dead. We thank God and praise Him for all He does, but we are only human. We scream. The chapel fills with the sounds we make, all the air in our lungs expelled in anger and sadness. We might break the glass in the windows. We might make the walls collapse. We might make the world end. We tear at our clothes, our hair, and grab each other by the shoulders and arms; we bring our foreheads together and breathe in each other's cries so that my breath goes into your lungs, and your breath into mine.

This is what I came to Dawes for: not only to honor Paul, to absolve myself of all my failings, not only to see God, to see the truth and the true believers, but to be seen by them, all of them, to prove that I am here, a part of things and indispensable. Even when my body feels on the edge of dissolution, like I am about to disappear, come apart, when

I seek to bump up against something that hurts or soothes, this has always reminded me I am here, I am real. I am among the real, the present.

But today that closeness, the sharing of breath, the physical touch—none of it is working. Amanda has her hands on my cheeks, our foreheads together, and my hands on her shoulders, her daughter between us touching us both, and the voices of everyone filling my ears and the place, and for so long this has all been almost enough.

"Enough," says Papa Jake, holding his hands up, and we fall silent. Around the room we all look so tired. Our clothes are torn, and our hair is a mess. I find Paul across the aisle, on his knees. "It is time to rest," Papa Jake says. "Soon we will talk about vengeance. Retribution against those who have done this. But for now, brothers and sisters, go home."

"Papa," a voice cries. "Who will take the gifts of the dead?"

Papa Jake has not forgotten. He is not a man who forgets. We, of course, have not forgotten either. A dead person still has gifts to offer, blessings he has accrued but not cashed in, that stay in his body until someone is able to absorb them. We all want to know who will be chosen to receive those lingering gifts, to lie on the grave site where Richard Moore rests and take them in. "Think of it like organ donation," Papa Jake said the first time he explained the process to Paul and me. "Why waste something precious when there are people desperate for it?"

Now he looks out at the congregation, evaluating or listening to the voice of God, and says Paul's name, and Paul, still on his knees, lifts his head. Someone beside him helps raise him up until he is on his feet. We applaud. Bless you, Paul, we say. At the front of the church, Molly Moore turns around and watches Paul. She turns around the other way, and I think she sees me. But it's hard to tell, and I stare back at her. I wave, and she doesn't wave back. Then Papa Jake dismisses us to our homes, our beds, and then Paul is beside me, handing me the truck keys, his wallet, his cell phone. "We can't bring anything with us," he reminds me.

"Am I going too?" I ask, confused as to why I have the keys if I am. People swarm around Paul, clapping him on the back, and he is nodding and smiling at all of them.

"Sorry, I didn't mean you and me," he says. "I just meant we, like whoever God chooses to soak up the gifts."

"Oh," I say, and he slides off his belt, steps out of his shoes.

"Can you carry all of this?" he asks. "I want to go in as unburdened as possible."

"I'll try," I say. Now I am carrying Lily, strapped to my chest in her wrap, and all of Paul's things too.

"Oh," he says. "Will you be okay with Lily all night on your own? Should I ask Amanda or Missy to come check on y'all?"

"I'll be fine," I say, and he pushes the wrap back so he can see Lily's face, and he leans over and kisses the top of her head.

"I love you," he says. "What's good for me is good for you. I'll get clarity tonight, I know it. I'll see you in the morning."

He turns and goes, back up the aisle, against the flow of the people, and he joins Papa Jake and Brother Lou at the front, and the three of them stand together silently.

As Lily and I are pulling out of the parking lot, I see someone running by, a jogger coming up on the road near the chapel. He passes under the orange pool of light from a street lamp. It looks like Colin Bell. I roll down the window, and the air that blows in is breath hot. I honk the horn of the truck lightly, just a tap. The jogger looks at me as he passes, and my stomach twists. It's Colin. He smiles but does not stop.

When I get home, I carry inside everything I have, though I've lost one of Paul's shoes somewhere, put Lily on her quilt with some toys, and turn on Paul's phone. I go to Instagram and log out of Paul's account, then reactivate my own.

All of my pictures pop up right away, but I don't look at them. Instead, I find Colin Bell and send him a message. I wait. I take off my dress and my underwear and walk naked into the laundry room, dump the clothes into the washing machine. I wish I could burn them, and I think someday maybe I will. I take a shower. I shave my legs. They are still loose, undefined, and I tell them to be patient, to hang on a bit longer. When I get out, I check the phone.

Where should I meet you? Colin has asked.

Twenty-Three

I am in my house with a man who is not Paul. The man is sitting on our couch, right in the middle where the two cushions angle down toward each other. I never sit in the middle, always picking one cushion, and Paul taking the other. But now I am in a chair on the other side of the room, with the coffee table between us. The man holds a glass of water; the hair on the back of his hands is dark. In another room lies a sleeping baby who is not mine.

"It's okay," I say as he looks around for a coaster. "Nothing can get ruined here. Or everything can. I mean, none of this is nice furniture. I didn't pick it out."

"How long have you been here?" he asks.

"Two years," I say. "How long has Jennifer been here?"

"Six months," he says.

"Wow," I say. "I didn't realize it had been that long." I remember her Reclamation the way Amanda remembered mine, though I don't think I even touched her as she got ready. I was a lady-in-waiting, quiet, an adornment. She didn't cry at all.

"Yeah," Colin says. He has his hands folded together,

226 | ALISON WISDOM

fingers interlocking, the gold class ring still visible, and he looks down at his thumbs.

"Did you expect it?" I ask.

"Expect what? For her to go?" He looks up at me and shakes his head. "Not then, but looking back on it, there were signs, I guess. She's always been a seeker, a searcher type. Always looking for something new, I mean."

"She's very young," I say. We are both old enough, I think, to count that as an explanation.

"My baby sister," says Colin. "And now I guess she's getting married."

"That means she's unlikely to leave," I tell him, and I hope my voice sounds gentle because I mean it to be—I want him to be prepared. We look at each other. "Then there'll be another baby," I say. "And then it'll be even less likely."

"Wait, another baby? There's a first baby?"

"Oh," I say. "Well, it's not really her baby. The guy she's marrying—it's his. Actually, right now I'm in charge of the baby."

"What happened to the mom?"

"She was having some difficulties," I say carefully. I want to protect Julie, though she will never know that I have, and probably feels I've betrayed her. "Anyway, the church made her leave. So I guess we're just, kind of, babysitting. But I assume when your sister marries Rob, they'll want her back?" I don't actually know this is true; when I've tried to ask Paul about it, he tells me to take it one day at a time. The days are so long now, with Lily of the Valley and her constant need, it's hard to do anything more than that, anyway.

"Wow," he says. "I'm an uncle. I guess?"

"Sure," I say. "Kind of."

He looks around, just now seeming to notice the swing in the corner of the room, at Lily's quilt she does tummy time on. The old makeup compact and a ball that squeaks when you squeeze it—I think it's actually for a dog—are still on top of it. "Is the baby here?" he asks. "Now?"

"She's asleep in my bedroom," I say. "Do you want to see her?"

"I guess not," he says. "I don't really know her."

"Me neither," I say, but I realize that's not really true either. At this point, I think, I know her better than any other person on earth does, and this strikes me as deeply sad. I didn't want her, and now I am the most important person in her life. I realize that besides Paul, she is probably the most important person in my life too.

"Why are you here?" he asks.

"Lots of reasons," I say.

"To be a waitress in a diner?"

I smile. "I'm not usually a waitress in a diner. I was just filling in the other day."

"What are you usually?" he asks. "A babysitter?"

"Just a wife," I say. "And a pretend mother."

"So you don't have a baby of your own?"

"Nope. Which is a problem here."

"So no baby means you're a bad wife?" he says. "Or a bad cult member?"

"Both," I tell him. "Do you really think this is a cult?"

"Do you?" he asks.

"It's a church," I say.

"That doesn't make it not a cult," he says.

"If it was a cult, I wouldn't be very free," I say. "But look at me! Extremely free."

"Well," Colin says, grinning, "you just said you weren't a good cult member."

I laugh. It feels so nice.

"Where's your husband?" He looks around, as if Paul might be hiding just out of sight, around the corner in the kitchen or crouching behind the chair I sit in.

"Oh," I say. "Someone died, and Paul got picked to lie on his grave and suck up all the blessings of the deceased."

Colin raises his dark eyebrows and lifts his chin, dark too, covered in stubble. "Naturally," he says.

"He won't be back until the morning," I say. Trouble, I hear Amanda's voice saying, her children buzzing around us as we climb into their van.

Colin nods again. "Okay," he says. "Seriously. What are you doing here?"

"I'm atoning for past mistakes," I say lightly.

"That's it?" he asks. "Go to confession. Say a Hail Mary. Get the fuck out of here."

"I'm not Catholic," I say.

"I think you could get away with it," he says. "Just this once."

"It's hard to explain," I say. "It's complicated." Try me, he says. I think back to when I was a gymnast, how my teammates and I couldn't imagine a life outside of that world, apart from the hands on our backs, on our legs, on our hips, tugging us and straightening us and bending us until we no longer had the shape of little girls but something harder and stronger. We saw the recreational gymnasts, the girls who only came once a week, and we marveled at them, wondered how they saw what we could do—what they could do, if only they tried—and chose not to. As we got older, we realized it wasn't that those girls chose not to do what we could; they simply weren't gifted. We were elite. It was an intoxicating thing, to be set apart. "If you're here, you're special," I say finally. "It's nice to feel special."

"It is," he says softly. He leans forward and takes the water from the coffee table and drains it. When he finishes, he holds it between his two hands like it is something warm and he is very cold. "When you messaged me, I looked through your pictures," he says. "You did have long hair."

"I told you I did," I say.

"We have mutual friends," he says. "Charlotte Newman, Phillip Goldstein. Some others too. We could have met sometime."

"We must have," I say. I think, again, of the creaking house. That night the house seemed to sway, and I thought here it goes, it's going to fall down with me inside it, but it didn't; I was just drunk, and the house was just old. Or maybe it was only later I told myself there was any kind of danger there that night. I had the outline of a memory and then filled it in myself, made it shake, made it rock.

"This is going to sound—bad, maybe. I don't know," Colin says. "I don't want to offend you."

"Offend me," I say.

He smiles, revealing one dimple. I want to touch it. "Is it possible," he says, "that we—hooked up? At some point?"

My face starts to burn, and I see myself climbing stairs, swaying, and my heart thumping with the pulse of music from downstairs. A hand reaching out, the dark-haired boy. I frown, hoping it distracts from my flushing cheeks. "You don't think you'd remember me?" I ask.

"I was an idiot," he says, "for so long."

He watches me as I stand and walk over to him. I could stop myself at any point. I could reroute, pick up his empty water glass and take it to the kitchen where Paul would wash it later. I could excuse myself to the bathroom. I could pull him up by the hand and tell him I'm sorry about his sister, wish him luck, hold the door open for him, and watch the night outside eat him up. But I don't want that, so I stand in front of him and lower myself down so that I'm straddling him. He puts his hands on my hips. I don't know if he has a girlfriend or a wife or children. I don't care. "Does any of this feel familiar?" I ask.

"Yes," he says. "Is this okay?"

"Yes," I say, though okay for who? Not Paul, not God. But I tell myself not to think about it anymore. *What's good for me is good for you*, Paul said. So I kiss him, and then we are kissing, and my dress is up around my thighs, his hands are pushing it farther up and up, and I let him, I want him to. We've been here before, I think. This doesn't count. When he lifts my dress up over my head, my skin chills in the cool air of the house, and we rearrange ourselves so that we are lying together on the couch, the weight of his body on mine, and I think everything that was falling apart is coming back together, and I relish it, the feeling of being here, here, here.

When Paul comes home in the morning, Colin Bell is gone, of course. He stayed for a little while, long enough to move to the bedroom, and that time, he didn't have to undress me because my dress was already gone. He jumped when Lily of the Valley grunted in her bassinet. "Jesus," he said, hand over his heart like an old woman, "I forgot she was in here." He peeked at her, said she was cute, but was otherwise uninterested in her. I showed him the watermark map of Europe on the ceiling. He had been to all the places I had been and more. "Maybe if I hadn't been here, I would've gone there too," I told him.

"Maybe so," he said.

When he left, I took a shower and put the sheets in the washing machine and then slept on the uncovered mattress.

I wake up to Paul's body beside mine. "Hey," he says in my ear. It's disorienting to have another man beside me now, identical in the basic ways, almost right but not quite—or no, he is the right one, and the other was the wrong one. "I already gave Lily her morning bottle. I wanted to let you sleep. She's in her swing right now." He pauses. "What happened to the sheets?"

"I got my period," I say. "I bled through my underwear and onto the top sheet, so I decided just to wash it all."

"Didn't your period just end?" he asks.

Shit. "I thought it did, but it must have just been a pause," I say. "Sometimes that happens. A false alarm. Tell me about the grave." I sit up. I put my hand in Paul's hair, rubbing a lock between my fingers. "If you shake your head, will dirt fall out?" I ask.

He laughs. "I didn't roll around in it," he says. "I actually got most of the dirt off before I came in. Papa drove me home and helped me put the dirt in a Ziploc." He nods toward the door to our room. "It's in the kitchen," he says.

"On the counter. So if you see it, don't mistake it for brown sugar or anything."

"Duly noted," I say. "Did God speak to you? Or did Richard?" Sometimes the dead spoke during the night, though not always. You had to listen very carefully, Paul said. Their voices are so faint because they are getting farther and farther from us and our world by the minute, and closer to God and His army of angels. By now, as the sun comes up, they would be impossible to hear at all.

Paul's face becomes serious. "Yes," he says. "Both. First of all, you'll get pregnant, Rosemary, both of them said so. And soon. We won't have to worry about you getting kicked out."

"Praise God," I say, careful to sound relieved.

"Yeah?" he says. "That would be a good thing, right?"

"Of course. What else did you learn while you were out there?" I ask, picturing the graveyard. It's a strange spot, at the intersection of the two roads that run through Dawes, the headstones visible as you drive by. Tall, short, boxy like little crypts. There are more headstones than I would have thought, but Dawes has lived many lives, seen many lives lived, and when I think about being here, our church and the many arms and hands it has reached into the town, I think about how many more lives it has left. Only one, Papa Jake says—ours. This is it. We are the fulfillment of its destiny. After us, the flood, the fire, the cracking of earth. We don't know what comes next for everyone else, and it does not matter. After us, there is nothing.

Paul shrugs. "I prayed a lot, but you know it's not a magic trick," he says. "There's a lot of silence."

"Of course," I say.

"There was one thing, though," he says. "Richard says the fire wasn't a holy fire. He said it was an evil flame. I asked God to tell me more, but He didn't say anything, so I'm assuming He didn't have anything to add."

"Creepy," I say. "Evil flame. Have you told Papa Jake?"

"Yes," he says. "He says he received the same message. But we don't know what it means."

"Bad luck?" I suggest. "Candle left burning? Electrical?" I think of Randall's church, the story we've told about it. But then I remember too what Jake said yesterday about vengeance. Someone will pay for this.

"I guess it could be any of those things, but they don't seem evil," Paul says.

"Just pray about it," I say.

"You know I will," he says, and smiles. "I missed you." He arranges me so my legs are across his lap, and trails a finger along my shinbone. My skin prickles. "It was a full moon," he says. "Did you see it?"

"Yes," I say. "It was beautiful."

Twenty-Four

All day my brain is full of Colin Bell, and there is no room for God or prayer or holy fires, evil flames, dead men. At first there is barely room in there for Lily. I just go through the motions of care—the feeding, the changing, the cleaning—and even going out with the stroller feels rote, mechanical. I am thinking of Colin Bell, replaying the night, beginning with him jogging past my car, passing under the streetlight, and ending with me closing the front door behind him. I imagined how he looked vanishing into the night, quick like a wink. This is how I know I was reckless: I did not care how he got out of our neighborhood or who saw him. The thrill of it and the dread.

But even though my brain feels crowded with Colin and our hands and legs and dark rooms, it worked; the rest of me is more real, solid. Paul comes out as I am kneeling in the backyard flower beds and watches me. "Your neck is pink," he says. "Do you want sunscreen?" He looks at my hands. "Or gloves?"

"No," I say. "I'm okay. I'll take a trash bag, though." I hold up strings of green weeds, and with a fingernail, I pierce the stem of one. The inside is wet. Paul nods and comes back out with a tall kitchen trash bag. He shakes it out and crouches down next to me with the mouth of the bag open. He is in sandals, and little blades of wet morning grass stick to his feet. I shove the weeds into the bag and pull some more. Beside me, Paul rearranges himself so that he is sitting, and he reaches into the garden next to me and yanks up a weed, then two, until he has a fistful.

"I'll help for a while," he says. We work side by side until we are sweating, until we are dirty. "You have a mustache," Paul says. "You look like a seventh-grade boy. Actually, you look like me in seventh grade." He laughs when I bring a finger to my upper lip. "A dirt mustache," he says. "Sorry, I should have clarified."

"I'm going to rinse off with the hose," I say, standing up. I brush off the seat of my dress, but my hands are dirty too, and I'm sure it leaves a mark. I uncoil the hose and turn it on, and the hose fattens up until the water comes out the end. I run my hands under it. I point it at my feet until the dirt is gone, but there are little blades of grass stuck to my feet now, just like Paul's. He's still sitting and pulling up weeds, but mostly sitting and watching me with the hose, languid stalks in his hand.

When I met Paul, he was just some guy, a friend of Tess's boyfriend who lived down the hall of his dorm. It was the spring then too; we were all going to watch baseball together, a hot afternoon game, and our school won in an absolute blowout, and we all went out for drinks after. Tess and I drank these blue frozen drinks that tasted the way sunscreen smells and took shots and then left together, giggly and wobbly. When we got home, I puked blue in our toilet, and it felt so terrible and so good to throw up, a renewal. "Paul likes you," Tess said as we recovered on the couch later, eating cookie dough straight from the container.

"What?" I asked.

"He laughed at everything you said all night," she said. "Even if it wasn't funny."

"Rude," I said, and she threw her head back to laugh. I reevaluated the night the best I could, trying to imagine myself the way Paul might have seen me, but whatever image I could pull up didn't look the way I felt. "I don't know," I said, but she was right: he called me the next day. After we slept together for the first time, I tried to imagine how Paul saw me then too, what I looked like as I undressed, what I looked like in bed, but still I couldn't grasp any of it, could only remember the way my body felt. "That's good, right?" Tess asked. "It means you were too in the moment to notice anything else!" I wasn't sure; something about it felt disconcerting, like there was an entire part of myself I couldn't quite get a grip on. I wondered if I was doomed to only know one half of myself, if one part of me would always be alienated from the other. Estranged, divorced. I've always counted on Paul to be that other half of me, to make me whole so I didn't have to try to achieve that on my own.

Now he is sweaty and dirty and handsome, his face already tanning, and it doesn't feel like we are here, in Dawes. It doesn't feel like we have a baby who is both ours and not ours napping inside this ugly house that, too, is both ours and not ours. It doesn't feel like I have cheated on my husband or had men's hands on my body to will it into conception or seen houses burn down or men cough up tumors. Instead, we are in the yard of our first home, the bayou rushing and brown a quarter mile away, jasmine blooming there too, and we are young and hopeful together, on the cusp of the rest of our happy lives.

I point the hose at Paul, covering part of the nozzle with my thumb so the spray fans out. I laugh as he sputters in the spray and stands up, laughing now too, dropping the weeds to the ground and charging me. He grabs the hose and turns it on me, and I run and slip and fall, and he rushes over to me, I think to see if I'm okay, but he sprays me again, and I lie there, the sun in my eyes, shaking with laughter. He drops the hose, which now runs like a tiny river in the grass beside us, and lowers himself on top of me. My dress sticks to my body, but I don't move; I let him look at me. "Is my mustache gone?" I ask.

"Yes," he says, and he lifts my wet dress over my head, my arms raising reflexively as he undresses me. He unhooks my bra, then pauses. The sun is warm, and I love it. "Is this fine?" he asks.

"Yes," I say. I pull off his wet shirt and then his shorts, and we have sex in the grass, the hose water still running underneath me, the sun still in my eyes. When we're both done, he pulls me up and we spray each other off again. Dripping, he goes inside, and emerges with one towel covering his lower half like he's just stepped out of the shower, and hands me another towel. "Those weeds," he says, and we laugh all over again.

Inside the house, when we are dressed properly again, I make turkey sandwiches for lunch. "You know," I say, thinking about Paul's hesitation in the yard, "it's okay that we had sex. We're married, after all."

"I know," Paul says. "I'm fine."

"You are?" I ask. I turn around. He's sitting at the kitchen table eating, and he shrugs when I look at him.

"Better than fine," he says.

"Maybe I got the dates wrong on the calendar, and I'm ovulating," I say.

"Maybe," he says. He takes another bite of his sandwich, chews, and swallows. "But you're right: we're married, and married people have sex, and you have to have sex if you want to get pregnant. Nothing to feel bad about."

"You're right," I say.

"It's amazing," he says, "how you can keep track of that all so well."

"God made bodies to be amazing," I say.

"Do you really think so?" he asks.

"Yes," I say. "Don't you?"

"Yes," he says too. "Miraculous."

"Shoot," I say, as I take a seat beside him at the table. "We had avocadoes for the sandwiches, but I forgot to use them. They'll probably be bad tomorrow." I can see them from where I sit, ripening on the window ledge over the sink, looking like dark eggs from some giant creature.

Paul shrugs again. "You could make guacamole tonight if you get an onion at the store."

"Good idea," I say. "I'll do that. Do we have chips?"

He nods, then stands up and takes his plate to the sink, my back to him from where I sit at the table. I hear the sink turn on and then off. "Hey," he says. "I thought you were on your period."

"It just ended," I say without turning my head. "Remember?"

"You said when I got home that it had just started again, and you bled onto the sheets."

I stay facing ahead and take a bite of my sandwich. When I finish chewing, I say, "I did. But I think that was the end." Now I twist in my chair so that I can see him. He's standing next to the sink, the clean plate and the dish towel he used to dry it still on the counter, the hem of the towel hanging off like a tail. When he notices it, he will fold it. Paul hates a mess.

"Gotcha," he says. "Maybe we should update the calendar."

"Is that not what the calendar says?" I ask.

"No."

"Ah," I say. "Well, things change. All kinds of things can mess up your cycle. Change in diet, travel, stress."

"You haven't done any of those things," Paul says.

"Stress," I say.

"What do you have to be stressed about?"

"Excuse me," I say. "Would you like a list? Lily of the Valley. Fires nearly every week. The fact that I'm about to get kicked out if I don't get pregnant."

"I think you want to get kicked out," he says.

"Paul!" I say. "I don't. I want to be wherever you are. If you're going to be here, I want to be here."

"What if I weren't here?"

"Then I would want to be wherever you were," I say.

"But I want you to want to be here," he says. "I want you to understand why I want to be here. I want you to choose this place, not just me."

"I have, Paul," I say. "I've done everything you asked."

"I just don't understand," he says, "how you could have

seen everything you've seen, experienced everything that's happened, and you still don't believe."

"I do," I tell him.

"Okay," Paul says. "Okay." I watch him as he picks up the dish towel and folds it into a nice, neat rectangle, no ends poking out, and places it next to the sink where it belongs.

Twenty-Five

I do not see Colin Bell again that week, as if the night truly did swallow him whole, a stone in the belly of the darkness. I look for him at every gathering, but he's never there. My period starts, and I am morose, moody, but I can't stop myself. I'm annoyed by the constellation of pimples that pop up on my forehead, by the bulk of the pads in my underwear, by every sound each creature in my house makes. It takes every ounce of my strength to stifle my irritation with existence in general and be cheery when Paul is around. When he's gone, I put Lily on her playmat and sink into my black moods; in a way, it's a relief. Then my period ends exactly five days later, as always, and my skin and mood both clear up. I stand naked in front of the bathroom mirror and examine my body, imagine Colin examining me. Lily of the Valley sits in her special reclining chair on the bathroom floor and watches, examining me too.

I find myself thinking of this wooden barrel in the chapel, which sits in one corner at the front of the church, to the left of the stage. I noticed it right away, maybe even the first or second time we attended a service; my senses were heightened then, the corners of everything extra sharp, the colors and the sounds and even the silence all so loud, I felt them pulsing in my ears, my throat. But I felt like I absorbed it all, taking the church and its people into my body, metabolizing them, turning them into what I needed for my survival. This was before I believed in anything but my own determination, my own desire to make things right with Paul. I think Papa Jake could sense that, that when he looked at me, he saw it like an aura radiating from my body.

I assumed the barrel was a trash can, the kind little country store restaurants had, but one day after a service, as Paul was talking to some of the other men, I walked up to it and peeked inside. It was empty and clean. When I looked up, Papa Jake was watching me, smiling. He walked over. "Curious?" he asked.

"Yes," I said.

"You'll find out soon," he said.

The next day, Papa Jake approached Paul and me before the service. "I have a task for Rosemary," he said.

Paul looked over at me, eyebrows knit together. "Of course," he said. "Whatever you need her for."

"You'll have eyes on her the whole time," Papa Jake assured him. "She's going to be right up here—" He pointed at the barrel, which had been moved onto the stage behind the pulpit. "Right here," he said. "The whole time."

"I'm sorry," Paul said. "I'm confused. Is she going to be in the barrel?"

"Sort of," said Papa Jake. "She's going to stand on a little step stool—Brother Lou is getting it right now—and she's going to keep her head in the barrel. The top half of her body, actually." He looked at me. "Okay?" he asked. "You'll want to reach your hands in, like you're reaching for the bottom, but I don't think you'll be able to touch it."

"Okay," I said. "The whole time?"

"Don't ask him, Rosemary," Paul said. "Sorry, Papa."

"The whole time?" I asked Paul. He looked at Papa Jake, who nodded.

"Yes," he said. "You might feel a little light-headed, but you won't be in any danger. There are spirit fumes in the barrel, and you're going to breathe them in. When the service is over, I'll come and place one hand on your shoulder. But you can't move, okay? When it's time for you to stand up, I'll come up behind you again and touch your other shoulder, all right?"

The pews were filling up now, and I saw the other men and women watching Paul and me, jealous, I thought, of Papa's attention. Or maybe they knew what was happening, that soon my upper half would be swallowed by the barrel like I was being devoured by some kind of beast. "All right," I repeated.

"There we go," Papa Jake said, looking past me at the stage, where Lou was giving him a thumbs-up, standing with one foot on a step stool. "Paul, would you like to escort your bride?"

"Of course," said Paul, and he took my arm and led me up the three stairs to the stage and then onto the stool. "Pray," he said. "And breathe deeply. I hope that God grants you a vision."

"Paul," I said, but he shook his head.

"Papa Jake wants to start the service," he said. "See?" Papa Jake was looking at us expectantly from behind the podium, adjusting the microphone that was hooked around his ear. "Put your head in," said Paul.

I did as he directed. "Farther," said Paul from outside, so I stood on my tiptoes and felt the rim of the barrel hard against my stomach as I draped myself over it, my ponytail flipping down, like it too was reaching for the bottom. There. Inside, it smelled like wood and something smoky. I touched the sides, for some reason expecting them to feel sticky, but they felt like dry tree bark. I imagined myself, how I looked to everyone else in the chapel, listening, ostensibly, to Papa Jake, watching me, my body performing its stillness, its posture of obedience. I would be watching too.

At first I listened to the muffled voice of Papa Jake, and then I tried to pray; I asked the Spirit in the barrel to show me something, but I saw nothing—only blackness when I closed my eyes, only darkness when I opened them, my fingers hanging down like those pale little crystals that grow in damp black caves, and eventually those fingers went numb and swelled. I stretched them, curling them in and out, shaking them loose. My vision went spotty, all the blood rushing to my head. I wish I could say it meant something to me, the darkness in the barrel, the wave of blood filling me up, the smell of wood and smoke and sweetness, but it didn't mean a thing. But there did become something pleasurable about hanging there, my feet on the ground but the rest of me suspended, blind in the barrel. It made me think of my bar work in the gym all those years ago, a lifetime, two lifetimes ago, how it felt to grip the bar with chalky hands, feel it bounce under my weight as I spun around it, arms outstretched and strong.

Finally, I felt a hand on my shoulder, and my body tensed, but I didn't move. I heard Papa Jake ask the women to stay, and then I heard more people arriving, sensed their presence near me, and then it was quiet. The women were still. Now I was desperate to stand, to straighten myself out, to blink in the light. Papa Jake put his hand on my other shoulder. "Close your eyes as you stand," he said, and I obeyed, though I didn't want to. My back ached. Someone put a blindfold on me, pulling out my ponytail so that it wasn't trapped under the knot. Papa Jake kept his hand on my shoulder and steered me a few feet away. More hands on my body, two more; they felt small, bigger than a child's, though smaller than a man's. Then they shoved me, spun me to the left, and I tripped. Get up, the women said. I did, reaching for a hand, but there was none there to help me, and I grabbed on to a skirt, like a child trying not to lose her mother in a crowd. Get up, they said. I stood, reaching for something to tell me where I was, and I touched something soft and bulbous, a breast, and I was embarrassed. I tried to see from under my blindfold, the thin line of light at the lower edge of it. Hands spun me again, and I fell to the floor.

Get up, the women said.

I stood more carefully that time, and the women passed me in a circle, twirling me as they sent me from woman to woman. They were saying something all together, a prayer, I thought, and it moved me to think they were standing there with me, present with me, but I couldn't understand the words. My head ached. I was dizzy and unsteady, trying to anticipate where I would be flung. Let go, a woman whispered as I spun into her arms, and I did. I gave my body over to the women, and each of them touched me with her own two hands, guiding me around and around.

Finally, they stopped, one of them grabbing me at my waist to steady me. Someone untied the blindfold, and I blinked. Papa Jake was standing in front of me, grinning. "How do you feel?" he asked.

"Good," I said, and I did. I laughed. Some of the women laughed too.

"Paul is waiting for you out front," he said. "You'll need to drink lots of water. Communing in the barrel takes it out of you." He turned away from me and faced the circle of women around me. "God bless you," he said to them. "You're free to go. You've helped a sister."

"Bless you, sister," the women said. They turned, some of them talking to each other and others descending from the stage, walking down the aisle and out the door. Papa Jake led me down the stairs too, holding me by the elbow, as though I were frail and old. "Well?" he asked.

I wasn't sure what to say. I didn't understand what had happened, but honestly I loved it—knowing I was being thrown but caught too. I loved the feeling of hands on me; disembodied, alien, they could have belonged to anyone. "It was interesting," I told him.

"Interesting," he repeated, nodding. "Did the Lord reveal anything to you?"

"I'm not sure. What were the women saying in the circle?"

"Saying?" said Papa Jake. "No one said anything. Did you hear something?"

"It sounded like they were praying," I said, "but it was in a language I didn't understand."

"Really?" he asked. We stopped at the double doors that led outside.

"Yes," I said.

"It was the angels," he said. "The Spirit let you hear them. Everything you breathed in from the barrel." He opened a door and stretched his arm out, like he was presenting me with a prize I had won. There was Paul, waiting for us, turning around as the door opened.

Later, when we had been here longer, I asked one of the women if they had really been silent during the circle. "Yes," she said. "We're not allowed to talk. We don't want to drown out the voice of God."

"Did you hear anything?" I asked.

"Nope," she said.

I was so grateful, so encouraged. The barrel, the circle, the women and their hands pushing and grabbing—all of those borders for my body to bump up against, to weigh me down, to show me I was present. I could be suspended in darkness, I could be hurtling through space, but the church was giving me something sturdy, solid. The architecture of my world, the hand under my back as I arched and reached, stretching to meet the mat on the ground.

And the church could be a voice too—one that instructed me, commanded me: get up, get up, get up. Paul was so pleased. "Give it all to God," he said. "Every part of yourself. Everything you have is on loan from God."

This explained so much to me: how my body had failed me before, its unruliness and disobedience, its constant dissatisfaction with the state of things. I had been treating it like it was mine when it hadn't ever been. I had tried giving it away over and over and over, to the wrong people. No wonder it fought back.

But look what I've done now—stolen it from the hands of God, held it fleetingly in my own feeble hands, as it would burn me if I kept it too long, like a hot coal cupped in my palms, and then when I could, I thrust it at someone else: *Take it, take it. Take this from me.*

I thought when I slept with Paul for the first time after Colin came over, I would feel guilty. I have been waiting for the shame to come as I know it should. I have been unfaithful; I have been lacking in faith. I try to get back to how I felt that day in the barrel, the day among the women, when I realized what I had done, how I had failed. I close my eyes and imagine the darkness of the barrel, but all I see is Colin Bell. Colin Bell in my house, Colin Bell in my bed, in my body. I try to regret it, but I don't.

TODAY THERE IS a wedding. It seems right that all this mourning be followed by joy. Tyler is to marry Erin, the childhood friend of Caroline's daughter, Ruth. In honor of the occasion, Tyler has shaved his mustache. I imagine touching that new clean spot, and then I think, again, of Colin Bell. I try to focus on the wedding. Tyler stands at the front of the church with both Papa Jake and Young Jake, his best man, short and square in an ill-fitting suit. Papa Jake looks immaculate in his own perfectly cut suit, nothing like what you would expect from the pastor of a small church in a small town. When Erin comes out, escorted by her father, I ask Paul how old she is.

"Old enough," Paul whispers. But she seems impossibly young in her white dress, and her ivory sandals with block heels, ancient and matronly, make her look like a little girl playing dress-up in her mother's clothes. But she's smiling.

Tyler is smiling too and so is Papa Jake, and around the room, we are all smiling because what a beautiful thing. We hold on to our husbands' arms, lightly, though, not lustfully—we are thinking of our own weddings, that strange and rosy time of being newly married, and now we exist in a different, richer realm, built by years together, an expanding world. How lucky we are. An image pops in my head of Lily of the Valley as a grown woman, or simply as an old-enough girl, getting married in a long white dress, white shoes. She will never have a Reclamation because we've already claimed her. She'll never have to belong to the world because she will always have belonged here.

When Erin reaches the men at the front of the room, Papa Jake raises his hands and we begin to hum, calling to God, bringing Him here to bless their marriage, and as we do so, Renee begins to sing from one side of the stage. Her voice is bright and sweet, and she doesn't stop as the lights go off and the feathers begin to fall on Tyler, Papa Jake, Erin, and her father. A waterfall of white on top of them. Erin looks up, and I can't hear her over the humming and the singing, but I see the laughter in her face, her body as the feathers catch in her hair. Tyler grins at her, and she points to the feathers; he nods and picks one out of her hair, holding it up to her between two fingers. She grabs it and puts it back, tucking it behind her ear. We all stop humming and laugh. Renee stops singing; she is smiling too. Papa Jake says, "It should always feel this exciting, shouldn't it?" Oh, yes, we say. It should. It is. For a moment, it is easy to feel that pleasure, but then when I watch Tyler promise to love Erin, to cherish her for all her days, I feel unease in my body, roiling and rising like floodwaters.

After, there is a reception in the high school gym; the football coach at the school is so close to joining us, he and Papa Jake play pickup basketball once a week, and he has opened it up for us. He stands near the door that leads into the rest of the school, his arms crossed over his chest, watching us. Tyler and Erin feed each other cake and dance to worship songs Kyle plays on the guitar. I wanted to bring the stroller to the reception, but Paul said it would be too much of a burden to drag it everywhere with us, so I am still wearing Lily of the Valley in the wrap on my chest, both of us, I think, sweaty and uncomfortable. She is awake and fidgety in the fabric, and I feel annoyed with her.

Paul brings me a glass of punch, pink and frothy, a little girl's drink. "Cheers," he says, holding it out. We have established a tenuous peace. We have moved on. We wait together for a miracle.

"Thank you," I say, tapping the little plastic cup against his and then drinking. "Does this taste funny to you?" I hold it out to Paul, and he takes a sip.

He smacks his lips and puts a finger to his chin. "It's fruit-forward," he says. "But also a little earthy?"

"Dork," I say, and he laughs. "I'm pretty sure it's made with Sprite."

"It tastes like mine, Rosie," he says. He hands it back to me and takes a sip of his own drink. "Maybe you're catching a cold. That does funny things to your taste buds."

"True," I say, patting Lily's bottom through the wrap.

We stand together, drinking the punch and watching the others. Some of the kids have found a loose basketball, and though the hoops are cranked up to the ceiling, the boys are dribbling and stealing and shooting the ball, tossing it up toward the hoop. It ricochets off, and one of them catches it and chucks it back up with one arm.

"This is going to end poorly," says Paul.

"What makes you think that?" I ask. I watch Amanda stride across the gym and grab the ball from one of the boys. She holds the ball on her hip like it's a baby. "Busted," I say to Paul, but when I look over at him, he's looking toward the open double doors, where a group of people have huddled. Someone shouts. Kyle has stopped playing and is moving toward the huddle. "What is it?" I ask.

"I'm going to go see," says Paul. He hands me his cup. I finish both our drinks and follow a few steps behind him. Everyone now has begun to turn toward the open door, the group gathered there. Erin holds Tyler's arm, looking past him. The feather is still tucked behind her ear, and I watch her reach one finger up to adjust it. Papa Jake is watching too, his arms crossed over his chest, though he hasn't moved.

The little crowd of people shifts, and through a gap, I see Colin Bell and his parents. But then Brother Lou stands in front of him, and he is gone from my sight again. "What are you doing here?" Lou asks. "You need to leave." He reaches a hand toward the Bells, and I hear the father tell Lou not to touch him. "This is a private event," says Lou. With Lily, I climb up a few rows of bleachers so that I can see, or rather, so that Colin can see me. From the corner of my eye, I spot a man coming to sit in my row, a few feet away. I look over. It's Papa Jake. He nods at me and winks, and I watch his gaze turn toward the Bells.

Mrs. Bell is looking around, lengthening every part of her body that she can, and I know she is searching for Jennifer, but she isn't here. Rob Friedrich is gone too. They must have slipped out the door on the other side of the gym as soon as they heard the Bells arrive. I imagine them hiding together in the locker room, Rob holding Jennifer to his chest as they wait, star-crossed lovers. "We're just looking for our daughter," Mr. Bell says, projecting his voice so that we can all hear him. "We just need to talk to her."

"We heard there was a wedding," Colin says. He's looking at Paul when he says this, and maybe he thinks Paul is the leader here or maybe he is drawn to Paul, the calmness he exudes; maybe he looks at Paul and thinks here is a man who will understand, here is a man just like me. "Is it Jennifer's?" he asks.

"No," says Brother Lou. "And even if it was, you would not be allowed to attend." Lou looks over his shoulder at Papa Jake, whose face gives nothing away. He is so good. He could be anyone sitting there. Colin follows Lou's line of vision, and I see him notice Papa Jake, and then I see him notice me. I look back at him. My cheeks burn, but I don't look away. He turns back toward Lou and Kyle and Paul, and I look down at the top of Lily's head, her scalp pink under thin hair. When I look up again, Papa Jake is looking at me, and my cheeks get hot again. "We just want to talk to her," Colin says, echoing his father.

"Hey, man," says Paul, stepping forward. He puts a hand on Colin's shoulder, and Colin lets it rest there. "She's good. She's happy. If she wanted to leave, she would."

"She couldn't be happy without us," Mrs. Bell says, her voice cracking, and I think of my own mother.

"Ma'am," Paul says, his voice gentle, "she is, though." Mrs. Bell shakes her head, angling it toward the ground, at her feet in black ballet flats, and she wipes her eyes before straightening back up.

"You need to go," Brother Lou says again. "You're ruining the wedding of another girl. Time to leave."

"Jennifer!" yells the father, and I think of when I first saw him in the back of the church, calling for her over and over. "Jenn!"

"She isn't here," says Lou.

"Come on," says Paul. "I'll walk you out."

He puts his hand on Mr. Bell's back; the older man shrugs it off and says, "I can walk myself out."

"Come on, Dad," Colin says. "Maybe he can help us." He looks at Paul, who shrugs.

"Maybe," Paul says. "If I can, I will."

Colin puts his arm around his mother's shoulders and guides her out the door. His father follows. My husband follows. Then the door shuts, and we turn away from the Bells and back toward each other. Tyler pulls Erin to him, and they laugh a little at the theatrics. Amanda throws the basketball back to her son and the other boys; she no longer cares. Papa Jake remains seated, but I stand up and climb down the bleachers to wait for Paul by the double doors.

Brother Lou lingers there too, but he does not speak to me, and I, of course, do not speak to him. "All good," Paul says when he returns a couple of minutes later. "Crisis averted."

"Will they be back?" I ask.

Paul sighs. "Who knows," he says.

"I wanted to call the cops," Lou says. "Next time I will."

"The cops wouldn't come if you called them," Paul tells him. "No offense. But if the Bells called the cops, then we'd have a problem. We need to get this figured out. Will you have Papa give me a buzz later?" Lou nods, and Paul turns to me. "Let's head home. You ready?"

"I just need to go to the restroom first," I say. "Can I give you Lily for a minute?" Paul waits while I unwind the baby from my body and takes her for a walk around the gym to greet people. He's so much better with her than I am, so proud to be the one holding her, so proud to have her fussed over.

When the door closes behind me, I am alone in the hallway. It's all gray, the floor, the ceiling, the walls except for a painted red line that runs all the way down the middle. Across from the bathrooms I see a glass trophy case, filled with little statuettes and pictures, all of them old. The boys' haircuts change, but not their uniforms, not their posture, not the straight lines of their mouths. There aren't any pictures of girls' teams. When I quit gymnastics, I threw away all my trophies and medals, though my mother dug them out of the trash and put them in a box in the attic, in case I changed my mind. "Hey," I hear, and I turn around.

"Hey," I say. "You're back."

"Not for long," he says. "Maybe another day or two. See if we can get to talk to Jenn alone."

"Well, I could have told you this ambush wasn't going to work."

Colin Bell smiles. "I didn't have your phone number to run it past you."

"It's hard to give out your phone number," I tell him, "when you don't have a phone."

"Right," he says. He takes a step closer so that he is standing next to me at the trophy case. He peers into the case at the pictures.

"That was my husband who walked you out," I say.

"I know," he says. "He mentioned his wife, Rosemary, and I said the girl who works at the diner? And he seemed surprised I remembered you. I said I was good with names and faces, and that I have a cousin named Rosemary." I keep staring into the trophy case. I can see his face in the reflection of the glass. Being so close to him in public makes every nerve in my body loose and wild, but the reflection of his face is calm, even amused. When I think of Paul—only briefly—his face is worried, his eyebrows knit together, his mouth tense and straight. Colin's eyebrows are soft and dark; his mouth is lovely, turning up at the corners.

"Do you really have a cousin named Rosemary?" I ask.

"No," he says. "He seems nice."

"Yes," I say.

"When can I see you again?"

"Now?"

In the biggest stall in the women's room, I unbuckle his belt and undo the button and zipper, and he lifts up my dress—there's so much fabric this time that it spills through his fingers—and the sex is fast and desperate and over soon, but it's enough. "My parents are waiting," he says, pulling up his pants.

"They'll wonder what happened to you," I say.

"I'm not sure I'll share it with them," he says. I leave first, thinking I should feel guilty—I know I should—but

I only feel relieved: to have seen Colin, to have been with him, to be reminded that I do not love him. I wonder if the guilt will come later.

I come out of the restroom, letting the door swing behind me, and there is Papa Jake, his back to me as he looks at the trophy case. He wears a long-sleeved white button-down shirt, and though it was probably crisp when he left his house that morning, in the summer heat it has wilted; it looks soft, inviting, but I know that's a trap. I would never touch it anyway. I step quietly in my thin sneakers, but he turns. "Hi, there," he says, as though he isn't surprised to see me.

"Hello, Papa," I say, keeping my head down.

"Paul and Lily of the Valley are waiting for you," he says.

"I'm hurrying," I say, though I am standing still. My back is to the bathroom, where Colin is. I imagine him with a hand against the door, ready to push it open. I will him not to emerge. I want so badly to turn and look at the bathroom door that my body itches, sweats. If Colin comes out of the women's bathroom, Papa will see him, and I'll see Papa seeing him, and then it'll all be over. Parts of me tingle at this thought—my fingers, my scalp, the tip of my nose. I am desperate for it not to happen. I am desperate for it to happen.

"Do you know the Bell family?" he asks. "From before?"

That listing wooden house in the night. "No."

Papa Jake nods. "For some reason, I was getting the message you did," he says. "But that Paul didn't know you knew them."

"I don't know them," I say.

"I'm not always right," he says, shrugging. I think of

another night, thick and hot, a boy and a rope. We both hear the double doors to the gym opening, and we turn. Here come Paul and Lily, Paul's shoes squeaking on the gray linoleum, the wrap draped over his arm. All those yards of fabric.

"You found her," Paul says.

"Where did you think I was?" I ask.

"Nowhere," he says.

"I told you I was going to the restroom," I say, and Paul looks at Papa Jake. Are we fighting? No, Paul's face tells Papa Jake. Rosemary and Paul do not fight.

"You ready?" Paul asks. He hands me the wrap, and I slip it on as the two men watch. I suddenly feel self-conscious, as if I'm removing clothing instead of adding another layer. When it's on, Paul hands Lily of the Valley to me. "Hi, there," I say to her as I wrap her up.

"Hey," says Papa Jake. "Actually, Rosemary, I wanted to tell you this." But he stops talking, and so I say, "Yes, Papa?"

"Julie Friedrich reached out to us," he says. "To Caroline. She wants to come back."

"Here?" I ask.

"Where else?"

"Wow," says Paul. "God bless her. How is she?"

"Are you going to let her?" I ask. "Come back?"

"No," says Papa Jake. "She doesn't belong here after all. She's where she belongs now, out there with the rest of them. Lily of the Valley doesn't deserve that kind of mother. We have to think of her too. We're all right where God wants us." Papa Jake casts a quick look in my direction. "For now, anyway," he says.

"Praise God," says Paul, who is smiling at Lily of the Valley, reaching into the wrap to find her little hand. She grasps his finger. "We've loved having Lily of the Valley with us. It does feel like it's what God wants us to be doing right now. Right, Rosie?"

"Oh, yes," I say. I glance over at him, but he is looking at Papa Jake, and it's like I'm not even here at all.

"Like I said, I'm not always right," Papa Jake says to me, as if Paul hasn't spoken. "Sometimes people end up here who don't belong here."

"Not your fault, Papa," Paul says.

"Of course not," I say.

"No," Papa Jake says thoughtfully. "I suppose not. But if your hand offends you, cut it off. If your eye doesn't see well, pluck it out." He takes my other hand, puts his fingers around my wrist and looks at me just for a moment, then releases me. I want to rub the place he touched, rid myself of his fingerprints on my skin, but Paul has my other hand, and so I do nothing.

"Absolutely right," says Paul, and I can hear he is uneasy.

"I'm not feeling well," I tell Paul. "I think you were right about my cold."

"Poor girl," says Paul. "Let's get you home. Papa, excuse us, please. We'll see you soon."

"Goodbye," says Papa Jake, but he doesn't move. He stays by the trophy case, trapping Colin inside the ladies' room, and I don't look back as we walk down the hallway, so for all I know he stays there and watches us until we step outside, back into the burning day.

Twenty-Six

That night, we are sitting at the splintery wooden table in the backyard, drinking lemonade Paul made himself, when he gets a call from Brother Pat. He laughs into the phone. "You're kidding," he says. "Well, I'm sorry we missed that." He listens and laughs again. "Sounds good. Yeah, we can plan a guys' night soon to celebrate. Shake the groom's hand for me."

"What was that about?" I ask after he hangs up the phone.

"Papa married Rob and Jennifer after we left," he says. "Right there in the gym. What are they waiting for anyway? And now that she's married to Rob, she truly belongs here. No one can make her leave."

"Jennifer's an adult," I say. "She can leave if she wants. And hasn't she always belonged here?" Lily reclines in my arms, and I shake the toy monkey that she likes, one with a rattle in his stomach, at her.

"You know what I mean," Paul says. "Rob's her family now."

"I'm sure they don't have a marriage certificate."

Paul stares at me. "They'll get one eventually," he says. "What's wrong with you? You're being very combative."

"I'm sorry," I say. "You're right. I'm really just not feeling well." I look down at the concrete beneath the table, and I remember the way my hair fell onto it the night Amanda cut it, how I wished the birds would take it, make it into something new.

"Did you do something to make Papa Jake mad?" he asks me.

"Me?" I ask, looking away from Lily in surprise. "I can't imagine what it would be."

"Maybe something about how you handled things with Julie?" He runs a finger down the sweating glass of lemonade, leaving a clear trail in the cloudy condensation. He looks up at me. I shake my head. "Or with Lily of the Valley?"

"What more could I have done? With either?" I shake the monkey again for Lily, and she smiles at it.

"I don't know," Paul says.

We are both quiet. I have the view of the star jasmine crawling along our fence, the little butterflies of flowers. Behind me, all he can see is the plain, weathered fence and a pecan tree that drops pecans every other year. Last year I let them fall and fall until the squirrels and the birds swarmed and glided in to nibble and peck at the nuts, until Paul asked me to please pick them up so we wouldn't attract any more pests. I did, and then I made a pie.

"It's just that there's something strange," he says finally. "Do you need to confess anything?"

"Did you have something in mind?" I ask.

"Not particularly, I guess," he says.

I think of Colin Bell. I don't feel sorry, exactly, but I am hopeful the time is coming when I will. I've always wanted to care about my weaknesses, but I rarely have. With Nick, right before we came here, I did, though. I've told myself it was God, convicting me. Something inside me had softened, made room for Him without knowing it.

Sometimes at night, when I can't sleep, I start to pray, but then instead I think of the men I've slept with, whose bodies I've used to betray Paul. I count them down, replay each memory and recite them to myself, a kind of litany. First I think of the places: the wooden house, my childhood bedroom with its paisley bedspread and the fairy lights tacked to the wall, the beach at night, the couch in the house I shared with Paul, the bed too, the other couch and the other bed in the other house. The handicapped bathroom by the Dawes High School gym. Then I think of the bodies themselves, of what I can remember about them; so much of them is the same, and I'm never sure if I have the details right, not that they matter. Then I think of myself with each of them, as if each time was experienced by a different version of myself, what I was wearing, how long or short my hair was, how old I was, how strong, how weak. I am alternately disappointed and amazed by myself, by these other women I was. My body feels loose again, untethered, I can feel the trembly way it begins, and I take a drink of my cold lemonade to add weight to my body and anchor me down. The drink is too sweet, but even that helps. I am here again.

From a backyard a few houses down, there are voices of

two little boys, the Crenshaw twins. It's hard to hear what they are saying, but they are playing, wild, and then we hear their mother. Time to come in, she says.

"Anyway," Paul says, studying me, "I just thought it was strange that he brought up Julie. And in such a strange way." Paul, who is constantly interpreting dreams and thoughts and messages and voices, is usually so straightforward. I used to feel hurt by things he said, the subtext of them, and he'd say, "Rosie, there wasn't any subtext." Everything has a subtext, I told him. But now it feels like there is something else lurking under his words, and I am wary.

"I don't know," I tell him. "I'm sorry. I have no idea." I make the monkey do backflips, and Lily surprises me by grasping it in her tiny fist when I hold it next to her hand. "Did you see that?" I ask Paul. "Look at her making her own decisions about her life!"

"Way to go, Lily girl," Paul says. She holds the monkey up to her mouth and sucks on its tail. I stand and put her in her little portable chair, and when she looks up from her toy, she seems surprised to have a different view. But I was making my own decisions about my life, she thinks.

"Maybe there's something else," Paul suggests. "Something he knows you aren't being honest about?"

I shake my head. "Paul, I'm sorry. I don't know. Really."

"Okay," he says. "It was just strange. That's all."

"Actually," I say. "I do have a question."

"Shoot."

"Will Lily go with Rob and Jennifer now that they're married?" We both look at Lily in her chair. She's dropped her monkey onto her lap and now sucks on her fingers, her little cheeks going in and out and her big dark eyes watching us like she knows we're making plans for her. Then I turn to Paul, but now he's staring past me, above me, like he's searching for something in the sky, in the treetops, his profile sharp and beautiful.

"I'm not sure," he says, still looking away. "One day at a time, remember?"

The days are long now, but this one is finally ending, the light in the sky dying a golden death. I can hear the Crenshaw boys still playing, and their tired mother. Boys, she says. Boys.

"Let's go in," Paul says, and I agree. One day at a time, one hour, one minute. I half expect our house to burn down that night, a punishment for my faithlessness or a prize for Paul's faithfulness. But Lily and I both sleep through the night, and when I wake up, the house is still standing, I have both my eyes, my body is lying solidly in my bed, and my husband is beside me.

THE NEXT AFTERNOON, Paul is out helping Papa Jake with a maintenance project in the chapel, and Lily won't stop crying. In the weeks she's been with us, I've learned to listen to her cry and deduce, more or less, what she wants. But this cry isn't just desperate or frustrated—it's full of rage or sorrow or both. Her face is red. Her fists are balled up. She is clammy from the exertion of displaying her unhappiness. If I hold her, she goes berserk, scrambling in my arms, but if I put her down, she screams even louder. "I don't know what you want," I tell her. I rattle the monkey for her, but it just pisses her off further. I try the swing, I try the stroller,

I try a bottle, which she bats away. I think of my first day with Julie, when she walked away from the house with Lily inside it. I understand that impulse.

I sit down on the couch, still holding Lily, who face-plants into my chest. My breasts ache, and when I touch them, they are hard. Stones, melons, coconuts. I put Lily on her quilt, still squalling like a little pink beast, and lift my dress over my head and toss it on the couch. I unclasp my bra and sit down on the floor beside Lily's quilt and scoop her up. She begins snuffling about my body like a truffle hog. I close my eyes, remembering what Julie looked like when she nursed, how Missy held Lily of the Valley, that one exposed nipple winking in the dim bedroom light. "Okay," I say out loud. I hold her up to my breast and use a finger to open her jaw, like she's a marionette puppet, and, gracelessly, I stuff my nipple into her mouth. She latches on and sucks, and my nipple feels like it's on fire, but the burning is almost pleasant, a relief, like when we used to take turns rubbing Icy Hot onto each other's sore muscles after practice. Lily's eyes are open, and she has one hand on my boob where she nurses, and we just watch each other.

A miracle, I hear Paul's voice saying in my head and my own echo, unable to call it anything else. What is a miracle if not something inexplicable happening? I look down at my breasts. The other nipple leaks uselessly, whitish tears dribbling down. With my free hand, I squeeze it, and an insistent arrow of milk sprays out. Lily of the Valley nurses furiously, and I cry. We are stuck with each other forever.

Twenty-Seven

I decide not to tell Paul about what's happened to my body. When he's around, I go into the bathroom, stand over the sink and squeeze my breasts until they feel fairly empty, like day-old party balloons. Then I prepare a bottle of someone else's breast milk for Lily of the Valley. I stick a folded panty liner in each cup of my bra in case I leak. But when he's gone, I nurse her. I realize I am again being unfaithful with my body, sharing it with someone else, not telling Paul. Every morning the next week, I consider stopping, but then I am outnumbered by baby and body demanding the release, and every day, I give in. Her little fingers flex and squeeze as she eats; I am being wrung out, emptied. If Paul knew, he would love it. He would be so happy, so proud. See, Rosie? he would say. Here is proof of God! A miracle, a gift. Now, surely, you can stay. All our problems are solved.

Now, surely, I can stay. All our problems are solved. If Papa Jake knew, how could he cast me out, separate me from Lily of the Valley? He couldn't. With this, I have earned my place here. But still, I cannot make myself want a baby, even this one attaching herself to my body over and over, and though I love Paul, I can't tell him. The miracle to make me stay will have to be something else. I dare Paul, I dare God: show me something else.

A WEEK OF secret nursing later, I start to feel worse, not morally, emotionally, but physically. I'm making the bed one morning, and when I bend down to arrange the pillows, I suddenly feel strangely tired, weak, and I get back in the bed I've just made. Soon, my body begins to ache too, and I wonder if it's something to do with breastfeeding Lily. Then I worry that maybe I shouldn't be nursing her at all, that I'm passing on some kind of illness to her, or she's passing along something to me. *She's not right*, I hear Julie whisper. That broken circle. *Anything could get in.*

"You okay?" Paul asks on our way to church. "You look—shiny." He waves a hand around his own face.

"I'm just hot," I say, turning to look out the window. "It's hot outside."

"We can ask Papa to heal you," he suggests.

"I think I'm okay," I say. "But we can if you want me to."

"Only if you want to," he says, and I think I hear disappointment in his voice.

INSIDE THE CHAPEL, Lily of the Valley and I sit behind Erin, the little bride, her new husband next to Paul across the aisle. She's sitting up straight, with her hair over her shoulder, except for one loose strand, which is tangled around a tiny pearl button. I scoot up and touch my hand to her shoulder, to tell her I'm going to unwind the little snare. It's then I notice there are buttons all the way down the back of the dress, from the collar past the waist, like the ticks of centimeters on a ruler.

Erin turns around and smiles at me.

"You have some hair tangled around a button," I tell her. "Let me get it for you."

"It's okay," she says. "It's just going to get tangled again."

"You won't be able to get it yourself," I say.

"I know. But Tyler can fix it later when he helps me change clothes before bed. I think the real solution is just cutting all my hair off." She smiles. "Like yours," she says and turns back around.

On our way home, Paul confides in me that Erin and Tyler have been arguing every day since the wedding. "It's not good to be having problems so early," he says.

"What sort of problems?"

"I don't think she understands how to be a wife," he says. "But she'll learn."

I think about the buttons down her dress, like a line of tiny round teeth, Tyler's fingers undoing them at night, redoing them in the morning.

"Of course she will," I say. In the back of the truck, Lily coos, and Paul smiles at her in the rearview mirror.

LATER THAT NIGHT, after days of feeling on the verge of illness, I teeter across the edge and become fully sick. For days, my throat burns when I eat and drink, but so does my stomach, as if everything inside it is acidic, but it's still hungry, so it's eating up everything, not just food but all my insides too, and whatever is inside me is going to devour everything in me until there is nothing left. I turn away orange juice and homemade lemonade, and so Paul makes me tea instead, hot in the morning and iced in the afternoon, and I drink it all, though it is bitter when it's hot and bland when it's cold. "More sugar?" he suggests, then takes it away and brings it back, sweeter. I eat bread and crackers. I wonder how anyone is a mother when she is sick. I think of Molly Moore, her pallid cheeks, thin wrists. Paul says don't worry about Lily, he's got her. He is always here, and so I cannot nurse her even in secret, and my breasts are demanding attention, filling and filling, relieved only when I can empty them in the bathroom. Lily looks at my chest longingly when Paul gives her a bottle, I think. "I know you're worried, Rosie, but she's protected," he says. "Papa put a shield of health around her. We don't have anything to worry about!"

He strolls her every morning, every evening, and when I watch them leave, I feel angry. My world has shrunk again, tightened.

She spends a lot of time in her swing, in her special chair, on her quilt on the floor of the living room. From this distance, I feel removed and objective, a biologist observing an animal in the wild. Subject reaches for the monkey or the compact mirror; prefers these items to the recently acquired squishy ladybug. Subject likes to put her fingers in her mouth instead of the pacifier offered to her. Subject's head looks perfectly round, no flat spots at all. I feel strangely pleased by this. I want to point it out to Paul, but I'm too tired. I'm also too tired to change her diaper when I know I should. She also shits so much more than she used to. At one point Paul brings her to me, naked, and shows me a rash on her bottom. The skin is red, irritated, rough when I run my finger over it. "You have to change her as soon as she poops," he says.

"I'm sick," I say, and he softens.

"You're right," he says. "I'm sorry." But still he stands in front of me with Lily of the Valley, a bundle of bare flesh, and doesn't move.

"Maybe run a bath for her," I suggest.

"Okay," he says. "Unless you want to?"

I get up from the bed and go to the bathroom, kneel beside the tub, adjust the knobs of the faucet until it's just right. Paul brings her in and places her in her bath chair; such a little girl and so many special places for her to sit.

Even though I'm sick, Paul has me stretch out on the bed or the couch every night and places Lily of the Valley over my uterus. She's growing, lengthening, getting heavier.

I worry that I'm not sick but pregnant; I'm worried that I'm not pregnant but sick. Here, all the options are bad. I try to count back to my last period. Without the calendar to look at, even with its fudged dates, I'm lost. I try to think back to when I had sex with Colin Bell and then with Paul. Not even two weeks ago. It's too soon for me to be pregnant.

One afternoon Amanda brings over homemade chicken soup, but looking at the stringy hunks of meat makes me feel sick, like the insides of something we shouldn't see. She examines Lily's rashy bottom, puts her on the quilt, and goes to our bathroom; I hear her rummaging through drawers until she comes back with a tub of thick lotion I've never liked. "Put this on her next time you change her diaper. But otherwise, she looks really good. Very healthy," Amanda says. She lowers herself to the floor beside Lily's quilt and hands her the squishy ladybug, and Lily frowns. She tries the compact mirror. This Lily accepts.

"Look how round her head is," I say.

"Very nice," she says, leaning over to cup a hand around Lily's skull. Her thumb rubs Lily's dark hair, then touches her forehead.

She tells me something scandalous has happened, and she has to fill me in. "What is it?" I ask. I'm sitting on the couch holding the bowl of soup, my legs tucked up under me, with an empty bucket Paul put on the floor before he left. "In case you need to throw up," he said. I told him I wished I could throw up. "When throwing up is the better option, that's how you know it's bad," he said, and kissed the top of my head.

"Molly left," Amanda says. "In the middle of the night. She took the boys and got out of here."

"Where did she go?"

"I don't know," she says, gesturing to the front door. "Out there." She says it like there are wolves lurking right on the other side of it.

"Do you know where she came from? Before here?"

Amanda frowns, rubs a hand over her swollen stomach. "Hmm," she says. "I do, actually. I think. I'm pretty sure she was a lawyer in Dallas. I think Richard was too."

"No," I say. "A science teacher."

"Huh," Amanda says. "It's weird he didn't know what was wrong with Molly, then."

"Science teacher and doctor are pretty different," I say.

"Both deal with bodies," Amanda says. "But I think the sickness was a punishment from the Lord anyway. Matthew thinks so too." Her eyes widen. "Oh, but not yours," she says. "Sorry. You probably just have a bug."

"Maybe it is a punishment," I say. What do I believe in? This, possibly: a God who punishes me because I haven't punished myself for all the things I keep hidden. I push the chicken around in the bowl, and the pieces bob like little sea creatures. I lean forward and put it on the coffee table and tuck my feet underneath myself again, more tightly this time.

Amanda is quiet for a moment. "What?" I ask her.

"The grocery store," she says. "Have you done something you need to be punished for?"

Franklin Aaron. Before Colin. That was in a different life, I think, but no, I've always been the same person, haven't I? "No," I say. "Old habits. You know."

"Good," she says. "Praise God. He put me right where I needed to be that day." She smiles. "You and Paul were so generous and kind when our house burned. I think I owed you one."

"I am thankful," I say.

"But back to your bug," she says, eyeing the untouched soup. "Maybe you're pregnant."

"I'm not," I tell her, but my stomach clenches.

"Well, let me just say whenever I'm pregnant, meat grosses me out," she says. "It feels like I'm eating my baby. I basically live off of peanut butter and jelly. And you're nauseous and you're tired."

"And my throat hurts," I say.

"So you're pregnant and you have a cold," she says. "That can happen."

In the window behind Amanda, I see a truck drive past,

but it isn't Paul's. "What did Papa Jake say about Molly leaving?" I ask.

"Oh, that's the other scandalous thing," Amanda says. "Papa told us that *Randall* started the fire that killed Richard! Randall wants us to think God would kill a father. Because if God would do such a thing, then surely we wouldn't worship Him, right? And the church would fall apart, and we would leave Dawes. But we know the truth. Papa received a God-thought about it."

"An evil flame," I say. "That's what Paul heard when he slept on Richard's grave."

"Interesting," Amanda says thoughtfully. "Is Lily of the Valley hungry? I'll make her a bottle."

She comes back with it a couple of minutes later, groans a little as she eases herself back to the floor, then scoops Lily up into her lap. Lily smells the milk, her hands searching, grabbing. Amanda slides the nipple into Lily's mouth, and her tiny body relaxes, melts into Amanda's arms.

"Oh," Amanda says, looking up at me again, "Papa Jake also says Molly was in on it. That she was having an affair with Randall and gave him a key so he could get in and start the fire, and she could get the boys out in time."

"No way," I say. But I think of when I touched her in the chapel, how she looked at me, how her skin burned beneath my hand.

"So someone asked if there would be justice for Richard," Amanda continues. "And Papa Jake said she's gone now, separated from the truth, and that's justice served. I can't remember his exact words, something about she'll get what's coming to her."

"Praise God," I say. "But what will happen with her

kids?" I think of them on the last night we mourned Richard, how they reached for their mother with anxious, needy hands but never cried.

"Well," Amanda says tightly, "a bad tree can't bear good fruit, right? I hate to say it, but you know." She shakes her head, casting the thought of the children out of it. Bad fruit. "Anyway," she says, "I think Molly's going to die out there. Get stuck in a burning building or something. God has a funny sense of humor like that."

"What about Randall?" I ask. "Did Papa Jake say he would be punished?"

"Of course. But he didn't say how."

We are both quiet for a minute. "I love the little sucking sound they make when they eat," Amanda says, looking down at Lily of the Valley. "It's so cute."

"Do you ever wonder what happened to Julie?" I ask.

"Yes," she says. "But she's not our problem anymore. She wasn't ever really one of us. She was just pretending. You want to know what I think?" She leans forward conspiratorially. "I think you're meant to be Lily's real mother. It's like everything that happened happened just the way it needed to so that this baby could get a good mom. Plus Julie said all that weird stuff about the baby not belonging to her. Maybe she was right about one thing. Have you received any God-thoughts about it? Any signs?"

"No," I say just as my milk lets down, breasts tingling, embers of warmth beneath my skin.

"If you are pregnant, it'll be like you have twins!" she says. "That would be so cute." Lily has finished the bottle, and Amanda puts it down and hoists the baby up against her shoulder and begins rhythmically patting her back. "But if you're not pregnant, well, maybe this is God's way of giving you a baby after all."

"What about Rob?" I ask. What about me?

"He and Jennifer Bell will have a new baby." She shrugs. "He barely even knows this one. I'm pretty sure Jenn doesn't even want her. No offense, Lily. Wow, she's a slow burper, huh?"

She tries a different position, like a ventriloquist holding a dummy on her knee, and pats Lily's back again. As she adjusts herself, her dress rises to expose two pink ankles. "They get so puffy," she says, seeing me notice them.

"I'm sorry, Amanda," I say, "but I just got so tired all of a sudden. Thank you for coming over."

Lily lets out a loud burp. "Ah!" says Amanda. "Perfect timing. You want her?" She hands her to me before I can answer.

"Rest up," she says. "Can I take this to the kitchen for you?" She points to the bowl of soup on the coffee table. I nod. "I'll put it in the refrigerator so you can heat it up later."

When she comes out, she squeezes my knee with her thin fingers and then pats it. "I'll be back again soon if you're still feeling badly," she says. "Or if you're pregnant and want someone to say 'I told you so.'"

"Thank you again," I say.

She walks to the door, but before she opens it, she pauses and turns around, keeping one hand still on the knob. "Oh, I remembered exactly what Papa said about Molly," she says, her long braid over one shoulder like a bayonet. "He said, 'They'll eat her alive out there, until she's nothing but dry bones in the dirt.' I knew it was something—vivid."

"God bless Papa's word," I say.

"Amen," Amanda says. "See you soon." She opens the door and closes it behind her, stepping out into the world.

I AM ALONE until Paul comes home to make dinner—spaghetti, meatless because I said the ground beef made me think of brains—which he serves to me in the living room. He's brought me a Sprite, a fountain drink he got at the church-owned gas station that sits at the freeway exit, and I crunch the ice between my teeth, though Paul urges me to drink it too. "The carbonation is off, I think," he says. "When I tasted it at the gas station, I thought it wasn't quite right, but I think it might still settle your stomach." I drink it anyway, then eat the spaghetti while Paul watches.

"Amanda says Molly left," I say.

"Yes."

"And that Randall burned down their house."

Paul nods without looking up from his plate of spaghetti. He holds it with one hand and twirls his fork in the noodles until his fork is wrapped completely, the pasta as fat as a fist. "We're worried it's starting again," he says.

"What is?" I ask.

"The persecution."

"A feud," I say. Paul shrugs. "But Randall wanted it to stop. Why would he burn down a house knowing that would start it back up?"

Paul chews, holding a napkin up to his mouth, and rolls his eyes. He swallows, puts down the napkin. "Who understands the ways of wicked men?" he asks. But it doesn't sound like his heart's in it. We are both quiet, and I wonder if he is remembering Randall's visit to our house. He points

276 | ALISON WISDOM

at my spaghetti. "Maybe it would be better to have some toast?"

I make a face.

"Eggs?" he asks. "I'm sorry, Rosie. This is so miserable. Can I pray over your body?"

"Yes," I say. And he stands up, and I can suddenly see a past version of myself, the night of Colin Bell, walking over to me, but when I get back to myself, it is Paul again, and I am gone. I am only this version of me, sitting on the couch with dirty hair, a baby's dried spit-up on my shoulder, tits filling dumbly with milk. He lays me down and kneels on the floor beside the couch. He places one hand on my stomach and the other on my throat. My chin tilts back. He prays for God to heal me, to restore my body, to replace the sickness there with life. I think of dry bones in the dirt.

When he is done, he raises me back up into a sitting position and sits beside me on the couch. "What did Papa Jake say about Molly?" I ask.

"That she was gone," he says. "That she worked with the townspeople to undermine us, and that resulted in the death of her husband. He's a martyr."

"Did he say she would get punished?"

"Ours is a God of justice, Rosie," Paul says.

"What did he say?"

He looks at me. We are so close I can see the pores of his skin, the beginning of lines in the thin skin around his eyes; Paul is still boyish, the kind of lucky man who will always look younger than his wife. I watch as the crease between his eyebrows emerges, giving him that baby hawk look of concern. "That God would judge her," he says. "But Papa wishes her and the boys well."

"Amen," I say. "Any sign of the Bell family today?"

"Nope," he says. "They're gone for now. But Papa thinks they'll be back."

A few minutes later, as Paul washes the dishes, I throw up into the bucket by the couch. "Finally," he says. He sits beside me and rubs my back until my stomach is empty, and my skin is light, and my body trembles. "My angel," he says.

Twenty-Eight

I cannot get well. Paul does not leave my side, except to care for Lily of the Valley and to attend services. He takes her with him when he goes. I eat only what he gives me until I tell him I don't want anything, and when he stops bringing me food, I stop eating. I drink what he gives me, until even that I refuse. He tells me I need at least to have liquids, but I don't want them. When my stomach is empty, I feel better. I lose hours, days. I wonder what happens to the milk my body makes when Lily doesn't nurse, if it just pools under my skin and then circulates through me like blood, the red and the white trapped in a loop together. Maybe this is the end of the milk, a short-lived betrayal like all the others; a brief compulsion I couldn't ignore.

People come by to watch Lily or take her out in the stroller, but at night she's still with Paul and me, her bassinet still on my side of the bed. Sometimes I get up when she cries and give her a bottle. Sometimes when she cries in the night I cannot get up, and those times, I reach over and rock the bassinet or hand her a pacifier or I just wait for her to calm herself. It's a skill, I tell myself, she needs to learn. I think of my mother, and I wish she were here. Then I think maybe she is here, like Jennifer Bell's mother, that she came looking for me and no one told me.

Finally, Paul brings me to a healing service, holding my elbow as I walk in shakily. I see people observing me, and I think of Molly, of her hard white bones on the ground, turned brown by windblown dust, and I wonder if maybe the bones are mine. I no longer believe I could be pregnant. If my body was not a suitable home for a baby before, it certainly isn't now. My insides feel poisonous.

We sit behind Erin and Tyler, with Missy and her family in the row behind us. Missy is nursing a baby hidden beneath a cover; when we sit down, she peels back the fabric, revealing Lily attached to her prodigious tit. "Thank you," Paul says, smiling. I stare. I don't remember when Missy got Lily. Then the baby disappears again beneath the nursing cover, only her bare pink feet visible. I wonder if Missy's milk tastes different than mine. Tess told me once that her husband tasted hers when she was breastfeeding her first baby. "He said it was kind of sweet," she said. "You think I should tell Starbucks?"

"Million-dollar idea," I said.

When Papa asks for the sick to stand, I rise from my seat, and Paul stands with me, his arm around my waist. I am not chosen, but the woman who is throws up onstage, and Papa Jake examines her vomit. With a gloved hand, he picks up something small and hard from the puddle on the floor, holding it up between pinched fingers. Her disease, Papa Jake says, and we all clap. The woman wipes her mouth and cries.

When we adjourn for a break, I ask Paul where Erik is. He cocks his head. "The one who's always sick?" I clarify.

"He died," Paul says. "I told you when it happened, but you must not have heard me. I'm not surprised, you've been so out of it. Yesterday was the third day. You didn't notice I hadn't showered? Andy Harris was picked to lie on his grave."

"Why didn't Papa heal him?" I ask.

"The angels wanted him," Paul says.

I can't concentrate on this, my thoughts too light to stay in my body and my body too weak to reach for them and weigh them down. Amanda comes to sit with us, and her daughter tries to hold my hand, but Amanda takes her hand away, peels each of her fingers off. I wonder suddenly if I am wrong and Amanda is right, if there is a little son or daughter trying to grow in the barren land of my body. If I had a daughter, I wouldn't let her touch me either. Then I think: I do have a daughter. I turn around to look at Missy and Lily, and Amanda says quietly, "She just has a cold."

"Lily?" I ask. "She isn't sick."

"No," says Amanda. "Missy. I thought you heard her cough and were worrying about Lily. But it's okay for someone to nurse even if she's sick. God protects the baby."

"Oh," I say.

Onstage, Papa Jake raises his hands, and we quiet down. Today he preaches about Richard Moore. Erik the Viking is dead too, but his death isn't relevant today. Richard Moore is a martyr, and Papa Jake preaches about his death, as if he only ever existed underground, unbreathing, unmoving. It's like he was born again in his death, into a new form entirely, into whatever Papa Jake has wanted to create. He doesn't have to contend with the reality of the man, only with his new version of it. The best canvas for painting is a blank one.

Oh, and we love the tragedy of it all, the theatrics, the drama. *Look what has been taken from us*, Papa Jake hisses. *A life, a father! We have been betrayed.* Yes, we say. The world wishes to harm us. *The world is everything and everyone who isn't here*, he says. *We can trust no one else.*

We have to fight back, someone calls from the pews. We nod, we agree.

But Papa Jake holds his hands up. *I will tell you when we need to act*, he says. *For now, let the anger you feel draw you closer in here, to each other.* He reaches his arms out, and we reach forward too, then place our arms around one another. *Let yourselves feel*, he says. *Let yourselves grieve. Those children are without their father. They are trapped outside with a demon dressed as a woman.* We weep for ourselves, for what we have lost. We cry for the world, lost itself. The entire chapel is filled with the sound of our grief, our anger, and Papa Jake stands on the stage and watches us. When our wailing turns into something brighter, fuller, we move, our sense of injustice propelling us, our indignation frothing like the sea-foam on the crest of a churning wave.

We make a tunnel again, the way we did the first time I touched Molly, our hands reaching for each other across the aisle. Paul stands across from me and our fingertips meet, shocking me when we touch. But he doesn't flinch, just smiles at me with no teeth. *Are you okay?* he mouths, and I nod. He jerks his head toward the entrance of the tunnel: *Go.* But I don't want to. *Don't you want to be healed?* Paul asks. I do, I do, but I don't want to be touched by Papa Jake. A rope, a boy, a pen of chickens. I pretend I don't notice Paul.

People dance down the aisle, through our tunnel, the tall men ducking and bending to fit beneath. Some men run straight through it and out the doors, like athletes running onto the field, soldiers rushing out into the clash of battle. Amanda runs through with her daughter but stops at the doors. She doubles back and pulls me out, and the tunnel collapses only a little, maybe not even at all, as if I had never been a part of it, holding it up. *Let him touch you*, she says into my ear. *He can heal you.* And for a second I wonder if she means Paul, but as she pulls me down the aisle, I see Papa Jake at the end of the tunnel, the double doors behind him closed tight. Amanda slows as we approach, and she pushes me toward him, into his arms. He holds me fully, arms around my body, the way a father embraces his little child. I keep my arms by my side.

He whispers to me, but I don't understand the words, and can't hear him well because around us everyone has begun to sing, and the lights go off and turn back on, and light falls from the ceiling, distilled into a shower that drenches us, sticks like snow in our hair, to our clothes. Over Papa Jake's shoulder I watch it glisten in the carpet. Suddenly, he pushes me away, like I have shocked him, putting an arm's-length distance between us. *I see*, he says.

See what? I ask. *See what?* There are so many options, so many damaging things he could see. My voice gets louder. I ask him again. But he has let go of me now, and I nearly fall before Amanda puts her arm around my waist, and then Paul is there too. He takes me and carries me out of the chapel like I am his bride, into the parking lot where I squint in the sun, and I am still asking Papa Jake what it is that he sees.

Twenty-Nine

In the morning, I feel better. Not well, but better. I am hungry and thirsty when I wake up, and I hold Lily of the Valley while Paul makes me tea. My arms feel strong again, like there are bones and muscles beneath the skin instead of only heat and air. After I finish the tea, Paul makes me an egg and toast, and I sit at the kitchen table and eat the toast. The egg is over easy, and the yolk is too runny, like a melting sun, and the whites glisten too much, so I leave those. Paul scrapes them into the trash and rubs my back. "I feel okay," I say.

"Thank God," he says.

"Yes, I do."

"I mean, really, though, Rosie," Paul says. "Papa Jake touched you last night, and today you're feeling better. You're being healed!"

I say nothing. "You are," he says. "And there's another healing service today, so Papa Jake is going to work on you again."

"Good," I say.

"It's great," he says. "Hey, I have to run to Papa's real

quick before the service, but I'll be right back, okay? Do you feel okay enough to give Lily a bottle?"

I nod.

"Want me to get it ready for you?" he asks.

"Paul, go! We're fine. I promise."

After he leaves, I carry Lily and her special chair into the bathroom so I can pee. When I wipe, there's blood on the toilet paper, and when I stand up, there's blood in the bowl, a lake of watery red. I roll my eyes—it feels unfair that I have been so sick and yet all this time my internal clock has been ticking away normally. It feels like my system should have had the decency to give me a break. I stick a pad into my underwear, then crumple the wrapping into a tiny ball and stuff it in the bottom of the trash can while Lily watches me skeptically. I scoop her out of her chair and take her to the bedroom, where I lay her on the bed and take off my dress and bra. I sit cross-legged and hold her up to one breast, and she latches on happily, and I feel the milk letting down, not the rush it once was, but something, still. I feel a pulse of disappointment that I am still bound to her after all, while at the same time I marvel at my body following its own set of rules. A miracle. The fact that I am right now both bleeding and nursing, one of those gray stone fountains in a garden, spraying water from multiple points: a fucking miracle.

The front door opens and closes, and I jump, jostling Lily, who snorts but continues to eat. "Rosemary?" Paul calls. "Have you seen my keys?" His voice getting closer as he comes down the hall. I pull Lily off my nipple, and she wails, and I am fumbling for my bra, and Paul is before me in the doorway to our room, staring.

"I think they're on the coffee table," I tell him.

"What are you doing?" he asks.

"Getting dressed." My boobs are out, the dress I was wearing a crumpled pool of fabric atop the comforter.

"You were already dressed," he says, and looks at Lily crying on the bed. "Don't lie to me, Rosemary."

"I'm sorry," I say, am always saying.

"Are you—feeding her?"

"Yes," I say. "I'm sorry I didn't tell you. It felt too, I don't know. Private, I guess."

"Too private," he echoes. "You've been so sick. You shouldn't be doing this."

"Amanda said it's fine," I tell him. "She said Lily won't get sick through my milk."

"Your milk," he says, staring. "Why?"

"God protects the baby."

"No," Paul says, waving a hand at us. "I mean, why? How?"

"A miracle," I say. "We were looking for one, right?" Lily is still crying. "Can I just go ahead and feed her?"

"No!" he says, coming toward us, scooping her off the bed. "I'll make her a bottle." This makes Lily even more upset, and her crying becomes throaty, irate. I hear Paul in the kitchen opening the refrigerator to get the milk, opening the cabinet to get the bottle. I put on my bra and dress and join them in the kitchen, where he's bouncing Lily in his arms, making shushing sounds into her ear. He turns her away from me when I walk in, so her face is hidden, and all I can see is Paul. Every part of his face shows his displeasure.

"I thought you would be happy," I say.

"I don't know, I'm kind of upset," he says. "You've been hiding this from me."

"I know," I say. "I'm sorry. I don't know why. I felt overwhelmed." The timer goes off on the bottle warmer, and I open the lid, hand the bottle to Paul. He sits down at the table, and Lily's mouth is opening, searching as he gets the bottle ready. Watching her desperation makes me feel more tense, more desperate, my boobs filling again uselessly. Never-ending. A miracle.

"Do you want me to stop?" I ask. "I can stop."

"I don't know," he says again. "It seems unnatural."

I think of the miracles Paul has wished for, all the things we've asked God for—every one of them a request for Him to subvert the natural order of things, to give us what shouldn't exist, to allow something to happen that never would. We demand the unnatural. We've traded in our lives for it, we insist upon it. How could Paul be so offended by the unnatural now?

"I'm sorry, I just don't know," he says when I don't answer. "But I don't care what Amanda says, you should not be feeding her when you've been this sick. You've probably infected her already." He looks at her when he says this, as if he's searching for a sign in her eyes that her insides are turning as toxic as mine have, but she continues to eat.

"She's fine!" I say. "I couldn't even feed her the last couple of weeks. You were always around."

"To take care of you!" he says. "You're welcome, by the way."

I roll my eyes. "Come on, Paul. Look. You wanted a

288 | ALISON WISDOM

baby. Now we have one. I'm feeding that baby with my body. I can't explain it. You can't either. But it's a fucking miracle! What more do you want?"

He's shaking his head. "I'm just worried she's sick," he says. "I'm going to ask Papa to heal her too when he works on you today."

"Okay," I say. "She doesn't want any more." I nod toward Lily, who has pulled off the bottle and turned her head away from it.

"I know," Paul snaps, lifting her against his shoulder and patting her back. "Go get ready for the service."

"I am ready."

"Fine," he says, and Lily burps. "What a good girl you are."

WOMEN COME UP to me in the chapel, taking my hand and talking to me in soft, low voices. The men speak with Paul, who pushes a sleeping Lily in the stroller. They commend him for taking care of both of us. Such lucky girls, they say. Paul and I smile at each other, an act. "Papa touched Rosemary yesterday," he says, "and already she's feeling better. Just a little more, and I think she'll be good to go. But Lily of the Valley seems to be coming down with it now." The women cluck and gaze down sympathetically at Lily, sleeping with her fingers in her mouth. They lead us to the front row of the church, where we sit on the opposite side of the aisle from the strangers who have come for healing, with Lily's stroller in the aisle. I think of Molly, how we used to gather around her too; we could hold her in the palm of our hands and close our fingers around her, trapping her body, snapping her frail bones. We should have held her tighter until she couldn't breathe at all, because now she is gone, a demon dressed as a woman, taking lives with her—her husband's life out of this world, her children's lives into another. Now it is me that we hold. And Lily.

Papa Jake lifts his hands, and we do our job. We call to God. "He's here," Renee says. "Here is He!"

I see nothing. I don't care.

"First things first," Papa Jake says, beaming. "There will be no more attacks on our family from here on out. Randall is gone. There is no one left to command our enemy. Finally, we are safe!" We all cheer. Thank you, Lord! I look at Paul, who nods.

"Papa went to speak with him yesterday, but he was gone," he whispers. "He just up and left. Too scared to face the music."

"God will judge him," says Papa Jake from the stage. "If He hasn't already."

"Randall didn't have anything to do with Richard Moore," I say quietly.

"Why are you defending him?" Paul asks, sounding angry still.

Up front, Papa Jake has paused to allow his people a moment to clap and whistle, to revel in the expulsion of an enemy. If this has really been a war, as Paul says, then we have won. We've survived. I listen for the relief and joy and hope that must be in their cheering, try to feel it myself, but instead everything feels as hollow as I do.

"Let's move on," says Papa Jake, holding his hands up. "Let's see what the Lord has for us today."

"I'm not defending anyone," I whisper. "No one just disappears."

"Some people do," says Paul.

"Rosemary," Papa Jake calls. I snap to attention with the same hot feeling of shame I remember from school, being reprimanded by the teacher for not listening, for talking while she was trying, just trying, to teach us. "Sister," he says, his eyes finding me. "I saw you stand yesterday. It's your turn now. Can you make it up here?"

"Papa," Paul says as I rise from my seat. "Lily of the Valley is sick too. Should I bring her up?"

"Rosemary first," says Papa Jake, studying me. I want to know what he sees. "I'll come down for Lily myself."

I walk up the steps and stand next to Papa Jake. "Are you ready?" he says to me. "This is going to change your life."

The last time I stood on this stage was when I put my head in the barrel. In that darkness, my life changed the first time. I changed. I look out to the people in the pews, to the family Paul and I chose, and they are watching me so expectantly; I see the hope I was listening for a moment ago, in their eyes on Papa Jake and on me, in the stillness of their bodies. I wonder what will come out of my body. I want to see it, and I am frustrated with myself for wanting it. I want to hold it with my hands. A miracle.

"What did you see?" I whisper.

"I'm about to tell you," he says in a low voice. "I'm about to tell everyone."

I LOOK AT my feet in their white canvas tennis shoes, dingy from years of Texas dust. The carpet on the stage is different than the carpet in the rest of the chapel. I don't know why they didn't pull it all up and replace it, but the carpet here where I stand is plusher and emerald green. Up here it is richer, more fertile, a breeding ground for miracles. The carpet below is flat and hard, the color of rust. "Look up," Papa Jake says, and I feel his hand on my chin, tilting my head back. He moves that hand to my throat and puts his other on my stomach, the same places Paul touched the other night when he prayed for me. I groan softly when he touches my bloated midsection, though his touch is light. "Oh, sister," he says finally, speaking loudly enough for everyone to hear him. "I cannot heal you."

We gasp. We have never heard Papa Jake admit defeat. I want to look at Paul, but I can't because Papa Jake's hand is still on my throat, and now he squeezes just a bit, a barely perceptible tightening, just a reflex. "How can I heal you," he says, "when there is nothing wrong?"

I try to look at him, but his hand is in the way, pushing my head back so I can only see the ceiling. There is a crack in it.

"You're pregnant," he says. He takes his hand away from my throat, and my hands fly to it, instinctively checking for damage. Of course, there is nothing there. Now both of his hands are on my stomach, pressing like he is waiting for a little thing inside me to answer, to respond to him when he presses, just as the rest of us have always done.

I look out to Paul, and he is shaking his head, shocked. For a moment I wonder why he isn't happy, rejoicing in the news, and then I remember my period, my body losing blood even now, and it doesn't matter how he reacts. Around him, men are clapping him on the back, and Brother Lou embraces him. I think of Colin Bell. It didn't count, I think. If he was the boy from the listing wooden house, it didn't count because it had happened before, everything was the same as before. A zero-sum game. It still is—I know there is nothing inside me, zero, less than nothing. Everyone is clapping, and Papa Jake is calling Paul up, and then he is beside me, Lily still in her stroller in the aisle. Every part of me goes light, and I am almost gone from here, and then I am. I leave them to address the problem of my body and everything they think is inside of it.

Thirty

I wake up on a little couch in Papa Jake's office at the back of the chapel to see Paul's face hovering over mine as he kneels on the floor beside it. When he sees my eyes open, he gently rests his head against my stomach. He looks up again first at me and then to the ceiling, and he thanks the Lord. "You're pregnant," he says.

"No," I say. I think suddenly of Amanda watching me poke at the chicken soup she'd brought. She must be remembering it too, feeling excited and vindicated—everyone loves to be right. She isn't right, but I'm the only one who knows that.

"I can't believe it," Paul says. "None of this is what I expected." He takes my hands, and I sit up so that I am leaning against a throw pillow. Something scratches me, and I turn around and see a tag still on the pillow, the little loop of plastic attaching it to the fabric. I rip it off, then fold the tag in half and in half again, and stick it in between the couch cushions. Paul watches me but says nothing. My abdomen clenches, and I'm not sure if it's the remains of my illness, cramps from my period, or dread. If I tell Paul I'm on my period, I run the risk that he'll check the calendar and see that the dates didn't line up. I would be caught, finally. But to let him think I'm pregnant seems cruel.

"Where's Lily?" I ask.

"With Amanda," he says. "Or Missy? Or maybe Caroline. I don't know. Everything was kind of a blur." He hands me a water bottle from the mini fridge by Papa Jake's desk. I twist the top open and take a drink, the water cold and bright. "So I guess when you were sick, it was probably just morning sickness," he says.

"That seemed too intense to be morning sickness," I say.

He shakes his head. "Richard told me it could last all day and be really awful. Apparently some women just throw up all the time."

"Richard?"

"Moore," Paul says without looking at me. He reaches into the split between the cushions where I put the tag, and he fishes it out and unfolds it.

"I know," I say, "but why were you talking about it with Richard?"

"Well, you know how Molly was always so sick? At first they thought it was just morning sickness. I guess she missed her period often. So he mentioned it then, and I've just always remembered it."

"Oh," I say. Molly and her bones in the dirt outside, Richard and his in the dirt here, with so much to say. Now at least I think we will never hear anything from either of them again.

"Or," says Paul, but he stops. He stands and tosses the

tag into a trash can next to Papa Jake's desk. "Never mind. I'm just in shock."

"It is shocking," I say. Maybe I could pretend to be pregnant for a month, and when my period comes next, I could say I was miscarrying. Though this idea comes with its own set of problems, it seems manageable.

"A miracle," says Paul. He kneels beside me again and takes my hands, and I think of a deep Texas sky, still and empty and vast, limitless, when he asked me to marry him. "This is it. Do you see it?" His eyes are bright, and his hands can't keep still, brushing a piece of hair behind my ear. "You're doing so much better already. You're just going to get better from here too, I know it. Papa healed you!"

"But you thought I wasn't sick," I say. "You said it was morning sickness."

"I think it was both things," Paul says, placing his hands on my knees. "I think you were sick, and I think you're pregnant. I think Papa Jake healed you, and God blessed you—us—with a child, and it's both things. Don't you see it? The miracle, Rosie!"

"But the fact that I am somehow making milk for Lily," I say. "That wasn't a miracle?"

He closes his eyes for a second. "It is," he says. "Okay? It is. It just isn't the kind I was looking for."

"Understandably," I say, and Paul laughs.

"It's incredible, isn't it? Everything that's happened to us here? I know you can see now, Rosemary. Right?"

I think of what I have seen. Flames and gray tumors in a jar. Specks and showers of light and glory and the gifts of angels, leaving pieces of themselves behind so that we might believe, an offering from their own beings, a sacrifice. Sustenance created from nothing. But also a girl's hair wrapped around a button on her dress and shoelaces wrapped around tiny ankles, tiny wrists, rubbed raw, throat raw too, worn from crying. Flames. A man—again—who was not my husband. And for what? So that I could weigh myself down, keep myself on the ground, in my body. Our bodies are big, dumb animals—oxen or cows, something to work, something to slaughter. What good has my body done for me? Who gave you your legs? Amanda's husband asked that night we stood on the street in the dark, watching their house burn down, a pyre for all the things they thought they loved, what they thought was theirs. Who put the breath in your lungs?

"I see," I say.

Paul closes his eyes and rests his head in my lap, and I stroke his hair, which is thick and straight and shiny, even though he only uses cheap shampoo. "Oh, Rosie," he says. He lifts his head again and rubs at his eyes, which are full of tears. "Okay," he says, standing up and rolling his shoulders back. "I'm going to go back in there. You just come out when you're ready. Okay?"

"Okay," I tell him.

"I hope the baby is okay in there," he says from the doorway. "I really thought you couldn't be pregnant. I thought you were just on your period, and then it would be at least a month until we could try again."

We have both lost track of my lies, lost track of what my body has done. What *we've* done, my body says. What we've done? We've done what we had to.

"I'm sorry, Rosie," he says.

"Paul," I say. "It's okay."

"Thank you," he says. "I love you." He opens and closes the door before I can tell him I love him too, and I realize that I don't know why he was apologizing, I don't know what I forgave him for.

Thirty-One

Paul, Lily, and I go home quietly, silent inside the truck. I look out the window; in the back seat, Lily clutches the squishy ladybug, whose beaded antennae rattle against each other with each bump in the road, and Paul drums his fingers along the curve of the steering wheel. His body is all energy, and I think of his hands in Papa Jake's office, grabbing at anything he could touch—this, of course, a feeling I understand. I could do something to help him, to reassure him, but I don't feel like it.

"How do you feel?" he asks finally.

"The same," I say. "Like puking."

"Do you want me to pull over?" he asks, slowing down.

"Nope."

"Morning sickness," he says, though it's the late afternoon now, and I say nothing. We pass the skeleton of the Wilders' house, a monument to the power of our God. I think of Paul's dream about Lily of the Valley, the tiny girl who felled a castle, all of Paul's dreams, the dread of them all.

"Were there any fires when I was sick?" I ask as we turn into the driveway.

Paul glances over at me in surprise. "No," he says. "Why?"

"I just wonder if they're over now," I say.

He frowns and shrugs. "Who knows the mind of the Lord?"

"Papa," I say. "And you. A bunch of other people."

"You know what I mean."

Paul carries Lily into the house in her car seat, and I follow behind. He turns the lights on and lifts her out of her seat and onto her quilt. He watches her, hands on his hips, as she finds her toes, then glances at his watch. "Does she need to eat?" he asks.

"Yes," I say. "Do you want me to breastfeed her? Or make a bottle?"

"Bottle," says Paul. "No more breastfeeding until you're better. I know what Amanda said, but better safe than sorry. I'll get the bottle and a clean diaper. You lie down."

I stretch out on the couch, my throw-up bucket still next to me, and close my eyes. I need to change my pad, since the lumpy one in my underwear is soaked through, but I don't want to get up.

"Shit," Paul calls from the other room. "Are we out of diapers?"

"I don't know," I say, eyes still closed.

"We are," he says, sighing. I hear him get closer and open my eyes to see him standing over me. He hands me the bottle. "I'll go get some. Will you and Lily be okay?"

I sit up. "We'll be fine," I say. But suddenly my stomach

churns, and I throw up into the bucket, my throat burning as everything comes up again. Between the blood and the milk and the vomit, there will be nothing left in me but bone.

"Maybe I shouldn't go," Paul says.

I shake my head. "Paul," I say. "It's fine. Morning sickness, right?"

"Right," he says. "Of course you're right."

WHEN LILY FINISHES her bottle, I carry her into the kitchen and put the bottle in the sink. As I do, I hear a buzzing sound from the table and turn around—Paul's left his phone there. I put Lily in the swing and turn the mobile on and turn my attention toward the phone.

Two new messages, the screen tells me. I slide the button to unlock it and open the messages app. There are only a few, since Paul has always been an avid text message deleter, and I scroll through the log: Brother Lou texting a group about a healing service, a recent back-and-forth between Paul and Papa Jake, none of it interesting—plans for a prayer meeting, plans for breakfast, a picture of a broken baseboard in Papa Jake's house that I know Paul helped him mend. There's a thread of messages from Brother Lou alone, only dates with no other text, going all the way back to early spring. Of course Lou's texts would be utterly bland, void of personality. Paul responded to all of these messages with only a thumbs-up.

The last text is a single message, no response from Paul, sent by Richard Moore, and dated two months ago. I open the text. It says: *begin with 3 tbsp, increase by 1 tbsp every two days, watch for vomiting. Split up into smaller doses*

if needed, administer throughout the day. Scale down by 1
tbsp as needed and start over from there. Mix with liquids.

I stare at the gray bubble. Was Paul sick? I open Paul's notes app, where there is only one note.

It is a list of dates, beginning about three weeks ago, the day of Erin and Tyler's wedding, and beside each date is a measurement. The first one is three tablespoons. The next date is two days after the first one—one tablespoon. It goes on. Two days later, one more tablespoon. The last entry is dated a few days ago. The measurement beside it is ten tablespoons.

I stand up and go into the kitchen, put the phone back where I found it. I pull out the ring of plastic measuring spoons, and look at the tablespoon. I imagine ten of them in a line on the counter. I go back to Brother Lou's messages to Paul, check the dates there to see if any of them match up, but they don't.

I open the phone calendar and look at the dates. Three weeks ago. What was happening then? Today I started my period. I finished my last period before I was sick—when? The day before I fucked Colin in the handicapped bathroom at Erin and Tyler's wedding; it was over by then, but just barely. So that was thirty days ago, give or take. What has happened since then? My blessed miracle tits started making milk. And I got sick. I look at the measuring spoons again. In the living room, the mobile's music has stopped, and the silence is punctuated only by the rhythmic groan of the swing as it moves back and forth.

I go into our bathroom and look in the drawers—there isn't much, since we don't have any medicine and Paul is so meticulous that he could never tolerate a crowded drawer—

searching for anything that might hold some kind of liquid, or even a powder. But this would be a stupid place to hide something. I rifle through his side of the dresser, I check under the bed, I stick my hand under the mattress and feel around. I go to the bathroom again and put on a new pad, and I take the old one to the kitchen and shove it down to the very bottom of the trash can.

I check the refrigerator, which is full of casseroles people have brought Paul since I've been sick. I open the cabinets and reach behind the stack of plates, the bowls. I stick my hand in each cup, open every piece of Tupperware. In the pantry, I shake a box of rice, a box of pasta. I examine the rows of the spice rack. There is one jar, in the back, without a label. It's a regular clear plastic container, and I lift it up from its corner and unscrew the red plastic top. I stick my finger into the whitish powder—it's fine, soft, like baking soda, and smells like nothing. I replace it and go into the living room where Lily swings. I sit in front of the swing and watch her be rocked back and forth.

I think about Paul's phone, the secrets he's hidden in it—the strange dates, the measurements. Then I think about the white powder in the spice rack. My brain ticks away, processing it all. In gymnastics, when we were first starting out, we learned all our skills piece by piece, tiny movement by tiny movement. First, we learned to point our toes and tighten our bellies. We would stand in place for twenty minutes lifting one leg at a time, our toes curled and our knees locked straight, over and over. After our coach taught us how to lift our perfect, lovely little legs, we learned to propel ourselves into cartwheels, into hand- stands, until we could do them without looking, landing on a line drawn in chalk on the floor. Then he put us on the beam where we sprung and flipped on its narrow surface. By then even the smallest flick of our muscles made sense to us. We memorized the single movements one by one until we could put them all together to make something bigger, more cohesive. All the small things added up to something big.

The front door opens, and there is Paul, holding a box of diapers under his arm. Paul, my husband. Paul, who still has a photo of a newborn horse he saw years ago. Paul, who once, uncomplaining, drove two hours to change a tire by the side of the road for my sister. Paul, who cries when babies are born. Paul, who showed me how to use chopsticks the first time we ate sushi together, who won the Houston Rodeo junior art show when he was ten for his painting of a little boy milking a cow, who always gave me the better seat when we went to restaurants, the one by the window, the one with the nice view. Paul, who loved me and asked me to marry him under a sprawling oak tree, the Texas sunset behind us the color of blood and wine. Sometimes when I look at him, I don't see Paul at all. Not a person but a jumble of memories in the shape of a man. When he looks at me, what does he see? A basket, a vase, an egg, a rope, a castle, a canyon. A pair of scissors, a frozen lake.

"How are you feeling?" he asks, brow furrowed in concern.

"Fine," I say. "A little better."

"Poor Rosie," he says, putting the diapers on the coffee table. He reaches a hand toward me, helps pull me up, and leads me to the couch. "I'll change her for you," he says. "Okay?"

"Okay. Hey, by the way, you left your phone here," I say. "I heard it buzzing in the kitchen."

"Oh yeah," he says, heading that way. "Thanks." A moment later, I hear him on the phone, but I can't tell with who. I listen. "Sorry, man," he's saying. "I forgot my phone when I went to the store. Is she okay now?" Nothing, and then: "Shit, okay. So everyone is heading over there now?" Listening. "Okay, yeah, we'll leave now. Can I bring y'all anything?" Lily squawks in her swing. "See you soon, man."

I go into the kitchen, where Paul is tapping away at his phone. "What's up?" I ask.

"That was Matthew," he says. "Amanda's water broke, but she's not due for, like, two more months. He called Papa, but couldn't get him, so he texted me. Anyway, we're all going to go over there and get things started."

"Oh no," I say. Paul opens his mouth to say something, but his gaze snags on the measuring spoons on the counter, the drawer still slightly open, and he looks up at me.

"Planning on cooking?" he asks. His voice is careful.

"Actually," I say. "I was going to make Amanda some cookies now that I feel a little better. To say thank you for the soup and the company." I walk over to the pantry and pull out the unmarked jar with the powder. I feel certain that when I look at my hand holding the jar, it will be shaking, but then I look, and it's not, even though my body feels quivery, loose. I turn to Paul. "But we're out of baking soda," I say. "And I wondered if this was baking soda?" I hold it out, and he stares at it. "Earth to Paul," I say, laughing. "Did you hear me? I don't remember buying it, but I thought maybe you did, while I was sick."

Paul hesitates and looks up from the jar to me. His dark

eyes are big and panicked, but then something inside him
resets. It's almost like he's shrugged the fear off like an un-
wanted jacket, and he's cooler, lighter now. He takes the
jar from me, holds it up and examines it. He takes off the
lid and sniffs the powder inside. He shrugs and puts it on
the counter.

"I don't know what it is," he says. "But let's just get a
new one at the store anyway." He claps his hands together.
"Okay," he says. "Can you be ready in, like, five or so? Do
you feel up to going? It would be good if you could."

"I think so," I say, though my insides feel heated and
sick; I am near febrile with anger. Paul is a liar. Paul is bad.
Paul is worse than me. In some ways, this is a relief, a welcome change.

"I love you," Paul says, watching me.

I walk over to him and kiss him with my poisonous
mouth. "I love you too," I say.

Thirty-Two

In the truck, I look out the window, and I hate everything we pass by: the burned house of Amanda and Matthew, the dead tree on the corner of the street that looks like a skeleton, the cemetery with its wrought-iron gate. So few years on the earth, never enough time, and I've spent too many of them here. I'm not pregnant, so I was only sick, and when I felt like I was dying, maybe I was. Maybe I could have died here, in this stupid, ugly town.

In her car seat, Lily of the Valley moans, the early stage of her tired cry. I twist around and pick up her ladybug and shake it in front of her face. She cries but then finds her fingers and sucks on them. I wait for my milk to let down at the sound of her sucking, but it doesn't. Beside me, Paul drives with both hands on the steering wheel, and he glances over at me again and again. "What?" I ask when I face forward again.

"Are you mad?" he asks.

"Yes," I say.

"At me?" He doesn't look at me as he asks, but I watch

him, and he grips the steering wheel tightly, every finger curled around it.

"I need to tell you something," I say.

"Okay," says Paul, his fingers loosening only so they can tighten again.

"I fucked Colin Bell," I tell him. "Twice."

He doesn't answer, but he pulls over. We're close to Amanda's new house, on a residential street, and a mailbox is right outside my window. I could roll the window down and slide a letter in if I wanted. "Jennifer Bell's brother," I say.

"Yeah," says Paul. He rubs his face with both hands, and then he puts them on the steering wheel again. "Fuck," he says without looking at me. "Okay. When?"

"A month ago," I say. "Just about. It's been hard for me to keep track of time these days."

"Goddammit, Rosie," Paul says. He slaps the steering wheel, but I don't even flinch. If there was a wall here, he'd punch it. He'd thrust a fist through the window if he could. I understand, I do—sometimes it feels good to break something. Maybe that's why I've done all the things I've done. They've felt good, haven't they? He turns now to look at me, his face reddening, every muscle in it clenched. But then he takes a deep breath. "I'm so fucking mad. I believed you, I trusted you about everything. But you're a liar." Now he sounds more sad and tired than angry. Maybe he really did trust me after all, I think, but this thought isn't enough to touch me.

"Yes," I say. "Sorry."

"Richard told me you were lying," he says, "said that I

should take away your calendar and check the trash to see if you were really on your period when you said you were, but I thought no, that's crazy, I would never do that."

I say nothing.

"But then I did, Rosemary," he says. "I figured out that you were lying about all that, and I knew you were unhappy and overwhelmed with Lily and no matter what you claim, I know you don't believe in anything anymore, and I panicked. So I made my own calendar. Did you know that?"

"No," I say.

"I mean, I just had to guess," Paul says. "It wasn't perfect. But I wasn't even mad. Really, I wasn't. I just thought okay, she's always had problems, I knew your faith wasn't perfect, but then I thought if I could prove it to you that all this is real, then you would come around, and we could have a baby, and things would be good." He shifts the car out of park and pulls away from the curb.

"Where are we going?" I ask.

"To Amanda and Matthew's," Paul says. "There's a baby being born, and we need to be there. I just can't believe this." He sighs, but I can hear in his voice that he's gearing himself up to be normal, getting into character. Good, honest Paul.

"I'm sorry," I say. We pass by a local woman outside her house, dragging a sprinkler to the middle of her yard. She looks up as we drive past, and we make eye contact. I lift my hand just a little. She smiles at me, and suddenly I want to cry.

"Actually, you know what? I can believe it," he says. I look away from the woman in her yard. "I should have known. The baby isn't even mine, is it? It's Colin's, isn't it?"

I want him to hurt. "I don't know," I say.

"It can't be mine," Paul says. "I was so careful. That's why—fuck. Forget it."

I don't answer, turning away from him to look back out the window. Everyone's lawns are already yellowing in the heat, and the worst is yet to come. "That's why what, Paul?" I ask.

"Nothing," he says. "Leave it alone."

Lily is quiet, the transition from awake to asleep so abrupt, it's almost laughable. Paul and I are quiet too, and I'm thinking about the texts, the note. *Richard says morning sickness can be pretty bad.* "Was Richard poisoning Molly?" I ask.

Paul looks at me and then back at the street. He slows for the stop sign but rolls through it and takes a right. The cul-de-sac of Victorians is right in front of us. Everyone is already congregating outside Amanda and Matthew's house, and Brother Lou is trying to organize everyone into a line that will wrap around it. Some people are already holding hands. "Paul," I say.

"I don't know," he says. "Surely not." I nod, but I feel the way I did all those years ago in the gym, when suddenly every small movement made sense, and I could put it all together. The bigger picture coming into focus. Lift the leg, and tumble.

"Paul," I say again. "Did Richard give you something to give me? Something that would make me sick? Is that what your calendar was for? So you could be sure I wasn't pregnant before you poisoned me?"

We park at the end of a long line of cars parked along the street. He turns off the truck and looks at me. Again, he is crying or nearly so. Gentle Paul, soft Paul. I am angry. I wonder if he thinks his tears can douse my anger, put out its flames. I keep my face still; I've had so much practice here. "Yes," he says. "I thought if you were healed, you'd believe in miracles again."

"I never believed in miracles," I say, but even after all of this, I'm not sure if it is true—that I never believed in them at all or I almost did or I wanted to very badly. Paul winces.

"I'm sorry, Rosemary," he says. "I'm so sorry. I thought I could fix things. That's why I was shocked about the baby. I would never have—done anything—if I'd known you could be pregnant. I love you! I do. I was doing this for you because I love you. I would never hurt you."

"But you did!" I say. "You poisoned me. And you could have poisoned Lily and any baby inside me too."

"No," says Paul, holding up his hands. "That's not what I'd call it. I prayed about it, and I felt like God had given me a clear answer, to go ahead. All those visions I had about you dying in a fire, all those dreams I had—they stopped when I started—when you started getting sick." He pauses. "Besides, if you had told me right away about the breastfeeding, I would have stopped. But you didn't. How could I have known?"

"Oh my God, Paul," I say. "This isn't my fault."

"It's not not your fault." He sighs. "Look," he says, putting a hand on my leg. It looks like a slab of meat, and I am repulsed. "Look. Sometimes the Kingdom of God requires you to do things you don't want to do. Things that maybe look bad to people who don't really understand the way we live. What's the saying? You can't make an omelet without breaking some eggs."

"So I'm the omelet," I say.

"I think you're the egg," he says.

"Right," I say.

"I think we can get past this," he says. "Don't you? We've both done bad things—you cheated on me. Again! But I can forgive you. I've done it before. Can you forgive me? I'll be responsible for the baby, even if it isn't biologically mine. God has blessed us with this baby, Rosemary. He won't punish the baby for our mistakes, I know it." He grins suddenly, a little bashfully. "Do you want to hear something amazing?"

"Yes," I say.

"Papa says it's a boy," he says. "We're going to have a son."

"Wow," I say, bleeding into the thick pad in my underwear. "You're right. That is amazing."

"Let's take a deep breath and go, okay?" he asks. "Together?"

"Together," I echo.

He undoes his seat belt and reaches for the door, ready for this conversation to be over, ready to get out of the truck—all the energy in his body directed outside of this small area. But I don't move and don't move, and finally he leans back in his seat again. He runs a hand through his hair, and it all falls back into place.

I look out at the people of our church in front of Amanda and Matthew's house. Lou has arranged them now in the circle that snakes around the house. The men must be in the backyard because I can't see any of them; the front yard is only women. This is the first time since I've been here that I haven't been a part of that body of women, and I am amazed by what they look like in their long dresses, only their backs and profiles visible. I recognize some by the colors and patterns of dresses they always wear, by their hair, by the way they stand. If one of them were here in this truck with Paul instead of me, she would recognize me too. There's Rosemary, she'd think, her short hair, the blue dress, how still she always stands, never moving, a statue, a vase, a perfect white egg. Night is falling, and the women glow in the dying light, bright like angels.

"That baby is going to die," I say.

"Don't say that," says Paul.

I imagine Amanda laboring inside her new home, Abigail downstairs, worrying about her mother. Gabriel tight and seething, keeping his eyes opened even while they are telling him to pray, pray. Troy with his own eyes squeezed shut. Amanda's body doing something it has done before, three times, but this time is not the same, though her body doesn't know. I can see it, Amanda pushing and straining in her bed. I can imagine it. I don't know.

"Come on," I say, and we get out of the truck. I go to the back and wrap the fabric of the carrier around myself, lift Lily out of the car seat and slip her into the folds of the fabric and secure her to my chest. I walk toward the house, expecting Paul to follow, but I don't hear him. I turn around. He's still standing where I left him, his hands in his pockets. The limbs of an oak tree hang over his head, its old roots pushing up against the sidewalk, cracking it in places. He kicks at the broken ridge of pavement. Around us the light is graying, the color of a tombstone.

"I'm so sorry, Rosemary," Paul says, looking up at me

and lifting his arms like he wants me to run into them. "Do you remember when we got lost in Big Bend?"

"We almost died," I say. I take a step toward him and then stop.

"Yes," says Paul, nodding. He sounds desperate and eager, seems relieved that perhaps I'm listening. "I didn't want to tell you that then. But all I could think about was how many things could have happened to us. A fall. A snakebite. We could've never found water. And I was so scared, but I didn't want to tell you. But it made me realize how fragile everything was, and when we got back to our car and then to the motel, I couldn't sleep because every time I closed my eyes, I saw you dead. Remember how scratched up your legs were? I kept seeing you with those scratches, but they weren't just on your legs. They were all over your body."

"Why are you telling me this now?" I ask. A burst of laughter comes from Amanda's yard. We both glance over, but when I look back at Paul, his eyes are already locked onto me again, like he never looked away.

"Because I would have done anything to make sure you were safe," he says. "I would have killed someone. I imagined it—I even came up with this one particular scenario where we found someone, some innocent man who had water, and I killed him so we could take it. And I imagined you thanking me. You understood, and I think I replayed it so many times in my head, the worst thing that could happen, that I started to think that you would do anything too, you would do what had to be done. You came to Dawes—you knew it had to be done, and you did it, and I thought that's it, she's doing what needs to happen. Destroying an entire life and rebuilding it. I just thought you would understand."

"After," I tell him. I am reeling. Paul reaches for my hand, and I let him take it. His skin is warm and dry, his fingers tight at first and then loosening, and I wonder if he knows I'm not actually pregnant, if he's already thinking of how, someday, he will let me go. "We'll talk about this after."

"Okay," he says. We walk toward the house. The dark is new still but full now, and the women glow even more brightly. Paul sees it too, the loveliness.

"Do you really think the baby will die?" he asks.

"Paul," I say. "The baby's not due for two more months. She needs to go to the hospital."

"God will protect her," he says. "Papa will protect her." I want to know who God chooses to protect, who Papa chooses, and why. It isn't me they choose, but then I hear Paul's voice saying, It is you, Rosemary; after everything, you're still here. Why do you think that is?

I walk over to the women and join the circle, putting a hand on the wrist of either woman beside me, and they part to make room for me. They smile at Lily of the Valley. On my left is Sandy from the diner, breathing heavily and rhythmically with her eyes closed. Erin, on my right, is still and quiet. I am facing Papa Jake's house. It is a beautiful house. Last year, Paul and a few other men painted it blue, the pale color of a duck egg. "The color of heaven," Papa Jake said. "It's a boy's color," Paul told me Jake's daughter, Ruth, said. "I wanted it pink." She is in the circle now, no bow in her hair this time, and it hangs down on either side of her face, wavy and bright like the silky ears of a spaniel. She stands beside Caroline, their fingers intertwined.

Caroline steps forward suddenly, leaving a gap that closes quickly as Missy reaches for Ruth's hand, and Caroline is in the middle of the circle, the pupil of an eye, and then she is in front of me. "I'll take her," she says, nodding at Lily of the Valley. "Just for now, okay?"

I have spent two years watching Caroline, as bright and cold as a mirror. But now when I look at her, I think of when she sang to Julie while she picked the glass from her friend's hair; I think of her Instagram page, her insecurities arranged so artfully, bite-sized pieces of her strange life offered for others to consume. *See?* she says as she holds them out to her old friends and classmates, to strangers. *It isn't bad, is it?*

"Just for now?" I repeat, and she nods and reaches out. I loosen the wrap from my body, revealing the little bundle of Lily, and Caroline unwinds the fabric, and it feels oddly intimate, like she is undressing me. Then she takes the carrier and, so much more quickly than I have ever been able to manage, wraps it around herself. I let her take Lily, who disappears within its folds, only the top of her dark little head sticking out. I touch it, her soft hair.

"Thank you," I say, and Caroline nods.

I turn and see Paul, who is walking up to the house. He touches my back as he passes and cuts the circle in half, goes up the front steps and inside. He shuts the door behind him, pulling it closed so carefully there is no sound. We stand still in silence for a few more minutes until Renee says into the dark, "Listen! Look! Here He comes! He turns the night to day! He brings the dead to life! He takes the ash and the dirt and the dry bones and builds His kingdom upon it!" Around the circle, women shield their eyes—a bright light descending. To me, there is only dark, one streetlight on and open like an eye. "The baby is here," Renee calls out. "Wait and see."

Brother Lou comes out then and tells us the baby is here, breathing and crying and very, very small. Another boy. Heart beating, skin pale but warm. See, says Renee. The Lord has shown me. I am a messenger!

We applaud, though not for Renee, but for a new life, for the miracles here, until Sandy, who now sits on the ground, cries out and points next door.

Papa Jake's house is on fire. The fire is a living thing, a hungry thing, and we all turn to face it, like it has called us each by name. The darkness has turned the pale blue house to gray, a building made of shadow, and the light of the fire fights the darkness. We cannot look away from the light.

In front of it, I see the shapes of Caroline, Lily held fast to her body, and her daughter, still holding hands. They do not speak or move. The front door of Amanda's house slams, and there are footsteps down the stairs, fast and frantic. I look to see Papa Jake. "What's happening?" he asks, his voice loud and sharp, and we do not answer. Our circle is still intact, though loose and no longer linked, and I think of Julie. *Those gaps. What if something got in?*

"A holy fire," says Renee. The circle of women disperses, and now we are all separate, our own islands in the sea.

Caroline turns to Jake, her eyes wide, pretty mouth parted. "We have to let it burn," she says. "How did this happen?" He goes to her, puts his hand on her back, an arm around Ruth's shoulders, his girls made of gold.

"I know," he says. "What else can we do?"

"Nothing," she says. I watch her rub Lily's back.

The fire is on the roof, the fire is visible through the windows, the fire is everywhere—a dragon, a serpent, a spirit. The men have come from the house and the backyard, and I see Matthew, Amanda's husband, and Paul too, coming down the steps and squinting at the light. *What the fuck?* I see him asking Brother Lou, who stands on the bottom step, as though the house is a boat, and the yard is an ocean drowning the rest of us. Who did this? Paul asks.

No idea, Lou says.

What do we do? Paul asks.

Nothing, Lou says, shrugging. It's just a coincidence.

An evil flame, I hear Paul saying in my head, a memory of another unexpected fire, how devastated and confused Paul had been when Richard Moore died. He had known about the other fires, had dreamed about them before they happened. But not that one and not this one. These were unforeseen.

There was a fire last night, Paul said, sitting on the edge of my bed, up for hours before me.

It's not here, Paul said when he found me at the window the night Amanda's house burned down.

I do so much for Papa, Paul said. *Even when I don't want to.*

I watch the fire devouring Papa Jake's house. Of course they have to let it burn. They will have to pretend that this was a holy fire like the others. I can already see how Papa will spin it. He will be perfect: he will be humble without his beautiful house but proud that God selected him for such a trial; he will miss his belongings because he's only human, but he will show his followers how it's done, how to live on faith alone, every move he makes a sermon. Oh, how they will love him.

You can't make an omelet without breaking a few eggs, Paul said.

I step away from the crowd, move beside a tree at the edge of the yard, watching them, listening. I move behind it, hiding myself. A sudden gap—anything could get in, anyone could sneak out.

The Lord of fire, Renee cries. He is in the flames! I see His face! Do you see it?

Yes, I hear people saying. There He is! His beautiful face! Caroline lifts her hands in the air, one an open palm, ready to receive a gift from the heavens, one still clasped to her daughter.

Someone else is yelling now, and when I peek around the tree, I see it's Paul. "Where's Rosie? Have you seen her?" Every part of his body looks like it's moving in a different direction, frantic, nervous, and Lou reaches both his hands up to steady him, but Paul shakes himself free. "She's in there!" he's saying. "Rosemary is in the house!"

No, someone says, we just saw her. She was just right here. Paul, I am here, behind the tree. I step out from its cover, but no one seems to see me. Maybe I have disappeared after all.

"No," says Paul. "I've had a prophecy. It's happening! She's in the burning house. Let me go!" He shoves Lou, who takes a stutter step backward, and runs toward the house. Lou sprints after him, diving as he gets close, tackling him, and they tumble to the grass. I wonder if Lou's thoughts look like mine: a feverish collection of memories featuring Paul, a carousel of all the iterations of Paul he's witnessed.

A boy with missing front teeth, a gangly teenager, a lost and broken man. I take another step toward them, but then Lou lets go, and Paul jumps up, tearing again toward the house. An impulse inside me buzzes, reminds me I should call out to him, stop him, when Papa Jake's voice rises above the din of the crowd, and the vibration I feel dies down. "Let him go," he calls to the assembled followers, holding up his hands. "Trust him! Trust the prophecy he's received. Let him go!" With this blessing, everyone shouts and claps for Paul, who is fast, unstoppable, using the strength and speed God gave him. He doesn't turn around. He keeps going—across the yard, up the steps, onto the porch, and into the house, leaving the front door swinging open.

In that moment, I worry that I am, somehow, in the house, that I'm tied to something inside it, just like Paul saw in his dreams, that I've lost track of my body and it's wandered away from me. That I walked in there when no one was looking, or that I walked in there and everyone was looking, and they just let me go. That I was led in. That I have always been in a burning house, unable to get out, watching the flames approach and rise. Paul does not come out.

I both dread it and desire it, for him to come out and find me, or to find me inside, save me. I think of Lou standing on the last step before the lawn started, like it was a small boat bobbing on the waves, the rest of us lost to the dark water. Now, back behind the tree's thick trunk, in the growing darkness, it feels as if I'm the one in a boat, sailing away, and Paul is drowning. But it also feels like Paul is the one in the boat, and I'm underwater, being pulled away by a riptide. Only one of us is being saved. I don't know who.

I hear someone coming toward me, grass crunching underfoot, and I turn. It's Franklin Aaron, not Paul, who has found me. "Are you hiding?" he asks, eyebrows rising. "Did you know your husband thinks you're burning in that house?"

"No," I say. "Yes."

"Why?" he asks, and I'm not sure how to answer. Why am I behind this tree? Why does Paul believe I'm in the house? You aren't in the house, I remind myself. You are here. It is a warm summer evening, and the air smells like smoke, and you are standing in the shadow of Franklin Aaron.

"Paul had a prophecy," I say, and Franklin nods.

"Don't worry," he says. "I don't think anyone will let him die in there." But I am unsure. After all, if it's what God wants, if it's what Papa Jake wants, who are any of us to stop it?

"I guess I should congratulate you," Franklin says. "About the baby."

"Oh, I'm not pregnant," I say, and he raises an eyebrow.

"You aren't pregnant, and you aren't hiding," he says, and seems to look at me with renewed interest.

"Right," I say.

"I'm leaving," he says. "Do you want to come?"

I realize that I do, that I want to be the one who is saved, the one who gets away. Paul, even among the growing flames, is where he feels he should be, and I am not. God will take care of Paul, and I will take care of myself. "For good?" I ask.

He leans back slightly, his feet still planted on the

ground, so he can see around the tree. "Yeah," he says, looking back at me.

"I think so," I say. "But what about Lily of the Valley?" Even as I ask, I know this isn't a question Franklin Aaron can answer. My breasts fill half-heartedly with milk. Even my body is ambivalent. She is my baby. She isn't my baby. She is Julie's baby. She was never mine.

"I saw Caroline with her," Franklin says with a shrug. "She's fine." I don't want to be her mother, but I don't want to leave her either. *Just for now?* I hear myself asking Caroline. It occurs to me that when I gave Lily to her, we both knew I was handing her over for good. Caroline was giving me the chance to go, empty-handed, unburdened. But now I don't feel unburdened; I feel still feel the weight of Lily of the Valley in my arms.

Maybe someday Julie will come back for her, or maybe someday Caroline will leave too, Caroline and her daughter who is getting closer every day to marriage, her chubby toddler and her older son, her old friend's little girl. "Starting over," she'll caption an Instagram photo of her daughter walking up a sunlit stairwell. She will delete the other pictures. Maybe one day soon the church will fall apart, and Papa Jake will become a realtor, a salesman, a dad who coaches Little League on Wednesday evenings and Sunday afternoons. Maybe I will leave, and I'll sleep beside Franklin Aaron tonight in Dallas or Houston or Waco, wherever we end up stopping, and I'll let him kiss me, let him touch me. Maybe Paul will escape the burning house and find me in my new life, or maybe he won't escape after all, and I will grieve him until one day I suddenly don't, or maybe I will disappear and belong to no one but myself. I can be alone. For a moment, I hope Lily knows I'm sorry to leave her, but then I realize she'll never remember me, and no one will tell her about me, and I have nothing to be sorry for. It will be like I never existed at all.

I think of the years I withheld my body from God, relinquished it, and then took it back again and gave it instead to Colin Bell. Then, just as soon as I thought I could repossess it, Lily had demanded it, and I'd given her a piece of myself and withheld another piece—a secret I kept from Paul. But then Paul seized it, all of it, without me knowing, tended to it carefully, like a garden, sowing it with poison, telling himself that because of him, someday it would bloom.

"Franklin," I say, "do you think Paul is trying to save me, or do you think he went in there to prove the prophecy he had is true?"

Franklin appears to think about this. "Does it matter?"

"I don't know," I say. "If I leave, I guess it doesn't."

"I'm parked right here. I think I can cover you if you stand behind me. You want to go?" He points at his truck, black with a rusted scratch along the side, like a giant clawed creature has sliced it with a long nail, like the truck has gotten away from something before.

"Yes," I say, and he steps out from the cover of the tree, and I step too, following each time he moves, and I feel silly. I cannot see over him, and so I do not look back at the burning house, at Amanda's house beside it, at the tiny girl born first into silence and then into sadness, who has no mother, who has three mothers, who is left behind, again. I do not look at our church family as they stand in the lawn and weep and rejoice at the destruction and creation;

it must be a gift because if it wasn't, what would that mean for them, their lives?

"Made it," says Franklin as he opens the door and I climb inside. He hurries around to the driver's side and starts the truck. A fire truck approaches, its lights dutifully flashing but moving slowly, as if it is weary or annoyed. We watch it together as it drives past us, and like small children do, we follow it with our eyes, turning in our seats. "Do you see that?" Franklin asks.

"Yes," I say. The house to the right of Papa Jake and Caroline's, where Kyle and Lou live, is on fire too, gray plumes of smoke pouring out the top windows like the entire house is a dragon, expelling flames with every breath, leaving nothing behind but smoke and burned bones.

"Matthew's house is burning now too," Franklin says. "Jesus. Can you see it from where you are?"

"No," I say, though I don't know, I probably could, but I've turned around, away from it. It feels like there is a fire inside my body as well, that desolate, beautiful landscape, the desert, the planes of ice, and it's cleaning me out. An act of destruction and creation, one life gone, leaving the place for another one, a new one.

"Where are we going to go?" I ask.

"Wherever we want," he says, grinning with pretty teeth. But then he glances down at my chest and something in his face changes, and he looks away.

"What is it?" I ask, but already I can feel my milk letting down, a wet circle growing on my dress. "Oh."

"Are you okay?" he asks, eyeing the small dark spot again.

"Yeah," I say. "It's breast milk. It'll stop soon."

"Oh," he says too. Something has shifted between us. I was a woman, then a wife, then something like a mother but not, now something like a woman but not, somehow none of the above, not fully.

"Let's just go," I tell him. "We'll figure it out."

Wordlessly, Franklin starts the car, the key doll-sized in his big hand as he turns the ignition. We drive away from the little nest of houses, glowing red and orange in the rearview mirror. As we turn at the end of the street, Franklin says, "I didn't really have a tumor. It was a gizzard, like from a chicken."

"Paul set the fires," I say. "Not these, I guess, but the other ones."

"And Randall is dead," he says. "Did you know that?"

"No, who did it?" Immediately I think of Paul, who has proved he could hurt someone if that was required of him. *I've done a lot you don't know about, Rosie.* "Was it Paul?"

Franklin shakes his head. "Tyler," he says.

"I can see that," I say. "This place is fucked."

"Yeah," he says.

Outside the window there are more burning houses, the flames bright and lovely and clean against the dark sky. "Who set all these fires?" I ask.

"I don't know," says Franklin. "What if no one did?"

"Can you drive by my house?" I ask. When we reach it, it too is burning, and it's in this way that we leave Dawes, silent in the truck, sirens in the distance, fires blooming on either side of us, on every street, like red and orange and yellow flowers.

Epilogue

When Paul and I had been dating for two years, we decided to go on a trip together over spring break. Our friends were driving out in a caravan of cars and trucks to Gulf Shores, Alabama, but we'd already been there. Not to that exact beach, but we had been there before in a greater, existential way. We were our own country together now, and it was a new land, so many corners to explore. So we went south, driving out to the desert.

It feels like a secret that Texas has mountains and a desert, the land down south glamorous and hard, as biting and strong as teeth. Big Bend is hours away, an entire day's drive, and the way out is long and resolutely not beautiful until suddenly it is. The hardscrabble cactus, the dry earth, the way the sky turns purple when the sun sets, and then suddenly the mountains are there, and they aren't giants the way the Rockies are, but imagine you've been on flat, straight ground for so long, your whole life, and then suddenly, there's the promise of going up. How tall and lovely those mountains would look then.

We checked in with the park ranger, who warned us of

the dangers of the desert and the mountains. Snakes, heat, cold, sheer drop-offs. He pointed to the calendar on the wall behind him. "Fire season starts this week too," he said, unsmiling. "Be careful." We told him we would, and when we walked away, we laughed. We set up our tent and ate ramen noodles we cooked on a camping stove, and we peed in terrible campsite bathrooms, and in the morning, we set out for the backcountry. We had permits and a map. We drove out an hour away from the trailhead and put our water in a cache, a locker right off the road, because this was the desert, where there was no water, and you were the only living thing out there who needed it. Then we drove back to the trailhead and started walking.

The first day was fine, long and hot and hilly. We passed other hikers, and when we slept that night, we heard people walking past our tent, through our campsite. I woke up scared, and made Paul crawl out of the tent, the headlamp around his head, but he could only see their backs; they had moved on. "You should feel sorry for them, not scared," he said. "They haven't found where they're going yet."

The next day we got up and hiked some more, and the earth beneath our feet turned orange, yellow, and the sun was so bright and hot, and there were no trees, just these bushes that crowded the trail and stung my legs as I passed. "Stinging nettles," Paul said. He knew so much.

We hiked for hours. Our water ran low, so we limited ourselves to a few sips each, and then it ran out. We saw no one. What kind of animals lived in the desert? Mountain lions? Coyotes. Snakes, yes. I watched the ground, the slivers of shadows created by rocks on the trail; if I were a snake, that's where I would be. But I never saw anything. Nothing else alive and moving. Only Paul and me.

In the desert, we stopped, looked at the map, and argued. "I think we should have turned here," I said, pointing at a black line. "Isn't that the water cache? That little blue box?"

"We did turn there," Paul said. "We're here."

"Are you sure?"

"You don't even know how to read a map, Rosie."

"We're lost," I said.

"How can we be lost?" he said. "We're right here on the map."

"But then we should be close to the water, and we aren't," I said. My legs itched and burned, and there was so much sunlight, I felt blind.

"Well, we must be," he said. "We have the map, and we're right here." But he folded it up before he even finished the sentence and shoved it into an external pocket on his pack. I rarely saw Paul mad. If he could have kicked something, he would have, but there was nothing out here but me. Usually he could fix any problem, solve for x no matter the equation. But here we were, in Texas, in the desert, on a trail—all these things physically real, true, tangible—but we could have been on another planet altogether, in another dimension, in another reality. I asked if we could use the position of the sun in the sky to tell where we were, and Paul groaned and said, no, that's how you tell time; you navigated by the stars, not the sun, and we weren't lost.

So what did we have? A map we couldn't trust. The sun in the sky. The only thing we had to orient ourselves was each other. I am here in proximity to Paul; Paul is here in proximity to me. This, at least, was a small comfort. Whatever was coming for us, we were together.

"So what do we do?" I asked.

"We just keep going," Paul said. He had been eating an apple, and he tossed the core far away, into the brush.

The sun was threatening to set, dipping lower in the endless sky. My head hurt. I was thirsty. My muscles trembled, and I was slimy with sweat, and then the sweat dripped into the scrapes left by the nettles and they stung anew. We'd been hiking for another two hours when we heard voices. "Listen," said Paul, and we stopped, his hand held up straight. I remembered the group who had passed through our campsite. The hours of daylight were longer now, but night would be falling soon, and there was no place to set up camp anyway. "Come on," Paul said and began running, his pack bouncing on his back, and I struggled to keep up as we ran toward the voices. Once I lost sight of Paul as he turned a corner, and I nearly cried. But all I had to do was follow him, watch where he had gone, and then there he was.

He was standing with a group of three other men, our age or maybe a little older, the packs on their backs smaller. They were already laughing together, with Paul, as if they had known him forever. Paul could fit in anywhere, be loved by anyone. Their legs were tan above their hiking socks and boots; one had long hair he pushed out of his face with a bandanna. He smiled at me as I approached, and I was suddenly self-conscious about how I looked. "This must be her," the long-haired one said.

Paul turned to face me and grinned. "Here she is," he

said. "Rosie, they have a GPS. We can get to our water now. It's super close."

"Thank God," I said. "I was worried we were going to die out here."

They laughed. "Were you really?" asked Paul. "Poor Rosie. I'm sorry. We're okay."

"Yeah," said one of them. "The maps are all wrong. Good thing we had the GPS. Otherwise we'd have been fucked."

"Come on," said the one in the bandanna. "Let's go."

As we hiked, they told us their car was parked nearby, just a few minutes' walk from the water cache; they had programmed that location into their GPS too, and they said they didn't feel like hiking after all, so they could give us a lift back to camp. "But once we get all our gear in the car, there will only be room for one of you," the long-haired guy said.

When we got to the locker, Paul and I drank greedily, though the water wasn't cold, and I felt worried it was suddenly going to dissolve into sand in my mouth. We walked to the road, and the men pointed at their car, tiny and toy-like in the distance. "Do you want to go with them, or do you want me to?" he asked. "One of us can get the car, and the other can wait by the road."

"What if they're murderers?" I asked.

"So you're saying you want me to go with them," Paul said.

"Well, they're less likely to murder you," I said.

Paul looked around. The road was long and empty, and the sky was turning purple and pink; soon it would be dark. "You could get murdered here," he said, and I laughed.

"You sound like a real estate agent," I said. "'This would make a lovely spot to be stabbed.'"

"It really would," said Paul. "'Imagine enjoying the beauty of the mountains while you bleed out.'" We stood there together looking out at the desert turning mauve and shadowed in the fading daylight, the mountains blank-faced and regal. The men stood in a little huddle down the road. "Who's coming with us?" one called.

"You, I guess," I said. "I'm not sure I'd even be able to find my way back to this spot."

"Are you sure?" Paul asked. He put his hands on my shoulders and looked into my face. He was worried, and this touched me. I leaned into him.

"There's not another option, right?" I asked. "We don't want to keep hiking." We both looked down at my legs. Some of the cuts had bled, and now the blood was dried. My body was sore.

"Okay," he said. "It will be two hours probably. I'll come back as quick as I can. I love you." He kissed me on the forehead.

"I love you too," I said and watched him as he jogged to catch up with the other men.

There was another thirty minutes of light left, and then it was dark: full dark, a waning moon that kept disappearing under fast-moving clouds, a million stars. I was cold as soon as the sun set, and I sat on the edge of the road, no part of me touching the dirt of the wilderness behind me, making myself as small as possible, hugging my knees to my chest, though it hurt to sit like this. I was scared, worried about Paul finding me. What if he had forgotten where he left me? What if he got into a car accident speeding to get back here? Or what if he never came back at all? I pictured myself sitting here all through the night, the light on my headlamp swinging wildly as I looked in every direction for danger, toward every sound I heard. Maybe I would be able to stand up and walk in the direction they drove off in, find them.

Or maybe I wouldn't leave at all. Maybe I wouldn't go after Paul. Maybe I would sit and sit and wait and wait forever, and people would pass me as they drove by, tapping their fingers against the window, saying look, did you see that girl on the side of the road?

What girl? I imagine a man answering. He is with his girlfriend; she's the one who sees me. She is pretty and athletic-looking in her hiking clothes, but her feet are bare. She's taken off her unwieldy boots for the drive back from the trailhead to their camp.

That one we just passed, she says. She was just sitting there on the side of the road all alone.

The man will look in the rearview mirror, but he won't see anything out of place. After all this time my hair will have grown long and wild, frenzied by the wind, dried in the heat until it is brittle. In the beginning, I will bite my nails out of nervousness and then eventually I will swallow the inedible shards just to have something in my belly, but later, I will let them grow and then use them to slash the throats of small animals to eat. It turns out I am adaptable, so adaptable. And while the dirt and the sun will have made my skin darker, it will have made my clothes fade and wear away until I am indistinguishable from the earth itself.

She was there, the girlfriend insists. We should turn around. What if she needs help? She thinks of me, of what she thought she saw: hair and eyes among the brush, arms and legs the color of the desert, the same dry texture. She has a fleeting and worrying thought that perhaps what she saw was a version of herself—the girl on the side of the road is, somehow, her—but realizes this is crazy. She saw nothing, or just something small and insignificant, and her brain gave it form. The desert is a strange place; the heat is doing strange things to her. Never mind, she tells the man.

I love you, the man says, reaching his hand over to squeeze her leg.

I love you too, the girl says, and they will drive away and leave me here until I become nothing but a bit of folklore, and then finally, nothing at all.

I was already feeling it begin to happen when suddenly there were lights coming down the road. I could see them from far off, and then they would disappear as they went down hills, reappearing as they climbed up again. Paul. I would not be alone. I stood up.

Acknowledgments

All my gratitude to my agent, Stephanie Delman, and my editor, Emily Griffin. Steph, you are a true star in every sense; your light and brightness have guided me so well, and I am so grateful. Emily, you are an incredible editor and one of the loveliest people I know—your work has made this book so, so much better than I could have ever imagined; thank you for believing in me and in Rosemary.

Thank you to the team at Harper Perennial—Karintha Parker, Lisa Erickson, Amanda Hong. Thank you to Olivia McGiff for the gorgeous, perfectly ominous cover.

To my film/tv agent Hilary Zaitz Michael for dreaming bigger than I could have guessed.

To Lighthouse Writers Workshop in Denver and Julie Buntin for crucial guidance in the development of Rosemary as a character.

To Britt Tisdale, my writing bestie for life.

To all the friends who have supported me, loved me, and made my life richer—Stephanie Matthews, Tara Madden, Liz Breen, Tucker Rosebrock, Brittni Austin, Leslie Bell, Ashley Winstead. Y'all are a gift.

To Discover Gymnastics, where I have watched approximately 520 hours of gymnastics and where I wrote and revised a good deal of this book. Thank you to the Super Twister/Hope Team moms for making the gym a fun place to spend hours every week and for helping me figure out the way this crazy sport works.

To all the people who care for my children while I work—the teachers at Our Savior Lutheran, my in-laws, Lannie and Don.

To Nsen, my best friend.

To Claire, my best sister. Did you see that this book is for you??

To my parents, Jack and Diana, whom I love so much.

To Margaux and Townes, my treasures, my perfect gifts.

To Josh. I love you. You are almost always right about almost everything, including this.

To anyone who reads this book—thank you. I am endlessly grateful.

About the Author

Born, raised, and based in Houston, Texas, Alison Wisdom has an MFA from Vermont College of Fine Arts and was a finalist for the 2020 Rona Jaffe Award. Her short stories have been published in *Ploughshares*, *Electric Literature*, *The Rumpus*, *Indiana Review*, and other publications. She is the author of *We Can Only Save Ourselves*.

About the Author

Born, raised, and based in Houston, Texas, Alison Wisdom has an MFA from Vermont College of Fine Arts and was a finalist for the 2020 Rona Jaffe Award. Her short stories have been published in *Ploughshares*, *Electric Literature*, *The Rumpus*, *Indiana Review*, and other publications. She is the author of *We Can Only Save Ourselves*.

DON'T MISS ALISON WISDOM'S GLITTERING DEBUT

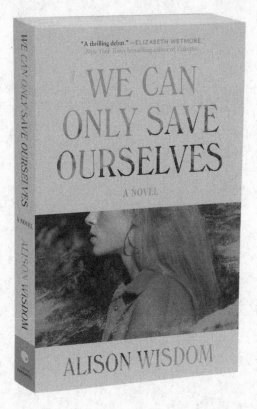

"In this tense, complicated novel, the loss of a daughter is observed through the singular, haunting voice of the town's mothers as they wage a daily battle for safety under the guise of conformity and belonging. . . . There are no easy answers in this thrilling debut novel by Texas writer Alison Wisdom, whose taut, steely prose reveals new complexities, questions, and dangers with each turn of the page."

—ELIZABETH WETMORE,
New York Times bestselling author of *Valentine*